"*Civil War Two* is a first-rate thriller, an epic history of a possible American future, and a compelling read you will be unable to put down."

> **–Paul DiMaggio**, Professor of Sociology,
> NYU Department of Sociology

"In the world of sociologists, Randall Collins enjoys a unique professional reputation. This is far from mere fantasy; it is a solidly built, scary hypothesis about a possible future of America."

> **–Georgi Derluguian**, expert on modern civil wars,
> Carnegie Scholar, and Professor of Social Research and
> Public Policy NYU Abu Dhabi

"In this perfectly timed and engaging prophetic novel, Randall Collins revisits themes central to his sociology—history, violence, war, emotions, human interactions—to give a troubling picture of the world ahead. A must for those looking for a most engaging read!"

> **–Michèle Lamont**, Harvard University, Professor of
> Sociology and of African and African American Studies

"In *Civil War Two*, Collins provides a believable and timely account of a country divided between secularists and religious zealots. The politics of romance and espionage, of human frailty and ambition, all jump from the page—Collins provides a masterful account of what a second US civil war would feel like from the inside."

> **–Randol Contreras,** University of Toronto, Assistant
> Professor of Sociology, author of *The Stickup Kids*

"Civil War 2 is a timely and compelling novel about what could be America's next Civil War. The writing is exceptional. Collins has created vivid characters that superbly weave his narrative and powerfully brings his story home—an engrossing read."

> **–Elijah Anderson**, Yale University,
> author of *Code of the Street*

"Collins has channeled his deep knowledge of human violence and the intricacies of combat into a taut and compelling *what if* fantasy that takes the cultural fissures of our nation to full scale rupture."

> **–Alice Goffman**, author of
> *On The Run: Fugitive Life in an American City*

CIVIL WAR TWO
PART 1

Also by Randall Collins

Nonfiction:

Napoleon Never Slept: How Great Leaders Leverage Social Energy
(with Maren McConnell)

Does Capitalism Have a Future?
(with Immanuel Wallerstein, Micheal Mann,
Georgi Derlugian, & Craig Calhoun)

Violence: A Microsociological Theory

The Sociology of Philosophies

***The Credential Society: An Historical
Sociology of Education and Stratification***

Fiction:

The Case of The Philosopher's Ring

CIVIL WAR TWO

AMERICA ELECTS A PRESIDENT DETERMINED TO RESTORE RELIGION TO PUBLIC LIFE,

AND THE NATION SPLITS

A NOVEL
BY RANDALL COLLINS

Civil War Two, Part 1: America Elects a President Determined to Restore Religion to Public Life, and the Nation Splits

ISBN: 978-1-7320605-1-7 (Paperback)
ISBN: 978-1-7320605-0-0 (eBook)

LCCN: 2018940925

Published by Maren Ink, San Diego, CA | Maren.Ink

Cover design by Maren McConnell

Book/eBook design and production by David Wogahn/davidwogahn.com, Carlsbad, California

C.S.S.A: Coalition of Secular States of America
U.S.A: United States of America

MAIN CHARACTERS

USA

President **Joshua Maccabee Jennings,** elected on a program to restore religion to public life in America

Secretary of Defense **Robert Madigan,** crusader for centralized computer control of the military

Deputy Secretary of Defense **Thaddeus Wolf**

General Curtis Harris, US Air Force, Chairman of the Joint Chiefs of Staff

Achilles Cruz, the most aggressive and persistent of the Union generals

John Gandhi Park, Korean orphan, old-style boots-on-the-ground soldier, opposed to computerization

Major Debra Zielkowski, Pentagon security officer

Capt. Tom Napoli, attack helicopter pilot

CSSA

Everett Rosenfeld, Governor of New York, Chairperson of the CSSA

"Big Bill" O'Leary, Mayor of Chicago, Vice Chairperson of the CSSA

Jordan Duplessis, Governor of California, former film star

Tim Birkenstock, Senator for Minnesota, secularist leader

Don Blastings, motorcycle-riding Governor of Montana, former talk show host

General Jefferson Gray, most respected officer in the U.S. Army, but loyal to his home state Illinois

General Mark McConnell, Marine Corps commander, he'd rather rebel than let the Corps be abolished

Ironman Johnston, health fanatic, commander of a brigade of former rehab boot camp inmates

Newton Crawford, former street gang leader, moving up through the ranks

Lt. Gabriel Napoli, former musician, in the midst of events

Marisa Santa-Ana, sex worker, spy, political climber

Time: an alternative universe, early 21st century

SECOND BATTLE OF GETTYSBURG

In the soft gray pre-dawn came the sounds of birds waking. Lieutenant Gabriel Napoli, Army of the Coalition of Secular States of America (CSSA), rolled over on the grass and raised up on one elbow, listening.

High-pitched chirps and twitters in the upper sound register.

Lieutenant Napoli, a musician before the war, thought: three octaves above middle C. Notes so high they'd be almost indistinct on a piano.

Another sound in the middle octave, a cool contralto, doves calling *whoo, hooo, hooo,* the pure breathy sound of blowing with one's lips across the mouth of a bottle.

Then lower down, a faint sound of wings flapping, a toneless drone, an army of birds all taking off at once from faraway trees. The sound grew, resolved itself into two, the dull bass drone joined by a high clattering, wavering slowly upwards and downwards a quarter note.

The whirling of wings, becoming less and less musical as it grew louder.

Napoli sat bolt upright. Helicopters, flying in formation.

Whose?

Ours would be coming from the east, back towards Harrisburg. These were coming from west and south, from the hills beyond Seminary Ridge.

★ / ★

From Hagerstown and the Chambersburg Road where Robert E. Lee had marched his army one hundred fifty years ago.

Lt. Napoli commanded a battery of SAMs—Stinger surface-to-air missiles. Last night his troops had dug pits alongside the Taneytown Road in the dark.

Now the dim light revealed where they had slept: a few yards from the cannon of the Gettysburg National Battlefield Park, pointing at the open field where the Confederate charge had come.

In those days a Napoleon Twelve Pounder could reach almost a mile with solid roundshot. The classic cannonballs were now piled up around the monuments in little pyramids of black iron globes. A Napoleon loaded with hollow shells filled with explosive or shrapnel was more dangerous, but its range was much shorter.

The Napoleons made a hell of a noise but mostly missed, unless advancing troops got within a few hundred yards, sprinting across the narrow killing zone to bayonet the gunners before they could reload.

Lt. Napoli's Stingers had a range out to three miles and were guided by infrared sensors that could spot an enemy helicopter by the heat it emitted even through smoke and bad weather. They weren't infallible but they were a lot more lethal than Civil War One artillery.

If I were firing those old cannon, it would be a lottery chance if my shells killed anyone. Now, a pretty good chance. Not a guaranteed killer. But better than fifty-fifty.

Napoli's troops were rolling out of sleep, stumbling for the SAM pits, prodded by sergeants. Some things never change. There was a voice at his elbow. Major Emerson checking the line in person.

"Morning, Napoli." Trying to sound calm. Knowing it was the first fight for Gabriel Napoli. "Looks like their first wave is coming in. A dozen Apaches heading this way. Maybe just a visit. Maybe a prelim to armor on the ground. Any which way, be ready."

Napoli nodded. Tight-lipped he asked: "Sir, any info what unit that is over there?" Gesturing with his shoulder in the direction of the helicopters droning.

"Eighty-second Airborne," Emerson said. Napoli thought his collar looked three sizes too big. "Up from Fort Bragg, North Carolina.

Funny how the army of the USA is based in the old South. Now the North is the Rebels, they're the Union."

Lt. Napoli said nothing, staring into space. The Major went on. "Know anyone over there?"

"Sort of."

"Well, get used to it, kid. Plenty of guys I knew at West Point are on the other side. They're probably saying the same thing about us. Just like Civil War One—Grant and Lee were in the same outfit in the Mexican War, and all that."

Gabriel Napoli was thinking of a day he was nine years old, wrestling with his brother in the backyard. The older boy, quick and aggressive, always went all out to win.

Gabriel winced again, his face again ground into the gravel on that bare spot in front of the shed where Dad kept the lawnmower.

The boys were together a lot. For some reason they didn't play with other kids. Mom and Dad were always hovering around, protecting, looking for reasons to keep them away from the neighborhood kids.

Or maybe they just didn't fit in.

Mom and Dad didn't allow them to watch TV. Dad was a music teacher, very high-toned, disapproving of the modern world. They did a lot of jigsaw puzzles, made airplane models. They knew every plane from every war of the twentieth century, most of them hanging on threads around their bedroom with the double bunk beds.

When Tom, the older Napoli boy, was a teenager he gave up military toys and went in for the real thing. When personal computers came in, Tom was online, not just surfing the web but running his own business—buying and selling guns.

Tom was always a hardass, Gabriel thought.

Major Emerson was talking, filling the silence that he took for nervousness. "Strange to be fighting on top of an old battlefield. They crammed in a lot more troops back then, we have fewer and spread them out further. Attacking head-on against our firepower would be suicide."

In the pits behind sandbag walls, Napoli's men were preparing the Stinger tubes for firing. Napoli wondered if they were even close to ready, but pushed the thought away, exhaling it out and away.

Each two-man team had a metal tube six feet long, like a section of sewer pipe. The operator held the pipe on his shoulder, most of it sticking out behind him to keep the fiery exhaust away from his body. The forward end had a bird-cage-shaped antenna on top, that sent signals to the operator's eye scope.

The whole thing weighed about thirty pounds and it took a muscular man to hold the launcher while his spotter helped with the loading. The missile itself was a long thin cylinder with surprisingly small three-inch fins steering it from the front. Once the missile was launched to a safe distance from the operator, the bottom stages dropped off as it accelerated to Mach 2—twice the speed of sound.

Stingers were finicky, fired by inserting a chemical unit into the handguard; the danger being that the unit could lose gas and malfunction.

Like so much high-tech weaponry, it was awesome when it worked, which wasn't all the time.

The two soldiers in the launch team nearest to Lt. Napoli were fumbling, their fingers strangely cottony and unfeeling. Not practicing any more. At last they were firing to kill. Lt. Napoli felt himself breathing harder.

They were dug in along the ridge road where the Union encampment had been. Armored vehicles were spaced along Cemetery Ridge for two miles down to Little Round Top. Abrams tanks, sixty-ton monsters, covered with layers of steel and ceramic protecting against armor-piercing and high-explosive anti-tank rounds, parked next to chiseled stone monuments memorializing the *Forty-first New York Regiment* and dozens of others.

Park Headquarters was just north of Gabriel Napoli's position, its postcards and exhibits frozen in time. Now the parking lot was crowded with military vehicles covered by camouflage netting. Behind them, the cemetery where Lincoln had made his Gettysburg address was mounded with hastily bulldozed dirt berms and the tents of the CSSA army.

Half a mile to the north, Gettysburg itself, the least changed thing in the whole environment: a little town then, a little town now, business dying in rural America, the agricultural crossroads replaced by a tourist attraction.

"Pickett's charge started over there, in those trees," said the Major, pointing across the shallow valley, living in history like so many professional soldiers, the past dignifying the present. "Fifteen thousand men kept their marching formation, over a mile of open ground, under fire all the way. They ended up here—" scarcely a hundred yards in front of them—"the ones who made it that far."

Napoli spoke. "I had an ancestor who died here."

"Did you? Who?"

"Brigadier General Garnett. He led the first brigade of Pickett's attack. He got all the way to that fence. They never found his body—there were too many dead piled up and torn to pieces."

"Oh yeah, General Garnett. There was a story about him, wasn't there?"

"Stonewall Jackson accused him of cowardice, because he pulled back from an impossible position at Chancellorsville two months before." The younger man looked all at once tired, as if he remembered not to tell the story too late to stop. "But Jackson was killed at the end of the battle. So Garnett could never have the court-martial to clear his name."

"So he welcomed leading a suicide charge. Better death than dishonor."

Lt. Napoli did not answer, thinking: Yes, he had seen where Pickett's charge had taken place, had walked across it from the Confederate side of the National Park to the Union side, with Mom and Dad. Tom was excited, slapping his younger brother's head and running away, himself chasing, unable to catch up. A nine-year-old boy chasing and an eleven-year-old striking like a cavalry raid and racing off jeering across the empty summer field.

As they had approached the Union guns, Mom had stopped, seemed to choke. What's the matter, Mom? Gabriel had said.

It makes me so angry, she said. She had a clear feminine voice with the softness of an old Virginia accent, so unlike the drawl of the deep South. From an old Richmond family, not like Dad. She was a small woman, very intense in her movements. Usually quiet, but when she spoke she always got her way.

Angry, he had said, at what?

All those lives. All those young men killed, fighting, for what? Her fists were clenched. The image was still in Gabriel's mind. He had not understood then. But now.

A thread from the past, twisting the present. A Faulkner novel seventy years after Faulkner. And stretching back seventy years before Faulkner, the Garnett connection. Mom's great-great-grandfather. A woman who didn't like the twentieth century, let alone the twenty-first. Emily Dickinson watching shadows marching slowly across the lawn.

Major Emerson was gone. Lt. Gabriel Napoli was alone with his battery of Stinger SAMs, the USA helicopters coming in.

Flying point at the front of the formation, the helicopter pilot was calling out orders to his troop. His voice, intermittent and laconic, punctuated a flow of unspoken thoughts. Gettysburg again. Ironic. Everyone must be thinking that. In those days, both sides moved almost blind. Met here by accident, where all the roads converge. Had virtually no intel. Jeb Stuart's cavalry, swinging wide to the east, circling the whole Federal army, out of touch with Lee for days. The eyes and ears of the army, fifty miles away, leaving Lee blind. Now we'd cover the distance in twenty minutes, radio the report in instantly, he thought, glancing around the arc of helicopters.

Our trouble is fighting troops with the same equipment, same training, same communications. Johnny Reb and Damn Yankee both spoke English. We both speak with the same electronics. We both used the same computer codes. Better to keep radio silence. Never know when they're hacking into our net.

As if on cue, CSSA voices broke in on the radio band. *"Hey, Red State rednecks! Come on and get wasted by somebody with a brain."* Another voice, a chorus: *"Jesus freaks." "Right-wing bigots." "Crazy religious fanatics."*

The helicopter pilot, unloquacious by nature, despising talkative people, kept silent. Other voices answered for the USA side: *"Blue*

State wimps." "Meet some real men, you liberal perverts." "Un-American traitors. Go back where you came from."

And a deeper voice, more threatening: *"May God have mercy on your souls."*

The helicopters were traveling low, terrain masking by skimming the hills and treetops. They dodged up and down, as low as a hundred feet, fifty feet.

The big danger was clearing the obstacles that masked them from the enemy. It was like road racing in a car, exhilarating to wait til the last minute to pull up before you hit the tree. Harder to do in formation with a dozen helicopters flying over 100 miles per hour. A lot of helicopter casualties came from collisions in maneuvers like this. The pilot was not worried. He had done it all before. Training was almost as dangerous as combat.

Enemy fire wasn't the main problem, yet. Trees and hills masked infrared sensors, and laser tags were no good against rapidly shifting targets.

Under five miles, he thought. We could hit CSSA tanks right now with our Hellfire missiles. Better to wait. Hellfires are radar-guided. The other side was probably radar jamming, just like they're trying to jam our electronic communications. They're jamming ours, we're jamming theirs. And if we turn our radar on, it will set off their HARMs—these were high-speed anti-radiation missiles, homing in automatically on radiation emission sources. Don't know how many they've got on this front. We could probably evade most of it. But wait, get in closer.

What else can they fire at us? Biggest danger is Stinger SAMs. They've got to be all over the place down there, cheap and mobile, man-portable and vehicle-mounted. Almost in their three-mile range now. Infrared guided, can't jam that. As soon as we get past these hills and trees, it'll be a race, us against them.

Hit them with our 70mm rockets. They're unguided so the enemy can't interfere with the guidance system. Just aim and fire. Old-fashioned warfare.

The pilot ordered his squadron to increase their altitude as they cleared the last trees. From the air, the row of tanks dug in along Cemetery Ridge looked like tines of a giant zipper lying open. The pilot had the sensation that the opposite row of the zipper was about to close.

At the north end of the zipper was a cluster of buildings surrounded by trees. Probably using the old Park Headquarters for military functions. Put some rockets in there. Should be a parking lot where those fake camouflage woods are. His memory flickered to a visit years ago to the Park Headquarters, with its exhibits, its big indoor 360-degree panorama painting of the battle of Gettysburg in 1863. The big round building was right where it should be. They're probably using it for munitions or something, thinking we would spare it. Give it a hit, he thought, hating the hold of the past. One battle obliterates another.

Bearing in on the enemy, his thoughts raced. Why attack here at Gettysburg again? Same strategic problem as Civil War One. Avoiding a direct attack along the coastal urban corridor. Hit Philadelphia and New York from the flank. Aren't we making Pickett's charge again? Not really; my helos have more firepower than all of Lee's army. But then, so do they.

The helicopters were at the edge of the trees. Seeing the field open up below, his memory flickered. Where we walked with Mom and Dad. Wonder where that little punk Gabriel is today.

He swooped the helicopter upwards, banking to the left. Gave orders to fire on the tanks, while he took out the buildings and missile pits at the north end of the line.

The thought flashed in his mind: General Garnett, who Mom was always talking about. Six generations back from me. They say he wanted to die. Bad attitude, makes you a loser.

Make the other guy die.

It's a calculated risk. No more frontal assaults. All high-speed maneuver now. But you have to meet the enemy somewhere. Be willing to take some casualties, take the risk in order to break them.

Rockets exploded on the battlefield, shaking the helicopters in the air. Captain Tom Napoli expertly rode the blast, veering towards Park Headquarters and the embankment just beside it.

★

Lieutenant Gabriel Napoli crouched beside a Stinger launcher, dug in along the Taneytown Road. Called out orders to his battery, peering into infrared scopes: "Track the lead helicopter, then get the others." The first missile fired, and was lost in the crash of battle.

Friction, or the Fog of War

In war, General von Clausewitz wrote, everything is simple, but carrying it out is hard. He should know; he was with the Russian army beaten by Napoleon on the way to Moscow in 1812, and he watched Napoleon's army dwindle away on the long march back through the Russian winter.

This difficulty Clausewitz called friction, the grinding of heavy forces as they move across the surface of the earth, rubbing against each other every step of the way.

In another metaphor, this is the fog of war. Originally it was the smoke of gunfire that covered the battlefield and made it impossible to see where anything was. No general could be sure his orders would be carried out or if the foe would be where he was supposed to be; no soldier could be sure who he was firing at, and a sizable portion of casualties came from accidents and being hit by one's own side. The victories and defeats of the Civil War of 1861-65 were fought under a dense fog of war.

Twentieth century wars had better intelligence and communications, but friction did not disappear. Planes still bombed civilians; unanticipated enemies popped up in sudden maneuvers. Tanks ran out of fuel and rumbled to a halt on the fields of France or the deserts of North Africa. Ammo was exhausted in the midst of battle. Helicopter strikes aborted for lack of repairs or from sand in their engines.

To this physical friction and informational fog must be added a third kind, the emotions of human beings. Soldiers under stress of combat did not always fire and didn't often hit their targets when they did fire. Officers did not always give realistic orders and troops did not always carry them out. Soldiers would forget to bring drinking water with them into combat, and supply officers could fail to provide warm clothes in the winter cold.

The idea gathered momentum that science and technology could do a better job of fighting than human beings.

Already in the Viet Nam war, Secretary of Defense McNamara used statistical controls to calculate air strikes and enemy body *counts. By the 1990s the transformation of the U.S. military was under way. Precision bombs and missiles were guided to their targets by computers in their noses.*

If humans were fallible, satellites with global positioning coordinates, transmitting intercontinental messages, and hooked to an array of sensors and weapons could hit targets with great accuracy, while their operators sat thousands of miles away out of the danger and stress of combat. The 2003 invasion of Iraq was run from an Air Force base in Florida.

The fog of war was disappearing. Though enemies hid and adopted guerrilla tactics of hit-and-run, their cloak of invisibility was being penetrated. Soon the murky battlefield would be fully revealed in the clear electronic light of day.

YEAR ONE.
A NATION DIVIDES

CONSTITUTIONAL CRISIS

Washington, DC. January.

Joshua Maccabee Jennings, newly inaugurated President of the United States of America, was communing with God in the Oval Office. "Send down your wisdom to the Supreme Court, Heavenly Father, as they hear the appeal of the law of Texas restoring prayer in the schools. Give them courage to do the right thing, and not to bow down to the forces of atheism and secularism threatening our great land."

The President prayed aloud, for he was not alone. His left hand grasped the hand of Louise Carter, his presidential secretary, and his right hand clasped Senator Bobby Jo Ingraham (Republican, Oklahoma) who had dropped in for a chat.

"We call on you, too, in this time of deadlock in our great Congress," Jennings continued. "Your people have been suffering too long without a budget. Three months and more our brave boys in the military, and the FBI, CIA and you name it, have gone without a paycheck. We pray you: end this time of fiscal famine; let it not go on like the seven years when Joseph was in Egypt. Deliver us from the tyranny of the special interests who make a mockery of our six-vote majority in the House of Representatives, and our 51-to-49 majority in the Senate. Give our Senators the strength to hold fast in your name, O Lord, and the wisdom to reach across the aisle to bring in the swing votes to the cause of God."

He squeezed the hand on his right a little extra and Senator Ingraham said aloud, "Amen!"

An aide entered the room, standing by the door hesitating at the sight of the prayer circle. "Sorry, Mr. President, but this couldn't wait."

"Come on in here, Jimmy Joe," Jennings boomed. "God doesn't stand on ceremony. Whatever you got to say, the good Lord will be happy to hear it." Without losing touch with either the Senator or the secretary, Jennings managed to reach around Louise, grasp Jimmy Joe's hand, and pull him into the prayer circle; Louise somehow transitioned from being squeezed under the President's long arm to holding hands in the chain on Jimmy Joe's other side.

"The Chief Justice is dead," Jimmy Joe blurted out.

"O Lord," Jennings called sonorously, "Your ways are mysterious and dark. You have seen fit to call Chief Justice Ernest home from his labors. Just this morning—when did he pass away?"

"Early this morning," Jimmy Joe said, "heart attack."

"Just this morning, before the dawn's early light," Jennings continued, "a man passed from the living, to that perfect world where Thou dwellest, O Lord, and we pray you receive him, whatever his sins. We pray for his family, and for those who survive him, and not least among them for his fellow Justices of the Supreme Court, who are now left split four-to-four." Jennings had preached many times in community churches, where the pastor's prayers were a public bulletin board, announcing the sick and bedridden, the passing away and the coming to birth, the travels and hopes of the congregation.

"Four men of God, and four atheists and secularists, and now you in your infinite wisdom have called away the swing vote. I think I see a little of your purpose, O God, giving me the opportunity to appoint a Christian to make a true majority on the Court. Just last week, as you know O Lord, I had a talk with Judge Tom Alexander, of the Federal Court in South Carolina. A mighty fine man, committed to restoring Christian values to public life in America. If it is your purpose, dear Lord, to send Judge Alexander to the Supreme Court, give me the sign, and I will see it done."

"And while you're at it, dear God, send us some help in the Senate," Ingraham added his voice. "Our majority is thin as a razor, and the Democrats will obstruct and filibuster the appointment like it's the end of the world."

"Let it be the beginning of a new world, we pray," Jennings resumed. "Let America be born again. But not my will, but Thy will be done. Amen."

The Governor of California's helicopter settled in for a landing. The Malibu coast loomed up, ready for its closeup. Surf pounded sparkling white and blue on rocky cliffs butting their heads into the ocean. On the bluff was the Governor's private mansion, a horizontal sprawl of low-angled roofs broken by oval skylights and patios decorated with tropical trees. The house covered two acres and had eight bedrooms, ten bathrooms, three pools complete with swim-up bar and twister slide, a movie theatre, a gym, and an eighteen-car garage full of antique cars.

Jordan Duplessis stepped out of the helicopter, spread his weightlifter's chest, and threw back his arms in a healthy stretch. The Governor was a self-made billionaire, his fingers in high tech, media conglomerates, with a little real estate and corporate raiding on the side. Long a famous figure in Hollywood, Duplessis had made himself available to the voters of California as a breath of fresh air. The usual politicians had aroused the usual failed hopes and recriminations. Duplessis stepped in, waving the fact of his never having held public office like a flag of virtue. He announced as a Republican but quickly established himself as a maverick: willing to spend money for the teachers and the highway construction industry, mollifying the unions, siding with the immigrants, squeezing the Indian reservation casinos for contributions; promising to cut taxes while balancing the budget with massive borrowing.

Duplessis was always hamming it up for the cameras and giving outrageous quotes, qualities that made him popular with the news media. Periodic scandal—his past sex life with a troupe of

Hollywood starlets; rumors of drug use in his younger years—just brightened the limelight. Energetic and happy, pumped up with self-confidence, Duplessis soaked in attention from the audiences that surrounded him, and beamed it back with a joke and a smile.

The Governor of California's official mansion was in Sacramento, but this was where he hung out. He could have used a state helicopter, but he preferred his own—he liked the dual identity, Bruce Wayne playing governor by day and Batman by night. His one concession to unifying his two lives was an escort of highway patrolmen, plainclothed in suits but cop-like nevertheless amid the open-collar shirts and gold neck chains of the Governor and his entourage. The officers were hard and fit and beneath their conservative blue suits was the bulge of pistol holsters.

A guest was waiting for Duplessis on the soft grass putting green next to the helicopter pad. He had slicked-back graying hair and a patrician aquiline profile. It was the Governor of New York, Everett Rosenfeld. He had made his reputation as a crusading District Attorney, cleaning up Wall Street, satisfying the public's periodic demand to do something in the face of periodic outrages. Rosenfeld was the kind of figure that often since the days of Teddy Roosevelt emerged in New York politics, out of the cynicism and machine politics and high finance from which an idealist reformer sprouted like a lotus from a swamp. Behind rimless glasses he gazed distrustfully on the California sunshine pouring from an intense cloudless sky and the dazzling sparkle off the ocean.

The men embraced, Duplessis' bearhug held at a distance by Rosenfeld's smooth cool greeting.

"Jennings is making himself dictator," Rosenfeld said. "He just announced he is breaking the budget deadlock by presidential order. He's ruling by decree. Democracy in Washington is finished."

"I heard there was some action on the floor of the Senate yesterday. Fist fight between the junior Senator from South Carolina and the senior Democrat from Nevada." Duplessis smiled. "Know anything about that?"

"One of those Christian fundamentalists called Sam Golden an atheist pornographer, a Las Vegas brothel keeper, and a string of other names."

Duplessis smirked. He had been not so far from the X-rated industry at one time in his life. "Clean-living guy wins by a knockout, huh? It wouldn't have happened if I'd been there."

"States are organizing constitutional conventions," Rosenfeld said, "Massachusetts, Vermont, Wisconsin, Minnesota, Oregon. We're meeting in New York tomorrow. You know what they're saying: If the President breaks the rules, he has lost his right to be President. If Congress is too split to impeach him, we'll impeach him ourselves. The People's impeachment movement. Realistically, it means seceding from the Union. Not everybody wants to say it, but that's what it boils down to."

"And you believe it will work?" They moved out of the bright sunlight into a sitting room, all lounge chairs and earth-colored sofas taking up about as much room as a good-sized house. A chrome and glass bar cart wheeled up, and a server who looked like a lifeguard poured drinks.

"Once a few states start pulling out, the rest of us are going to get hammered if we stay in the Union. Congress is deadlocked, for now. But it gets undeadlocked every time a state withdraws its Representatives and Senators. Vermont doesn't make much difference in the House, but losing its two Senators will bring Jennings' crowd that much closer to a working majority in the Senate. Even a filibuster isn't going to protect us much longer. The Christian Right will push through its Supreme Court appointment and enact whatever it wants. We can't sit on the fence when the fence is being torn down beneath us." A gust of warm wind tried to displace Rosenfeld's perfectly coiffed hair, and failed.

"Not every Republican belongs to the Christian Right."

"Of course not. But centrist Republicans can only stay alive in the party if they're the swing votes who can appeal to moderate voters. Once the Democrats are out, they don't need you. You just become the new left-wing minority for them to beat up on."

"The tipping point," Duplessis said, holding his drink, pretending to sip it. "The old teeter-totter is about to seesaw. And you want California to tip over along with you."

"It's inevitable. The country is breaking up between the Red states and Blue states."

"And you think the Blue states are going to put together a new country—a new Confederate states of America, only in the North and the West, while the South gets to be the Union?"

"Confederacy isn't the name we will use, obviously. But that's the general idea."

"Funny thing about these Red and Blue states," Duplessis said. "Red used to mean Left. Some liberal news network deliberately changed it around—it wouldn't look good for the Democrats if their strongholds were called Red states. As I recall, you guys were pinkos back in the fifties. How about calling this new confederation the Pink States of America?"

"It's not about Right and Left. It is a broad-based coalition, defending American values. The heart of the Constitution, the separation of church and state. The first Americans came here for religious freedom. All the other freedoms come from that. The freedom for everyone to be religious in their own way; or not religious, if that's what they want."

"I don't know that the Pilgrims would have agreed with that. Didn't they think they were setting up God's country?"

Rosenfeld forged ahead. "Freedom of conscience, freedom of speech. Freedom of the media—" he gestured Hollywood-wards "—freedom to consume the media anyway you want."

Duplessis grinned two perfect rows of dentist-whitened teeth; he had only been kidding, he knew what was important. The Christian Right in Congress was pushing a bill to prohibit sex and violence in the media and video game business.

"Look—" Rosenfeld leaned forward intently. "Birkenstock is righter than he knows." This would be Tim Birkenstock, Senator from Minnesota, the archetype of the dedicated liberal. He had been the first to advocate seceding from the United States. "It's like a light bulb going on. Being in the same country with those Bible fanatics is what causes all the trouble. Pull out, start our own country before we're under a Christian dictatorship."

"Don't you think we'll have a civil war? Jennings will fight to preserve the Union. He thinks it's a God-ordained nation."

"Even hotheads have to cool down after a while. And the Pentagon is unraveling—half the officers hate the Secretary of Defense anyway, for the way he's replacing the military with computers. It will be a standoff. This isn't the backwards rural Confederacy. And we're not the slave owners. We're the ones who are in the right."

"Sure," said Duplessis. "They think they're in the right too. Sounds like the formula for a knockdown drag-out."

"It's a hand that can be played. A very winnable hand."

Rosenfeld nudged his drink against his lip, warily not drinking. "Let's get down to business. A dozen states are holding conventions, voting to pull out of the Union. A bandwagon is rolling. There will be more. Especially when we go ahead with the next step, a national convention, where we'll establish a new federation—" he stopped himself, disliking the ring of confederacy, "—a new coalition of states. Every state across the North and West, and some of the Midwest, will feel the pull. Once they vote to pull out, they'll have to throw in with the others. I don't think there will be much of a civil war, if any, but it's the size of the coalition that means safety for all of us."

He looked at Duplessis pointedly. "Even California."

Duplessis shrugged, an ambiguous curl to his lips. "I believe we'll wait."

"Why wait?"

"Til the national convention is about to happen. Til the clamor gets big enough up and down the state. We have our own Bible faction here, you know. If I call a state convention now, there'll be an anti-convention movement. Not a majority, but enough to be trouble. If I wait until it sounds like everybody is demanding a convention, it will happen—like rigging the Academy Awards, it has to be done during the last week."

"All right, so you don't want to get in early. Just checking. You're going to be the biggest state in the coalition."

"I had a staffer look it up. Virginia wasn't the first state to pull out of the Union in 1861; it was one of the last. Not until after Fort Sumter. It was the biggest state in the Confederacy, and it got to have the capital, too, at Richmond."

"So that's your price? You want L.A. to be the capital?"

"As a matter of fact I don't. You know what people say about California, back in your end of the country. They think L.A. is the toilet bowl of pop culture superficiality. We have people up in the San Francisco Bay area who think the same way—who'd be just as happy to see L.A. bombed into rubble." He grinned at Rosenfeld. "Of course there are lots of people across the country who feel the same about New York City."

"New York would be a logical center for the Coalition," Rosenfeld said. "The world's greatest city. And home to the United Nations. Jennings and his fanatics have already alienated the international community. He'll push them into our arms. The Coalition could start a movement for world government, and we'd be the center."

"But New York has the same problem Richmond had for the Confederacy. Too close to the front line. Our army would have to be concentrated in front of it, tied down in its freedom to maneuver— Yes, we do read books out here occasionally."

"If not New York or L.A., then where?"

"Chicago. That's where the constitutional convention will be, isn't it?"

"It hasn't been settled yet. For one thing, Illinois hasn't called their own state convention yet."

"I know you guys think it's a vast wasteland between the Hudson River and San Francisco—flyover country, isn't that what you call it? But you're going to have to stop talking like that. The Midwest is the key. You'll need those states to hold this new country together. The Rust Belt. The collapsed steel mills, the closed auto factories. This is a chance for them to rise again. It will be another World War II for them—the wartime economy, full employment, good wages. And it would do a lot for the aircraft industry down here in Long Beach and up in Washington state."

"That's a terrible reason for a war," Rosenfeld said. "Defense industries are fine if you don't have to use them. Do you have any idea how destructive war really is? It's not like the movies."

"Don't make speeches to me, Everett. Do you want California in the coalition or don't you?"

"Of course we do." Rosenfeld thought: does he think he'd look good in a general's uniform? A Napoleon complex. God knows what he'll do as time goes along.

"If California comes in on the coalition, Nevada will come in—it's Sin City, the Christians would crucify it. Hawaii, the leisure entertainment economy. We're a cultural entity out here. They'll follow California."

Rosenfeld sat back, letting the Pacific sparkle behind plateglass windows, letting Duplessis talk.

"But Illinois should be in the forefront. Chicago is right in the middle of the country and would make a good symbol."

"Not entirely," Rosenfeld said. "Big Bill O'Leary is about to be indicted by the Feds." O'Leary was Mayor of Chicago, the most powerful politician in Illinois; the Governor of the state was merely a figurehead. "The FBI has been investigating corruption in Chicago, and they're going to announce their indictment soon. O'Leary will claim it is just a political ploy to distract attention from Jennings' crimes. Big Bill is busting his balls to organize a secession convention right now."

"Chicago will be the capital city. That doesn't mean O'Leary gets to be president. I don't think he'd cut quite the right figure."

"Who would? Birkenstock would be the obvious choice, but he's too extreme. And he won't be unhappy about not getting it. He's ready to be John Brown, he doesn't have to be Abraham Lincoln."

"Who then? Someone with stature." Both men shrugged self-deprecatingly. Rosenfeld went on, "Someone who stands as close to the center as possible. Someone good at crossing over between Republicans and Democrats. Someone larger than life."

Duplessis was thinking: he's offering me the presidency; he wants this thing enough to give away the presidency of a new nation.

"Let's wait and see." For the moment Duplessis would rather be kingmaker than king. "Let me know if there's anything I can do."

Two governors wandered back along endless verandas and Pacific views to the helicopter pad. "What about these rumors I've been hearing?" Duplessis said, by way of small talk. "That the Chief Justice was murdered. Poisoned. A setup to throw things into crisis. The question is, who did it? The CIA, the NSA, the White House staff—?" He noted Rosenfeld's snort of disgust, went on, having gotten a rise. "After all, *cui bono*, who benefits? Jennings comes out on top because it gives him a chance to take command in the deadlock.

Or it could have been the people who hate Jennings so much they'll even kill the swing vote on the Court. Not that our nice people would dirty their hands—"

Duplessis puffed out his muscular chest, purposely dwarfing the pale complexioned New Yorker, "—but they could have hired a Mafia hit man. The girly men wouldn't do it themselves but they must know somebody, if they come from Jersey or New York or Massachusetts. Ever notice, that, Everett? Liberals and the Mafia always live in the same place."

"Come off it," Rosenfeld said. "See you in Chicago."

The country was polarizing from week to week. Across the Blue states of the North and West, state conventions were taking place. Some had already seceded, others were still debating, hesitant or genuinely torn.

Red states began to pass legislation that had been stymied by liberal opposition or overturned by the courts. Recitation of the Pledge of Allegiance was mandated in schools, legislators loudly reaffirming the phrase "one nation under God". The Ten Commandments were restored to court houses that had removed them, and some states ordered them displayed in all public buildings. Liberals bemoaned the fall of the separation of Church and state.

The country was separating like an emulsion in a centrifuge, liberals flowing North and West, conservatives flowing South. Each flow drained away the opposition in the other's stronghold, making it easier for the militants to get control. Moderates and those who genuinely could not make up their minds were bewildered.

Crosses erupted on public property. Manger scenes sprouted in front of city halls, somewhat incongruously since it was now three months after Christmas. In some cities, the crosses were torn down again. Manger scenes were found rearranged each morning, with atheist slogans painted on them, Charles Darwin taking the place of the baby Jesus. Vigilance groups formed to guard them.

Old horror stories were resurrected and repeated. The college librarian who prohibited students from displaying "USA" stickers on their book covers the day after 9/11/01 lest it offend non-American students, was excoriated again in one speech after another by Red State politicians. Conservative legislators passed laws and imposed draconian penalties for flag burning and desecration of national symbols. Blue State militants responded with a rash of flag-burning demonstrations across the upper tier, from New York to San Francisco. Secessionists brought extra supplies of American flags to trample and burn, while marchers made a point of cheering Mexican flags, Canadian flags, any foreign flag. Jokers marched with skull-and-crossbones flags, Mickey Mouse flags; in Boston the American flag was torn down and replaced by a flag proclaiming Red Sox Nation. More serious marchers displayed a World Unity flag, a globe with "Peace" above and "RELIGION DIVIDES, SECULARISM UNITES" below.

Abortion laws were being tightened across the Red states. Police were no longer enforcing laws requiring demonstrators to stay back or refrain from hassling women entering abortion clinics. Encouraged, demonstrators began to block the entrances, sitting down in the technique of passive resistance imitated years before from the civil rights movement. Little factions in the crowds—like Maoist radicals who hijacked nonviolent demonstrations in the 1960s—smashed windows and forced indoors. Several clinics were wrecked, and doctors and nurses had to be rescued by the police. Red State governors deplored the violence, then issued emergency edicts closing the clinics as a public safety measure. The last remaining medical personnel who had been willing to perform abortions left the Red States and traveled North, to heroes' welcomes.

The wave of demonstrations crested and receded. State legislatures had made their pronouncements. The secessionist constitutional convention was convening in Chicago. All attention shifted there; the rest of the country took a deep breath and watched.

YEAR ONE, CHAPTER TWO.
REVOLUTION IN MILITARY AFFAIRS

The Pentagon. March.

"Point that thing the other way," Marine Corps General Mark McConnell said from the front row. "I'm on your side."

A soldier with outsized goggles over his eyes covered the auditorium. The new prototype assault rifle in his hands looked like a standard M4 carbine but encrusted with electronic eyes on the barrel and boxy protrusions near the trigger as if it housed a nest of cell phones. More electronics bulged from the soldier's helmet.

"It wouldn't matter if it was loaded," the soldier said. "Because these sensors on the gun and my goggles connect me to the big computer. The Frankenstein monster you call HOME." Colonel John Gandhi Park pulled off the helmet and looked human again. "I can't fire without the computer approving my target. What kind of a soldier does that make me?"

"It makes you the soldier of the future," Secretary of Defense Robert Madigan said. "An unbeatable soldier. Small arms are going to be one hundred percent accurate."

"In theory," Gandhi said. "In the real world, something always comes up."

From the podium Thaddeus Wolf, Deputy Secretary of Defense, paused laser pointer in hand, his tailored gray suit framed against the multicolored graphs of the PowerPoint on the screen. He had a way of half-closing his eyes when he talked to officers in uniform that conveyed what he thought of them.

"Look, Colonel," Wolf said, "this is the direction the military has been going for twenty years. Jet pilots don't pull the trigger anymore, it's done by the computers flying on an AWACS a hundred miles away. Now it's the infantry's turn. Quit dragging your feet and get into the twenty-first century."

Gandhi threw the assault rifle onto the exhibits table. "HOME is going to choose all the targets and fire all the weapons. We might as well not have officers any more, because there's nothing left for us to lead."

The auditorium stirred uneasily, a melange of uniforms of all the services, Air Force blue, Army green, Navy khaki, red-trimmed olive green of the Marine Corps. If you asked them what they were there for, they would have said something that sounded like *"tittifwisk."* This was the TTFWSC—Transformational Task Force for Weapons, Sensors and Computers. Its purpose was to sound out reactions from experienced combat officers to the latest high-tech reforms. Veteran task-forcers assumed it meant getting everybody on board with what the SECDEF wanted to do.

"We'll still have military managers," Wolf said. "Some of you will have a career in this organization."

"I don't give a damn about career," said McConnell, the Marine. He was Clark Gable handsome, strong jaw and cheekbones, an erect confident way of holding himself that cast him for the hero parts in the cinema of life. "You can't run a war thousands of miles from the front. We need boots on the ground. That's the lesson we learned in Iraq—in case you didn't learn it."

"We're not getting rid of boots on the ground, Mark," Madigan said. "We're turning them into high-tech boots."

"You're cutting off our hands," Gandhi said. "We do the fighting, we're the ones who get killed. We need to decide when to pull the trigger."

"I resent that, John," Madigan said. "We're doing everything we can to protect you. Friendly fire will be impossible. Our computer files will combine all the sensor inputs. You can't miss. What better protection is there than that?"

"It's an insult to the fighting man. We'll be dragging a computer around the battlefield. Setting it up, feeding it ammo, cleaning it, clearing out jams. We'd be nothing but servants for robots."

"Infantry aren't called grunts for nothing," General Curt Harris said. He was Chairman of the Joint Chiefs of Staff, Air Force blue uniform with bushy eyebrows and four stars on his shoulders. The Air Force was the first service to go over to computerized remote control, and Harris had little sympathy for what he regarded as the old-fashioned services. He was the only uniformed officer sitting on the stage with the civilians.

"This so-called transformation is going to destroy us," Gandhi persisted. "No army ever won who didn't believe in what they're doing."

"We'd be happy to accept your resignation," Wolf said. "We only want people who belong on the team."

"I've been on more fire teams than you'll ever see on your TV tube. Rear echelon MFs."

"Don't you challenge my commitment." Wolf stepped down from the podium into the pit of officers. "I'd give my right arm for the service."

"I already have," Gandhi said. He thrust his uniformed forearm in Wolf's face: the flesh-colored tube of a prosthetic arm projected from his sleeve, ending in a shiny steel clamp. "You want to step outside, Mr. Deputy Secretary? Or don't people like you ever step outside of anything?"

"Forget it, John," Wolf said. "I won't fight a cripple."

The crowd teetered on the brink of something, holding its breath.

Madigan motioned everyone to sit down. "We've aired our differences enough. Unless there's anything new, that's it for today."

The Marine remained standing in front of the podium. "I've got something," McConnell said. "Is it true this new system means abolishing the Marine Corps?"

"Correct," Wolf said. "I know there's a lot of sentiment about historic organizations. But they're out of date. If it makes you feel any better, we're abolishing the Army, Navy and Air Force too. All officers will be assigned to joint operations. Don't say you're surprised. Navy and Marine planes fly off land bases, same as the Air Force.

Every service has its own helicopters and drones. There's a lot of bureaucratic duplication and excess procurement. Now that HOME is going to run everything, it's time to cut the superfluous fat."

"The United States Marine Corps is superfluous fat? Who fought on the front line at Guadalcanal and Okinawa? And Kuwait and Fallujah?"

"With all due respect for the Marine Corps' distinguished past," Wolf interrupted, "that's history. We're moving into the future."

"What will happen to Camp Pendleton?" This was McConnell's own command, the Marines' big West Coast base, in southern California. "What about the Marine Corps Air Station in San Diego?"

"They'll be folded into the unified military service. Don't worry, General, officers of your experience will get commensurate positions in the new organization."

"I'd rather see Pendleton shut down than some other insignia on it," McConnell said. "Don't underestimate what the Marine Corps will do to survive."

"What do you have in mind?" Madigan said.

"You'll find out. There's a lot going on around the country. If you don't want the Marines, there are others who do."

Achilles Cruz, Colonel of the US Army, Reserves, sat in a bar in downtown Denver, staring thoughtfully at his whiskey glass. He was in civilian clothes, a business suit looking more than a little rumpled. It was his only suit, and he had been wearing it to sales meetings in one Western city to another for two weeks. His brother-in-law's chemical supply company kept him on the payroll, but not at all lavishly. Cruz had left the Army three years before, feeling blocked in his career, hoping for business prospects that did not pan out. He was listless and bored. His companion at the bar was conservatively dressed in blue suit, white shirt and dark tie, a middle-aged man but flat-bellied and fit, the look of a high-ranking police official.

"Security is always a big issue," he was saying, "especially these days. But I don't know that the Denver Police Department has an opening for a man of your rank and qualifications, Colonel Cruz."

Cruz grunted. He was used to hearing it. "I appreciate your honesty," he said. "I hear there's a former military man on the governor's staff. You happen to know him?" He took another sip of his whiskey.

"Yeah. That would be Freddie Weston. Seems to me he had service in the Gulf War. Ever run into him?"

The sound of distant shouting came from the street. An insistent repetitive rhythm: *juh-juh-juh. juh-juh-juh. JUH-SHUH-JUH.* Growing louder.

"Another demonstration," said blue suit. "Heading down Fifteenth to the State Capitol."

"Happens a lot everywhere, these days," said Cruz, not looking up. "Big trouble is coming."

"A bunch of college kids from Boulder. We can handle it."

"Down the road a few months," said Cruz. "It's growing."

"You may be right," said blue suit, standing up. "Want to take a look?"

In the street was a parade of marchers, chanting. *Jennings must go! JENNINGS MUST GO!* The chanters were thicker at the front of the crowd than the rear. The sound crested, went down the next block.

In the distance, the chanting stopped. A portable loudspeaker blared sharply, a leader's voice starting a new chant. *Free Colorado! FREE COLORADO!* It was picked up by the crowd.

Then came the sound of confused shouting, and the metallic resonance of police bullhorns.

The two men in suits came out on a plaza before the Capitol. The crowd had unfurled a banner, COALITION OF SECULAR STATES OF AMERICA. To Cruz's practiced eye, it looked like about eight hundred people, an undisciplined battalion. Here and there waved the rainbow emblem flag of the CSSA.

A counter-demonstration carrying small American flags was blocking their way. Perhaps four hundred in all, a couple of rifle companies minus their rifles. They shouted in rhythm too: *USA! USA!* The two sides stopped thirty feet apart, shouting at each other.

Three or four individuals from each side ventured into the intervening space, the cement no-man's-land, gesturing with their fingers and hurling insults.

This went on for five minutes, ten, fifteen. Momentum had stopped. A line of police officers in riot gear stood at the side, impassively waiting. Veterans of demonstrations, waiting for boredom to do its part.

The two sides were chanting at each other: *FREE COLORADO!* against *USA! USA!* The two sounds remained surprisingly distinct for a while, then began to meld together as the crowds became hoarser, losing energy. Individuals at the back of the crowds were beginning to drift away.

A young man in jeans, stripped to the waist and with a bandana over his face stepped into the empty space with a large American flag draped over one arm, and a bottle of kerosene. The flag flared up on the cement, red-white-and-blue licked with orange flames.

The front line of counter-demonstrators ran forward. The CSSA line surged raggedly to meet them. A half minute of pushing and shoving took place around the space where the flag was charring on the plaza. One knot of counter-demonstrators was striving to stamp out the flames, while a little circle of opponents tried to hold them off with linked arms. Punches were thrown, most missing; at best someone grabbed an arm or tackled a leg.

The flag was still burning. But the circle of its protectors was winnowing, becoming more isolated as its numbers fell.

The configuration of the plaza had shifted. Where a few minutes before there were solid masses, the crowds had suddenly dispersed. More than half of them were running, centrifugally, although the CSSA demonstrators were falling back more than the counter-demonstrators.

A hard core of about fifty or so of the USA faction were advancing. Little knots of action opened up, separated amidst the surrounding space. Five counter-demonstrators had caught the bare-chested young man in the bandana, and had him down on the cement, pummeling and kicking at him.

The fleeing CSSA demo left its bravest or more foolish members behind, like seaweed on a beach behind a receding tide.

Where an isolated individual was caught by a half dozen counter-demonstrators, the eddy of attackers swirled around him, or her. Where a little group of three or four stood their ground, the attackers flowed by, like waves past rocks, seeking softer targets.

The all-against-all mêlée beloved of filmmakers was nowhere to be seen. In the absence of strong military discipline—and sometimes even then—crowds of fighters are rarely capable of effective violence, except when ganging up on an isolated victim.

Momentum was on the side of the USA counter-demonstrators. The bigger group of demonstrators had melted away before a smaller one; their activists had won emotional dominance over their counterparts on the CSSA front line.

The police finally went into action. After the counter-demonstrators drove their opponents from the plaza, the police advanced, capturing defeated CSSA demonstrators and dragging them off to arrest. The cops were better rehearsed than the amateurs, but the pattern was similar. A knot of four or five officers, a cluster of black beetles in helmets and shields, would descend on a single demonstrator, knocking him to the ground, pummeling him with batons, pinioning his arms behind his back and hauling him away. Or occasionally her, women being a minority of the active front line but nevertheless present here and there, and the police—all male—were equal opportunity as far as making arrests.

The crowd of USA counter-demonstrators who had retreated to their side of the plaza when the riot began now crept forward cautiously, observing and cheering from a safe distance.

Achilles Cruz had barely moved from his position, fifty yards off to the side of the confrontation. Something in his demeanor kept him from being a target. The crowds had run past him; the little knots of attackers hounding their isolated victims had swirled around him. He looked at them dispassionately, a practiced observer of human tides. He was waiting. The monsoon was yet to come.

★

In the Secretary of Defense's office, Wolf said: "Colonel Park is the last of the barbarians. We need to clean out the military of men like him."

The SECDEF office was a series of connected rooms where flags sprouted in clusters.

At one end of the spacious central room, the Secretary's fortress-size desk was backed by a wall portrait of a historic predecessor, honored by the red-white-and-blue flag of the USA at one side and the spread-eagle-on-blue flag of the DOD at the other. Down at the end of the room was a map of the world, continents in green, oceans in blue, ice caps in white; another clump of flagstaffs surmounted by gold eagle finials: a spot for official swearings-in and ceremonial photo ops.

The officials took their usual places at a conference table. It was the right size for an informal dining room in a wealthy mansion, polished dark wood covered with silver water pitchers and gilt-rimmed coffee mugs with the DOD eagle crest.

"The big problem is McConnell," Madigan said from the end of the table. The Secretary was a nondescript, medium-size man with rimless glasses and thin slicked-back hair. "He has thirty-five thousand troops at Camp Pendleton. Reports are he's been meeting with Marine commanders from Hawaii to Arizona. That would make a total of seventy thousand troops for this secessionist Coalition. If McConnell talks the Navy bases in southern California into going along, he'd have a sizable force of aircraft. In fact, the biggest force in the CSSA."

"The CSSA," General Harris snorted. "They won't last long. We could nuke New York and L.A. and that would be the end of it."

"Don't even joke about it." Madigan eyed him sternly. "If I thought for a moment you were seriously considering it, I'd fire you. Immediately."

"Okay, conventional weapons. A precision surgical strike. Take out their ringleaders. The FBI knows where they are. Get a couple of F-16s in their airspace, swoop down on precise GPS coordinates, and that's the end of it. The Israelis do it all the time with the Palestinians."

"This secessionist movement is more than a few politicians. Creating martyrs would make it worse. Ask the Israelis."

"Then what do you suggest we do?" Wolf said.

"Wait," Madigan said. "Now is our chance to put everything under control of HOME. Nobody can run to Congress and tell us we have to keep the Marines or the Navy. Crisis is always a good time for big changes—usually it's the only time."

Wolf eyed Madigan with respect, one shrewd organizational politician admiring a shrewder one. "You're right, Bob. HOME isn't operational yet. It could use some debugging before civil war starts. Nobody is going to be in very good fighting shape for a few months anyway."

"There's another job, too," Madigan said. "We need to get rid of a lot of people. The diehards resisting HOME. When we combine the services, there'll be another round of dissenters. We might as well clean them out now, don't let them hang around slowing things down."

"How about the disloyal ones?" Harris said. "The secessionist sympathizers. Put them on trial for treason. And arrest McConnell before he leaves the building."

"Take it easy, Curt," Madigan said. "We want to keep people calm around here, not rile them up. It will make less stir if we just say their jobs have become redundant."

"And let the atheist symps go over to the enemy?" Harris said.

"It's better than having a gun battle in the Pentagon. Handle it honorably, the way they did in 1861. They drank a toast and said, see you on the battlefield. The better forces are going to win anyway. You don't doubt that, do you, Curt?"

"No, of course not."

Madigan turned to Wolf. "That incident with Colonel Park this morning. How many more are there out there like him?"

"A few," Wolf said. "Our surveys show twenty-three percent of Army officers disagree with computer control, and forty-seven percent approve. The rest—"

"Surveys don't always tell the truth. A lot of them are covering their ass. This outfit is full of yes-sayers who'll find a way not to go along."

"The Computer Security office can search all emails," said Wolf. "That will tell us what they're really saying to each other." He called over a tall young woman in Army uniform standing in the entrance alcove, lean athletic torso with flax blonde hair pulled back in a tight ponytail.

"Major Zielkowski will take care of it," Wolf continued. "I want a list of everyone Colonel John Gandhi Park has been talking to. And who else they've been talking to."

"Yes, sir," Major Debra Zielkowski said. It was the first time she had been in the SECDEF's office. She hesitated. "Isn't that against the rules, sir—monitoring private email?"

"The rules are changing, Major," Wolf said. "Computer security is the heart of our operation. You're a team player, aren't you?"

She was a team player, all right, Debra told herself. She had come over as a child from the Ukraine when communism collapsed. Her mother refused to speak Ukrainian anymore, the moment she got off the plane. This is my country now, she had said, in a heavily accented English that she never lost. Her mother often repeated the story to Debra, the last time when Debra got her commission at West Point. "Yes, sir," Debra said. "We're a team, sir. We don't let each other down."

"All right. I want to know Park's movements, where he's been, who he's seen. Track his cell phone calls." Wolf smacked a fist into his palm. "If HOME were up and running, we'd have this already. The computer keeps track of every communication sent, every weapon fired. We'll have a record of what every soldier is doing, who talks to who, and what they said. HOME won't just direct battles, it will be a complete security system."

"We're not there yet, Thad," Madigan said. "If Park is organizing a revolt, I've got a simpler solution."

"Namely, what?"

"Let Park smoke them out for us. Call him in. Tell him I'm open to listening to him and whoever else thinks like him. Let him know I don't necessarily think he's crazy, but he's got to calm down and prove it's more than just the opinion of a tiny extreme."

"The rest of them might not come," Wolf said.

"Have Park followed as soon as he gets the message. Report everyone he's meeting with. Copy Major Zielkowski so she can track his network."

She stood by at attention, all serious concentration. She didn't wear glasses but she looked like she was reciting in a classroom. Behind the Secretary, floor-to-ceiling windows at intervals opened the office's back wall to the Potomac, she supposed, except that they were closed by the slats of mini-blinds. Across the river somewhere was the Lincoln Memorial.

"I want a squad of MPs. Out of sight, but ready to cover the hallway as soon as Park exits my office." Madigan leaned back in his chair with a tight smile. "I think Colonel Park is going to do more talking than is good for him."

"I'm going to enjoy watching you square off with Park again, Thad," General Harris rasped. "He almost nailed you with that prosthetic hook of his."

"He's a barbarian," Wolf said, unable to let go of the insult he had rendered to the face of another human being. "A mad dog. Men like that ought to be shot."

Without taking his feet off the desk, Lt. Colonel Brian Sanchez reached out and gently pushed the door shut. "You know, Gandhi, you'd be a good-looking guy if you didn't look so angry all the time."

John Gandhi Park was Korean-American, high cheekbones in a broad, clean-featured face. But his brows were always curled in the beginning of a frown, his mouth set hard, his high straight forehead furrowed vertically above the bridge of the nose in an everlasting scowl. Something in his eyes was ambiguous, a quick way of glancing around, and a habit of tuning out immersed in his thoughts, second-guessing himself. He made people uneasy.

Brian Sanchez leaned back in his chair and laughed. "Yeah, you'd be a real Hollywood idol if you'd lighten up. All the women would be throwing themselves at you. Wouldn't they, Deb?"

Major Debra Zielkowski looked at Gandhi Park with a flicker of alarm. Until now he was just a name, an assignment. "Cut it out, Brian," she said. She tried to concentrate on her computer screen. Was she going to have to enter this into her data base, that she herself was one of Colonel Park's recent contacts? The network algorithm didn't have room for exceptional circumstances. Keep your mind on your work, she told herself.

"Don't mind Debra," Sanchez said. "She's in love with her computer."

Gandhi did not look in her direction. "Brian, I need your help. We need to get the officers together who've been in combat. You can locate everybody who's here in the Pentagon, can't you?"

Sanchez took his feet off the desk. "Why come to me? I'm in Computer Security. I'm working for the chief bad guy."

"We were in combat together. A band of brothers. Remember?"

"That was then. Now I've got a cushy desk job. Surrounded by beautiful babes, who are secretly in love with me."

Debra gave him a rueful look. "Keeping on dreaming, Brian."

"I can't do this alone," Gandhi said. "A lot of officers agree with me, but hardly anyone wants to speak out. I'm sure the Marines are on our side. If we got enough together we could go to Congress. Or President Jennings himself."

"And tell them what?"

"What combat is really like. Why controlling everything by computers isn't going to work. Wolf and Madigan and their crowd can be replaced if enough of us speak up."

"The trouble with you, Gandhi, is that you don't know what the Pentagon is really like."

"I know it's a bunch of computer jockeys who are totally out of touch with reality."

"That's inaccurate," Debra joined in. "We have better information than any frontline soldier. All you can see is what's in front of you, and you don't see that very well."

Gandhi noticed her for the first time. "I suppose you know all about it, young lady." Women in the military, that was half the problem. Women, and men who act like women, sitting in offices and trying to run things.

"Let's not get personal. We're going through a military revolution. We're lifting the fog of war."

"You'll be a great general some day, Major," Gandhi said sarcastically. "The kind of general who thinks if everything is okay at headquarters it must be okay in the field. The kind that thinks soldiers are numbers without emotions."

"We're aware of soldiers' emotions," Debra said. "We're putting sensors on their battle dress to monitor their body signs—blood pressure, heart beat, glucose level. It all goes into the computer so it can tell when troops are stressed and performing below capacity."

"So what? You might know when men are in trouble, but you don't know what makes men fight through trouble. You can't create morale by sitting at a keyboard in your office."

"What you call morale, Colonel, is just a cliché old soldiers have been repeating around the fireside for thousands of years."

"Some things never change," Gandhi said. "You win by imposing your will on the enemy. You have to break him down, and you never let him break you down."

"That's mysticism," Debra said. She made a wry face, an adolescent smarty-pants putting down a dumb classmate.

He took a step towards her. "If you've been there, you'd know what I'm talking about. War is about dominating the enemy. All the high tech in the world is never going to change that."

"War is about material forces," Debra said. Men didn't intimidate her. If she stood up, she would be taller than this outraged Colonel, even in her flat-heeled shoes. "If we destroy their assets before they destroy ours, we win. That's what our high tech does."

"Tell that to the Taliban. We blasted the hell out of them with our high tech, but we didn't impose our will on them, and they outlasted us. We lost our will to fight before they did." Gandhi dropped into a swivel chair.

"Give us time. Once our computers get enough information on the guerrillas, we'll beat them."

Gandhi leaned forward intently, almost touching the knee of her Army uniform trousers. "Let me tell you a true story. I was leading a battalion rooting out jihadi terrorists. There were a couple hundred of them dispersed in caves and gullies—one of those arid Third

World landscapes, a few scruffy plants but lots of boulders and some cement and plaster farmhouses, little village clusters here and there. What you theoretical soldiers would call a granular environment—plenty of cover, poor sightlines, lots of possibilities for moving from place to place, playing cat and mouse. Our job was to spot the enemy and draw them out, so we could hit them with precision air strikes. After about ten hours of this we were getting tired, when we ran right into them—suddenly the place was swarming with jihadis. We called for air support right away. What we wanted were A-10 gunships or Apaches but they didn't come. I found out later they were back at base refueling."

He paused, tuned into his inner vision, remembering. Debra wondered what it would be like to have a device that could project images in someone else's mind onto her computer screen.

"What we got was an airstrike by what was available, two F-16 fighters. They had the coordinates we sent them, and they came in and dropped a couple of five hundred-pound bombs right on them. The trouble is everybody was moving—the jihadis were already on the move, and we were on the move because there were more jihadis than ourselves in that particular spot. One of those bombs sent a bunch of boulders crashing and blocked the gulley where we were taking cover. Then the F-16s went back to reload, or maybe they were at the end of their fuel. Anyway, they disappeared and the jihadis came down on us in a old-fashioned firefight. I lost fifteen men and had a bunch more wounded, including myself. Thank God we were hand-carrying enough firepower to drive them off. We didn't rely on long-distance backup—it did us more harm than it did the other side."

"I'd call that a system failure," Debra said. "A command computer would have allocated close air support with better attention to refueling schedules. They should have monitored more carefully which ground troops were engaged and which weren't, so they could get backup to the right place at the right time."

"If we'd gone in with larger ground forces, we wouldn't have been spread so thin. I would have had enough to take on the jihadis, without having to depend on whether air cover would screw up or not. And the reason we didn't have more was this whole idea of replacing boots on the ground with machinery, flying in just in time from long distance." Gandhi looked at Debra angrily. "This isn't a commercial inventory saving shelf space. War isn't a business. It needs to be run by warriors. Not by civilians wearing army uniforms."

"OK, computer systems sometimes make mistakes. But so do humans," she said, trying to stare back. She caught sight of Gandhi's prosthetic arm for the first time. "If you'd called in your position faster, Colonel, you'd still have your hand."

"My hand!" Gandhi held up the prosthetic clamp, looked scornfully at the device on the end of his arm. "I wouldn't mind losing it to the enemy. But I'd like to get my hooks into that computer operator. And all the other computer jockeys who think they can play God."

"Hey, Gand, you sure don't live up to your name," Brian Sanchez said.

Colonel Park gave a little grimace of a smile, relaxing. Only his close friends called him Gand—his boyhood nickname. He had been born Gandhi Park. His father was a Korean immigrant, his mother a civil rights enthusiast from an old New England family. Both parents were admirers of Martin Luther King and nonviolent direct action. Then when young Gand was nine years and the idealism of the 1960s was turning into the frenzy of the 70s, he lost his parents in a plane crash. He was adopted by neighbors, a prominent Irish-American lawyer with a devoutly Catholic wife, who insisted that Gandhi be baptized with a proper name. He went through his teen years as John Gandhi Park, never answering to the name John without a scarcely visible twist of his lips—half defiant, half mourning for young Gand and his family who were no more.

"Enough reminiscing," he said. "Are you going to help me, or not?" He was asking Sanchez, but out of the corner of his eye he caught something flickering in Debra's face. He swung around, fastened onto her perplexed glance.

"I'm a loyal American," Gandhi said. "I have no intention of going over to the CSSA. The US Army is my home. I just hate to see it commit suicide."

"You don't have much time," Debra said. "The Secretary is going to call you in this afternoon."

"To can me? Or listen to what I have to say?"

"You'll have a chance to make your case."

Gandhi turned to Sanchez. "Are there any high-ranking officers who'll back me up? What about Jefferson Gray?"

They all paused. Lieutenant General Jefferson Gray was the most respected officer in the services. A combat officer who won every battle. Who had survived every reform, without joining any wave of rhetorical enthusiasm and without compromising himself.

"Jeff Gray plays the hand he's dealt," Sanchez said. "If you want my advice, I'd say do the same."

He stopped Gandhi in the act of opening the door. "I've seen a lot of reformers come and go. I know the Pentagon better than they do. You think this latest computer system is going to fail. You'll never convince them. So let it fail. If you're right, you'll still be here to bail us out."

"I can't keep my mouth shut," Gandhi said. "Watch my back, if you can."

Secretary of Defense Robert Madigan's office held pride of place on the outermost of the Pentagon's five concentric rings. The blinds on the back wall were open, offering vistas over the Potomac toward the seat of government in Washington, DC.

"I'm willing to hear you out, John." Secretary Madigan indicated a sofa where Colonel Park should sit. They were in an alcove near the entrance hall, the sofa tastefully upholstered in pale gold, a glass-topped coffee table, Persian carpet under foot, green house-plants in Chinese porcelain vases. This would be no official repri-mand, the subordinate officer standing in front of his superior's mas-sive desk, just a comfortable chat. Madigan sat at one side in a wing chair covered in silver fabric. General Harris sat on another chair at the far end, flanked by Deputy Secretary Wolf, making a wide semi-circle with Gandhi at the focus. Wolf looked abstracted, avoiding eye contact. He had been instructed to keep in the background, not to stir up this morning's confrontation with Gandhi, unless the Secretary gave the signal.

Gandhi launched into his critique. The others sat in silence until he was done. Some of the vehemence was draining out. Gandhi had come for a fight, but the enemy was eluding him, sitting quietly in plain sight.

"That's very well said," Madigan began. "But I'd like you to see something, John." He led the way to a side room.

On the wall above a bank of computers were two large round screens side by side, one green and other blue. The green screen was marked like a navigational compass. The blue screen carried messages and images.

"Colonel Park, meet HOME," Madigan announced. "Officially, it's Hyper Organization Military Efficiency. It's much friendlier than you think."

Gandhi shrugged noncommittally.

Madigan punched a few keys. The green screen centered on a large unmoving blue dot, surrounded by a scatter of smaller blue dots, some moving, some stationary. A touch on an icon displayed the view from the interior of a helicopter, swinging through 360 degrees.

"That's from the cockpit of a transport helicopter, sitting outside here on the helipad. It tracks every weapons platform, every vehicle around it, at whatever distance you want."

Another flick. A map of the Potomac River banks and adjacent areas, with blue icons moving across it—blue forces, friendlies.

"HOME can also track hostiles. We aren't completely set up yet, but let's try a training exercise at Ft. Benning."

The green screen was now looking out from the interior of a tank in the Georgia countryside. Its central icon was ringed by blue icons representing friendly tanks; another flick to a coarser scale showed the airspace for miles around, displaying the positions and movement of supporting aircraft. Red icons showed the location of hostile forces, both ground and air.

"HOME has better eyes and ears than any human," said Madigan. "Radar, thermal imaging, laser beams, GPS. It can penetrate clouds and see in the dark. We're adding senses humans never had. Chemical tests that can smell out weapons and who's fired them. Photo archives that can remember every face and match it with live video feed, combining visuals from UAVs and security monitors. You know where your enemy is, and you hit exactly that spot. And where all your support is, all the time, and how much weaponry they have to support you. Wouldn't you like to have that in your tank or your helicopter?"

"It'd be too much of a good thing," Gandhi said. "Troops would spend so much time looking at it, they wouldn't do any fighting."

"That won't be a problem. HOME doesn't just provide target acquisition, it provides execution. It tracks targets for you, aims all the weapons connected to it, and even fires them."

"The Army that gives away its freedom of action to a computer is giving away its soul. The Army that does that is going to lose."

Harris said, "I didn't know you atheist rebels believed in the soul."

"If you're talking about the CSSA, I'm as loyal as you are. I've fought for my country and I'll fight for it again if you give me a chance. But I'm not going to fight for a computer."

"I understand you, John," Madigan said. "There are things that computers can't do—not yet, at any rate. We need quick-thinking officers who can react on the spot. You, and a lot of good men like you, have been doing it for years."

Gandhi continued to scowl, refusing to be cajoled.

"But you need to understand my position," the Secretary went on. "There is more to this than integrating battlefield information and optimizing our response. The computer isn't ultimately in control, you know."

"Who, then?"

"Behind the HOME computer system is a human being. That's me," said the Secretary, "or the Chairman of the Joint Chiefs"—indicating General Harris—"or the President. This isn't a science fiction movie, where a giant computer named HAL takes control away from humans. We decide what is going to be hit. And—you may not like this, John, from your battlefield point of view—sometimes what is not to be hit."

"That's just the problem," Gandhi said. "Political decisions over-riding military realities. Like when President Bush ordered a stop in February 1991, just when we had the Iraqi army on the run. We would have saved thousands of lives in Iraq if they let us finish the job in the first place."

"War has changed," Madigan said. "Victories aren't won just on the battlefield. Now it's a war for hearts and minds. We use satellite hookups that transmit battlefield sensors instantly to command computers. The 24-hour news media and the blogs and the internet postings use the same technology we do. Nothing stays secret very long. The media will ferret out every mistake. You can do a thousand things right on the battlefield, but if one civilian gets killed, that's the big story."

"Computers aren't going to help that," Gandhi said. "They can interpret signals the wrong way. Like the aerial sensors in Iraq that picked up guns firing in a village, and called in air strikes. It turned out to be a wedding party. Not knowing that Iraqi villages celebrate weddings by firing guns."

"So the computer system doesn't always have all the information it needs. What's the answer to that, more information or less?" Madigan said. "Soldiers on the ground commit atrocities too. Their emotions are on edge; they've been ambushed and their buddies blown up by roadside bombs set off by someone within sightlines. It's understandable how they mistake a civilian for a guerrilla. And then they get themselves into a hole by shooting a whole family and trying to hide the bodies."

Madigan shook his head sadly. "These are human reactions. We understand that. But that's how you win a battle and lose a war. The news media find an atrocity story. The enemy picks it up and makes a propaganda coup out of it. The people we're fighting for become enemy sympathizers. That's how we lose hearts and minds."

"And you think this computer is going to save them?"

"If more centralized control will cut down civilian casualties, it is worth it. That's all the more reason why military action needs civilian oversight. Now we can do that in real time, not wait until things go wrong to court-martial some poor grunts."

HOME glowed unblinkingly from the wall behind Madigan. Gandhi started to point at it with his prosthetic hand, caught sight of the metal clamp silhouetted against the calm blue and green screens. He dropped his arm abruptly.

"You can't just win hearts and minds and forget about winning battles. We can be the nicest guys in the world, always letting the other guy take the first shot and the last shot too. But if we lose the firefight, we lose everything else. Intruding politics into war is a formula for losing."

"This is a democracy, John. That means the people decide, through their elected officials. That means Congress, and the President. In America the chain of command is civilian. The military doesn't overrule it."

"That's a funny argument right now," Gandhi said. "Exactly where is the legitimate chain of command? Some people question President Jennings' authority. They say he's acting in violation of the Constitution and the Supreme Court. You're his political appointees. If Jennings' authority is in question, so is everything you're doing here."

"I knew you were a traitor," Harris said.

"I'm not going over to the CSSA," Gandhi said. He stood up, feeling the anger flood through him. "But if there's a civil war coming on, I have to question, in good conscience, what you are doing to our military. Real soldiers won't fight in a robot Army. I hear you are forcibly retiring a lot of officers. They won't all go peaceably. I know I won't."

Madigan looked over at Wolf. The Deputy Secretary took up the argument in a goading tone. "We've had reports questioning your mental stability for some time, Colonel Park. I'd say you're just an isolated individual, unable to adapt. Your mental faculties are an unfortunate casualty of battlefield stress. I doubt if any other officer of repute would go along with you."

"Say what you like. There are a lot who think like me."

"Who, for instance?"

"So you'd like me to make out a list? That would be convenient."

Madigan shrugged, indicating the door. "You're behind the times, John. Take an honorable retirement—while you still can."

Debra Zielkowski pushed through an excited crowd in the corridors of the Pentagon. The entire floor around the Secretary of Defense's office was restricted and you were supposed to have a badge with a high-level clearance to enter the area. Under normal conditions even one-star and two-star generals could not get through the guards. But this afternoon the checkpoints had broken down. Guards were surrounded by a hubbub of angry voices; some had gone over to the dissidents, others were flustered and cowed by the pressure of numbers. In one place Debra saw a scuffle where the guard was relieved of his firearm and knocked to the floor.

The crowd was thickest outside the Secretary of Defense's office. The corridor was wider here, with a spotlighted display on the opposite wall showing the gold-rimmed seal of the DOD alongside a historical sequence of official medallions and honorific emblems. The outer walls of the Secretary's office were floor-to-ceiling dark wood paneling, with a large brass name plate on the main door. Was Brian Sanchez here? Debra thought of asking officers she knew, but maybe she had better not say his name out loud. It might be recorded by surveillance and go into his record—and hers too. Of course she had the proper security badge and the right to be here. She saw Brian at the edge of the crowd.

Brian shook his head. "It wasn't me that done it. I'm just here for the show."

Nevertheless the corridor was filled with Gandhi Park's friends and Wolf and Madigan's enemies. There were generals who had been with Gandhi in the field in earlier days, and respected him as a better battlefield soldier than themselves. They knew they had been promoted ahead of him because he was too outspoken and that he would never rise above the rank of colonel. Junior officers repeated stories about him. Now they were inside the forbidden zone, things falling apart, the center not holding, something unleashed upon the

Pentagon chain of command, a feeling of who knows where things were going but a turning point was at hand.

There were sounds of a struggle, cursing, a crescendo of voices. Pushing to the front, Debra saw Gandhi Park in the midst of four MPs, two on each arm. Gandhi wrenched himself free and floored one MP with a swing of his metal hand.

The line of MPs—about fifteen of them across one side of the corridor—drew their pistols.

From the crowd of uniforms, Army green with a few olive Marines, pistols were pointed at the MPs. Someone aimed a M4.

The crowd, tightly packed, rearranged itself, the armed men at the front, others backing away, giving them room. The MPs crouched in firing position, arms extended, both hands steadying pistol grips, elbows locked. They looked uncertainly from the cluster arresting Colonel Park to the crowdfront twenty feet away. The Secretary of Defense retreated to his office door, deputies peering from behind him.

The standoff went on an eternity in the time distortion of adrenaline pumping through human bodies. In clock time it lasted about fifteen seconds.

From the back of crowd came a ripple of voices: "Jefferson Gray! It's Jeff Gray!"

The crowd parted for a bronze-skinned man with silver-white hair, the three stars of a Lieutenant General on his shoulders. He stepped into the space between the opposing gunsights. His habit of standing very erect made him look taller than he was.

"Soldiers!" he called out in a strong clear voice. "If you're looking to shoot somebody, start with me."

Both sides turned to him, recognizing General Jefferson Gray. He was not the ranking officer in the Pentagon—that would be General Harris, Chairman of the Joint Chiefs of Staff, who at the moment was squeezed uneasily in the knot of bodies in Secretary Madigan's mahogany doorway.

"I've been in the military a long time," Gray said in a voice that carried above the quieting audience. "If it's going to degenerate into a barroom brawl, you might as well kill me, because I don't want to look at it." He swept an arm slowly across the arc of guns aimed by the two opposing lines. "Who wants to shoot first? You? Or you?"

Guns lowered as his gesture swung past each bearer. Barrels pointed to the ground, returned to their holsters.

"No one? All right then, put your weapons away before they get dirty."

Contagious smiles softened the faces of the officers, breaking the tension. The MPs stood more easily. Gray went on.

"I don't have to remind you that officers handle their disputes in a honorable fashion. There are a lot of issues that divide us. Maybe we'll have to settle them on the field of battle. We're professional warriors. Let's act like it."

Madigan stepped from the doorway. "Colonel Park is under arrest."

"What's the charge?"

Madigan hesitated a barely discernable fraction of a second. "Attempted homicide."

"Treason," Wolf called out behind him.

"Refusing a direct order," said General Harris.

"Is that so," said Gray. "Who did he try to kill?"

"He said he'd kill *me*," Wolf said.

"No doubt it was a figure of speech," Gray said. "You know how soldiers talk when they're trying to make a point."

"All right, treason," Wolf said. "Insubordination. Refusing an order."

"Whose order did he refuse?" Gray asked, turning away from Wolf. "Yours, Mr. Secretary? Yours, General Harris?"

The Secretary's group looked from one to another.

Wolf began. "Colonel Park has questioned the existence of the chain of command—"

Madigan cut him off. "We don't need to go into it now. It will come out at the court-martial."

"Court-martial, is it?" said Gray. "Perhaps you recall another famous trial, the trial of Captain Dreyfus of the French Army. It brought down the government. Are you sure that's what you want?"

"Alright, Jeff," Madigan said in a deliberately casual voice. "We'll discuss this privately." The MPs had backed away from Colonel Park, unsure what to do.

Jefferson Gray went on, holding the floor. "Colonel Park is a rough-spoken man. A tough, honest soldier. Ever hear of William Tecumseh Sherman? Toughest soldier in the Union Army. He hated civilian control, hated politics. He hated political generals. But his country needed him, and we needed his service. He won the war for us, Sherman and Grant.

"Ever hear stories about General Patton cursing people out? He didn't always follow the chain of command either. Look it up some time, what he did in 1944, after leading the breakout from the Normandy beachhead. He wasn't waiting for orders, he was rushing to cross the Rhine and end the war—and get to Germany before the Russians did. Patton didn't care about rank when something needed to be done. He'd be down there in the mud, directing traffic, moving his tanks along. When they ran out of fuel he cannibalized other units. He'd take over another division's fuel dump at gunpoint, as long as his tanks didn't slow down."

Gray smiled, imagining the scene. Half the crowd laughed along with him. "Patton was in trouble all the time, with someone or other higher up. But he was a better general than the ones who reprimanded him, and they knew it. When we ran into trouble in the Battle of the Bulge, who did we turn to? Patton.

"Now some say we don't have room for officers like that any more. No more Shermans, no more Pattons, no more Colonel Parks. Is that really so?" Gray scanned the assembly, looking each officer in the eye. "I don't think so."

Secretary Madigan broke the silence. "On reflection, a court-martial would serve no useful purpose. But I believe Colonel Park's service is at an end. There is a serious question as to his sanity."

Gandhi Park looked at him contemptuously. "The truth looks crazy if you're blind. Anyway, I'm gone. I resign."

Gandhi turned on his heel. Dozens of officers followed. Others exchanged glances, or tilted their heads back and lifted their eyes to the ceiling.

The constitutional crisis had not been mentioned. But it hung in the atmosphere like humidity saturating the air before a rainstorm. Sides were being chosen in the Pentagon. Not everyone was announcing. But more than a few offices would be vacated in the days to come.

Secretary Madigan was behind his desk in the depths of his office, door closed, surrounded by a knot of deputies. The room was dim, lamp-lit, window blinds to the river closed again. General Harris was indignant. Madigan cut him off. "I'm just as happy to see them go. So what if they fight for the CSSA against us? If they want to fight against the military of the future with the Army of the past, it will be a lesson for everyone."

YEAR ONE, CHAPTER THREE.
SECESSION

Chicago. March.

Two weeks before the convention there was a shootout in Chicago.

The U.S. Attorney, Colby Hunter, took his stand across from the Mayor's office on Clark Street, surrounded by dozens of FBI agents.

"Got the indictment, Clyde?" he asked his deputy. "Big Bill O'Leary is going to face so many charges he'll be in prison for the rest of his life."

"Got it, chief. Fourteen counts of influence peddling, offering government appointments for bribery, demanding and receiving kickbacks; multiple counts of rigged elections going back for years."

"Make the arrest as quickly as you can," Hunter said. "Don't call the media until we've got him. We'll make the announcement once we've got him in the Federal Building."

There was a roar of motorcycles as a large convoy of Illinois state troopers pulled up and fanned out along the side entrance of the Mayor's Office. Scores of blue-uniformed Chicago police began to spill onto the sidewalk. O'Leary, a thick, jowly man, walked out boldly in their midst. He smiled sardonically at Hunter across the street.

"He wouldn't try anything," Hunter said. "It's all for show. Let's make this arrest."

But it was not entirely for show. As the U.S. Attorney and his cluster of FBI agents stepped off the curb, shots rang out, echoes reverberating off the high building walls of the urban canyon. It sounded like the St. Valentine's Day massacre but in fact consisted mostly of firing in the air. No one carried anything heavier than pistols, and in the heat of confrontation these mostly produced misses firing high at a range of twenty feet, a distance that steadily widened after the initial jaw-to-jaw as the two sides backed apart. Fortunately no bystanders were hit; everyone else was wearing kevlar body armor and there were only a few minor wounds.

While President Jennings and his Attorney General Bull Drummond pondered what criminal charges to add to the indictment, O'Leary's District Attorney charged the head of the local FBI office with attempted murder, along with a list of every Special Agent in the region. It was showdown in Dodge City, really a ploy to get the Feds out of town.

The next day Chicago police massed a thousand uniformed officers in front of the Federal building on State Street, with SWAT team snipers in prominent positions, all posing for the TV cameras. The FBI agents were allowed out the back of the building onto Dearborn Street and into a fleet of waiting cars directly to Midway airport where they were whisked back to Washington and out of the sovereign state of Illinois.

Jennings contented himself with pronouncements, deploring the breakdown of law and order, pouring on the rhetoric—utter, despicable, cowardly attack, brave men, will not be taken lightly, God in His good time. Awaiting the decisive break. Waiting to put the onus on the other side when it came.

★

Projected on the wall behind the speakers' podium at the convention hall across from Grant Park in Chicago was a gigantic image representing the states that were forming a new nation. It a long skinny snake of a country, stringing together every state of the East from Maine down to New Jersey, then running west from Pennsylvania between the Canadian border and the Ohio River, turning northward along the Great Lakes to Wisconsin and Minnesota. Off in the West was another block, running solidly down the Pacific from Washington State to California and Nevada. Arizona and New Mexico were represented in faint, ghostly colors: they were wavering and not yet decided, although the pro-secession factions in those states had sent delegations to observe the proceedings. There was a noticeable gap between the two blocks in the upper plains and mountain states of the West, from the Dakotas across to Montana and Idaho. Optimistically, these too were drawn in faint colors, although they had not sent delegations.

Other than the giant map glittering on the wall, and the cameras and cables of the media entwining everywhere, the convention hall had a rather bare-bones look. No colorful balloons, no little flags on the table, no bunting draping the white-skirted podiums, since no one knew yet what the colors would be. Just a democracy of chairs filled by a mass of people, for once taking politics with utmost seriousness.

By the time the Founding Convention had begun in late April, most of the issues had been thrashed out at the state level. What remained were the nuts and bolts, what kind of organization it would actually be.

The big symbolic issue was what to call the new government. Confederacy or even Federation were out; no one wanted a replay of the old South, and ideologically it was the opposite of what most Blue-Staters believed in. One proposal was the Democratic States of America.

Governor Everett Rosenfeld liked the name. Looking even more silver-haired distinguished than ever, he made an impressive speech on American values, much like the one he had repeated in Duplessis's Malibu mansion.

Privately, Rosenfeld had pointed out to other delegates that making the new government as similar as possible to the old USA in its organization and ceremonial trappings would help bring over officers and troops of the US armed forces to protect them in case of civil war. They would not have violated their oaths if we constituted the true legitimate state; and it would appeal to all those persons torn in their loyalties who hated the thought of leaving the USA however much they disliked the direction it was taking under the Christian Right. To that end he advocated adopting the same Constitution, the same Bill of Rights and amendments, adding a few to strengthen forever the wall of separation between church and state.

Rosenfeld wound up his peroration. "We are the true United States of America; the other side are the betrayers. In the end, people of good will, the true Americans stranded on the other side will rejoin us."

Senator Tim Birkenstock followed. Sandy-haired, with the gaunt body of a marathon runner, he spoke in a high-pitched voice that choked up at times with sincerity and outrage. He agreed on retaining much that was good in the old Constitution. But it needed explicit provisions so that the problems of the USA would never be repeated. The electoral college must be gotten rid of, so there is direct election of the president. There must be wording so that strict

constructionists on the Supreme Court could never go back to original intent of the founders as a criterion for what the constitutions
means—it must clearly express the rights we have learned to value
only in the last fifty years.

"We made a revolution in human rights," he declared, "starting
in 1956, the day Rosa Parks refused to sit on the back of the bus in
Montgomery, Alabama. We refuse to go back to the old America, the
America of segregation and second-class citizenship, the America
ruled by white Anglo-Saxon heterosexist Christian males. America
is the wrong name, a chauvinist name, a name hated by fighters for
freedom and human rights around the world. The name for a nation
of polluters, a nation with the death penalty. America is the name
for two whole continents, North and South America, which we have
usurped as if we were the only states in America.

"What we are," Birkenstock wound up, "is a coalition. The coalition of black and white and brown and yellow, the coalition of gay
and straight and lesbian and bisexual and transgendered, a coalition
of many faiths who agree to keep those faiths private so that they do
not offend each other. We are a Rainbow Coalition; let that be our
name, let that be our flag."

Protracted debate followed. It centered on two main points: the
name of the new government, and the presidency. In the end, it was
decided, attempting to stick to the most basic points of agreement,
to call themselves the Coalition of Secular States of America. The
Constitution would be similar to the USA, and would retain much of
its language. The electoral college was abolished—no more stacked
delegations, no more hanging chads, no more winning the presidency without a majority of popular votes.

The question soon veered to the issue of whether to have a president at all. We needed an executive to organize the nation for defense in the present emergency. There was no time for a lengthy
presidential campaign. Besides, the bad example of Jennings ruling
dictatorially gave the presidency a bad name.

Duplessis, with the support of Mayor O'Leary, argued for a tri-
umvirate: power to be split among three co-leaders, with the informal understanding that they would represent and have chief authority over East, Midwest, and West respectively. Birkenstock argued

against; triumvirates have never worked out; look at the ancient Romans. In the end they decided there would be not a president but a Chairperson, elected by the constitutional convention, and thereafter by Congress sitting as a body of the whole, Senators and Representatives together.

Duplessis had finally agreed; a bit to everyone's surprise, he supported Rosenfeld for Chairperson. O'Leary was to be Vice Chairperson. Seasoned politicians nodded their heads. Duplessis was positioning himself, staying aloof in case things went wrong, preserving his options for the future.

The day after the Chicago convention came to an end, and the Coalition of Secular States of America had come into being, President Joshua Maccabee Jennings made a speech.

Jennings appeared before the television cameras, a tall awkward man of formidable bulk, his white suit disheveled, red-faced, white-haired, white-bearded and wearing a black string tie. "It is with sadness that we all hear this news," he said. "Is this the end of America and what it stands for?

"I address all of you—so-called Blue States and so-called Red States. I address especially those of you who have shaped this new Coalition of Secular States. You are still states of America. You may deny it, but it is in your bones, it is in your hearts.

"Some people have called me a dictator. Is that fair? I did what had to be done in this time of emergency. If Congress will not pay our brave boys in uniform, the Executive branch must pay them. If Congress cripples the Supreme Court, it cripples itself. But it will never cripple the United States of America. My responsibility as President is to keep America going.

"I am a Christian, like so many Americans. Now some people speak evil of Christianity. They say it is dictatorship. They say it's racism and imperialism and all the other isms. Is that fair? What is the essence of Christianity, but the message 'Love thy neighbor as thyself?'

"I'm not ashamed to be a Christian. I say it in public. Neither should you be ashamed, nor should you make anyone else ashamed to speak out who they are. I'm not ashamed to be an American, and to speak proudly of it. I can't understand how some of you think religion is something we should keep hidden away, not to be mentioned.

"Isn't it strange that the most private matters of sex are talked about in public, on television, in the schools, but it's considered wrong to express one's religion, and one's love of country? What kind of values is that? Isn't that idolatry, like the people who worshipped the obscene rites of Baal? We're living in Sodom and Gomorrah. If you read your Bible, you know what that means—if we don't mend our ways God is going to send down fire and brimstone to destroy us.

"You may not like me, but I was elected fair and square. Our appointment for the Supreme Court is being carried out under the rules. We are upholding the Constitution; we have not abrogated it— the abrogators are among yourselves. Sooner or later you will see that, and cast them aside. We will welcome you back. We are not giving up on America.

"America is still strong. We will fight for our country, if we have to. But never fear—we will not attack you first. If war comes, you'll know who is to blame.

"Providence moves in a mysterious way. The withdrawal of these obstructers from Congress, the removal of disloyalists from our midst, may prove a blessing. Without them, we will reestablish a working Congress. We will have a working Supreme Court. If we are outvoted by a majority of Justices, we will accept it. We will obey the law. We only ask that the rest of us obey the law when they are outvoted.

"This is democracy. Come back, America—and may God save us all."

YEAR ONE, CHAPTER FOUR.
FORT SUMTER IN MONTANA

April.

The Missouri River breaks out of the northern Rockies between walls of dark rock gorges, and flows eastward into a winding valley to meet the high flat plains at Great Falls, Montana. Patches of snow remain in the spring, clumps of low trees dotting the prairie, lonely barns, silos, squat corrugated tin sheds. Attached to every isolated gas station is a small garish casino, revenue source in a tax-poor state.

Interstate-15, following the river, comes down into a bowl at Great Falls. Now there are more trees on the skyline broken by brick church towers. A divided highway turns east, interrupted by traffic lights, the usual malls, oversized advertising signs, car dealers, motorcycle lots: cheap transportation for low-paid airmen.

After the commercial district comes Malmstrom Air Force Base. It too is nondescript: low tan buildings behind chain-link fence topped with barbed wire; a base parking lot full of campers; a water tower is the highest structure visible. Beyond the base is the open prairie. All nondescript, calm, boring.

And hidden. Malmstrom AFB is home of the 341st Space Wing, and its mission is to aim, and if need be fire, intercontinental ballistics missiles with nuclear warheads.

They have not yet been fired. During the Cuban missile crisis in 1962, they were on full alert, aimed over the north pole at the Soviet Union, well within their range of eight thousand miles. A Minuteman ICBM is on display inside the front gate at Malmstrom, a slim white bullet sixty feet high aimed at the sky. This is a dud; the real ones are underground, two hundred nuclear missiles spread across hundreds of miles of Montana prairie.

Out there in the emptiness are twenty missile alert facilities, minibases monitoring information from early warning systems and capable of opening the underground silos and raising the missiles on their hydraulic lifts. Each missile has its own launch facility, a hardened bunker with its array of keys and codes, arranged so that two airmen operators must each separately work the launch mechanisms as a precaution against mistaken disaster. There are periodic drills and checks, and each two-person team is rotated in and out by helicopter. The duty is awesome and boring, boredom being the sign of peace.

The main action at Malmstrom AFB consists in periodic crackdowns by base authorities on drunken driving and smoking marijuana on duty. The Missile Security Forces Squadron, less than one hundred airmen armed with pistols and automatic rifles, guards the missiles against threats on the ground. Its duty too is peaceful and boring, and its members too are among those busted in rank, put on restriction, or discharged for intoxication and drugs.

Midafternoon on a dull Tuesday in April, a knot of men in lumberjack shirts and windbreakers slowly accumulated at the parking lot outside the Malmstrom AFB visitor center, just next to the main gate with its high roofed canopy and its guard hut between inbound and outbound lanes.

There was the usual gaggle of female relatives in the visitor center, signing in to see their spouses, or waiting for them to come out. A pair of blue-uniformed guards from a private security company lazily checked IDs of vehicle drivers entering the gate.

A middle-aged woman driving a large motor home pulled up to the gate and inquired about the hours for tourists at the base museum. Annoyed, the security guard pointed to the visitor center parking lot off to the right, and told her to back up. The second guard came out of the hut and advanced down the line of traffic, motioning to back up the queue so the woman could move her camper.

At this moment, one of the men in a checkered lumberjack shirt stepped behind the first guard, pulled a pistol and swung it hard, hitting him in the back of the head. The guard slumped to the ground.

The side door of the camper opened and let out three more men, carrying shotguns and pistols. Running to the rear of the camper, they caught the second guard from behind, forcing his arms in the air and relieving him of his pistol.

Inside the visitor center, three airmen were sitting on duty behind the counter, engaged with questions from a group of tourists. Suddenly there were guns pointing at them; hands up, they were marched out from behind the counter, unable to give any alarm.

In a few minutes, there were five hostages, arms trussed behind them, on the floor of the camper, and a little caravan of campers and pickup trucks were passing the main gate. They headed up the base road and divided, some towards the staging area of the Missile Security Forces Squadron, others towards the flight control tower and Base Headquarters.

For several minutes, the road in front of the gate was thick with vehicles entering the base. Their occupants had been idling on nearby streets, waiting for a signal to move. The night before they had been hanging around the seedy north side of Great Falls, with its railroad tracks by the highway, junky looking boxcars, its equipment rental yards, motels and roadhouse bars. It was a little army of a hundred men or so, and more than a few gun-toting women.

The caravan passed into the base. Behind it left a few guards of their own, clearing the visitor center and turning away all further traffic from the hut at the main gate with hunting rifles.

A banner in hand-drawn lettering was draped across the gate:

LIBERATED ZONE — FREE MEN OF AMERICA

The Governor of Montana received the call from the head of the State Police while out riding on his motorcycle.

"Governor? We have a Code Red emergency."

Governor Don Blastings slowed his big Harley to 70 miles per hour and shouted over the highway noise into his helmet radio. "Code Red? I'll be right on it. Where's it at?"

"I don't think you can take this one in person, Governor. It's at Malmstrom AFB. A group of militia calling themselves the Free Men have taken over the base. At least they're inside, with hostages."

Gov. Blastings slowed his cycle to the side of the road. "Have they got any of the nukes?"

"Don't know yet. It's only been an hour. We have two dozen Highway Patrol cars around the base. The militia has reinforced the front gate with a machine gun, probably taken from inside. Do you want us to move in?"

"Not yet. I'm heading back to my office. See you there in twenty minutes. And get the National Guard commander there." He wheeled the Harley around and accelerated to top speed on the mountain road down into Helena, Montana.

Don Blastings was, for a while, the most popular elected governor in the country. Running as an independent on his own Liberty platform, he had trounced long-standing Republican and Democratic candidates two years before. His hallmark was unhesitating outspokenness, here's what I think and wishy-washy politicians be damned. Before politics he had made his name as a casino operator, then as a talk show host who got proponents of rival positions to square off with boxing gloves in the studio. He proclaimed minimizing taxes and interference in people's lives. His state budget was based on expanding gambling revenues. On the expenditure side, he opposed government funding of higher education—buying credentials for rich people, he called it. He had fought with the legislature over public school funding, too, vetoing bills until he got legislation which gave Montana parents the nation's widest mandate to home-school their children, "free of the bureaucratic lockstep of the educational establishment," was the way he put it.

He raised some hackles by declaring organized religion to be a con game, and organized charities nothing more than stock market schemes for their administrators; "if you give ten bucks to a beggar," one of his widely quoted lines went, "you're cutting out the ninety percent that goes to the middleman." Blastings's popularity had dropped a bit as time went on, and his opinions in favor of legalizing marijuana and prostitution cost him some of his constituency. Still, no one could stand up to his energetic honesty in open debate.

He wasn't running for reelection, he said, and that made him free to speak his mind—"unlike some people I could name," he crowed.

At the Governor's office, there was more news from Malmstrom. "There's been more shooting," the State Police commander said. "Looks like the Missile Security Forces have been disarmed. Base Headquarters has its own guards and is still holding out."

"Yeah, the base is full of technicians and maintenance personnel," said Blastings. He sat behind an oversized desk made to look like rough-planed logs with the bark side left on. The office walls were paneled in knotty pine bracketed with display cases of Old West pistols, flintlocks, and repeating rifles. "Missile Security is about the only fighting force they've got in there. How'd it get taken so quickly?"

"Must be sympathizers inside. There's a new base commander who's been cracking down on the airmen, and a lot of them are facing charges over drinking and drugs. Also there's a push to ban pornographic magazines and videos on base, and get rid of prostitution off base."

"Same old story," said the Governor. "The Feds are into their Bible crusade, and G.I.s are the easiest to put the screws on."

"We've got reports from people who escaped through the side gate. Most of the enlisted men are just staying out of the way while the security detail fights. We do know some of the airmen from the Missile Security Squadron gave weapons to dissident airmen. And the Free Men militia were in cell phone contact with airmen who directed them inside the base."

"Some of these Free Men are probably veterans," said General Martin, the National Guard commander, "These militias usually are. I'll bet good money that some of the men who attacked Malmstrom today had served there. Might even have been discharged for bad conduct."

"And I hear," said Blastings, "that officers at Malmstrom have been at each other's throats over the budget crisis and the Pentagon reforms. Some have been quitting, and the rest are waiting for the right moment to make up their minds which way to go. And that moment is now."

The Governor had gotten up from his log cabin desk and was pacing the room like a big cat on the prowl. "What about the nukes, Ted? Are these Free Men going to be able to operate them?"

General Ted Martin shook his head doubtfully. "There might be a veteran or two who knows something about it, but it's a pretty specialized task. You need a team of experts."

"What about the dissidents inside the base? Would they be able to re-program the missiles, to hit targets here in America?"

"Sure they could. That's what they're trained to do."

"As long as there's fighting inside the base, it's not going to happen," said the State Police commander. "The missile launch sites are all over the countryside, and their crews are rotated in and out by helicopter from Malmstrom. The operators out there now are cut off and won't do anything unless the whole operation gets reorganized and targets are reprogrammed."

"OK," said Blastings. "We've got to make sure that we come out in control of Malmstrom. Ted, start moving National Guard units in around the base. But don't go in until I give the word. I'll get the Free Men to hand it over without more shooting. The big question is: what are the Feds going to do?"

"One of their bases is under attack," said General Martin. "They'll send in reinforcements."

"Not after they hear what I have to say," said Blastings. He turned to his secretary. "Get President Jennings on the line."

"Let him wait," Joshua Maccabee Jennings said. "Keep him on hold a while."

He turned to the National Security Advisor, Pat Buckley, who had just been giving a summary of National Guard forces in Montana and neighboring states.

"How long before they can get those forces to Malmstrom?" said Jennings.

"About a thousand troops are in the vicinity and can be there this evening. Full strength will take a couple of days."

"Then there's the nukes. Can we destroy them or disable them, to keep them out of enemy hands?"

"We'd have to get expert technicians out to the launch sites. They can't fly helicopters out of Malmstrom as long as there's fighting on base. We could send in some nuclear techs from other bases. Nearest would be Minot AFB in North Dakota, or Warren AFB in Wyoming."

"Not sure that's going to work. Those states are politically iffy, and they have some of the same kinds of crazies as Montana. None of those states attended the CSSA convention, but they might waver now."

"If you want total loyalty, there's a space wing with nuclear weapons at Schreiver AFB outside Colorado Springs."

"OK, get them on alert. But you say this mob at Malmstrom won't be able to turn the nukes around and aim them at us any time soon?"

"Assuming the Montana National Guard is going in there, there's danger that a dissident chain of military command could be established within a couple of days. If enough technicians defect to their side, the missiles could be reprogrammed by then."

Jennings mused for a moment, chin on hand. "What about paratroopers and assault helicopters? How long would it take to get those boys in there?"

"We could start moving them up from Ft. Carson, Colorado, or bring in airborne from Fort Campbell, Kentucky. It's a bit of a chess game. It depends on how fast the other side is able to bring in their reinforcements. If Blastings calls on the CSSA, they could bring in forces from Fort Lewis, Washington, for instance."

"And there's the political angle. I hear that some of those bases are pretty torn up right now, with all those malcontents against our reforms."

"Since you mention it, Mr. President, I'd have to say the cohesion of our forces is rather iffy. Still, if we start right now, we can probably have a couple of battalions on their way to Malmstrom in two days. Special ops units could get there in smaller numbers by tomorrow. Shall we go ahead?"

Jennings shook his head. "No. Put them on alert, get the loyal units ready. But keep it quiet."

"OK. I'll call General Harris"—the Chairman of the Joint Chiefs of Staff—"and tell him you want to speak with him."

Jennings stopped him. "No, let's leave Curt Harris out of this for the time being. He's too much of a hothead."

The National Security Advisor looked at the President quizzically.

"We're on the brink of war," said Jennings. "There is no stopping it now. It is God's will. But I want the onus to be on them. We are men of peace. When war comes, let the other side force us into it."

He rose heavily. "Keep Governor Blastings on hold for a few more minutes, while I go relieve myself."

Jennings returned looking pleased and picked up the phone.

"Donald, you old hound dog, where you been keeping yourself?"

"At the moment," said Blastings, "I've been keeping myself pretty busy with Malmstrom AFB. You're aware of the situation, Mr. President?"

"It's a breach of law and order by a gang of outlaws, as I understand it. Of course you'll give us full support in restoring lawful authority, won't you, Governor?"

"Lawful authority would be fine," said Blastings. "But there's a question right now across the country as to just where lawful authority happens to be."

"Lawful authority by the will of the people of the United States, by the Constitution, and the grace of God, rests with me, Governor. Now I'm asking you—"

"That's not the way we see things in the state of Montana," Blastings interrupted.

"Hold on, Donald. I have to tell you I'm federalizing the National Guard, so they can help the United States government restore control of its property at Malmstrom AFB."

"I've already called the National Guard under my personal authority as Governor of Montana. And I promise you they'll follow my orders."

"Are you aware, Governor, of the legal implications of what you just said? That you are putting yourself in a state of rebellion—"

"Damn right I am. The sovereign state of Montana is claiming all military bases on its territory, and will resist any attack on them from outside."

"The sovereign state of Montana, is it? It seems to me you have a long way to go. You can't even keep public order."

"It seems to me," Blastings said, "that any state with its own nuclear weapons is as sovereign as you can get. And if we're attacked, I'm ready to use them."

Jennings paused. "Nuclear weapons," he said finally. "Tell me the truth. Do you have nuclear weapons? Or not?"

The slightest moment of hesitation. "I sure do," Blastings said. And under his breath: *Or I soon will.*

The Free Men of America, if truth be told, were more of a slogan than an organization. For forty years, dissidents had been heading for the hills, withdrawing to isolated farms, turning cabins into forts. Homemade flags were flown over barbed wire compounds, proclaiming defiance to tyranny by the U.S. government and resistance to paying its taxes. The enemy was encroachment by anything big and modern. It was a melodrama of family farms holding out against agricultural corporations and environmental restrictions in the national forests; small town dentists squeezed by insurance companies and fed up with welfare deadbeats. A succession of culprits featured in their rhetoric: once upon a time it was the world Communist conspiracy, then the United Nations flying over in mysterious black helicopters, then the hated liberals; but now the betrayers were both mainstream political parties. Notorious shootouts with the FBI created martyrs.

Though not religious on the whole, American freedom fighters sympathized with cults if they were far enough removed from mainstream churches. The burning of the Branch Davidian compound at Waco, Texas—a branch of the Seventh Day Adventists, an extreme breakaway from an older extreme—was a memorial of what the hated Feds would do to us all. The Free Men were inheritors of a long tradition of utopian communities and gun-carrying individualists on the diminishing American frontier.

What were they doing at Malmstrom AFB? Most of the previous history of their kind had been a posture of violent defense, not attack. Even when they blew up the Federal Building at Oklahoma City in 1995 it had been a hit-and-run, an act of vengeance, not a taking of enemy territory. They were not organized to hold territory; an anti-government, they were incapable of setting up a government of their own, or even a functioning military chain of command. It was amazing enough that they had put together one hundred Free Men in one place for a concerted attack on Malmstrom AFB.

If truth be told, the Free Men were not exactly clear on what they wanted at Malmstrom. It was more the time than the place that attracted them. In the atmosphere of crisis and revolt across the country, these cultists of permanent revolt could not sit still without doing something. Sheer emotional magnetism drew them to Malmstrom and its nukes.

What were they going to do with the nukes once they got them? No one had thought that far. Any huge crisis, focusing the normally scattered attentions of the entire populace onto a single story, is like an emotional cyclone. The period of weeks when emotions are most intense is a hysteria zone, and it sucks the already hysterical over the edge. Every crisis has its main players, its dedicated opponents, but at this moment they are intruded upon by a buzz of batty individualists, bizarre seekers of a place in the charged-up public attention space. Such were the senders of anthrax in the weeks of security hysteria after 9/11/01, and the much larger swarm of hoaxters in the same period, the heat of crisis drawing the bugs out of the woodwork.

Such were the Free Men of America in the week after the constitutional convention of the CSSA, while the country held its breath, waiting for the shoe to drop.

Governor Don Blastings was conferring with representatives of the Free Men of America at the front gate of Malmstrom AFB. The Free Men had no elected officials and no leaders, but a trio had come forward to do the talking.

One was the middle-aged woman who had driven the mobile home beginning the assault. She had short curly hair, orange colored from too much home bleaching, and wore big dangly earrings with some kind of Indian symbol.

"I'm Zona," she said. "No fixed address. We're highway free. My camper is my home."

Rube introduced himself, a trim man in his early sixties, wearing a polo shirt and tinted glasses. A pistol was stuck in the back pocket of his jeans. "It's short for Ruby Ridge," he said. "Ruby Ridge Wilson is the name I took after the Feds executed Randy Weaver's wife, so as I'll never forget."

The third was a young man with a buzz cut, heavily muscled in a camouflage- mottled T-shirt, and a serious face. He introduced himself simply as West.

"I'm Don Blastings," said the governor. He was wearing his motorcycle gear for the occasion, black leather jacket and leggings. He was flanked by the National Guard chief, holding back a few steps away, in combat dress, downplaying his insignia. The rest of the

National Guard kept a distance, standing in deliberately casual, un-military groups across the street.

"We know who you are," said Zona, prolonging the handshake. "Say—would you mind autographing this for me?" She held out a plastic drink holder and a marking pen.

The governor obliged. "I just want to say to all of you—congratulations. Mighty good work." He swung around to make eye contact with all three, raising his voice to be heard by the row of Free Men who stood behind the entrance barrier with rifles in their hands.

The governor went on. "We're here to help you any way we can."

Body postures of the men with guns stiffened. West scowled slightly beneath his buzz cut.

"Don't know that we need help, Governor," Rube said.

"Don. Call me Don."

"Okay, Don." Rube made a gesture of opening his arms, palms up. "We can handle this ourselves."

"What about supplies? Anything you need?"

"Yeah. We could use ammo. And food."

"Some of us are vegans," Zona put in. "They've got these Meals Ready to Eat in there. But that stuff can poison your body. And there's nothing organic in the base cafeteria."

"We can do that," said Blastings. "I'll have my personal trainer bring in my week's supply of natural food. What else? How about weapons?"

"What you see." Rube shrugged towards the men with hunting rifles and shotguns.

"We can resupply bullets if you let us know the makes. But what are you up against? I hear they're holed up in the Headquarters building. Control tower still holding out?"

"We'll smoke 'em out of there soon. Hard to get in close to the Headquarters, though. They have a couple of machine guns."

"We can get you some heavier weapons," said Blastings. "You'll need them. The Feds are on their way. I've talked to Jennings himself."

Smiles lit up the faces of Zona and Rube. This was attention, big time. Even West looked a little smug.

"He tried to fox me," Blastings went on. "But I can see where he's going. Sneak attack, probably tonight. Air cavalry. Special ops, parachuting in. Or make a distraction in one direction, while they rope in from helicopters out on a corner of the base."

The Free Men looked concerned. The line of men at the barrier crowded forward around the trio of negotiators.

Blastings went on. "Have you got the firepower to drive off armored helicopters and gunships? Here's what we need to do." He motioned to General Martin to step up, into the conspiratorial group.

"This is Ted. He's here to reinforce you. We've got anti-aircraft artillery, surface-to-air missiles, armored vehicles."

Hands were shook all around. Blastings put up his hands, calling a stop. "Let me get one thing straight."

All eyes were on the governor.

"We're not here to replace you. I don't want you to withdraw. I need you. We're going to fight them side by side."

A cheer went up.

"Remember," Blastings said. "Side by side."

The National Guard had driven through the gate, a long procession of armored vehicles, heavy trucks, towed and self-propelled artillery and rocket launchers. They took up positions around the Headquarters compound and the control tower, and spread out around the base to defend against air assault.

No attack came that night. The Free Men stayed awake, exhilarated with the taste of full-scale battle provided by the soldiers around them. They chatted far into the night about the merits and quirks of weapons, the soldiers bragging about the precision of their infrared sensors and laser guidance systems, the militia beginning to look a little self-consciously at their hunting rifles, some even putting them to the side, out of sight.

Next morning the control tower gave up. Blastings made sure the entire Free Men contingent was there to watch them cross the tarmac with their hands up. Rube and West were unsure what to do with the captives. As they hesitated, National Guard troops took the air controllers into custody and marched them away. Blastings and Ted Martin shook hands with the Free Men again, all around.

Base Headquarters was still holding out. The National Guard set up machine gun positions and rolled a tank into view. But after a token rattle of machine-gun fire, and an answering rattle from the Headquarters gunners, General Martin called a halt. It was largely for the benefit of the Free Men. As the standoff continued through the afternoon, they drifted away from the front lines, leaving the boring business of confrontation to the professionals.

The second night, the Free Men were again on alert, expecting attack. But there were fewer of them now on the front lines, or elsewhere on the base. Familiar faces were missing. The feeling of being hangers-on in the midst of the soldiers was growing. On the Governor's orders, the National Guard had taken over the base perimeter. Anyone who wanted to leave was allowed out; no one was let in. The Free Men were gradually winnowing away.

On the third day, Blastings suggested a victory parade.

"Is this enough of a victory?" said Rube. "Headquarters is still holding out. Why don't you open fire with some of them rockets?"

"Cause we're not cold-blooded killers," said Blastings. "We're not the FBI or the ATF. We can starve them out in a few more days. And it looks like Jennings is losing his nerve. We've beaten him already. It's time for us to march out and tell the world what we've done."

"A parade would be nice," said Zona. "We can drive out in the same vehicles we came in on. With my camper at the front."

"You bet," said Blastings. "And we can all get a little sleep."

In fact, Blastings had slept in his bed every night. But the Free Men were exhausted, on edge for three nights in a row, including the night of adrenaline-pumping anticipation before they had first taken the Malmstrom gate.

"How about the TV people?" Rube said.

"There are hundreds of them outside. I've been keeping them away. Newspapers, photographers, everything."

"I don't want to talk to them," said Rube. "They always twist your words." Zona pressed her lips together and shook her head slowly. West just looked stern.

"Leave the talking to me," said Blastings. "Nobody gives me any guff. All you have to do is look good for the cameras, and back me up."

The parade took place that afternoon. The fifty or so Free Men of America remaining in Malmstrom AFB exited the front gate in their vehicles, waving their hunting rifles and shotguns defiantly. Zona drove the first vehicle, her gigantic camper, with a big banner that said: WE LIBERATED MONTANA—NOW LIBERATE AMERICA.

Governor Blastings rode on the back of a National Guard flatbed truck with Rube and West. Blastings stood in the middle, holding the two Free Men's fists in the air, like a referee signaling a boxing victory. It was a gesture made famous during the governor's talk show days.

Inside the fence of Malmstrom AFB, everything except the embattled Headquarters compound was now in the hands of the Montana National Guard.

The evening news was full of pictures of Governor Blastings and the Montana Free Men. As the video clips were run over and over again to the point of satiation, the announcement came that President Jennings was delivering an emergency address. He came on the screen looking like a baboon on stilts, his face gaunt and craggy.

"My fellow Americans," Jennings intoned, "As you know, Malmstrom Air Force Base has been invaded by a gang of thugs. They call themselves the Free Men of America, but they are wrong about that. No American would ever attack this great country of ours. And they can hardly be free, since they attack the bulwark of our freedom, the wonderful men and women of the US Air Force.

"But however evil they may be, in the big scheme of things they are only little sinners. They are misguided and crazy. As good Christians, our sympathy and our prayers should go out to them.

"There is something far worse than these little men. Governor Don Blastings, as you have seen, has put himself in league with them. I ask you: why would he do that?" Pause for dramatic effect.

"Because Blastings has now put himself in control of the nuclear weapons at Malmstrom AFB." Another pause.

"Governor Blastings told me himself that he possesses nuclear weapons, and that he will use them. Against us, the people of the United States of America."

Questions were now allowed from the assembled press corps. What did Blastings say? When? How many nuclear bombs? Aimed at what targets? Jennings stuck to reiterating his statement, letting the simple message sink in.

Most importantly: what do you plan to do?

"It is a matter of strategy," said Jennings, "and I can't go into details. But let me tell you this about that: I will take appropriate action to defend the people of the USA. We are faced with a Coalition of the Crazies. But your government will protect you against Blastings and these madmen."

"You'll have to deny it," said Everett Rosenfeld. They were in Governor Blastings' office in Helena, momentarily the headquarters of the coalition of the dissident. Blastings strode about the office in his motorcycle boots, too pumped up to stand in one place, the upstart hosting the big shots at a urgent meeting at his behest. Duplessis eased his weightlifter's bulk in an overstuffed leather chair, regarding the scene through half-closed eyes. O'Leary sat with one elbow on the table, hand cradling his bulldog chin.

"It puts us in the wrong." Rosenfeld stood, cool and elegant. "Explain that it was a misunderstanding, that he didn't catch your words."

"It wasn't a misunderstanding," Blastings said. "He heard me right."

"Fine. Very honorable. Tell the press you were quoted out of context. You would never use nuclear weapons, under any circumstances. It's Jennings and his crowd of fanatics who are talking irresponsibly."

"That ain't true," said Blastings. "I did say I would use them if I had to. And I meant it. If they're going to attack Montana, I'm going to deter them with everything I've got."

"It's a sensible position," said O'Leary. "Jack Kennedy did the same thing with Khrushchev."

"Right," said Blastings. "They're the ones who are threatening me."

"Threatening all of us," said O'Leary. "You're not the only target, Don. We're in this together."

"Wait a minute," said Rosenfeld. "You don't have control of Malmstrom yet. Those nuclear weapons are only a possibility until that happens."

"Everett has a point," said Duplessis, opening his eyes. A stuffed moosehead loomed from the wall over his head. "Don, you're not the only one outside Jennings's USA who can get his hands on nukes. We've got some at Vandenberg AFB in California. Not to mention what the Navy carries. You've even got some at your nuclear submarine base in Connecticut, Everett. Even though you're too coy to mention it."

"I intend to dispose of those submarine-launched nuclear missiles as soon as we can negotiate a safe way to do it," said Rosenfeld.

"The fact remains, Don, that several interested parties have nukes, and we're all embroiled in this dispute with Jennings together," said O'Leary. "The CSSA has them, and so do North Dakota and Wyoming. Those states are making feelers right now to join the Coalition. We have to strategize this thing together."

"But I'm the only one who's willing to use them," Blastings said. "That puts me in the driver seat."

"What are you talking about?" said Rosenfeld.

"I'm sending in tanks to take control of Malmstrom Base Headquarters. I'm calling Jennings' bluff."

"What do you think Jennings is going to do, stand by and let you do it?"

"Frankly, yes. He's not going to drop nukes on us just to keep me out of Malmstrom. I've got him figured. He's not going to be the first to strike."

"That's not to say he won't send in conventional troops," O'Leary said. "What have you got out here? A National Guard brigade and a half dozen tanks. They're got the whole US Army. When they roll, you're not going to be able to stop them. You need troops. The CSSA is the only one who can provide them."

Blastings stopped pacing. "I could put together a coalition with North Dakota and Wyoming, maybe Idaho and some other northern mountain states. The Free Mountain States of America. What have you got to offer?"

"That's a dream," said O'Leary. "You can't do 'nothing but nukes.' Believe me, it isn't going to work. You need conventional forces, too."

"Join us," said Rosenfeld. "We're going to win this thing. Together, we're too big for Jennings to attack. The CSSA is going to make up an unbroken arc from southern California up the Pacific coast, all the way across to New England. We've got the bulk of the population and the economy. Nobody can beat us. We will be safe together."

"You'll play a big part of our strategy, Don," O'Leary chimed in. "You're right, we should play hardball right now. And Don has the ball. Tell the press that you've got the Malmstrom nukes. Tell them that it's purely defensive, and that we want to keep it that way. But Jennings is threatening us, and we can't be held responsible for what happens."

"You can't be serious," said Rosenfeld.

"It's worth taking a shot," said O'Leary. "See what we get from it. If it doesn't work, we can always cut a deal."

"It's a matter of right and wrong," said Rosenfeld. "Do you have any idea what a nuclear attack can do? You wouldn't wish it on your worst enemies."

"We're not talking about all-out nuclear war," said Blastings. "Threaten a limited nuclear exchange. If they have any sense, they'll back off."

"Don't go there," said Rosenfeld. "Once that gets started, there's no telling how it will end. And even a single nuclear attack is immoral. It's worse than terrorism."

"Of course we're not going to drop nukes on Washington, DC," said Duplessis. He sat up and flexed. "But it doesn't hurt to let them worry about it for a while. And since we all have nukes, from California to Connecticut, we can show them that we're in it together."

"We can get the same results if we send conventional forces to reinforce the defense of Malmstrom AFB," Rosenfeld said.

"Okay," said Blastings. "Let's go ahead and do that. But you need to back me up on my own terms. I want all of Malmstrom, and I'm going to take Base Headquarters today. We've got the ball in our court. We've got the momentum. I'm going to use it."

Rosenfeld took his arm. "Look, Don. You know how to handle the Free Men. That was nicely done. But Jennings is something else. This is the big leagues. He's not just playing hardball with you. He's playing jujitsu. Whatever move you make, he's going to twist it to his advantage."

"What do *you* propose?" Blastings dropped into the governor's ornamental chair, a smirk on his face.

"We've got to be completely straightforward with him. Challenge him to be as principled as we are. Tell Jennings that we will do anything possible to avoid nuclear war. Get him to make an agreement."

"That's fine, Everett," said Duplessis. "You go ahead and talk to him. Be principled. I think the rest of us are in agreement. While you're doing that, we'll send reinforcements here to Malmstrom. And go ahead with cleaning up Base Headquarters."

"Give me some time," said Rosenfeld. "Give me forty-eight hours."

"Twenty-four," said Duplessis.

The four men scanned each other's eyes.

"All right. Twenty-four."

Blastings burst into a laugh. "This is great. Good cop, bad cop routine. We'll make a great team."

It became a war of news releases. Both sides accused the other of making nuclear threats. Both disowned any intention to be the first to use a nuclear weapon. But no one was going to tie their hands in the face of what an untrustworthy enemy might do, and what they would do in response. Neither was going to back down to nuclear blackmail.

The media were full of speculation, the web full of rumors. Jennings was lying. Troops were poised on the Montana border; outside of Chicago; special ops were already in New York City. Nuclear bombers from southern California were spotted circling over Dallas. A hostile submarine had raised a nuclear launch tube in Chesapeake Bay. Federal troops had been secretly ferried to Canada and were about to take Minot AFB in North Dakota. The US Navy was about to bombard San Diego.

In the midst of this, USAF fighter planes from Colorado buzzed the airspace over Malmstrom AFB. (This was true.) Also true: CSSA troops were sent into Montana from Washington State, from California, from the Illinois National Guard. The Montana National Guard at Malmstrom was reinforced, outnumbered, shunted aside. (This was not reported.) The governor of North Dakota offered to send nuclear technicians from Minot AFB to Malmstrom, to help get the nuclear weapons "properly dispositioned," as the ambiguous phrase went. The offer went both to the CSSA in Chicago, and to Governor Blastings in Montana, and was quietly accepted by both.

The Coalition of Secular States of America was abuzz with excitement. Delegations from the states of the upper West, who had so far held aloof, were crowding into Chicago. Idaho and Wyoming checked in, offering their air bases. South Dakota and Arizona had been badly split, but their governors too were on the phone with O'Leary and Duplessis and Rosenfeld, getting assurances, sliding away from neutral and accelerating into the rush of decision.

The CSSA was becoming a collection of strange bedfellows. The acronym became increasingly popular, the words no longer spelled out, blurring the secularist fight against the religious state that was Jennings's USA. It was no longer what the fight was about, but that the fight was on.

Atheists, militant anti-fundamentalists, liberal spiritualists and secularist Jews were allied with Bible-reading ranchers from the isolated plains and breakaway congregations of apocalyptic cults, and even a compound or two of harried Mormon polygamists.

Environmentalists allied with critics of the Environmental Protection Agency. The politically correct were arm in arm, temporarily, with PC-haters.

What held them together was the intense feeling of the moment. Normally the world is full of conflicting opinions, single-issue interest groups, movements in varying degrees of militancy and mobilization. Taken in the aggregate, they cancel each other out, a gridlock where nothing is done, cars stuck on the highway with their windows open and their drivers shouting at each other fruitlessly. War is a horrible thing in reality, but at the moment a war gets started, it produces a wonderful simplification. At the polarization point just before the fighting starts, multi-sided conflicts are boiled down to two-sided, and everyone faces the same clear choice: which side are you on?

Violent conflict wreaks havoc with ideological purity. Whatever specific grievances a faction had held, days or years before the crisis, are suddenly bleached away. The question of war or peace has already been decided. Now it only remains to join one mass of surging enthusiasm, or the other.

It is a magic moment, and it will not last. A year or two later, sometimes sooner, more than one enthusiast will fall back in wonder why they had thought war was the way, and whether their bedfellows were the right ones. But for the moment they are on an emotional high, and such questions belong to a mundane world far beneath their feet.

The following afternoon a formidable array of CSSA tanks were in position across from Base Headquarters at Malmstrom AFB. Surface-to-air missiles on their mobile launchers were dispersed around the runways, pointed to the skies, ready to repel any last attempt at rescue, or the bomb strike that would escalate into full-scale war. The media, which had been kept outside the base perimeter, were invited in, making a little circle around Governor Don Blastings, and CSSA Vice Chairman Big Bill O'Leary, who had flown in for the occasion.

Blastings made a little speech. He was holding a bullhorn, for the benefit of the USA loyalists inside Base Headquarters, while a phalanx of microphones stretched up to his podium from the media below. He was here to announce Montana's formal accession to the

CSSA. (cheers) It was a solemn moment. We had not chosen war. We were pushed into it. He was full of respect for the gallant airmen of the USAF, and there was no dishonor in their surrender. Five days holding out showed their courage. He was sure they were familiar with the Abrams tanks lined up here (cameras panning), and they must know what the depleted uranium shells they fired would do to the walls in front of them. (closeup of tank gun muzzle) They had sixty seconds to come out.

News reporters all over America were breathlessly launching into summaries and mini-commentary.

Suddenly an announcement filled every screen. Hold for the President of the United States and the CSSA Chairperson, Everett Rosenfeld.

On a split screen appeared Rosenfeld from Chicago and Jennings from the White House. Per arrangement, Jennings began reading first.

"My fellow Americans, we have reached a three part agreement. First, and most important, we have pledged there will be no nuclear war." Jennings raised his hands to heaven. "If the good Lord wants to destroy us, He'll do it in his own way. But we won't do it to ourselves."

Jennings gave a little snort and a shake of his white-bearded head, then continued. "Nuclear weapons will stay where they are, on whatever bases they might be at the moment this agreement is made, namely now. Their alignment will not be changed to targets inside the United States or on the territories claimed by the CSSA. Come what may, Americans will never visit the horrors of nuclear attack on each other."

Rosenfeld underlined the point solemnly. "Nuclear war is the most horrible thing that has ever happened to humanity. It happened only once, on those unspeakable moments at Hiroshima and Nagasaki. I only saw it on film, but it burns in my memory. The blast that turns buildings to dust, the heat that incinerates man, woman and child. The radiation poisoning that goes on for years. The ground on which nothing will grow. We have vowed it will never happen again." Rosenfeld paused, silver-haired eloquence quieted to absolute seriousness. "If we are destined to fight, fight we will; but it will be with conventional weapons, never with nuclear ones."

The second point of agreement, read out by Jennings, was that all military bases were now to be regarded as under the control of whichever state they were located in. In all states adhering to the CSSA, US forces would transfer control of the facilities in an orderly way to properly designated representatives of the CSSA military forces.

The third point was read by Rosenfeld. All military personnel, on any base whether on territory claimed by the CSSA, or in states adhering to the USA, would have free choice of which side of the conflict they would join. Free passage was guaranteed for any officer, enlisted personnel, or civilian employee of the military who wished either to go north to the CSSA, or south to the USA.

Jennings had the last word. "Why are we doing this? This is war, much as we hate its coming. But if God wills it, we will fight a good clean war, a godly war. There will be no bombing of civilians, no children exposed to nuclear radiation. No fellow soldiers on the same base shooting it out, no war of assassination in the bunks of warships, no sabotage of planes by their own comrades. We'll separate, make a clean break, and start out clear. America can afford to fight fair. I know the right side will win. Bring it on."

Before signing off, Jennings held the cameras for an afterthought. He looked a little less rumpled, now the concession-making was over. A familiar smile crossed his face. "Y'all know there was a War between the States once before. It was a terrible thing at the time. But as we look back at it, it was the greatest thing in American history. God grant that we will see those days again—this time with a better outcome."

Outside the compound at Malmstrom AFB, US airmen were coming out of Base Headquarters, shouldering M4s and machine guns, putting their weapons on the ground, then lining up to salute their CSSA counterparts. Salutes were returned on all sides.

"That takes care of that," Blastings said to O'Leary behind a cupped hand, while the media flocked momentarily to watch the transfer of troops. "But why did Rosenfeld let Jennings do so much of the talking?"

"Knowing Jennings, it must have been part of the deal. Take a note, Don. Everett Rosenfeld knows how to trade in his ego to gain points."

At the White House, after the press conference was finished, Jennings huddled with Defense Secretary Madigan and National Security Advisor Buckley.

"It was a better deal for us than they know," Madigan said. "Nuclear weapons are a thing of past. Our modern precision munitions are just as devastating on military targets, and a lot cleaner. No collateral damage. With proper targeting, no civilians are hit. And we're much further ahead than they are in modern weapons systems."

"It will be a truly honorable war again," Buckley said. "As you told us, Mr. President, it was the greatest thing in American history."

Jennings was unusually pensive. "God will test us with the baptism of fire," he said. "Let us pray we will be worthy."

YEAR ONE, CHAPTER FIVE.
HACKERS' WAR

The Pentagon. April, one week after the Malmstrom AFB crisis. Early morning.

"**H**oly Mother of God!" said Major Brian Sanchez. For once he sat bolt upright at his desk. "This can't be for real. Debra, take a look at this."

Major Debra Zielkowski peered over his shoulder at the screen. It alternated between flashing:

> URGENT — TOP SECRET

and:

> DEFCOM 1 — CODE WHITE

Then the message:

> TO: Maj. Gen. Wilson Wood, USAF, Commander,
> Andrews AFB, Camp Spring MD
> Maj. Gen. Herbert Delarkey, USAF, Commander,
> Langley AFB, Hampton VA
>
> FROM: General Curtis Harris, Chairman of Joint
> Chiefs of Staff
>
> COUNTERSIGNED: Robert Madigan, Secretary of
> Defense
>
> ORDERS: Prepare fighter wings for imminent
> strike on Bolling AFB, District of Columbia,
> and Ft. Belvoir, Arlington VA.

Traitorous forces have taken over these
installations. They must be destroyed before
essential control systems are subverted and
turned against us.

ATTACK targets simultaneously at 0800 hours
precisely.

ABSOLUTE SECRECY is mandatory.

Repeat: maintain ABSOLUTE SECRECY until
targets are destroyed.

LOCKDOWN Andrews AFB and Langley AFB to all
incoming and outgoing traffic.

All voice and data links are COMPROMISED at
this time. Encryption is unreliable due to
traitors inside the system.

SHUT DOWN all email servers and voice links
and

DISREGARD ALL COMMUNICATIONS from outside
base.

CONTACT ONLY THIS ADDRESS if attempt is made
to countermand this order.

The electronic signatures of Gen. Harris and Secretary Madigan were attached.

Sanchez scrolled further. Following were replies from both Langley AFB and Andrews AFB, asking for confirmation of orders. Time stamps showed confirmation was almost instantaneous, reiterating the need for secrecy. It added:

WARNING: ALL COMMUNICATIONS SYSTEMS ARE
INSECURE due to traitorous insider activity at
Bolling AFB and Ft. Belvoir systems centers.

SEAL OFF all external connections until
further orders FROM THIS ADDRESS ONLY.

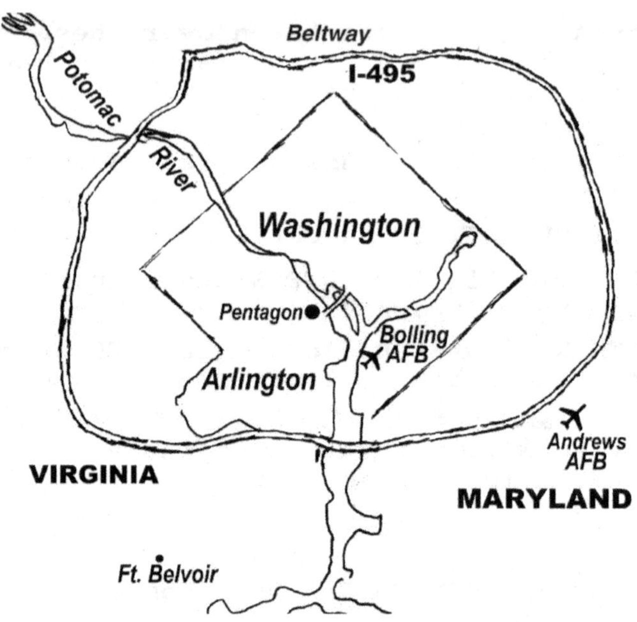

"Bolling Air Force Base?" Debra said. "That's where the DIA is located." The Defense Intelligence Agency, center for gathering all information on enemy forces, from all sources including remote electronic sensors as well as human intelligence reports.

"And Ft. Belvoir houses the Information Systems Command, the Intelligence and Security Command—the heart of defense technology and logistics. Not to mention Army Criminal Investigations," Sanchez said. "Looks like somebody figured out one hell of a way to get their records expunged."

"We need to verify this," Debra said. She started to type on her keyboard, stopped, went to the door. "If the system is compromised, we need to do this in person."

A minute later she returned with Captain Shirley Jones, a short, heavy black woman from computer security enforcement. Jones inserted her control card into the computer, and ran a program accessible only to those with the highest possible security clearance. "It checks out," she said. "Harris and Madigan's electronic signatures are correct."

"Couldn't somebody have forged them?" Debra said.

"*Hypothetically*—" Capt. Jones drawled out the word, "anything is possible. But they'd have to get through half a dozen security checks. Not too many people could have done it. *I* could do it—but not too many others."

"We better check with Grotweil," Sanchez said. Brigadier General Grotweil was the ranking computer officer for the Secretary of Defense's office. Grotweil had just last week put them on the job of double-checking security of transmissions from the Secretary's office.

"Go ahead and call him," Debra said. "I'm taking this directly to General Harris."

"He'll bite your head off," said Sanchez. "He doesn't like people second-guessing him. And this is supposed to be need-to-know only."

"The attack is supposed to happen at 0800 hours. Just the time when everybody at Bolling and Belvoir will be at work. It's not a nighttime attack when shifts are low. Thousands of intelligence and security personnel will be wiped out. And it's 0610 already."

"Like I said, Harris is one mean SOB. If you're on his shit list—"

"I'm going anyway."

Twenty minutes later Sanchez received a call to report to the Chairman of the Joint Chiefs' office.

Brigadier Grotweil was there, along with Gen. Harris, and Thaddeus Wolf, the Deputy Secretary of Defense. Madigan, it transpired, was out of town, on an unannounced trip to military bases in Texas.

"Major Zielkowski," said Harris, "tells me the two of you have uncovered orders given out in my name."

"I have some further information," Sanchez said, moving towards a computer console. "A series of follow-up orders giving attack detail to the flight leaders, and targeting missiles and bombs onto key assets at Bolling and Belvoir. If you will allow me, sir, I'll call up the screens."

They peered at the offending messages, while Harris cursed at length.

Grotweil immediately began sending out countermanding orders.

There was no response.

"Our orders are being overridden," said Grotweil. "Nothing is going through to Andrews and Langley."

"Check all other air bases," said Harris. "Make sure no one else has received orders like these. And get Madigan on the line."

A quick check of communications showed nothing but routine contacts with other air bases.

"We can't assume this check is reliable," Wolf said. "Obviously there are traitors in our midst. CSSA moles who delayed going over to the other side so they could hack our computer system. They've penetrated out command-and-control links, and now they're sending out false orders, turning our own weapons against ourselves. Any orders we send get blocked or portrayed as coming from enemy sources."

"What the hell can I do about that right now, Thad?" Harris demanded. "We've got to stop Andrews and Langley from bombing our intelligence centers. And fast."

"That may be only the tip of the iceberg. We can't rely on our computer system to convey our orders. We need to shut down the whole system."

"Are you out of your mind? We can't run anything without computers. You know that yourself—you pushed for this HOME system that runs everything."

"Excuse me, sir," an aide interrupted. "We've tried to get through to Secretary Madigan.

"So put him on!" Harris snapped.

"That's just it, sir. His encrypted line is not responding. We've tried calling his aides but they're shut out too."

"Get the idea, Curt?" Wolf said. "Traitors are everywhere. They knew Madigan was going to be away, and they're interrupting all our normal communications. We can't trust anything."

"There's no time for that," Harris said. "We've got to act right away. You said shut down the computers. OK, shut them down. And start phoning all bases that can have fighter planes over DC in the next half hour. Call the Naval Air Station at Norfolk and tell them to hit anything that takes off from Andrews and Langley."

"It might be safer to hit them on the ground before they take off," said Admiral Midhoff, the Chief of Naval Operations.

"Wait a minute," said Wolf. "Whoever is hacking our system would be happy to have us do that. Whether our planes blow up Bolling and Belvoir, or we bomb Andrews and Langley, it's all fratricide. Let's see if we can't get through some other way to call off the attack."

"Phones at Andrews and Langley are not answering," said an aide. "We've been trying for ten minutes."

"How about personal cell phones?" said Harris. "Anybody have Wilson Wood's or Herb Delarkey's private numbers? Or anybody else on the staff we can get through to."

"They've been ordered to disregard all external communications," Grotweil said. "But we'll try it."

"Meanwhile, let's see if we can bust in a message through the front gates," said Harris. "Send an MP company out there to Andrews, with orders from me personally to the C.O."

"Unfortunately," said Wolf, "they may take that as confirmation that their orders are correct, and that the traitors are attacking them. Also, I doubt if MPs have enough armament to break through if the air base is going to resist."

"Damn," said Harris. "We don't have any heavy units stationed near enough to get in there in time. But at least we can break into Langley. Call Fort Eustis and tell them to get over there. They're right next to each other at Hampton."

"Those are just training and headquarters troops," said Admiral Midhoff. "But I've got the amphibious warfare center across the bay at Norfolk. I guarantee that Air Force base security won't stop them from getting in."

"All right," said Wolf. "Get the SEALS over there as quickly, and quietly, as they can. We want to calm those bases down, not fight them, if we can avoid it."

Grotweil had a report on the cell phones. "General Wood's cell phone is turned off. General Delarkey's answering service says that our call is very important to him, and he will call us back at the first opportunity."

Harris cursed.

"But I do have some cell phone numbers for officers at Andrews AFB."

"OK," said Wolf. "Does anybody here know any of these personally? They're going to have to recognize your voice if this is going to work."

Shoulders shrugged as the list went around the circle.

"I know a couple of them," Major Zielkowski said. "Major Tom Murray, in charge of base security. And Lt. Colonel Rod Ambrose, deputy operations officer."

"Good," said Wolf. "How do you happen to know them?"

"I'd rather not say," said Debra.

"Consider that an order, Major," Harris said.

"I met Murray at a party. He was more friendly than I wanted him to be. In fact, I slapped his face."

"Well, he'll remember you," Sanchez put in.

"And Ambrose?" Wolf asked.

"He invited me to dinner with his wife, when we were at a National Defense University seminar. He was very friendly too."

"Call them both up," said Harris. "We need to get you inside that base ASAP."

"Start with Murray," said Wolf. "He could bend the rules for you, if he thinks it's a personal message, lovers saying goodbye in a big crisis. And he could escort you personally through the gate. Once inside, you can ditch him and talk to Ambrose. If you convince him, he's got enough authority to stop the attack."

Ten minutes later Debra was on a helicopter making the quick run outside the Beltway to Andrews AFB. She transferred to a civilian car and drove a few minutes to the main gate. She parked fifty yards away and walked along the stopped cars that jammed the roadway leading up to the gatehouse. It was placid looking amidst the well-trimmed shrubbery. Security officers were turning away a line of civilian employees. A handsome, rather vain-looking officer came around the security barrier to meet her. It was Major Tom Murray.

"The question is," said Brian Sanchez, "who done it." He was back in his familiar posture, feet up on his office desk, chair tipped back and hands clasped behind his head.

"A computer search should solve that," said Debra. "The security staff is working on it right now. Trace the message back to the computer that originated it, and find who had access at the time the message was sent."

"Unless the hackers got into a zombie computer, and erased their own presence. A delayed message could have been left weeks ago."

"The links can be traced if we work at it long enough," said Debra.

"I've got a better method," said Sanchez. "In twenty questions or less, I will come up with the culprit. Question one: insider or outsider?"

"Insider. It had to be someone who had access to Madigan and Harris's electronic signatures."

"Question two: there could be two kinds of insiders. Was it a defector, who left us for the CSSA, taking along his or her access code? And maybe left a Trojan horse inside our system, so they could get back in via a private entrance. Or is it a sleeper, a defector who hasn't left yet, lurking here in order to do damage from within?"

"Good question. We'll have to check out both possibilities."

"Question three: So maybe it was an outsider after all. And this brings up more possibilities: A, it could be somebody at a CSSA base over on the other side—someone just like us, who knows all about the system because it was one single system until one week ago. It could be somebody in their cyberwarfare division trying to penetrate our system just like we used to penetrate foreign enemies.

"B, it could be a private contractor in the defense business. A lot of our advanced technology was built in California or New England. They would know how to hack it because they built it."

"And they still have links to loyal contractors in Texas and Virginia," said Debra. "They could get in by that route. DOD has been changing our own codes since the split-up, but there are so many contractors that it will take a while to get them all sorted out."

"Correct," said Sanchez. "So it could be a civilian hacker. There are a million people out there with Top Secret clearances."

"And point C," said Debra, "is just plain amateur hackers. Teenagers. After all, they do most of the hacking."

"I don't think they could do this one. They're mostly thrill-seekers. Personally, I think it's someone right around here." He raised a finger melodramatically. "Question four: is it—Shirley Jones?"

"Why her?"

"It has to be somebody with a high enough security clearance. She not only has TS access, she has SCI clearance, that's walled off from the most super-sensitive sectors in this playground. I happen to know that Shirley Jones has both Crypto and ESI clearance." Sanchez made a ring with thumb and index finger, pinkie in the air. "Extremely Sensitive Information, you know. She has all the access lists and codes. She can even change the codes—though it would take a couple of collaborators. And furthermore, she confessed: she told us that she *could* have forged the command signatures."

"Doesn't the fact that she said she could do it prove that she didn't? She didn't act like someone covering her tracks."

"Unless she was deliberately trying to throw you off, because she knew you'd think like that. You're not subtle enough for this business, my dear."

"Don't be ridiculous," said Debra. "She's just as loyal as we are."

"We haven't caught her yet," said Sanchez. "But we have to be on the alert. Look for even the slightest slip in her story. Spies weave a web of cover—it's where the tiny details don't fit that gives them away."

"I think we need to look at everyone who had high enough access to forge the signatures."

"Now," said Sanchez, "we come to the really important questions. Question number five: What did you actually do when you were with Major Tom Murray yesterday morning? And how exactly did you ditch him for Col. Rod Ambrose, and thereby save the world?"

"Twenty questions is supposed to be yes or no answers."

"Okay. Question six: Were you alone with Major Murray? Answer: yes. Question seven: Major Zielkowski, when you were alone with the aforesaid, did you engage in bodily activities such as to arouse—"

"Cut it out!" said Debra.

There was a knock on the door. Without waiting for an answer, an armed security officer stepped into the room. "Major Sanchez? You are ordered to report to the Secretary of Defense's office. I will escort you. You are not to speak with anyone along the way."

"Thank you for your cooperation, Sanchez," said Secretary Madigan. "You understand, the entire matter is to be treated with absolute secrecy. No hint of the threatened attacks on Bolling and Belvoir must reach the media. It could create unease among the public. And very likely set off a round of copycat attacks. They would probably be ineffective, but they would muddy the waters and make it harder to trace the real perpetrators."

"My lips are sealed," said Major Sanchez, "sir."

"And remember, this entire investigation is confidential. You may go."

Deputy Secretary Wolf and General Harris glowered from their chairs. Grotweil sat expressionless in the background.

"I've had my doubts about revealing this attack to President Jennings," Madigan said. "He likes talking in public too much to be good at keeping secrets. But he needs to know what we're up against. I've told him as little as possible about what steps we're taking, and I've gotten his approval for whatever emergency measures are needed."

"All right, to sum up," said Wolf. "We're looking for individuals who have both motive and capability to carry out the attack. We are checking out all defectors with high enough access to penetrate the top command codes."

"And traitors who are still here as sleepers," said Harris. "Everyone who is on record as a dissident."

"And we need to find out who their contacts are," said Wolf. "Whether or not they're in on the plot, they're all weak links. The whole network needs to be rooted out."

"We have two prime suspects already," said Grotweil. "One of them is Captain Shirley Jones. She has the right level of access, which very few others do. She verified the signatures on the attack order, as Sanchez confirmed. And she is one of the few people who knew Secretary Madigan was out of town when the false orders were given. That simplified matters by keeping top command out of the loop."

"OK, so she had the capability," said Madigan. "What about motive?"

"We're checking into that," said Grotweil. "The other suspect is more on the motive side. Colonel John Gandhi Park."

"That's pretty obvious," said Harris. "Dissidents don't get any more blatant than that."

"We can all testify to the scene he made in this office," said Wolf. "And the threats he made in public."

"Col. Park resigned his commission after that incident, and lost his security clearance," said Grotweil. "So it's not likely that he personally could have done the hacking. However, Park did not actually defect to the CSSA."

"Where is he now?" said Madigan.

"When the split occurred, Park offered his services to the Governor of Maryland in the National Guard. Park got command of a company of loyal infantry and put down a riot in Baltimore. That helped keep Maryland in the Union. As a reward, the Governor put him in charge of reorganizing the Maryland National Guard. Reports are that Park's troops are guarding the border with Delaware and Pennsylvania."

"He could be a sleeper," said Wolf. "That's a sensitive position for a potential turncoat."

"I don't like the man any more than you do, Thad," said Harris. "But Park is not exactly a computer expert. In fact, he hates high tech. He's just a hotheaded infantry grunt."

"That's where the networks come in," said Wolf. "He could collaborate with technical experts. His motivation plus their access. And he seems to be a friend of our own Major Brian Sanchez, right here in the SECDEF's own computer security detail. And possibly a friend of Major Debra Zielkowski too."

"I had no evidence of their friendship when I put Sanchez and Zielkowski on the job of checking top command security," said Grotweil. "The number of email messages between Park and either of them is zero."

"They're just part of the picture," said Madigan. "We still have to check out who was friendly with the defectors who went over to the CSSA, and who could be providing access to remote hackers. And we need a graduated level of response."

"How do you mean?" said Harris. "If they're traitors, throw the book at them."

"Look, Curt, we could shut down the whole system right now. Make everybody give up their access cards, and go through security clearances again. Re-key the whole system. That would take a lot of time, and put us out of business for the interim. It's the most secure solution, but it also eliminates the possibility of catching anybody

red-handed. So let's take a little more risk. We keep the system going, and deny access to the biggest security risks while we're checking them out. Where we have less to go on, we can downgrade their
security clearance to a lower level of access."

"But for the prime suspects," said Wolf, "there's no reason not to
go ahead and arrest them right now. And don't tell anybody about
it. That way, if the news gets out, it will prove they have a network
engaged in breaching security. We'll have a trail to follow."

"Arrest them on charges of treason in time of war," Harris said.
"Try them before a military tribunal and execute them. No long
drawn-out public trials giving away information on how our security system operates."

"We don't have to do that any more," said Wolf. "Let the CSSA
hamstring themselves with legal formalities, if they want. That's one
more advantage for us."

"Let's not get ahead of ourselves," said Madigan. "There's still
the question of who is in on the investigation. Our problem is there
are too many enforcement agencies who have an official hand in
this. Besides our in-house security units in DOD, there is the NSA,
CIA, Homeland Security, FBI, NIPC, and a bunch of CERTs. Not to
mention CYBERCOM." The SECDEF ran off a string of acronyms
including the National Information Protection Center, Computer
Emergency Response Teams, and Cyber Command. "If they all get
into this, it raises the chances of warning off the perpetrators. Not to
mention getting in each other's way, and letting things slip through
the cracks."

"Let's keep it in-house," said Wolf. "It needs to be a much smaller
group. Traitors have penetrated our highest security procedures.
Defectors are all over the place. Sleepers are undoubtedly inside every enforcement agency."

"It's the old question," said Madigan, "who guards the guardians?"

"We need a special investigating group with authority to override everyone else's domain, to rescind anyone's security clearance,
and to order arrests when necessary," said Wolf. "We need to start
with a core group that we can absolutely trust, and then expand the
circle of security as we clear out the traitors."

Madigan looked around the room, eyeing each man in turn: Wolf, Harris, Grotweil. "This is one circle we can trust. Thad, I'm putting you in charge of the investigating group, with authority to bring in whoever else you deem fit, pursuant to your investigations."

"You can count on me, Bob," said Wolf. "I'm already on it."

Madigan raised an eyebrow slightly. "But there's too much work to do without bringing in other agencies. We'll need deeper background checks for all high-level personnel in DOD. The FBI and the usual agencies can cooperate in this. They don't need to know too much about what they're looking for."

"I'll start by eliminating the prime suspects," said Wolf. "Capt. Shirley Jones will have her SCI and Top Secret security clearances downgraded to Secret. She can keep working for the time being under surveillance. Col. John Gandhi Park is to be put under arrest on charges of treason."

In the following days, Debra was called in for questioning by four different investigative agencies. A fifth showed up at her apartment unannounced; they seemed to know her routines and when she would be home. Many of their questions were the same ones. Was it organizational duplication, she wondered, or were they trying to catch her in some inconsistency of detail?

"Can you believe it?" she told Brian Sanchez. "They kept asking me about you. About who your friends are, who you talk with. And about us—what kind of relationship we have, whether we ever see each other outside the office."

"And you said, fat chance of that, huh?"

"I told them that you're a big joker and as harmless as a teddy bear."

"Well, thanks a lot."

"And they asked a lot of questions about Shirley Jones."

"I'm not sure I want to hear this," said Brian. "They're not through yet. The less I know about anything connected with Captain Shirley Jones, the better."

"But Brian, she's in trouble. I just saw her in the corridor. She said they've taken away her higher clearances, and she's not working on password security any more."

"Well, I guess that could be construed as a line-of-duty communication, so we won't call on her any more if we have to verify a signature. Somebody else will have to help us avert the next plot to blow up the Pentagon."

"That's not what I mean. Brian, she's done nothing. She did her duty. I told her I'd try to help her."

"Stop it, Deb." Brian put up his hands. "I don't want to be questioned about what you've said to me about Shirley Jones. I don't want to get caught lying, or leaving anything out. So stop." And contrary to his usual talkative disposition, he turned to his desk and began to work.

Next day Debra was called in again, this time to Deputy Secretary Wolf's office. Brigadier Grotweil was there, along with a man in civilian clothes. His face was drab gray, almost the color of his well-tailored suit, and the skin hugged the bones of his face unusually tightly. He was introduced as C. J. Clements, Special Deputy to the Deputy Secretary of Defense.

"I understand that you've had a number of communications with Captain Shirley Jones," Wolf said. "Suppose you repeat to us what transpired between the two of you the morning of the Bolling-Belvoir attacks."

"Yes. I've been through that," Debra said. "I knew she was the duty officer that morning. So I called her in and asked her to verify the electronic signatures. She said they were genuine."

"But you didn't believe her."

"I thought she was telling the truth—I mean, that those really were the correct electronic codes. And that's true, isn't it?"

"Then why did you go over everybody's head, directly to General Harris?"

"Because it was an emergency. Because he was the only one who could know for sure about the orders. And because there were less than two hours to stop the attacks."

Special Deputy Clements spoke in a flat voice which nevertheless had an unpleasantly penetrating edge. "Was there anything about Captain Jones' manner that made you doubt that the matter should rest with her verification?"

"No. Yes—what I mean is, I couldn't believe the order could be genuine. I mean, it could have been—but it was too important not to check it further."

"We have a statement from Major Brian Sanchez," Clements said, "that Captain Jones made some further remarks. Captain Jones said that she could have forged the orders. Is that correct?"

"Yes. But—"

"Then why did you withhold this information from us?"

"It was just her way of speaking. She just wanted to make the point that it would be very hard to forge the signature, and that only somebody with very high SPI clearances could have done it. It was her way of emphasizing that she thought the signatures were genuine."

"And you say you believed her. But you didn't believe her, so you went to General Harris. Which is it, Major?"

"Look, I believed she was honestly performing her duty as an electronic security expert. But I still thought she could have been mistaken about the possibility of forgery."

"Are you aware that Captain Jones has had her security clearance removed? And that she is under investigation in regard to further possible penalties, quite severe ones?"

"Yes, she told me in the corridor yesterday." She turned to Wolf. "Sir, with all due respect. You need to do something about this. It's an injustice. Shirley Jones is a loyal American. I'll swear to it. I'll take a polygraph test."

"Justice is precisely what we are after," said Wolf. "You will have opportunity to testify further. I should point out that all investigations, both involving Captain Jones, and those involving yourself or any other person, are confidential and are to be treated as such. Haven't the investigators who have questioned you reminded you of that requirement?"

"Yes, they all did. But that doesn't mean I'm supposed to tell one investigator I haven't talked to another investigator, does it? Aren't we all on the same side here?"

"It appears from what you have just said," said Wolf, "that there are further breaches that will have to be considered."

After Debra was dismissed from their presence, the security cabal conferred. "How deeply is Major Zielkowski involved in this?" said Wolf. "Just a naive dupe? Or something more?"

"I've checked all Zielkowski's emails with Jones in the past year," said Grotweil. "Ninety-seven point six-four percent of them were official line-of-duty messages. There were a two suspicious ones about meeting for lunch. Then a cancellation. We're looking into it."

"What about Major Tom Murray at Bolling AFB security? If they engaged in one deception, they could engage in another."

Clements answered. "We're interrogating him now. The fact that he broke security at his base, against an urgent order from the top command, gives us a way to make him sweat."

"See if there is anything deeper in his prior relationship with Major Zielkowski. He may have something on her."

"Playing devil's advocate for a moment," said Clements, "Major Zielkowski was the whistleblower in this case. Without her, the military bases very likely would have been destroyed. The inconsistencies in her case may be minor and inconsequential. Not every lead goes somewhere."

"So it appears," said Wolf, "on the surface. But sometimes the person whose presence on the scene seems most innocent turns out to be the culprit. You may remember the Leopold-Loeb murder case in Chicago back in the 1920s: two super-smart kids who thought they could outwit the police and get away with the perfect crime. It turned out the murderers were always hanging around the investigation. That's what brought them to the attention of the authorities. Zielkowski thinks she's some kind of scientific hotshot too."

"Fair enough," said Clements. "We also need to ask the question, *cui bono?* Who benefits? What would Zielkowski have to gain by turning in the plot, if she were working for the CSSA?"

"A good question. For one thing, she might have expected that the attack couldn't be called off, that it would go through even with her intervention. She might have been giving herself cover in any subsequent investigation."

"But she did personally stop the attack by getting through to Murray and Ambrose at Bolling AFB."

"She might have been going out there to warn them that the plot was discovered, once she knew Major Sanchez saw the order. We need to look further into that. Find out about Ambrose too. Start with his cheating on his wife. That will give us a hook into him."

"We've accessed Major Murray and Col. Ambrose's emails," said Grotweil. "So far, there is nothing in them relating to Major Zielkowski. We are checking if Murray and Ambrose discussed anything sensitive between themselves. We do know that they have met for lunch."

The meeting broke up. After Grotweil left, Wolf motioned Clements to stay. "What about that guy?" Wolf said. "Is Grotweil deliberately holding out on us? After all, he put Zielkowski on the job in the first place. And Jones is under his command."

"We're checking on him," Clements said.

"Look at this." Debra motioned to Brian Sanchez. "It's addressed to both us. From Secretary Madigan. You must have the same message."

```
TOP SECRET

TO: Major Debra Zielkowski
    Major Brian Sanchez
FROM: Robert Madigan, Secretary of Defense
Thaddeus Wolf, Deputy Secretary of Defense for
Security
General Curtis Harris, Chairman of the Joint
Chiefs of Staff

RE: Commendation
```

> Dear Debra and Brian:
>
> You are hereby commended for your outstanding
> action on [date deleted] in overcoming a
> threat of the highest order to the heart of
> our defense installations. By your actions,
> the lives of thousands of military and
> civilian personnel were saved, and grave
> impairment to our national strength averted.
> Your initiative and courage have been
> exemplary.
>
> Under ordinary circumstances, your heroic
> actions would amply merit award of a
> Distinguished Service Medal. You will well
> understand the circumstances that require your
> action to be kept in strictest confidence.
> Nevertheless, please be assured of our
> profoundest gratitude and respect, and that of
> your fellow servicemen and women.
>
> electronic signatures of Secretary Madigan,
> Deputy Secretary Wolf, and General Harris
>
> NOTICE: This message is to be held in
> STRICTEST CONFIDENCE. Delete upon receipt.

"That's a relief!" said Debra. "It means we're off the hook."

"They didn't say the investigation was called off," said Brian. "I wonder how long ago this thing was written up. And by which of Madigan's many assistants? The left hand doesn't know what the right hand is doing."

"Brian, you're so suspicious. Can't you take a moment to be happy? Even though it has to be kept secret, of course."

"Right. We're not in it for the glory. Just for the satisfaction of doing our duty."

"As a matter of fact, yes. Even you, Brian, deep down inside."

"Have you ever considered," said Sanchez, "why they've kept us in the same office, even though they've been investigating both of us?"

"Why not? We work together."

"Hasn't it occurred to you that they want us to talk to each other? Then they call us in separately from time to time, and find out what we report about our conversations—compare them for inconsistencies and breaches and so forth."

"But that was yesterday. Now we have this commendation."

"Which we're supposed to delete and not show to anybody."

"Wolf knows about it; he signed it."

"I think he's just stringing you along. My baby girl."

"Keep on talking like that," said Debra, "and I will turn you in."

Later that afternoon, Debra returned from a break, and inserted her access card into her computer. The message came up:

ACCESS DENIED. SECURITY CLEARANCE REVOKED.

Brian Sanchez was not in the office. She went out looking for him. Nowhere.

People seemed to be avoiding her as she hurried through the halls of the Pentagon. A few clipped answers: no one professed to know anything about Major Sanchez.

Finally she caught a glimpse of Captain Shirley Jones. She was not in her usual office, but had moved to a cubicle in a large room down the corridor from the computer security station where she had formerly worked.

"Sanchez has been picked up for interrogation," Shirley said. "By a squad of armed guards. Possibly under arrest."

"But why? Because of something I said?" Her stomach felt hollow. Or because of something Brian failed to report that she had said, and which they knew about, and caught him for covering up for her?

"It's because of his friend Col. John Gandhi Park. They were pretty good friends, weren't they? Didn't Park come in regularly and discuss his plans with Sanchez?"

"Yes, but Park was just a hothead. You can meet guys like that in a bar every day. It's just a lot of talk."

"Well, you told the investigators yourself about Sanchez and Park."

"How do you know all this, Shirley? I thought you had been cut out of the loop."

"I'm back in," said Shirley. "I got my security clearances back. At least some of them."

"That's wonderful." Debra gave her a hug. "I knew they couldn't keep on being mistaken about you."

"Listen," said Shirley. "I shouldn't be talking to you. But I heard you went out on a limb for me."

"I didn't know I had so much influence."

"You don't. But I appreciate your trying. Look, they don't want you. You're just small potatoes. They think they've got the perpetrator nailed down—John Gandhi Park. Sanchez was his inside connection, or part of it. We're closing in on the rest of the evidence now."

"We're closing in—you're working on this investigation?"

"Doing a damn good job, baby. Just take my advice: don't go out on a limb for Sanchez. And don't tell anybody I told you so."

"Of course not, Shirley. But Brian is my friend—"

"Get another friend. Don't you see, Major? Suspicion is like a contagious disease. If you're in contact with someone who is infected, you become infected. Didn't you just lose your security clearance?"

"How did you know about that so fast?"

"I know. Take my advice. You need to quarantine yourself. Cut off any connection with Sanchez."

"It's not going to work," said Debra. "You can distance yourself from all your friends, but the investigators know what your relationships have been. You can drop your old friends but they can always accuse you of faking it just to cover up. The best way to prove you're honest is to be honest. Isn't it?"

Captain Jones shook her head sadly.

Shirley Jones returned to her keyboard. Things seemed to be moving sluggishly. She felt sluggish herself. She considered herself tough, a no-nonsense person. She had risen a long way to this position, and she wasn't going to give it up. Out of the ghetto. No matter what it took. Hell or high water. Whoever gets hurt along the way. Why was the computer taking so long? Words hung back for seconds before her keystrokes appeared as letters on the screen.

Keep your mouth shut and do your job. She cleared the program and brought up another one. It was tantalizingly slow. Icons disappeared, leaving blank sections of the screen, like brain synapses gone dead; then reappeared; they had only been sleeping. Maybe I should take a break. Get some coffee. Finally the program came on. It was a list of passwords to be checked against failed attempts to use them to access higher security levels. She worked for a few minutes, noting instances of possible break-in attempts and tracing their connections. Portions of the data seemed to be missing. Strange. She had gotten her SCI clearance back for password files, although not her clearance for *Crypto* and *Extremely Sensitive Information*. Was her clearance blocked for particular topics? It was possible.

She considered whether she could break into the higher level clearance, using her existing access to leverage a higher level. Hackers did it all the time. It was one of their favorite techniques. Even legitimate technicians sometimes have to do it just to perform their job. Remember a story about an FBI technician who was shut out from connecting a new laser printer because the security level had been set too high. So he hacked his way into the higher clearance. Better not try it. They're probably watching me, seeing if I'll slip up.

There was another blank in the data. Pain in the butt, she thought. She scrolled back up to where the previous blank had been. It was larger. The blanks were growing. She scrolled down. Now the other blank spot was much larger. Its edges were expanding before her eyes, like a blot of invisible ink soaking away the contents of the screen.

She left her cubicle and checked next door. The same thing. Whatever program was running, blanks were appearing of screens, links were dropping, computers were freezing up.

"It's a virus attack," said her neighbor.

The rest of the afternoon and evening were spent by the entire computer staff cleaning out viruses and getting systems running again. In the small hours of the morning, the wave of malware had been contained. Forty minutes later came another round of electronic assaults. This went on intermittently throughout the next day, and the next. Worms lodged in one place propagated themselves in other computers and other programs. Servers were bombarded with millions of nonsense messages, hogging their attention and shutting out other traffic. Source computers for the attacks were traced and neutralized. Others took their place. It was like an electronic battlefield fighting against a swarm of insects, army ants marching through cyberspace and gobbling up everything in their path. Driven back in one place, they came on again in another.

On the second day of the virus attacks, Grotweil was in Wolf's office. General Harris and Special Deputy Clements were there.

"We're getting it under control," said Grotweil. "The rate of new attacks has declined by 48.63 percent, and 72.38 percent of estimated vulnerabilities have been closed. We're checking for worms implanted with a time delay, to go off in the future. We've got countermeasures in place for anything that eats up hard drive space. Of course, new attacks could happen at any time. New kinds of malware are always being invented. But we should be getting back to the normal, non-crisis rate of cyber attacks per day, which is, according to my figures—"

"Never mind that," said Harris. "What took us so long to launch our own attacks against CSSA computers?"

"We've only had two weeks since the two computer systems began to separate from each other," said Grotweil. "Until our own computers were sealed off, anything that we launched against the CSSA could have leaked back into our own system."

"But they thought of it first. They got the jump on us. Now we're playing catch-up, while they have the initiative," Harris said. "We're supposed to do that to them."

"It doesn't matter in the long run," said Wolf. "When our forces are ready to strike, our firepower will decide this war fairly quickly. We can afford to wait until everything in the system has settled down."

"Regarding our ongoing investigation," said Grotweil. "These virus attacks are coming from outside. The access level necessary to get in for these kinds of attacks does not require any extremely high security clearances. I estimate that four thousand three hundred twenty-six defectors could have done these. And it could be the CSSA cyberwar division."

"And your point is?" said Wolf.

"The hackers are not necessarily insiders at all. Our investigation needs to take a new direction."

"That's not the way I look at it," said Wolf. "These attacks are coordinated. On their first try, they went for maximal gain, not by destroying our system but by subverting it. They tried to use our command system to attack our own bases. To do that, they had to leave the system intact. Haven't you wondered why we didn't receive cyber attacks right away?"

"The same reason why we didn't launch attacks on them right away," said Grotweil. "Danger of self-contamination."

"That's probably what they wanted you to think," said Wolf. "Now they know the big attack from the inside failed, so they've fallen back on a crude external attack. Since they can't use our system any more, they're trying to smash it or at least temporarily jam it."

"We have a list of high-level defectors who could have provided entry for CSSA experts. General Jefferson Gray, for one, had access to the highest command codes. We changed the codes, but there was a window during which they could have inserted their Trojan horse."

"What do we learn from the timing of these new attacks?" said Clements. "It's not just Park or Sanchez, since they were in custody before these attacks began. And it's probably not Zielkowski, since she had her access denied. Shirley Jones could be involved, since she had most of her access restored just before the attacks began. The whole group could be implicated in the overall plan of attack, but it looks like their active part in it is over. We could release them all now, and keep them under surveillance. Tell them they've been cleared. That could lead us to their networks."

"I'll go along with that," said Harris. "Except Park. We've got enough to nail him anyway. Whatever his involvement in these particular episodes."

"We're at a turning point," said Wolf. "The scope of the investigation has got to expand. We've concentrated too narrowly on high-level clearances. Now we need to go after everyone with enough clearance to be instrumental in the virus attacks."

"That's a huge number," said Grotweil. "Even if we confined it to persons whose computers were used in the transmission, they could simply be zombies in somebody's botnet."

"There's a way to winnow them down," said Wolf. "Look for the intersection of access and motive. We need to launch new security checks on everyone who could be implicated. Ferret out CSSA sympathizers. Check their religion, especially for outspoken secularists and atheists. Anyone who was involved in the movement against transformation of the modern military, the anti-RMA crowd. Natives of the Northern states and Pacific Coast who might be feeling nostalgia for home. And of course find out who their friends are, and how their friends check out on loyalty criteria."

"We don't have all that information in electronic form," said Grotweil. "And I'm not sure we can get all of it from their email."

"Old security clearances aren't good enough any more," said Wolf. "Most of the investigations were made prior to the secession crisis, so there is no information about their sympathies to the CSSA. We'll need new security checks on everybody."

"It will be a massive job," said Grotweil. "Nothing else is going to get done around here for a long time. I'm estimating nine and one half months, minimum."

"General Grotweil," Harris said. "Cyberwarfare is just as deadly as conventional warfare. You ought to know that. We're fighting for our lives here."

"Once we get a sufficient group of loyal officers," said Wolf, "we will proceed to set up military tribunals. They will operate is strictest secrecy under a new SCI clearance that I am creating. It will be called TE: *treason enforcement*. They should be prepared to recommend the death penalty."

As the weeks wore on and spring turned to summer, Secretary Madigan's office was swamped with complaints and requests. Complaints about the heavyhandedness of Wolf's investigations. Questions about Special Deputy C. J. Clements. Who was he anyway, and how did he get so much influence? Requests to override reclassification of security clearances. Generals and Admirals from all over the Pentagon and from bases across the country were protesting. Careers of long-trusted personnel were being wrecked. Ordinary operational efficiency was being stymied.

"You might as well arrest them as take away their security clearances," a general protested; "either way, they're casualties as far as organizational strength is concerned."

Madigan shrugged off most of the requests and told his interlocutors they needed to cooperate with Wolf.

Brigadier Grotweil paid a call. "I'm in a bind," he said. "I need more personnel to carry out computer security checks. But I'm losing effectives every day because these background investigations are making them suspects."

"How do you know they're not?"

"Everybody who works for me fits our own security protocols. We've run it through statistically. The probability of disloyalty in my organization is cumulatively below 0.04 percent."

"Wolf has added further loyalty criteria that you don't have in your system."

"That's just the problem. Excuse me for saying so, Mr. Secretary, but I am the professional here. These political people need to get out of the way and let me do my job."

"Unfortunately," said Madigan, "in the present situation security has a strong political component to it."

"Be that as it may. I need more personnel with high-level access. If I don't get them, the computer security operation itself is going to grind to a halt."

Madigan frowned. "How many do you need?"

"At least thirty SPI, Crypto and ESI clearances."

"Bring in your list. I'll have somebody check it—outside of Wolf's office."

Later Wolf showed up. He looked tired.

"We have a serious problem," he said. "Grotweil."

"What about him?"

"His loyalty. The whole pattern is falling into place. He's been covering up for traitors. And I hear he has been going over my head, Bob."

"He's been in here, Thad. You don't have to be reminded, he works for me too."

"Asking for illicit clearances, right?"

"If you want to call it that."

"Look," said Wolf. "This is what we have on him. The background checks show, first of all, that he is not a practicing Christian. Or any other religion. He doesn't even attend funerals. Second, he is from Massachusetts, and he studied at MIT. He did not belong to ROTC. He came into the service via a special program for computer scientists. He used to belong to a group that played poker on Saturday nights. The group broke up during the secession. His friends are all atheists, and they're all from the North too. Three of his poker buddies are now working for the CSSA. At least one of them is in their computer security organization."

"Has he ever expressed any sympathy for the CSSA?"

"We're still checking on that. It's not in the files so far."

"Personally," said Madigan, "I don't think that Grotweil is interested in politics. Or in his poker-playing friends very much either. I can just imagine the conversation around the table."

"I know he's been your guy, Bob. That's what makes it hard for you to see. But the pattern is right there in black and white. We assign a point for each suspicious item in the investigation. Grotweil's score is way up in the higher echelons of suspects."

"What do you want to do?"

"I want him arrested, before he can do any further harm."

An aide knocked, entered. "Mr. Secretary, President Jennings is on the line."

"Don't go, Thad," said Madigan.

After a few rhetorical greetings, Madigan turned on the speaker phone. "Wolf is here with me now, Mr. President," he said into the handset. "I think it's important for him to hear what you've just told me."

"Thad!" Jennings' voice boomed. "I wish I was there in person, but I'm tied up. Consider your back slapped by this old bear-hugger." The president's belly laugh echoed throughout the room.

"What I was telling Bob about," Jennings continued, "concerns Colonel Park. John Gandhi Park, he calls himself. Mother and father must have been religious people, though they might have started him out with the wrong religion. But Hindus can be a stepping stone to God the Father."

"Mr. President," said Wolf, "Colonel Park is under arrest. As the result of my investigation. It is the most serious possible charge—he is implicated in the computer-subversion attack on our DC-area bases. It's one step from bombing the White House."

"From what I hear, Thad," the speaker phone boomed, "the evidence is all circumstantial. You don't have him red-handed."

"With all due respect," Wolf said. "Evidence of his disloyalty is palpable. We have witnesses to that."

"Well, let's just add another witness. Myself. Colonel Park is a true Christian. I happen to know this, because Johnny Park came to one of my prayer meetings. I talked to him. He was in difficulties—in a quandary. He's a man who wanted to serve his country, but he couldn't see his way forward under his superior officers. I advised him to give his heart to Jesus, to let Jesus make the decision for him. That's what he did."

"Mr. President—" Wolf began.

"Let me finish. I know you don't see eye to eye with him—nor you neither, Bob. I know he's had some run-ins with both of you. But he's an honest man. He speaks his mind."

The President paused to let his words sink in. "I want Col. Park released. He's done good work for us on the front lines in Baltimore.

That's only forty miles from where we sit, as I'm sure you know. He helped keep Maryland in the Union, and that's mighty important for anyone like ourselves here in the District of Columbia. And we're going to need him when that atheist army comes down the pike. I want him released and restored to his position in the armed services."

"I'll see to it," said Madigan.

"Thanks, Bob. And Thad—come round some time. We need to have a little chat."

Two days later Wolf was called into Secretary Madigan's office. General Harris was there, along with Grotweil. Wolf was not asked to sit down.

"I'm lifting your security clearance," said Madigan. "Your investigative unit is being moved under direct authority of my office. You're out of the loop, Thad."

"You can't do that, Bob. If you try, I'm going to the news media with the whole story," said Wolf. "Security breakdown at Pentagon. High-level cover-up. Corruption all the way to the top. Treason."

"I wouldn't do that if I were you." Madigan held up a handful of files. "I have three dossiers here."

Wolf sat down, unbidden.

"The first one," said Madigan, "is my own. Highlights include the fact that I am from California. That I attended Cal Tech. That I worked for a big defense contractor in Southern California which is now at the center of CSSA electronics warfare. That I am not religious. That I had friends who are defectors to the CSSA. And that my daughter is a lesbian. Total rating: loyalty highly suspect."

Wolf started to say something. Madigan held up his hand, waving him off. "The second dossier is General Curtis Harris. Harris is from New York City, which gets extra low loyalty ratings. His father was a Democrat, and he seldom attends church. He has often been heard to take the name of the Almighty in vain. He attended the Air Force Academy, which is good. However, his appointment to the

Academy was recommended by Senator Philip Rosenfeld, father of the current Chairperson of the CSSA." He looked around at Harris. "Neither one of us would get a security clearance today, and given our access at the time of the attack on Bolling and Belvoir, we should probably be arrested."

"And the third one, I suppose," said Wolf, "is mine."

"Not exactly. Although the name Wolf is on it. Theodore S. Wolf."

"No—Ted?"

"Your son."

"He's only fifteen years old."

"More or less the modal age for a hacker, isn't it?"

"What do you have on him?"

"For one thing, we know he hacked into Pentagon computers a year ago."

"It couldn't have been any real damage," said Wolf. "I never received any complaints about it. It was just mischief."

"We didn't think it necessary to tell you. But we kept it on file. More up to date, we know that he hacked into our system two weeks ago, at the time of the virus attacks. One of the viruses was traced to your own home computer, and your access code."

"Well, obviously I didn't do it. I wasn't going to hack myself."

"We didn't think you did. It appears that Ted borrowed or copied your access card and your personal codes. We have him in custody, and we're questioning him about it. You must have been careless in leaving them around the house when you were sleeping or showering or something. But carelessness in this kind of emergency is culpable, too. You're a weak link in the chain, Thad."

"When exactly did this virus get into our system?" said Wolf. "Was it on the first day of virus attacks?"

Madigan turned to Grotweil. The latter said, "It was on the third day. Around four thirty-six a.m. I can get more exact information."

"So it was just a copycat attack," Wolf said. "He's not part of any enemy network. He must have picked up from me that the attacks were going on, and I suppose he thought it would be fun to get in on the excitement."

"Do you talk about your work at home?" said Madigan.

"Of course not. But Ted is a bright boy. He infers things."

"We're going to throw the book at him, Thad. Charge him as an adult. We can make it look pretty bad. If we have to. If this thing goes public."

Wolf contemplated a moment. "He can take his medicine. Ted will testify that I had nothing to do with it."

"Are you so sure about that, Thad?" Madigan leaned forward, looked him full in the face. "Do you really think he loves you as much as you say you love him? Or that he even likes you? How much time have you ever spent with him? One whole afternoon in the past fifteen years? Five consecutive minutes of conversation?"

"I resent that," said Wolf. He looked stunned. "Maybe I haven't been such a good father. Who can be, in this business?"

Madigan was silent. A long moment passed.

"If I resign, will you drop the charges against Ted?"

Madigan shrugged. Wolf turned to Harris.

"We'll think about it," said Harris.

Wolf turned to Madigan. "Bob?"

"Okay. Now get the hell out of here."

After Wolf had left, Madigan addressed the others.

"I'm calling off the investigations. Wolf's security unit is abolished. Destroy their background check files. And get Special Deputy Clements as far away from here as possible."

"I could store the background checks," said Grotweil. "Or we could turn them over to the FBI, or one of our in-house agencies."

"It would do more harm than good," said Madigan. "I've got a better plan. We will shut down our entire computer system. Reconfigure an entirely new system with new access codes. It will have a completely different security structure. That way nobody from the CSSA, and nobody from the period before the split occurred, will know how to access it."

"That's going to slow down any military operations," said Harris. "We're going to have to do a lot of telephoning and note taking for a while."

"Hopefully it won't take too long. And when the new system is operative, it will be vastly superior to what we had before. It will be a truly computer-centralized system. Human error will be minimized, since the computer will collect information directly from mechanical sensors, and it will guide the execution of combat operations, all the way from logistics through weapons firing. You know the plan. Remember why it's called HOME: Hyper Organization Military Efficiency. Now is the time to put it into operation."

"What about spies and hackers?" said Harris.

"HOME will be much less dependent upon human inputs, or on human execution. It will deal with the world objectively, not subjectively. Hackers will be incapable of introducing wrong decisions or misinformation. And it will assess its own security risks."

"That sounds great, Bob, once the thing is up and running. But we're still in the midst of a serious hacker problem. Some of the breaches may have come from insiders. Are we just going to let them go?"

"Look, Curt, I know it runs against the grain. If someone hits you, it's a primitive human reaction to strike back. But rationally, it is just too expensive. Consider Wolf's investigation as an experiment that failed. Paranoia is killing our organization. Suspicion is the worst kind of virus. The only rational solution is to cut our losses. Fall back and start over again with an invulnerable system."

"Okay," said Harris, grudgingly. "But it burns me up—traitors getting away with something."

"We don't even know that for sure. And it's too costly to find out. Let it go, Curt. We're moving on."

"One other thing that bothers me about shutting down to reconfigure the entire system," said Harris. "Isn't that going to give the enemy a huge advantage? He'll be operative while we're not."

"The other side has the same problems we have," said Madigan. "We're practicing cyberwar on them too. We know their computer system just like they know ours. Sooner or later they'll have to make a move like we're making. We'll be ready to fight before they are."

They got up. The conference was over.

"Let's face it," said Madigan. "Neither side is well enough organized to carry out any significant military operations for a while. Just some minor clashes with small arms in Baltimore and Denver. Nothing that local forces can't handle."

YEAR ONE, CHAPTER SIX.
McCONNELL'S MISSOURI RAID

Northeast New Mexico. June.

The base commander of Cannon Air Force Base was missing. Sprawled in arid northeast New Mexico at the border town of Clovis, Cannon AFB was the CSSA's nearest base to Union territory—if it could be held. Its fighter wings would be a mighty counterweight in the balance scales, whether aimed east and north at Union airbases in Texas and Colorado, or swung around westward to menace CSSA strongholds in Nevada, Arizona and California. Depending on which side got control.

The C.O., General Harrelson probably took off for Texas, McConnell thought. Waiting until the last minute to see if CSSA forces really would arrive. Well, here we are.

McConnell scanned the C.O.'s private quarters, trying to form an impression of how he had left. The rooms had a rumpled look. The last occupant had been rummaging around looking for something. If he'd left in a hurry, wouldn't it look more normal, undisturbed, coffee still brewing and all that?

A movement on the other side of the bedroom door brought him to alert. A hand was pointing a Glock 9mm pistol through the doorway. A cop's gun, he thought.

McConnell's Smith and Wesson .357 magnum weighed comfortably in his hand. He cocked the hammer for a smooth, unjerking shot. Practice shooting on the firing range did not necessarily translate into hitting a live human target, and police often fired wildly in shootouts at less than seven feet—the closest confrontations pumped the most adrenaline and produced the worst misses. Both gunmen were inching forward around the doorjamb.

But it was not a gunman, but a gunwoman, dressed for a nightclub in stiletto heels with silver straps accentuating curves of the instep. A body-hugging cobalt blue party dress came down barely to the top of her well-turned thighs, and her bare arm extended the gun against McConnell's chest. He held his gun steady in the two-handed grip, the barrel almost touching her cone-shaped breasts.

"Mind your manners, General," she said accusingly. Her hair flowed wildly over shoulders and bust, tawny-blonde with an orange tinge contradicting the heavy black arch of eyebrows and her theatrical eyelashes, a botched bleach job. High cheekbones with rouge-accented hollows; pouting lips glossed deep red. "I'm the Queen of the West."

McConnell flashed his dentally perfect grin; he too had photogenic cheekbones. Gunmetal nudged nippletip. "Lady of the night, you mean. Something General Harrelson left behind?"

She shoved her gun defiantly into his diaphragm. The fingers of her free hand snapped a business card in front of his face.

Marisa Santa-Ana

Consulting

Security, Communications, Countermeasures

She dropped the card and scraped her red-clawed hand across his cheek. Her inch-long fingernail extensions were painted with red, white and blue stripes. "I don't come with the office."

"I didn't think you came for free."

"You can't even afford to be around me." Her pistol barrel sketched a dance step on his hard muscled belly, descending to the crotch. "General *bandido*."

McConnell lowered his left hand from the pistol stance and rested it on the pelvic curve of her invitingly full-dimensioned hip. "Now that we know each other, let's drop the hardware. All right now, one, two, *three*."

Loud clanks on the carpet. Both had thrown their guns clear, out of reach.

She pulled his face towards hers and attacked his mouth. Her tongue darted inside. A sharp pain, and she pushed away. She had bitten his lip.

"Don't get any ideas," she said. "What goes around, comes around."

He licked away a trickle of blood, rust-tasting, viscous. "Consulting, countermeasures. I bet you have a lot of business these days."

She stepped inside his arms again, giggling, nibbling at his ear, taking little playful bites. "I'll tell you a secret, *mi corazon*. I know the brass on every airbase in the Mountain Time Zone."

McConnell petted the back of her neck, pushing up the tent of hair, stroking her ears and face. "There's a different dividing line now. Which side are you on, Marisa?"

She pushed off, palmheels straight-arming his chest, and commenced to prance back and forth, preening. Pulling out a cell phone, she began checking for messages.

McConnell snatched the phone and tossed it onto the sofa. "I like a lady who's been around. No expectations. Not even about where you'll be tomorrow night."

"I'm in the CSSA zone now. Maybe I'll stay. Or I can go back to the other side, if you want me to." She put her hand on his zipper.

They were in the bedroom, clothes strewn across the floor. She squirmed on top of him, full length, snuggling, kissy-kissy. An orange-blonde halo of soft hair shrouded their faces, a secret hideaway. "I can find out anything. *Mi Generalito*."

"Tell me something I don't know."

"Dyess AFB has gone for the Union. Holloman AFB for the CSSA." Dyess was in Abilene, Texas; Holloman in Alamogordo, New Mexico.

"BFD, Marisa. Everybody knows the rule, which way the state goes, the base goes. Any military assets wrecked on their way out?"

"Holloman AFB shot it out with Fort Bliss across the Texas-New Mexico line. It's pretty much no-man's-land now." She rolled off and begun to lick and stroke him. She raised her face after a few perfunctory licks, her hand rubbing him fast and hard. McConnell lay back, letting her work, unmoved. He would take her when and if and on his own terms.

"What about here at Cannon? Didn't General Harrelson talk about keeping it for the Union? And redrawing the border of New Mexico at the east side of the Rockies?"

"*Si, si*. He said that. He's gone to Dyess. They're in a mess over there, half their officers are leaving."

If we move fast, we can take Dyess AFB while they're too disorganized to keep up security, McConnell thought. If it's true. He pushed her hands away and slid his face down her belly. "You're too rough, too hard, too fast. Let me do it. Like this."

She was shaved to black stubble except for a crown-shaped tattoo where her delta would have been. At first she leaned her head forward to watch him lick, not lying back with eyes closed in ecstasy or pretence of it: her gaze keeping his sexual performance at a distance. She began chattering, a professional stream of Spanish endearments and English obscenities.

He raised up for moment, fingers squeezing her clitoris.

She was trying to keep from breathing heavily, and making herself a little breathless in the process.

"Who else was in on Harrelson's plan? Anybody who's still here?"

Her calm cool was breaking down. "No. Yes. Ask me later. What kind of bed talk is this?"

She was moaning and squirming under his tonguing, deep trembling in the musculature of her legs and buttocks. She pushed hard against his mouth, then again- again-again, exploding with a crashing sigh, a brief thunderclap. "Don't lick me any more," she burst out, sitting up. "I can't take another one like that."

She propped herself against the bedstead, demanding a cigarette. "Tell me something. Tell me anything, *Generalito*. Make me laugh."

"We banned the nukes in this war. Maybe we need to ban you."

"Not my game," she purred. "Women make love, not war."

She crept upon him as he lay. She was licking and murmuring again, flicking her hair across his face, dragging cool pendulous breasts across his chest. She straddled him and began bouncing up and down, like a painted carousel horse rising and falling on its pole. McConnell let her work, a little game of controlling each other's orgasm. She began to chatter again.

"The great General McConnell. I heard your name around. If you're so great, what are you doing out here in the New Mexico desert?"

"Looking for a cheap trick."

"Watch your mouth. I worked as a police decoy once. Trapping Johns on the street."

"You think you'd do better by going over to the Union? They burn ladies like you at the stake."

"I could like it here." She was getting tired of pounding up and down without result. His hands went over her body appraisingly. When her rhythm slowed, he pulled her hips down like covering himself with a pillow, and began to thrust upwards. She crouched forward on his neck, heads close together. "Now we can talk," she whispered. "Where are you going after you leave Clovis?"

"C'mon, Marisa. Wait til I catch my breath."

"No, really, *papi*. Will you still be here next week?"

"Probably not. Old friends at Colorado Springs are expecting me to drop in." Harmless information, McConnell thought. They're already expecting an attack to the north. He rolled Marisa over on her back.

"Harrelson might come back from Dyess," she said, twisting her face to the side, tantalizing him. "With a lot of help."

"I've got help coming too." He pumped harder, trying to force her orgasm. "Maybe you can give a party for everybody."

Her fingernails dug into his back. "I heard your next move is Fort Bliss. On Texas territory. Your first attack on enemy turf."

"Somebody is always first, Marisa. Shut up a minute." He furrowed her vigorously, listening for the shortening of her breathing. He let his legs and buttocks go on riding her, letting the rumbling of his muscles take over, until her body set off contagiously from his own. She began rocking like a car on a bumpy road. Then her full body shuddering, eyes closed, mouth open, gasping and panting out short yelps.

Abruptly she stopped: one last full-body spasm, as she shrugged off the drumbeat rattling her from within. Getting control of her body, McConnell thought. She knows who turned who on.

"Get out," she said. "You bore me."

"I thought we had an understanding."

"Get out. I'm Queen of the West. I'll let you know if we have a deal." She became absorbed in studying her makeup in the mirror.

McConnell dressed quickly. Passing through the living room, he saw her cell phone where he had thrown it, picked it up.

At the front door, she came running after him, nuzzling both cheeks, uttering a stream of Spanish endearments.

From the helicopter, the pink parched earth blotted with cloud shadows looked like a Salvador Dalí painting. McConnell was flying southwest towards Holloman AFB, two hundred miles across some of the hottest and most beautiful land in America. Billy the Kid country, he thought, where rival syndicates of ranchers and politicians fought it out with hired gunmen in the 1870s. This isn't the first time someone has tried to set up competing governments out here. At Cannon AFB, it was hard to tell which side anyone was on. New Mexico was a giant poker game where all the cowboys wore six-guns and everybody's cards were marked.

A few days ago there was a remote-control battle at Nellis AFB outside Las Vegas. The drone operators were split between CSSA and USA, so they sent all the Predators up to shoot at each other, like a big video game. Everybody had a good laugh, shooting at each other from adjoining screens. Then the USA guys left, and we've got Nellis because Nevada belongs to us. We're on a roll, McConnell thought. Let's keep it rolling.

In his pocket he felt a cell phone. Marisa's. He scrolled through the address book: abbreviations, all sorts of area codes and electronic addresses. He would have someone check it out. He reached for his own cell phone, checked the contact for Brigadier General Frank O'Mara, C.O. of Holloman AFB. Not one of Marisa's recent contacts, at any rate.

Before leaving Cannon, he had considered ordering Marisa kept off base, then thought better of it, and gave orders that she not be allowed to leave base or communicate in any way. To enforce it, he had assigned around-the-clock surveillance by a pair of male and female guards. The woman was the most straightlaced marine he could think of, all muscles and glower. She'd probably enjoy putting the strong arm on someone like Marisa.

Still, Marisa wasn't the only one to worry about. Anyone could see the thousands of marines and their materiel flowing into eastern New Mexico, and ask: what were they here for? What was their next move? Only McConnell knew, and he was flying out of town not to be overheard. Electronic communications everywhere were insecure. What the hell, it's better like this.

Passing a girdle of dark mountains, the helicopter descended toward a vast expanse of rippled sand. White Sands missile range, where the first A-bomb was tested back in 1945. The most uninhabited part of the country. Late-afternoon shadows pockmarked hillocks with deep gray, streaked by blowing sands that made the desert look like it was weeping.

The helicopter hovered in for a landing at the edge of the dunes where a car waited. There was a paved road, covered by snow drifts, pushed back here and there by the futile efforts of a snow plow. Only it was ninety degrees in the middle of summer, and the drifts were whiter and cleaner than snow, and it didn't melt and refreeze as black ice or turn dirty by being shoveled into gritty piles. Mile after mile of pure white gypsum sands.

Frank O'Mara gripped McConnell's hand. An old classmate from the War College at Carlisle; someone he could trust. Holloman AFB was ten miles away across the sands. It was their missile range.

They walked away from the driver, up and over the nearest dune. The sand slithered below their feet in mini-avalanches, making every step a double effort.

"It's dangerous out here if you lose your sense of direction," O'Mara said. "The dunes are always shifting. You can see the ripples moving before your eyes. If you go very far, your footsteps are gone before you come back. There are no landmarks because nothing looks the same very long."

The pure white sand was seductive, geometry in motion, not a speck of ugliness anywhere. McConnell gave a sudden whoop and took off down the steep slope. It was like sledding on your feet. Down into the hollow, where the shadow curved a blue-shaded parabola across a sand-cliff, gently changing angles never stopping, bringing out the three-dimensionality of this desert world that made ordinary eyesight feel like the flat page of a newspaper. He charged up the opposite side, fifty feet tall though it felt twice the height by the time his legs had slipped and scrambled to the top.

He sat puffing on the sand ridge while O'Mara circled more perspicaciously along the crests to reach him. In the distance, a little depression on the surface of a long soft dune dimpled like a navel. "This must be a great place to bring a woman," McConnell said as his friend arrived.

"It is. It's like being in the waves and troughs of a slow-moving ocean, only you can't drown. All you can do is get lost." O'Mara lay back, luxuriating in the soft yielding hollows of warm sand. "So what are you going to do, Mick?"

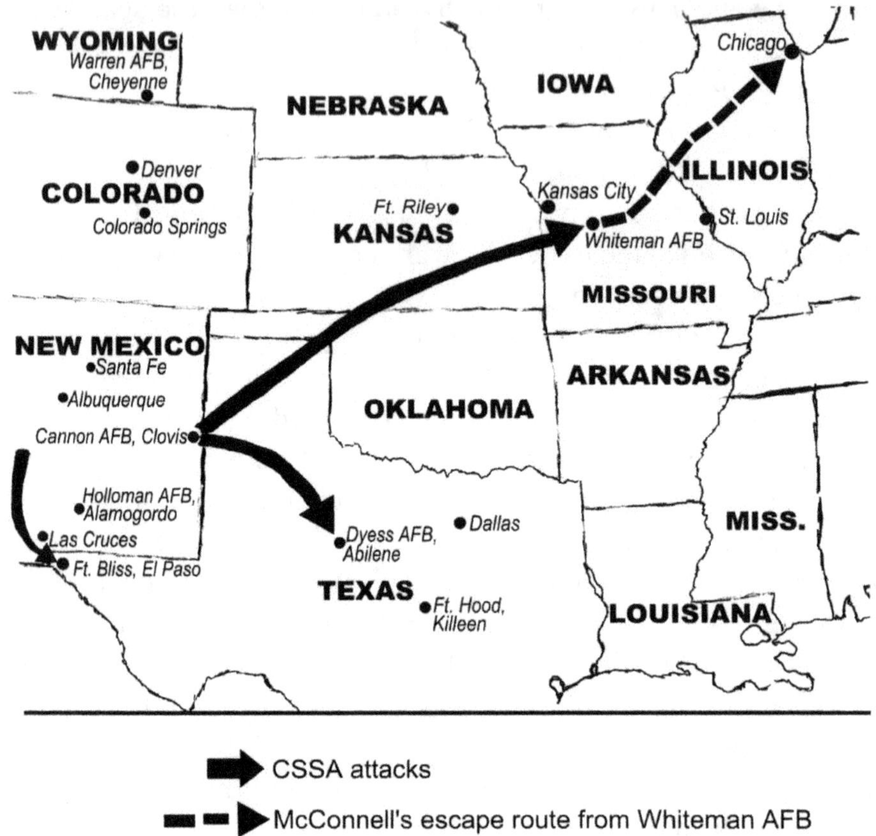

"Three simultaneous attacks. Fort Bliss, for one." McConnell drew a map in the sand with his finger. At El Paso just at the New Mexico border, Fort Bliss stuck like a knife point into CSSA territory, only a few hundred miles westward to the populated region at Tucson, Arizona, or threatening to roll north up the central axis of New Mexico along the Rio Grande through Las Cruces, Albuquerque and Santa Fe.

"Why bother?" O'Mara said. "It's an isolated outlier for the Union army, five hundred miles from their nearest reinforcements at Fort Hood. We can command the highways from the air."

"Because," McConnell said, "it's where Patton and Black Jack Pershing took off from in 1915 to chase Pancho Villa into Mexico. I always thought it would be cool to go on that mission. But seriously—" he kicked into motion a little avalanche down the slope, "we're going to take it sooner or later to secure our defenses, and this would be the right time to catch their attention."

"While you go where?"

"Second prong of attack: Dyess AFB." He drew another arrow in the sand, this one due east from Alamogordo into central Texas.

"Makes sense. It's the biggest Union bomber base in this part of the country. That would certainly reduce the threat to CSSA high value targets everywhere."

"Knocking out Dyess would redress the balance. Help put our air forces even with theirs. Turn the war into a stalemate. That means victory for us."

"So it's an airstrike. And you want Holloman's fighter wing to do it."

"Partly. You're only seventy-five miles from Fort Bliss, so you'd be the logical jumping-off place for that campaign."

"I'd rather hit Dyess. Fort Bliss is an artillery base, the center of their air defense artillery. They don't have a lot of mobile ground forces, but it could be costly to take them from the air."

"So we'll take them from the ground. I'm sending a marine battle group eastward through Las Cruces, with advance elements already at Holloman, as you know. Then we'll turn quickly and jump down on El Paso. Helicopters winging in from three directions, including Mexico. They're used to drug-chasing operations."

"And you want Holloman to provide air cover?"

"Just a base for marine fighters I'm bringing forward."

"So who's going to knock out Dyess?"

"That will be a combined operation between Holloman and Cannon AFBs. Our fighters versus their bombers, probably caught on the ground. Should be a piece of cake."

"Fair enough," O'Mara said. "And the third prong is Colorado."

"Nope. Too heavily guarded. I'm going after Whiteman AFB."

"Whiteman? And you think Colorado Springs is heavily guarded. Whiteman AFB is in the center of the biggest field of nuclear missile launchers in the country. And where the crown treasure is kept, the B-2 stealth bomber fleet."

"That's what makes it a great target. Imagine the headlines. A long raid behind enemy lines, plucking the golden fleece from the teeth of the sleeping dragon."

"Get real, Mick. This isn't a nuclear war. Everybody knows both sides have enough nukes to destroy the world."

"That makes the B-2 even more dangerous. It's so unstoppable and so accurate that it's more destructive with conventional bombs than old-fashioned nukes were. It could penetrate any defenses we could put up, even the most hardened, deeply buried targets."

"Whiteman AFB is in the middle of Missouri, across seven hundred miles of open plains. You would have to thread the needle between half a dozen Union bases between here and there. Even in their computers down while they sort out this hacking mess, somebody's radar would pick up your planes."

"I'm not going in with fighters. That's what they're defending against. It will be a helicopter-borne force, hugging the ground."

"Somebody will see you."

"And call in where? Nobody will know where we're heading. We'll hide in the open."

O'Mara clapped him around the shoulders, playfully threatening to push him off the precipice of the dune. "You wild-ass SOB. What's the timing?"

"The Whiteman mission will spring first. It's farthest away and I want everything to be quiet when we arrive. Then near-simultaneously, the strike on Dyess. The Fort Bliss attack will be in position to launch the same day."

"And I don't have to guess which attack you're going to lead. Crazy Mick. Are you sure you aren't just doing this on a dare?"

"It should be fun," McConnell said. "Six hundred fifty miles of the most wide-open spaces in America. If we're ever going to cross it, the time is now."

The caravan of fifteen unmarked vans and pickup trucks set out from Cannon AFB at 1500 hours. McConnell had ordered a staggered start.

The ground portion of the Whiteman expedition would have twelve hours to cross the western corners of Texas and Oklahoma and the length of Kansas, to arrive at its rendezvous south of Kansas City at 0300 hours, three o'clock in the dead of night, just fifty miles short of its target. It was to stay off the Interstates and use minor roads—not really much of a slowdown in this part of the country, where towns were little more than crossroads without traffic lights. But their orders were to avoid speeding beyond the local custom, which could be over 80 miles per hour. The vehicles carried a total of one hundred troops and their weapons under tarps and in duffle bags; their T-shirts and cargo pants were in fact regulation uniforms but would not look much different from rough young men of the gritty plains.

The first part of the route would be roundabout, feinting towards Colorado Springs, three hundred miles due north. The mission was top secret, which in itself was enough to call attention to it at Cannon, with all its spies and dubious loyalties. The mission's official orders were to cross into Texas, head north bypassing Amarillo on the west, and then loop into Colorado from the southeast. In fact, once it got north of I-40 the caravan was to split up on little country roads, heading toward Missouri, refueling at ordinary gas stations along with way.

Including the ground component added more risk, McConnell knew, but it was better to have a multi-pronged attack, and ground vehicles provided backup for contingencies. The helicopters would go off later, traveling the whole way in darkness. At up to 180 miles per hour, they would cover the distance in under four hours.

Whiteman AFB had thirty-two hundred troops, but most of them were administrative and maintenance personnel for the stealth bombers. Base security forces would be around two hundred, no more than fifty of them on duty at one time. Some would be dispersed out in the eighty-mile-wide ring of missile launchers rather than on the base itself. Their heaviest weapons would be machine guns. The base had a wing of Apache attack helicopters and a wing of A-10 gunships, but these would not be scrambled unless the approaching force's cover were blown completely. McConnell calculated that four hundred marines landing from a fleet of helicopters, plus the land backup, would be enough to overwhelm initial resistance and immobilize Whiteman's combat assets on the ground.

McConnell had dedicated eight CH-53 Super Stallions to the mission, capable of carrying fifty troops each. He had borrowed two Pave Low III's from a Special Operations group in Arizona—ultra-fast long-range helicopters named after their Precision Avionics Vectoring Equipment i.e. PAVE. Their ordinary combat range was five hundred miles without refueling, but that was out-and-back. Ferrying troops one-way to their destination, they could cover the distance to western Missouri and still have some fuel left over, probably, to make it to the safety of CSSA territory inside Illinois. They could refuel at Whiteman AFB, if successful. If unsuccessful, they would not be coming back.

McConnell was impatient for their 2300 hours departure. Idly he recalled that during the Iranian hostage crisis in 1980, eight Special Forces helicopters, earlier versions of his own, had been sent to rescue the hostages by swooping down on the US Embassy in Tehran. But a helicopter had crashed into a refueling plane in the Iranian desert and the mission had aborted. Not this time.

Storm clouds were gathering to the east, white cottonballs clustering in the sky, their undersides gray with moisture. So much the better. He thought of J.E.B. Stuart's raid in 1862, when Confederate cavalry galloped into the middle of an invading Union army in Virginia under cover of a thunderstorm, paying a night visit on the commanding general's headquarters and stealing his dress uniforms. We'll bring Jeb Stuart up to date, McConnell told himself.

Cumulus clouds merged into a mass of smoky gray, low on the flat horizon of the Texas panhandle. The empty narrow road was a straight line to the vanishing point in the distance. Marine Sergeant Dante Jones felt the hot wind from the passenger side window turning cooler by the minute.

Dark clouds were sweeping right to left like smoke from a forest fire, except there was nothing growing here taller than roadside weeds alongside ploughed fields, dotted by rolled-up bundles of yellow hay. Dante grinned. The stifling heat was an exotic sensation for a farm boy from Washington, and made him feel exactly like a marine. The abrupt change of temperature was exciting too, especially since they were driving right into the teeth of the storm.

"Bring it on!" he said out loud. The driver, Corporal Jessie Ramirez, grunted assent.

The lower part of the cloud was gathering three miles to the left of the road, forming the base of a giant mushroom. Its top was a huge ballooning canopy filling the sky in every direction. The clouds were rushing in toward the mushroom's center, mixing and swirling inside the storm-cauldron, and then propelled furiously upwards and outwards. The top was spectacular roiling white-streaked gray but underneath the bottom of the mushroom, a few hundred feet off the ground, it was dark as night.

Nature's atom bomb, Dante thought. Thunder crashed; almost immediately the truck was hit by the blast of a machine gun. The air filled with clear white crystalline shells that rattled on roof and hood. Windshield visibility was like looking up into a high pressure shower nozzle. A hailstorm. Dante hastily cranked the window while the truck slowed, axel-deep on a roadbed of bouncing iceballs.

The tattoo of hailstones lessened to a monotonous patter. "Fuck this," Dante said. "Speed it up. It's 1700 hours and we're not even out of Texas." Ramirez laughed and accelerated to 60, then 70. The ragged edge of the dark cloud was passing over a cluster of silos in the distance, black roiling clouds now distinct from softer gray cottonballs like a chemical mixture resolving back into its components. White sky was becoming visible, framing the edges of the storm as it passed away to the west. Rays of the declining sun lit up the higher part of the cloudscape while the lower edge still hung black on the horizon. Furrows of ploughed fields converged at infinity, grooves filled with white hail glinting against brown earth.

Monster number one, met and conquered, Dante thought. He remembered TV ads of a marine in fulldress uniform, bright sword in hand, scaling a castle tower. This was what he had enlisted for. He glanced back at the van behind them. Others were making their own way, through their own adventures, towards a common destination.

Argonauts, a band of heroes. Sailing off into the unknown. "Bring it on," he said again.

Nightfall found them in Kansas. If anything, flatter, emptier feeling. At infrequent intervals, trucks like theirs passed both ways on the roads, marking the time like beats of a metronome, hypnotically slow. When they stopped for gas, the truck hood was cratered as if it had come through a firefight.

The sign in the filling station window said HAILSTONE DENTS REMOVED. A common occurrence.

In a little town, big enough to have cross streets with trees and houses with wide-roofed porches, a car pulled out from a vacant parking lot and fell in behind them. What's the speed limit? Dante thought. The car was a four-door sedan. Outside of town, it set in motion a rotary flasher. It pulled alongside the truck—now traveling alone—and motioned it to the side of the road. Dark empty fields, the humming of crickets. The crunch of footsteps approaching. The cop aimed a flashlight inside the driver's window.

"I didn't see no speed sign," Ramirez said. "What's the ticket?"

"How about you boys gettin' outside?" The night was hotter once the car stopped moving. "Mind if I take a look in back?"

Ramirez looked at Dante. "I don't know about that, sheriff. What's the trouble?"

"No trouble." The cop was leathered, fifty-ish, in steel-rimmed glasses. A pistol sat on his right hip. "Just this route is sometimes used by drug smugglers coming up from the border, heading for St. Louis."

He opened the back shell of the truck. Two more of the marine team were sitting on the floor. He motioned them outside. Dante nodded and they complied. Four to one should make this cop nervous. In a minute he would be heading for his car radio for backup.

The officer pulled at one of the bulging duffle bags. It moved only slightly, heavier than expected and made a clanking noise. The barrel of a 40mm machine gun protruded under the flashlight beam.

Alarmed, the officer began to run. Ramirez cut him off while two marines pinioned his arms. Dante stuck a M4 carbine in the cop's chest and motioned to Ramirez to take his gun.

"Shit! Dante. What do we do now?"

"Don't lose our heads. First, turn off that cop light."

They decided to tie up the cop with plastic handcuffs and standard Enemy Prisoner of War blindfold, and trussed him in the back of the truck. One of the marines drove the patrol car into a field.

It was 2320 hours.

Dante was on the cell phone. He got through to Captain Zabrisky, commanding officer of the ground force, thirty miles away on another Kansas byroad. "Uh Zero. How ya doing tonight? This is Dante."

Deliberately nonstandard nomenclature for a mission, but cell phones were the easiest way to communicate, more reliable range than encrypted radio and less likely to sound military.

"All up and up, Dante. Any trouble?"

"We just picked up a passenger."

Momentary silence on the line. "Where you at?"

Dante reflected, checked the map. Would it be giving away too much to mention a place? "Tell you what. I'm heading for Clark, Kansas. About half an hour from now."

"Okay, bud. We'll go into town together and lift a couple of cold ones. Don't get started til I get there."

They parked the truck in a little dirt road a few miles west of their destination. Lights came down the highway, going their direction. The car slowed a little, seemed about to turn, then continued on. A passenger car. Farmer looking for his road? Did he see us here? Probably a drunk. I'm imagining things, Dante thought.

The prisoner was kicking and squirming, rocking the truck. "What's the matter with him? Dyson, go shut him up."

Dyson returned in a moment. "He wants to take a crap."

"Let him wait."

"Christ, Sergeant, we're the ones who have to ride in back with his smell."

"Okay, what the fuck. Hurry up." The smell of fear, Dante thought. He had heard that cops could smell a burglar trapped in a house, it was so strong. Now we've got a cop shitting in terror.

Dyson led the prisoner off into the field, M4 in hand. Vehicle lights came down the road. Reached their position, passed. A farmer's truck.

Time: 0017 hours. Dante reached for his cell phone. Orders were to minimize calls, emergencies only.

Another light appeared, slowed to a halt. Captain Zabrisky's van.

As Dante explained the situation, Dyson came running up. "Fuck it all. I lost him."

"Whadya mean, lost him?"

"I untied his hands. Whadya think, I'm going to take his pants down for him? I could hear him dumping and splattering, like diarrhea. Stunk something awful. I gave him a little room. When I turned around, he was gone."

"Couldn't you see him in your NODs?"

"The batteries were dead."

Zabrisky sent four men to search. Dante put on his night observation devices and scanned the field. Corn stalks in uneven ridges. No farm buildings in sight. His watch showed 0031 hours.

Dyson and Coglin came back, the rest of Dante's squad. No prisoner. No sign of him. 0043.

Zabrisky called the other two marines in. "To hell with it, Sergeant. Let's get moving. We've got time to make up."

"What about the cop?"

"How long is he going to take to reach somewhere?" Zabrisky said. "And what does he have to tell? You guys mention where we're going?"

Dyson shook his head. "Shit, I don't even know where we're going."

"Let's hope Clark, Kansas isn't much of a place," Zabrisky said. It wasn't, just a couple of grain elevators. No lights anywhere. They roared through at 100 miles per hour, heading for the Missouri border.

Out on the Kansas plains, Lou Vogler was up early, reading the Bible and praying for America. He had just begun Daniel 3:15 when the shudder of flapping wings came. Angels? He lowered the Bible but held onto it steadily, his companion of many days on a tractor and many hours of early morning comfort. He went out of the parlor onto the front porch. Angels bathed everything in light but this night was dark, moonless.

The flapping grew louder, approaching. One, three, a dozen, a multitude. Dark shapes passed overhead, blotting the star-spangled sky cleansed by the end of the storm. Hope gave way to fear. He knew them for what they were.

Vogler went back inside, turned to Psalms. Though I walk through the valley of the shadow of death, I will fear no evil. Nevertheless a shudder went through him. The Angel of Death. It had passed over, did not touch this house. Not here, not now. But always somewhere. Where? He began to pray.

The Pave Lows went in first. Designed for Special Forces operations, fastest and nimblest of the helicopters, they skimmed in at 200 miles per hour, relying on sophisticated avionic sensors to keep them masked barely above the contours of the rolling terrain. A dozen troops roped down from forty feet above the ground at Whiteman AFB base security headquarters; another squad dropped behind the main gate, to let in the column of vans and pickup trucks waiting outside the double perimeter of wire and surveillance cameras. Behind the Pave Lows came the bigger, more lumbering Super Stallions, spilling four hundred marines onto the apron in front of the base operations control tower. It was 0330 hours, 3:30 in the morning.

When McConnell arrived they had taken the base security office and located the duty officer's command post. Casualties were entirely one-sided. The marines had the momentum and the security troops were dazed. Like sleepers suddenly wakened, although in fact they had not been sleeping but merely in the bored comfort of routine, some were disarmed before they knew what was happening. Others startled violently into clumsy action and were shot. The duty officer reached for his sidearm and was killed by a trio of marines unloading on him simultaneously. In the security command post the monitors were flashing:

> ALERT — URGENT — PERIMETER PENETRATION —

but there was no one operating them. McConnell took a detail and went to look for the C.O.'s office.

The office was empty.

No, the highbacked chair behind the desk was turned away. It began to swivel towards the intruders: Marisa.

She lounged deep in the padded chair on her shoulder blades, stiletto-shod legs splayed provocatively. Her head lay back and eyes half closed in a supercilious way that managed to give the impression of looking down on them while slouching below.

"What are you doing here?" McConnell said. "I thought I left you under tight escort at Clovis."

Marisa slithered to her feet and began to preen. "I turned them into pussycats."

"I know, you're the Queen of the West. I'm not surprised you got your hooks into the man, but how'd you get rid of the woman? Poison her?"

"I took her first. Super-straight broads may look impossible to a man, especially if she's ugly. It's not hard for a woman. She thought I was being friendly when I hugged her and kissed her ear and stroked her hair. When I got my hands inside her clothes she was wild. Then of course the guy wanted in on the action. No one can resist me, male or female. *Mi Generalito.*"

Had she warned anybody? Still, the base had been caught by surprise. She couldn't have been here long. Must have hitched a ride in one of the helos, God knows how.

"Since you know everything, where's the C.O.?"

"General Johnny? There's a gentleman who knows how to treat a lady right. A lady who needs some relief after a long helicopter ride."

McConnell walked around the desk. The phone was on the floor behind the chair. "Who were you calling?"

"My mother. She's worried about me since you took my cell phone."

"How much does your mother get paid? A cut of your take?"

"How much are you offering, big boy?"

The marine squad began to look embarrassed. McConnell was about to send them away.

"You know, Marisa, I can't decide whether to waste troops on arresting you, or shoot you myself."

The barrel of an M16 poked through the door. Then from the side door, another. McConnell and the little detachment of three marines were surrounded by half a dozen men wearing the blue berets of base Security Forces. Disarmed, the marines were herded against the wall. Captives of the U.S. Air Force.

Marisa pranced up to most menacing guard and took the barrel of his M16 caressingly in her hands.

"Hold it, ma'am. Stay where you are."

But Marisa was not one to do what anyone told her, nor to stay put for more than a few seconds. The guard tried to pull the gun away but she pulled it forwards, rubbing the barrel muzzle in her crotch.

"Do you know who I am? I'm the Queen of the West. Don't tell me what to do."

She wore a tight red sheath that buttoned up the front, only now it was unbuttoning. She glided from one guard to another, her face haughty as a queen, pursing her lips at them scornfully. She bent over and kissed a gun muzzle, *tzuk, tzu-u-uk*, a sucking motion.

She did a little stutter-step in front of a young-looking guard and pulled the automatic weapon from his hands. The red dress sloughed off on the floor. This left her in a see-through white lace body corset with the tops cupping her breasts just below the nipples. She cradled the gun pubic level between the curves of her hips, her thumb hooking into a white garter that held up her sheer stockings. She looked from one blue beret to another, eyeball-to-eyeball around the row of stunned faces. "This is boring. Get out of my way."

She began a hip-shaking dance, elbows swiveling her arms in counterbeat to the pivoting of her torso. The gunbarrel swept a complete circle of the room, her finger on the trigger.

"Hurry up, I'm losing my patience." She loosened off a rattle of automatic fire.

The entire room ducked, guards and marines alike: then heads raised cautiously, breaths exhaling. The shots had hit the ceiling.

Marisa began wriggling out of the top of her corset. She backed up to the guards squad leader, buttocks leading, pouting over her shoulder. "Be a gentleman and unhook this thing." He put down his gun and complied.

Troops came running, filling the room with a fresh set of guns, barrels for the moment horizontal and steady. More marines. The Air Force guards were disarmed, unresisting.

McConnell went up to Marisa and tore the M16 from her hands. "I should have shot you when I had a chance."

"But you love me too much, *Generalito.*" She turned away, nose in the air, lips pursed in a mock kiss.

Sounds of distant firing came from outside. They left the security forces tied in plastic handcuffs.

McConnell had assigned separate task forces: setting up a perimeter around the base to repel relief forces, by ground or air; another seeking out security forces inside the base, preempting or neutralizing them. There was firing a mile away, at the alert crew facility, hardened bunkers with their own landing pad. It was unnecessary to blast them from their underground shelters, only to make them keep their heads down while the raiders completed their mission. The nuclear launch control center for the missile fields, too, they left alone, not even approaching it. Nukes were not what they were after.

The most heavily protected part of the base, McConnell knew, was the weapons storage area, a square mile beyond the main runway. It had its own double perimeter of security wire, its own guard posts and security gate, next to the hot cargo pad. And no wonder, since this was where the nuclear bombs were stored, along with other explosive payloads for the Air Force's prize long-distance heavy bomber, the B-2 stealth bomber. The marines lobbed a few shots in their direction, to keep them on the defensive. It was impossible to stop them from calling for aid. Let them call, making themselves inevitably the supposed center of the attack. Adding to the confusion.

The main target was in a row of hangars along the apron opposite the control tower. Already the marines had the doors open and canopies of lights turned on. Each B-2 sat in pampered glory in its own air-conditioned hangar like a megastar presiding over a vast Hollywood sound stage.

An improbably wide span of gray-black wing resting on retractable wheels, a stealth bomber from the front looked like a gigantic manta ray, without tail or fuselage carrying only a tumor-shaped cockpit flanked by ominous black mouths of low oval air intakes. Twin jets rippled the top of the wing, their engines buried inside to conceal their induction fans and hide the heat signature of their exhaust. Without abrupt angles and flat surfaces, made of signal-reducing alloys, coated with radar-absorbent skin, the stealth bomber could invisibly penetrate any air defense. At almost two billion dollars apiece, it was the most expensive plane ever built. There were only twenty B-2s in existence, and their loss could not be replaced for years.

Marines were setting explosive charges as McConnell came up. He caught a conversation between a marine sergeant and a CSSA Air Force technician brought along from Arizona. "I can't destroy these beautiful things," the tech was saying. "You know how many years it took to get them up and running? I don't even want to watch."

"Then get your weepy Air Force butt out of the way," the marine said. "We'll turn them into high-tech junkpiles in about ten minutes."

"Hold on," McConnell said. "We're not just destroying these planes. We're taking them with us."

"All of them, sir?"

"Some of them." He waved the marines back to their task. "Go ahead and set up the explosives. But wait until you get orders for demolition. We'll let you know which planes."

The Air Force technician looked relieved but skeptical. "These things are different from every other kind of plane, sir. Not many people know how to fly them."

"That's why we brought pilots with us who have experience." One of the last Super Stallions was unloading clusters of men in CSSA Air Force uniforms. Duffle bags were being unpacked, flight suits put on. "Also we dug up some technical crews to get these things ready to fly. Are you one of them?"

"Yes, sir!"

It remained to find out which B-2s were recently maintained, on alert, fuelled up. A marine detail looked for maintenance records.

Sounds of battle around the air base had quieted to an intermittent rattle. The sky was beginning to pale. Almost 0500 hours. How much longer before relief forces arrived?

Marines dragged a captured maintenance technician into the hangar where McConnell had his temporary battle headquarters. He stood rigidly at attention. "Name, rank and serial number is all you'll get, sir. Raymond Durfee, Senior Airman—"

The marine sergeant bullied him towards a shack-like interior room full of files and monitors. "Where's the records kept, in there?"

"Geneva convention says, name, rank, and serial number—"

"You might just stay in here while this plane blows up. Less you help us get it off the ground."

McConnell ordered the sergeant to give the man some distance. Still, time was tight. Would a more psychological approach work?

He was about to launch a friendly chat when the staring eyes of the men around him made him realize a new arrival had joined the group. Marisa had flounced up with her hip-swaggering walk, red dress semi-buttoned.

"Leave the poor man alone. You big bullies." She draped herself on the captured airman's neck. Then she led him by the hand, reluctant-bewildered, into the cubicle and shut the door. Abruptly the door opened again. Marisa's face appeared, all fresh red lipstick and large theatrical eyes. "Ten minutes, General," she mouthed.

McConnell shrugged. Who knows? A new twist on the good cop, bad cop routine.

A renewed sound of fighting came from the far end of the apron. A hangar full of A-10 Warthog gunships had opened and one of the Warthogs had wheeled into the open. Union Air Force reserves had apparently reached some of their weapons, and the plane's occupant was raking the field with its heavy Gatling gun. Fortunately the gun was under the nose pointing down and could not get much range unless the plane took off. Marines' automatic weapons fire bounced off its armor, while the demolition and flight crews backed into cover of the B-2 hangars. Finally a marine caught the Warthog with a shoulder-launched missile and the plane stopped moving. One of the raiders' Super Stallions was damaged, inoperable.

Colonel Kilson, McConnell's deputy commander, brought further news. Whiteman AFB had been reinforced by a fighter wing of F-16s, they were mostly up in maintenance, and could be quickly fueled. Were there enough F-16 pilots available to fly them out to a friendly base? They would have to go unarmed, since the weapons bays were still largely in enemy hands. But it was only two hundred miles to Illinois—

"The B-2s are our priority," McConnell said. "That's what we came all this way for."

"But if we can't get them out? F-16s will be more use in the kind of fighting we're going to do. And a whole lot easier to fly."

"Capturing F-16s is too easy," McConnell said. "We came here to make the world sit up and take notice. These are the only B-2s there are. Now the CSSA is going to own them."

"If there isn't time, General—"

Marisa flounced to the hangar door, posing herself with arms outstretched against the backdrop of B-2 wingspread, her cheek narcissistically nuzzling her shrugged shoulder. Her scarlet closeup momentarily eclipsed the world's most dangerous plane. A marine sergeant scurried around her apologetically. "She's done it, General. We've located the maintenance records."

"How many planes are ready to fly?" McConnell thought Marisa was waiting for him to catch her eye. He was not going to be first.

"It looks like four or five, with an hour or so of preparation."

"We have three pilot crews. Pick the most likely planes and get them ready."

It was 6 a.m. and the summer morning was clear and warm. Clouds were a high white ripple across the sky, and soon there would be Union fighters streaking out of them, firing rockets. The only good thing is they don't know what they're looking for. He ordered the undamaged Super Stallions and Pave Lows to be refueled and moved into hangars, under cover but ready to go.

Where would the relief force come from? It all depended on how messed up their communications were, and how ready to scramble they would be. The nearest Union fighters were at Eglin and Tyndall AFBs in the Florida panhandle, eight hundred miles away. Even farther were Langley AFB in Virginia and Seymour Johnson AFB in

North Carolina. But F-15s and F-16s can fly Mach 2.5, 1500 miles per hour, so they could get here in a hurry, once they started. There were AF reserve and Air National Guard bases closer which had fighters but their readiness was iffy. Much slower were attack helicopters from an army base; nearest was Fort Riley, Kansas, about an hour away flying at top speed, 180 miles per hour. Fort Campbell, at the western tip of Kentucky, was headquarters to an airborne division, but it would not be capable of moving in a few hours. But Fort Campbell had a Special Operations aviation regiment, and they were less than two hours away by helicopter—they had Pave Lows, too.

It was 0630 hours already. How long does it take for the alarm to get out, get filtered through the proper channels, get men into aircraft and aircraft into the air? McConnell tried to imagine messages going up to a readiness center: at the Pentagon? Or at STRATCOM in Colorado, treating this as an attack on a nuclear base? But the raiders had stayed away from nuclear weapons and launch sites, and NORAD was focused on countering missiles incoming from space. Were there conflicting messages in the system?

It was hard to estimate, McConnell knew, how much progress the USA had made in recovering from the cyber attacks. Probably they're still half blind—that's why they're taking so long to get here. Could an enterprising commander at Ft. Riley, or at a Special Operations base like Hurlburt Field in the Florida panhandle, hear the news and launch an emergency reply on his own? It was a gamble. The Pentagon style over-centralized everything. Everything but the Marines. Or were there others as daring, other McConnell prototypes out there, about to fly over the horizon?

At 0740 two of the B-2s were ready. They were starting their engines on the apron while a third was being hauled from its hangar by a truck with boom attached to the giant wing's front wheel. The third of the two-person crews was taking their places in the cockpit. A couple of F-16s had also been readied, for good measure, and were already out on the two-mile long runway.

McConnell gave orders to begin helicopter evacuation. As soon as the captured B-2s were clear of the hangar area, demolition of the remaining stealth bombers was to begin, along with the F-16s to be left behind.

In the confusion of machines, rotating, taxiing, revving, roaring, accelerating, at first a new presence went unnoticed. A half dozen Union attack helicopters, Apaches, had come in low over the base, heedless of CSSA air defenses which had lapsed at this moment of impending departure. Air-launched rockets exploded on the apron. Designed for penetrating tank armor, they were easily effective on the huge boat-like Super Stallions just beginning to lurch clumsily airborne. One CH-53 burst into flames in front of the control tower. Another Stallion rose thirty feet off the ground, then settled down slowly like a deflating rubber boat, its tail on fire.

Almost simultaneously the demolition charges began to go off in the hangars. There were so many blasts in different directions that most of the marines seemed unaware of which were friendly and which were hostile, or indeed of the fact that hostile forces had arrived. The Apache crews, too, seemed overwhelmed by the extent of the destruction going on below, unclear what their targets were. The Apaches circled away to a two mile distance to regroup.

The CSSA Pave Lows, more agile, were aloft, releasing infrared decoy flares to mislead the Apaches' missile guidance. On the ground, the vans and light trucks of the marines land force were still covering the Stallions' retreat with shoulder-launched missiles. One of the Apaches, standing off in the distance, took a hit. Other SAMs went astray, misled by CSSA's own decoy flares.

One of the B-2s was aloft, followed by another accelerating down the runway. They were not particularly fast, limited to subsonic speeds because their design was based on deceiving enemy sensors rather than withstanding the pressures of breaking the sound barrier. The Apaches seemed to hesitate. Were these Union planes, making their escape, or enemy aircraft? When a third B-2 reached the turn onto the end of the runway, an Apache swooped in and unloaded on it, releasing its rockets under visual control. The runway was blocked by the wreckage.

More F-16s were out of their hangars, heading towards takeoff. Colonel Kilson had interpreted McConnell's grunted assent as license to take as many fighters as he had F-16 pilots. But now the Apaches, in a feeding frenzy, were going after the F-16s, stuck in the takeoff queue like ducks in a shooting arcade.

Demolished aircraft were all over the field, encouraging the Apaches to aim at any aircraft down there. Friendlies and hostiles no longer mattered; it was like the holiday atmosphere of a rioting crowd burning their own neighborhood. One, then two, of the Super Stallions were aloft, accelerating to the top speed they could muster, evading the Apaches by flying in different directions.

Three Super Stallions remained, temporarily unseen under cover of the huge Warthog hangar at the far end of the apron. Remaining marines from the demolition crews were running through the smoke, looking for evacuation berths. McConnell was distributing them into overcrowded payload space, directing the overflow to the ground vehicle fleet.

A bright red dress suddenly asserted itself in McConnell's field of vision. Marisa. Eager hands were ready to pull her into the nearby helicopter's crowded cargo bay. McConnell cut in front. "Where do you think you're going?"

"I need to come along. I have something to tell you."

"If it's so important, tell me now."

"Union forces from Fort Sill and Fort Hood are launching a ground attack on Cannon AFB."

"When?"

"It's part of the plan to break away and form a new state, Eastern New Mexico. The base will be part of the Union. Then Holloman."

McConnell calculated quickly. Cannon and Holloman's fighters would swing the balance back to the Union, if this were true. Order an evacuation at Cannon? But he had fifty thousand marines moving forward from California, less quickly than his advance force, of course. Was he caught out, away from base just when it was under attack? J.E.B. Stuart joyriding around the Union army instead of aiding Lee at Gettysburg.

"When?" he repeated.

"I don't know yet. They're already starting to move at Ft. Hood."

She knew about the CSSA attack on Fort Bliss. But it didn't sound like she had tipped off the other side. He would have to gamble. The Fort Bliss attack would draw off the Fort Hood forces, at any rate take away their surprise. Which now no longer existed, thanks to Marisa. If her latest report were true.

A helicopter from Whiteman AFB's own Apache fleet had been commandeered by a couple of marines and was now aloft, steering into the midst of the U.S. Apaches and launching its own missiles against them. Commandeered weapons in the heat of battle carry no enemy markings, so the shock of betrayal seemed to throw the U.S. Apaches into a visible shudder of confusion in the sky. One Union helicopter was already down; then a second, knocked out of the air at range so close the Union gunner could see the rocket released. Its companion fired back, and the CSSA-flown Apache exploded and went down.

Three U.S. Apaches of the original six attackers were left, and they seemed unsure what to do. On the ground, one of the CSSA Super Stallions lifted off successfully and made its escape. Two left.

The stream of marines running for escape vehicles had thinned to a trickle. McConnell put his foot on the loading ramp.

"You're doing a great job, Marisa. Such a good job that you should stay here and go on doing it."

She stamped her stilettoed foot petulantly. *"Hijo de puta! Puto! Haven't I done everything for you?"*

"Sure," McConnell said, as the helicopter moved. "Just having you around makes me nervous."

Over the fields of central Missouri a pair of F-15s appeared, with that dart-in-the-sky look when one aircraft passes another at high speed in opposite directions. Their vapor trails unreeled past the CH-53 like puffy white strings. Before the Union fighters had a chance to turn around, the helicopter pilot went diving toward the surface looking for cover. They had been flying at almost twenty thousand feet, beyond the eleven-thousand-foot hover ceiling of the Apaches. Hopefully those had given up pursuit. The checkerboard of green and brown fields came rushing up towards the CH-53, mile-regular squares broken here and there by irregular belts of dark forest green, gashes in the simple geometry promising rough ground, promising possible cover.

An image of the crash site they had passed over just outside Whiteman AFB flashed into McConnell's head. One of the B-2s was smashed belly down, looking like a black bat with broken wings gruesomely spread by a taxidermist. It had not been hit by enemy fire. It was merely a difficult plane to fly, sent airborne after hasty maintenance preparations. Of the three stealth bombers taken from their hangars, one remained. It was nowhere as fast as the F-15s, but if it reached flight altitude it was capable of evading radar, infra-red, electromagnetic, acoustic and any other monitoring devices the Union fighters had.

By comparison, the Super Stallion felt as naked to the fighters as a dancer in a strip show. Not entirely naked; they had jamming devices to prevent missile sensors from locking onto the helicopter. To McConnell, there was something teasingly audacious about being in the open. They were slowed, heavily loaded with extra troops, and the fighters must already have seen them in the bright clear morning below the clouds high above. They had only to find them again and open fire in the old-fashioned visually-aimed way. High tech having countered high tech, they reverted towards the past, almost like WWI dogfights, almost like a cavalry raid seeking cover of the woods.

One of the Pave Lows came circling back like a cowboy protecting his herd from wolves, dispensing electronic chaff to mislead the rockets. So far there were only two enemy F-15s, hunting seven helicopters that had gotten airborne from Whiteman AFB, five of them heavily loaded with troops, plus the two Pave Lows. McConnell's helicopters had orders to disperse, heading north into Iowa, east into Illinois, any direction if necessary. There was a CSSA air base just east of St. Louis, Scott AFB, but it was mainly an air mobility base, without fighters. And it was so close to the border that it would not be safe from determined Union assault. McConnell had ordered the B-2s to head for Chicago, another two hundred fifty miles north. The helicopters would find safety where they could.

At any rate, they could not hover in the trees long, they had not only to evade but to cover distance. Some of them would probably not make it. They were dice thrown in the sky, chancing which ones would take the attention of the predatory F-15s and let the others escape. Some farmhouses had rows of trees as windbreaks and oases of shade; some property lines were marked by walls of stately poplars and chestnuts. McConnell's helicopter darted from tree-line to tree-line. The F-15s seemed to have gone elsewhere. More Union fighters could be on their way, but the CH-53 gained altitude and throttled all-out toward the Missouri River.

Dendrites of streams, the shape of green candelabra, tributaries to the river, signaled its closeness. Their water was not visible from the air but only the little forests fed by ground moisture, swamp willows in the depressions of dried creek beds. The Missouri itself came into sight, twisting between sandbanks, dirty greenbrown, paralleled briefly by the straighter concrete river of Interstate-70. Vehicle traffic still flowed on the man-made highway, oblivious of the war now beginning, if no longer the torrent of cars and trucks of the days when St. Louis was a crossing point toward Chicago and Indianapolis and Louisville instead of the enemy frontier.

Again the checkerboards, flatlands safely passed and finally giving way to green hollows and grassy ridges, the up-and-down roller coaster that led to and away from the banks of the mighty Mississippi. The bluffs of Hannibal, Missouri were below, where Samuel Clemens had stored up boyish adventures that made him famous as Mark Twain. As the helicopter crossed eastward, a flight of white birds in triangle formation crossed beneath them flying west.

O'Hare airport was not a military field, but on the north of Chicago it was both reasonably safe from Union attacks and a huge airfield that could handle the big stealth bomber, and more importantly, give it proper publicity. McConnell's CH-53 had acquired as escort a couple of CSSA F-16s by the time it came in over the dense suburban grid and settled down next to the one B-2 that had made it through. It was the golden prize of the expedition, the purchase of all their blood and treasure, and McConnell was not going to let any civilian air controller tell them to set down anywhere else than here, the spot dictated by military necessity.

It's a war of perceptions and morale, he thought. Napoleon said the moral to the material was three to one; at this stage of the war, when the CSSA was barely fluttering off the ground, it was more like ten to one.

A crowd of reporters greeted them on the tarmac. McConnell answered questions at a bank of microphones set up where the silhouette of the stealth bomber framed the background.

He said it was California aiding the Midwest, symbolizing the unity of the CSSA. Benjamin Franklin said if we don't hang together we'll all hang separately. In answer to a question he extolled the unparalleled range of the B-2s; from their base in Missouri, the geographic center of America, they could bomb the factories and homes of Los Angeles and fly back without refueling. Same as they could with Boston or New York. Chicago, the capital of the CSSA, was closer to the front line but now it had its own B-2, capable of hitting Texas or Florida or North Carolina, as the need might be.

Yes, it was just about invisible, invincible because invisible. That's why the commando raid had been mounted, all the way from San Diego at one far corner of the continent, to Whiteman AFB at its center. The decks were evenly stacked now. We aim to conquer no territory, we have only to endure to win.

A reporter asked about losses. McConnell said that his own Super Stallion had survived ground fire, Apache rockets, an F-15 chase and emerged with all aboard unhurt. There were others in the fleet—

At that moment another Super Stallion hovered in towards the tarmac. It settled down next to them, metallic teammates standing shoulder to shoulder at the end of the game. The engines cut, the rotors hushed into an expectant moment of near silence as the rear loading ramp lowered. First down the ramp was Marisa, carried on the shoulders of muscular young marines, cheering team captain and mascot. A crush of reporters ran to the spot, live TV feed carried in harness and news cameras held overhead, while she waved and smiled, playing Marilyn Monroe amidst her happy admirers.

Marisa reached the interview area at the same time Big Bill O'Leary emerged from the terminal. He was a solidly built man with a strong square jaw, pugnacious mouth, a wedge-shaped nose like the prow of a ship. Dark hair graying around the edges, combed straight back and receding a bit from his high forehead. His eyes always looked like he was in a stare-down contest; not a smiling or genial face, the demeanor of an old-fashioned politician who ruled not by popular image but by hard bargaining and coalition-making.

There was a brief quandary: who should have the center of attention, the handsome CSSA leader, the hero of the raid, or this dazzling figure in a tight red wrap with the flamboyant mane of tawny-orange hair?

With sure political instinct O'Leary solved the impasse before a dramatic pause could turn into an embarrassing one. He stepped between Marisa and McConnell, put an arm around both necks and hugged them to his chest, while adroitly locating the angle of the cameras. They obligingly went through a series of poses: three faces cheek-to-cheek, O'Leary holding up their raised fists in a double-championship pose, O'Leary kissing each. McConnell found himself arm around Marisa's waist while both waved their free hands to the adoring crowd.

When questioning resumed, it was much the same set of replies. O'Leary, uncoached, echoed the unity of California and Chicago, and even managed to quote Ben Franklin. The captured B-2 was gestured to, treated as a backdrop for more poses, extolled as a symbol of evil forces destroyed (the rest of the Whiteman B-2 fleet) and an ace in the hole for peace.

Surprisingly, Marisa had the sense to keep silent, mostly. "General McConnell will have to tell you my part in everything," she answered almost every question. He described her as Security Consultant to CSSA forces. Did that mean her work was classified? You could say that. Was she a spy? That was the kind of question it was not possible to answer, McConnell had to answer. Marisa only smiled and posed with lips pursed in a kiss, Marilyn-like eyes almost closed, secrecy itself wrapped in a bright red curve-hugging dress.

By the end, O'Leary had started referring to Marisa as an essential element in the plan, alluding to secret enterprises launched under perfect cover at CSSA headquarters in Chicago whose story could not yet be told. He and Marisa posed, arms around each other's waists, then giving each other a military salute. McConnell felt himself pushed to the sidelines. At last, he stepped into the middle and raised Marisa's and O'Leary's arms simultaneously, then the three of them bowed like a dance team and made their way inside.

Through the evening and into the next day, the picture began to fill in. McConnell relinquished publicity to O'Leary and concentrated on military reports. Fort Bliss had been attacked and taken. Union troops had started out from Fort Hood, direction not entirely clear. Their advance helicopter units heading west towards El Paso had been hit from the air by fighters from Holloman AFB and turned back. Dyess AFB had been attacked by CSSA fighters, destroying an undetermined number of bombers on the ground. All three prongs had been successful.

At what cost? There was no good information yet about the other operations, but the Whiteman AFB attack had cost six out of the original eight Super Stallions. The two Pave Lows had escaped, with their small crews and a few passengers. Three CH-53s had been destroyed on the ground at Whiteman, unloaded, but another three had been hit in the air, with their complement of troops, including most of the wounded carried away from the ground battle. Of the fifteen trucks and vans in the ground component, thirteen had made their way to CSSA territory, crammed with the troop overflow lucky enough not to have found room in the helicopters. Two of the three B-2 pilot crews had been lost. Altogether, two hundred-plus of the marines and air force technicians who had started from Cannon AFB were safe in Illinois; somewhat more than that number were casualties, captured, or missing.

But the news was dominated by pictures of the B-2 on the runway at O'Hare, along with photos of McConnell's handsome physique. The raid was described as miraculously casualty-free, taking McConnell at his word when talking about the escape of his own CH-53, and he did not go out of his way to remind them of the rest.

The popular press was obsessed with Marisa, sounding out rumors and conjectures that grew more and more extravagant. She made herself available for photo ops but always surrounded by plain clothes security provided by O'Leary. Officially he was Vice Chairperson of the CSSA but in the Midwest he was in his fief. She said little but now she was deferring all questions to O'Leary. "He's the big boss," she said. "The man with the big hammer."

This set off another spiral of conjectures and imaginations, in which McConnell began to play the part of the jilted lover, or maybe even quasi-adulterer.

Jason and the Argonauts is how it began, McConnell thought. The band of brothers. Then it turned into Jason and Medea. The golden treasure was brought safely home, but the second part of the story was darker than the first. He had captured fame, but already he was something of a has-been. He would have to do something bigger.

Almost lost amid the big news stories, a smaller item was picked up from the Union networks. A fast-moving US Army force from Colorado had struck northwards into Wyoming and captured Warren AFB in Cheyenne. Only one hundred miles from Denver, it would have been hard for CSSA forces to protect. As part of the Space Command, Warren AFB was a missile base, like Malmstrom and Minot. Under current conditions of nuclear stand-down, not of much military significance. But Union forces, too, had shown they could be aggressive. The leader of the attack was an unknown Brigadier named Achilles Cruz.

YEAR ONE, CHAPTER SEVEN.
GATHERING FORCES

Western Pennsylvania Mountains. Flashback: late March

Ironman Johnston chewed a mouthful of unhulled sunflower seeds while he scanned the exercise yard. Several dozen inmates went through bodily contortions beneath a cold gray sky, dressed in blue denim jumpsuits. Around the corners of the yard, by the chain-link fence topped with barbed wire, guards in black ski parkas kept watch, thick rural-fed white men with PENNSYLVANIA DRUG REHAB BOOT CAMP STAFF across their backs.

"Number three-oh-seven!" Ironman called out in a high piercing voice. "Pick it up. Quit dogging it. Or I'll give you another hundred reps." The cloud of breath hung in the morning cold.

Ironman swallowed the rest of the sunflower seeds, hulls and all. The roughage was good for your digestion. Ironman was six foot three and weighed one hundred sixty-five pounds, all sinew and tension. He glanced at his watch, a plain black Casio with a stopwatch, on his left wrist below a thin copper band for channeling atmospheric magnetism. Enough time for a hundred one-arm pushups, before breaking for his seven a.m. yogurt shake with herbal supplements.

He lowered himself to the winter-dead grass and began pumping, his right arm twisted behind his waist, doubling the pace of the inmates. Defying the cold, he wore shorts and a cut-off T-shirt baring his rippled abs.

Your body follows your mind, Ironman programmed himself, his inner voice chanting the mantra as he pistoned up and down, your body follows your mind.

Number 307, a muscular young black man with a shaved head, blew out his breath hard, and increased the speed of his calisthenics.

"Pick it up, everybody!" Ironman yelled. "Keep my pace!"

A brick came flying from somewhere behind him. It grazed his cheekbone, leaving a gash. Ironman lost his balance and collapsed on his chest. Immediately he raised himself again on his left arm, and finished his hundred pushups.

The inmates had stopped, standing in a ragged semicircle, staring at him with hands on hips. Silence except for the sound of heavy breathing.

Ironman deliberately pulled himself erect, slowly eyeing the group. "Whoever threw that, step forward."

Inmates' eyes glanced sidelong at each other. No one moved.

"If the man who threw that doesn't step forward, all of you are going to the hole." It was a five-foot-square bare cement cell, with just a sewer outlet in the middle of the floor.

Everything suspended, even the sounds of breathing.

"All right. You're going to the hole. But first you're going through me."

He motioned the first inmate in line towards him. It was a scrawny white teenager, the scruffy look of a methamphetamine addict. He halfheartedly put up his fists in imitation of the Camp Director. Ironman slammed him on the chest with both palms, knocking him all the way to the chain-link fence. Putting anything in your body that made you weaker made Ironman disgusted.

The second inmate was number 307. Four inches shorter than Ironman but outweighing him by eighty pounds, the inmate apparently knew something about boxing. He circled warily, feet dancing, fists and elbows pumping slowly in a tight defensive guard in front of his chest and face.

Ironman backed him toward the fence, then kicked him in the knees, knocking him to the ground. Ironman went down on him from behind, pinioning his arms in a full nelson, using his armpits as fulcrums to leverage the back of his neck until the head was ready to snap. Ironman pushed the half-conscious body away and regained his feet.

"Boxing is OK for your reflexes," he said loudly. "But a good wrestler always beats a boxer. Don't forget, the knees are the weak point." He was pleased to deliver instruction, felt himself calming down a little. Use your anger, don't let it use you, Ironman told himself.

He motioned the third man forward. A young black man, tall and slim, the chiseled physique of a basketball player.

They wrestled, circling for a few moments in the up position, using their arms to keep the other away from one's body, grabbing elbows and twisting free, torsos leaning forward with legs well back against a takedown. They went down on the dirt amid patches of dead grass, first one on top, then the other. Both wrestled well, the man on the bottom struggling to get to his knees and rise to escape. The man on top struggling to keep the man on the bottom lying flat where his thighs were useless, on the defensive. The man on the bottom trying to angle an arm inside the other's limbs, seeking a fulcrum for a sudden move that would leverage their bodies into a reversal putting himself on top.

Muscles strained against muscles as their positions froze and stalemated, twenty seconds, forty, a minute. Both men were panting hard, fatigue cramping their movements. Blood from Ironman's cheek wetted the inmate's shoulder, red streaking black. They writhed together erotically.

With a ferocious grunt Ironman got a hand under the inmate's armpit and levered him onto his back, snaking his right arm around to catch the back of the neck in the crook of his elbow for the pin. Ironman shoved his left arm between the other's legs, splitting the crotch, immobilizing him from rolling sideways while stretching his own body at right angles out of the way of the other's useless kicks. These were real wrestling moves, not a silly choreographed TV exhibition, nor the Hollywood cliché of the kick from beneath which knocks the man off the top and brings a last-second reversal of fortune. Ironman had him pinned, but would not loosen his grip, tightening the pressure around the inmate's neck, waiting for him to give up. The black man moved the only part of his body within reach of a target—his head. He caught Ironman's right ear in his teeth and bit.

Ironman gave an orgasmic shriek and rolled off. A bloody half-circle bitten out of Ironman's ear hung by a shred of skin. As the inmate sat up, panting in exhaustion, Ironman threw himself on him, full frontal chest to chest, choking his throat with both hands.

Two black-parkaed guards stepped forward, gingerly flanking their Director. Ironman usually knew when to stop, but a death at the boot camp would mean the end of the program. Sensing their presence, Ironman banged the inmate's head sharply against the dirt, and released him.

The man opened his eyes and spat feebly at Ironman.

Ironman motioned the guards to pull the inmate to his feet. "Was it you that threw the brick? Tell me, you'll get the same whether it's yes or no."

The black man panted out the words groggily. "Yes, devil white man. I'll kill you for sure next time."

"Throw him in the hole for three days."

One of the guards spoke. "Excuse me, Major Johnston. I think this man has a concussion. He'd better get medical attention." He was about to say, and so should you, but he knew the Director well enough not to.

Ironman's face wrinkled with scorn. He dropped his shoulders, expelling a breath. "All right. Take him to the medical bay. When he gets out, throw him in the hole."

The guards got the inmate's arms draped around their shoulders and began to walk him away. Ironman stopped them.

"What's your name?" he said to the inmate.

"Newton Crawford."

"All right, Crawford. When you get out of the hole, I want to see you. We could use another guard. You might just be ready for a promotion in this organization."

★

Western Pennsylvania mountains. May.

Ironman Johnston stared at every face, making eye contact, unsmiling.

"You will be issued guns tomorrow."

Ironman held a M16 by its barrel, slanting toward the oppressive rain-threatening sky. Every eye followed him, every inmate in blue denim uniform, most of them black-skinned, head-shaved, scarred by tattoos clumsily erased from limbs and torsos, necks and faces. Gang postures were forbidden by boot camp regulations. Lined up at attention in the exercise yard, quasi-military, their eyes followed the gun muzzle, the curved ammunition clip, Ironman's finger resting on the trigger guard.

"That doesn't mean this rehab program is over. It means that as of tomorrow, you are soldiers in the 7th Battalion, Pennsylvania Volunteers."

Some faces turned quizzical, a slight dropping of a jaw, raising of an eyebrow. Uncharacteristically, Ironman recognized their reaction without immediately punishing it.

"Some of you are thinking, when did you volunteer? I'm thinking, you were heading down this path when you did the things that got you into rehab."

He pointed to a short, heavily muscled black youth. "Tell it, Sutphen."

"Like, a war be going on, y'know?" Though strutting was forbidden, Sutphen took the opportunity to direct a series of shoulder shrugs around the denim-clad audience, choreographing his words with a rhythmic dance of head shakes. "Like, y'all niggas ain't signing up for no white man's war. But let me tell you. You signed up for death when you came into this life, this life on the street. You can go back to that death, when they let you out. Or you can jump death right now. Don't matter what they call it. Soldier, gangbanger, convict number zero-zero."

One more stutter-step and he clipped to a halt. "Ya know what I'm saying? This for real, man."

He ended by looking straight at Ironman, chin raised an imperious moment, then fell into expressionless military attention.

All eyes fixed on the gun. No one seemed inclined to speak after Sutphen, though Ironman's face gave them license.

His receptive gaze shut off. He tossed the M16 to Newton Crawford, tall and tight in a guard's jacket. Crawford did not expect it but he snatched the gun gracefully out of the air, holding it aslant by the barrel, mimicking Ironman.

"These are real guns," Ironman said. "Not the cheap junk you buy out there on the street. You are going to learn to kill the enemy with these weapons—M16, M240 machine gun, anti-tank rockets, mortars. That means learning when to fire and when to hold your fire. That means no blasting off just to make a lot of noise. It means no dancing around showing off you have a pistol butt sticking out of your pants."

Tight-lipped, Ironman eyed the group. "Some of you think you're pretty tough guys. You say you've killed someone already. I'm not going to make you put up your hands, because I don't want to see that many liars around here." The crowd laughed, breaking into sidelong glances.

"Some of you may have gotten off a lucky shot from a car window while you're driving by. Some of you maybe snuck up on some guy on a corner and shot him in the back. If that's what you've learned, you're going to unlearn it. Starting tomorrow, you're going to learn to fight as a unit. That means crew-operated weapons. It means covering each other, while you move and lay down suppressive fire. It means taking casualties, if you have to, and keep on holding your position, not running away as soon as the action gets hot."

He gestured to Crawford, who tossed the M16 back to him, sharply, like a parade drill. Ironman caught the gun almost without looking at it.

"Crawford will be First Sergeant. That means he can recommend anybody for promotion or demotion. You can go up to corporal, staff sergeant, you name it. And it means you can be busted all the way down. If you mess up, we'll take your gun away. You can get busted below the rank of private, here. You can get busted right out of the 7th Pennsylvania Volunteers, back into some other rehab where you're not coming back out."

He turned the unit over to Crawford for calisthenics. It was a warm summer day, fragrant in the wooded hills of western Pennsylvania. One of the guards approached Ironman. A white man, a native of the rural community where the Pennsylvania Drug Rehabilitation Boot Camp was located. "Uh, Major Johnston, sir. We were wondering where the guards will fit. I mean, in this army scheme."

"Like everyone else," Ironman said. He popped a handful of organic sesame seeds into his mouth and began chewing them carefully to a pulp. "For now, you are NCOs. You can move up or move down, depending on how you perform."

"You mean you could put one of them—one of those ghetto hoodlums—over one of us?"

"If performance merits it."

"But Newton Crawford—he's just an uneducated thug. Doesn't even have a high school equivalent."

"This is the army," Ironman said. "Crawford has passed harder tests than you did."

"Well, okay, that's my point, Major. We didn't enlist in any army. We are hired staff of the Pennsylvania Rehab project. Maybe those kids have signed up for the duration, but we didn't."

"I'm asking you now. Sooner or later we're going to have a draft. Would you rather end up in a second-rate outfit full of draftees, or be a real soldier in a first-rate fighting unit?"

"Uh, what's the pay?"

Ironman looked disgusted. "I'll ask somebody. Better than getting no pay at all, because the Pennsylvania Drug Rehab Boot Camp is going out of business, as of tomorrow."

"I guess we'll stick and see how it goes," the guard said. He sidled up to Ironman, low-voiced. "One thing we better watch out for is giving these kids live ammo. Some of them are just waiting to take a potshot at us. Especially you, Major."

Ironman spat out the chewed seeds. He strode into the middle of the exercise field, towing the guard by an arm. A whistle blowing shrilly from Ironman's lips brought everyone's attention. "Mr. Barnes has something to tell us," Ironman said loudly. "Barnes, repeat what you just said."

"Uh— shut up and listen, all of you! You're going to get live ammo—but you better watch out. Anybody who doesn't keep their gun pointed where it's ordered is going to be shot." Barnes looked uneasily at the guards, mostly all white, clustered at the gates of the yard. "Shot by the guards."

"Not quite accurate," Ironman said. "As of tomorrow, there aren't going to be any guards. Everybody will be a soldier, some of them will be NCOs. Some of you are going to be officers."

Barnes made one last effort to retrieve the situation. "And you'd better obey your officers, because we are armed and ready to shoot—"

Ironman had the M16 again, extended in his left hand by mid-barrel, offering it to the crowd. "Get out the way, Barnes," he said, "before you get hurt." Barnes backed away quickly to the safety of his compatriots. "Today there's only one combat weapon here. Tomorrow everybody gets one." He turned slowly, displaying it like the holy sacrament, dangling the ultimate drug before long-deprived addicts.

"We obey orders, because that's how we fight. That's how we win. One man with a gun means nothing, even if he has the only gun there." He tossed the M16 to Crawford.

"Anybody want to shoot anybody here? If you're going to, let's do it now." He gestured to Crawford to carry the gun around the onlooking ranks. "Because tomorrow, if we get to tomorrow, you're only going to fire on orders." Hands moved to faces, pondering cautiously; others were frozen in place.

No one reached for the gun.

Crawford offered the M16 back to Ironman. He gestured to Crawford to keep it. "Keep them exercising, First Sergeant."

Of the cluster of guards, most had left through the gate. Ironman turned his back and checked his watch. It was almost time for his daily detoxing, cleansing impurities from his body by colon hydrotherapy.

Washington, DC. July

"What I don't get," said Jennings, "is how a mere civilian like myself can see what you professional military experts can't see no better'n a hole in your own head. You gotta move fast. Hit 'em before they're ready. That's how you win this war."

"We've been over this before, Mr. President," Secretary Madigan said. They sat at the mahogany table in the White House Situation Room, a row of aides behind them along the walls. Dull gray carpet and matching gray swivel chairs gave the basement room a dim oppressive feeling that the fluorescent-lit ceiling panels did nothing to relieve.

"We can't do what's technically impossible," Madigan went on. "Delivering a brigade of mechanized infantry isn't like ordering a package off the shelf. This is an integrated combat system. You need transport, logistics, air support. All the components have to be in place or it doesn't work."

"What about airborne? They can move pretty darn fast, can't they?"

"They move fast when they're in the air," Madigan said. "But once they've made their parachute drop, what you have is a lightly equipped battle force somewhere inside enemy territory. You need to hook up with them quickly with ground forces or they're going to be cut off. And once they're out there they have to be supplied just like everyone else. As I said, it's an integrated package. Let me show you on PowerPoint."

Madigan gestured to an aide to start up the sequence on the wall-mounted viewing screen. Jennings cut him off at the first brightly colored flow-chart. "Hold off on that pretty little toy a minute. I want to talk this out man to man. Not the both of us talking to the wall." Reluctantly the screen went dark.

Jennings continued. "I hear you telling me, Bob, that we can't move nothing til we move the whole ball of wax. So how about that Marine Corps rebel out there in the West—McConnell? Seems he had no trouble hitting three of our bases. If he can do it, why can't you?"

"The Whiteman and Dyess attacks were just raids. We could do the same thing to them if there were any point to it. A raid doesn't hold any territory; it's just in and out."

"What about losing Fort Bliss?"

Madigan shrugged. "Look at the map, it's an isolated outpost. We have to concede it to them for the time being. We'll get it back, along with a lot more enemy territory, when we get everything mobilized."

"The way I'm looking at the map," Jennings said, "Utah and Colorado are isolated outposts too. Are we going to write them off, too?"

"The enemy can't move troops that far from the West Coast without air superiority," General Harris said. The Chairman of the Joint Chiefs of Staff, heavyset in his Air Force uniform, looked like a menacing blue Buddha. "That's why we've been shifting fighter squadrons from the Southeast to our Central and Mountain Zone bases. Before either side can take anything on the ground there's going to be an air battle."

"Okay, Curt," Jennings allowed, "good move. But now you're telling me we don't have fighter forces to cover an attack in the East?"

"We have enough to hold them," Harris said. "The rebels are shifting some of their fighter wings east too. We'll match them plane for plane if we have to."

"I don't like the sound of this," Jennings said. "If the Air Forces are equally matched, it's a stalemate. And we can't put the Union back together just by holding them off. That's why we need to go on the offensive. Don't we have an edge somewhere?"

"Of course we do," Madigan said. "We're going ahead with the transformation into a full-scale integrated fighting force. The rebels are clinging to old-fashioned separate services. Once our HOME computer system is up and running, they'll be overmatched."

"And how long is it going to be before that happens? I seem to recall you fellas ran into a pack of trouble with that fancy computer system. You got it straightened out yet?"

"Security was severely compromised, as you know, Mr. President," Madigan said stiffly. "We are having to reconstruct the whole system. General Grotweil can fill you in on the details."

Jennings waved Grotweil to a halt before he could begin summarizing a sheaf of reports. "Just give me the bottom line, General. How long before our forces are operational again?"

"It's a complicated question, Mr. President. I'd have to break it down to a series of estimates. And of course the estimates interact with each other mathematically—"

"So what you're telling me is you can't tell me when you're going to be ready. How about three months from now?" A negative-looking shrug from Grotweil. "Six months? A year?"

"Ninety-five percent confidence interval should be within a year," Grotweil said. "It chiefly depends on—"

"A year is a lot longer than we have to save the U. S. of A.," Jennings said. He waved his long arm at the world beyond the walls. "Do you have any idea of the political pressures that are building out there?"

Madigan intervened, protecting his subordinate. "I don't play politics, Mr. President. I just report on what is possible and what is impossible, by our best estimates. If you're not satisfied with any member of my team, I'm ready to submit my resignation."

"I appreciate that, Bob," Jennings said. "I truly do. But politics is my job. That means winning the hearts and minds of our fellow Americans. The politics I'm most worried about isn't down here below the Mason-Dixon line. I can handle those buzzards. And I'm not too worried about this coalition of the godless over in New York and Hollywood and those other sinkholes of atheism. We'll flush 'em out when we get there. It's the politics of the border states that worries me. We need to move the war way past Maryland, so they don't feel like a halfway place, waiting to fall one side or the other. They need to feel secure inside our front lines, and that means we have to strike forward."

None of the Pentagon team said anything.

"Now I'm going to respect your judgment, Bob," Jennings went on. "You all say our regular military isn't ready to move out, and won't be ready until we have a full-scale reorganization sometime next year. So be it. But we have forces who aren't regulars, and I'm going to use them. I mean the state militias, and the troops they've been recruiting in this emergency."

"Normally we call up the states' National Guards into the regular military in time of war," Harris said. "Just now things are a little screwed up, but we'll get them organized before long—"

"While you're playing with your computer system," Jennings said. "I've asked our more patriotic governors to get their state forces ready for action. The governors of Maryland and West Virginia have been specially helpful."

"So I hear," Madigan said. "Our materials command has been getting requests from them."

"And I'd like you to honor their requests, as best you can. The most important thing here, I'm going to say it again, is speed. I know they're not going to be high tech. But if we can truck a few thousand National Guard troops up the road to Philadelphia and New York, we could make a big dent in the other side. Maybe even collapse their whole house of cards. We may not be so very ready, but sure as God punishes sinners they can't be near as ready as we are."

"I wish I was riding with them," Harris said. "Just for the hell of it. But professionally, I have to say it won't come to anything without the Air Force."

Madigan gave a microscopic shrug. "I hope there's a political payoff in it, Mr. President. Because I don't see that kind of lightweight operation accomplishing anything militarily."

"It's in God's hands." Jennings stood up. The meeting was over. He pulled Madigan aside as the others went out the door. "You know this Brigadier Achilles Cruz?"

"Not personally. I have the report on his attack in Wyoming. Yes, I admit it's a successful use of National Guard troops. In a very chaotic situation."

"Argument's over, Bob. I just want to make sure General Cruz gets the kind of command he deserves."

"You want him for this Philadelphia attack?"

"No. Governor Curry has a Maryland officer lined up, and I kind of owe him for the way he's helped us through these last months. I want Cruz to get a major command out there in the Rockies."

"I'm not sure how well he can handle the technical side," Madigan said. Jennings grinned at him intently, a big arm draped around the Secretary's shoulders. "But under the circumstances, he may be the best man for the job." He disengaged himself from Jennings' grip. "I'm not incapable of factoring the political side into the equation."

YEAR ONE, CHAPTER EIGHT.
BATTLE OF I-95

Northern Maryland, approaching the Delaware border. July.

The bridge at Havre de Grace was intact, unblown. Brigadier General Gandhi Park was surprised, but not very. *They're as incompetent as we are,* he thought, *hope they're more so.* This would be the logical place to stop the attack, where I-95 crosses the mouth of the Susquehanna River, over a mile wide. Beyond the long low causeway of the railroad bridge, the wide flat shore of upper Chesapeake Bay looked tranquil, undisturbed. *We could probably have loaded the troops on Amtrak and got off in Philadelphia at Thirtieth Street Station.*

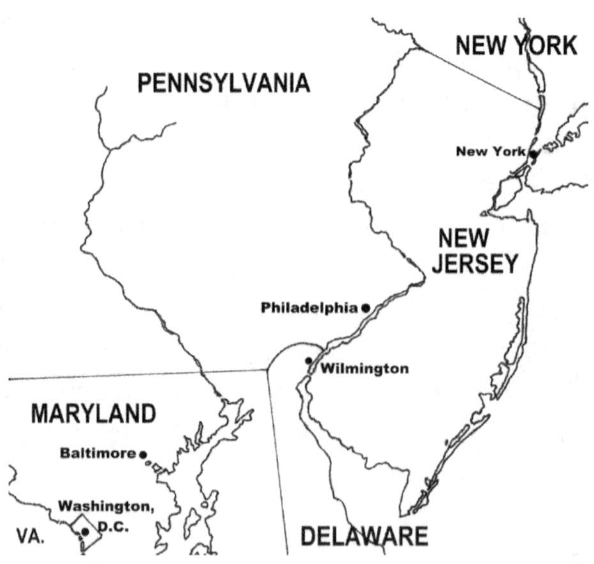

Gandhi rode in an armored staff car, a Humvee, but the rest of his brigade were in the long columns of trucks filling the lanes of the Interstate. A force of thirty-five hundred troops takes hundreds of trucks, with their supplies and auxiliary equipment, even though they were carrying no weapons heavier than machine guns and mortars. With proper spaces between vehicles, the column covered the highway for five miles, slowed by its sheer size and the need to stay in formation. If the CSSA had any air power on this front, we'd be dead, Gandhi thought. Not that they don't know we're coming and what route we're taking.

The news has been full of it. Still, that cut both ways, and the news from New York was all about the CSSA's own debate. Whether they should advance into enemy territory, or just a few miles this side of the border to a natural defensive position at the Susquehanna. Whether to take the moral high ground by strictly remaining inside their own borders, waiting to be attacked. Militarily it made no sense to pin yourself down to a particular place—as if the Pennsylvania National Guard were going to meet us on the I-95 at the Delaware border—but at any rate the Havre de Grace bridge was open. Politicians! Gandhi thought.

He got through to the theatre commander, General Agnew. "Terrific news, my man," Agnew said. He had made a local political career in Maryland on the strength of having served in the Vietnam War, and many years of making speeches had infected his rhetoric. "We'll drive on through to Philly before those pointy-headed wimps know what hit 'em."

"The problem is," Gandhi said, "we're out of sync." He explained General Agnew's plan back to him. Gandhi's own brigade would be over the Susquehanna and into Delaware in half an hour; behind it on I-95 another brigade was coming, under Brig. Milton. They were the middle of three prongs. Another brigade, Easton's, was coming up on the right by a circuitous route; it had crossed Chesapeake Bay on the bridge at Annapolis to the Maryland eastern shore, and was making its way up the lower Delaware peninsula on minor roads.

The first phase of the maneuver was designed to circumvent any holdup by the enemy at Havre de Grace; now Easton's columns would be converging with Park's force at Wilmington, but coming in late behind him. Easton was moving much slower than Park's brigade on the Interstate.

"While I've got the initiative, sir," Gandhi said, "it would be good strategy to keep pushing ahead."

"Good thinking, good thinking," Agnew said. "That's just what I would say."

"Instead of waiting at Wilmington for Easton's brigade to catch up."

"Hold on now, Johnny boy," Agnew said. "I want you to keep checking with me, before you do anything. Let me know when you get to Wilmington. I have another trick in my game plan."

Gandhi did not bother to ask what it was. He would act on the situation as it unfolded and let Agnew know. He had another concern: the left prong of attack, Avery's brigade, was moving on US-1, a parallel road west of I-95, and should be crossing the Susquehanna at the next bridge, ten miles upstream. "There's another problem," Gandhi said. "Avery's brigade is slower than everybody. As you know General, they're supposed to converge on Philadelphia from the west. But at the rate I'm going ahead, and the rate they're hanging behind, there isn't going to be any converging attack."

"Sure enough," Agnew laughed. "You got the Interstate and Avery got stuck with the surface roads. We could speed him up—shift Avery over to the Interstate, since your bridge is open."

"That wouldn't help," Gandhi said. "We've got two brigades on the Interstate already. And we're going to have too many piling up at Wilmington as it is. What I suggest, sir, is to take my brigade off I-95 at Wilmington. I'll take the country roads up the Brandywine Valley, and turn east on US-1 into Philadelphia. That way I'll be the attack on the left flank, instead of Avery."

"So you want to be the first to carry the ball, hey Johnny?" Agnew chortled. "I like that. I like my boys to show initiative. Avery will be a reserve force behind you, when he comes up. But someone has to cover the front door into Philly, so don't you leave I-95 until Milton or Easton is there in Wilmington behind you."

"I could split my brigade to cover both approaches," Gandhi said. "Keep one battalion moving north on the Interstate, and send the other two battalions around to the west. That way we won't slow down any."

"Not yet, not yet," Agnew said. "I want Easton to be available to cross the Delaware if any of the bridges are open. Those chickenshit liberals don't know how to run a war. If Easton can get across to the New Jersey side, he can roll right up I-295 and into Philly from the east. Or keep on going into New York, if they're stupid enough to leave the road open. We're running our option play, see? Either way, we'll keep 'em guessing."

It was a good plan, on paper, though Gandhi doubted it would play out as written. It never does. He told Agnew they would soon find out if the two bridges over the Delaware below Philadelphia were still open, and reiterated the need to move quickly inland once his own brigade reached Wilmington.

"Bring it on! And God bless America!" Agnew said. "But be sure to keep me posted."

Gandhi Park's truck column had ground to a halt. His Humvee drove up the shoulder to the head of the line, at the toll plaza entering the state of Delaware. A lieutenant on foot approached the command car. "General, the toll booths are still operating. And I don't think all our trucks have the correct change. Some of them may not even have money."

"For Chrissake," Gandhi growled. "This is a war. Stick a gun in their face and tell them to open all the gates."

The lieutenant looked shocked. The reality of war in his own country had not yet hit him. "Go on," Gandhi said. "The State of Delaware can make their revenue some other way."

At Wilmington, Easton's brigade was still hours behind. The long span of bridge over the widening mouth of the Delaware River was blocked; there would be no dash up I-295 or the New Jersey Turnpike on the other side. The bridge was not down; rather than destroy valuable property, CSSA troops had merely hauled a series of heavy trucks and buses onto the lanes and disabled them, jammed sideways one behind another. An advance scout radioed back a report from the smaller bridge at Chester; it too was blocked. Word on the Walt Whitman Bridge and the Ben Franklin Bridge, in Philadelphia itself, was unclear; the CSSA was keeping open their options, since these bridges were lines of reinforcement, or of retreat, for themselves.

That meant the attack would have to come entirely on this side of the river, Gandhi thought. He was ready to press on, but General Agnew insisted that he wait until at least one of the other brigades, Milton's or Easton's, was on hand. Both arrived in midafternoon. An ordinary passenger car could have driven the distance from Baltimore in an hour, but an army's movements are never so simple. Wilmington was becoming a bottleneck, crowded with army trucks, spilling onto the streets of the modest downtown as well as clogging the I-495 bypass.

General Agnew arrived by helicopter, now that the city was secured. He had the wide body and thick neck of an ex-football player, and his aides looked like a crew of assistant coaches. They huddled with the brigade commanders in a downtown city park. "Here's my new plan," he said. "Easton! You keep on going straight up I-95, past the Philly airport and into the city. That's a feint, get it? Enemy troops will be expecting you. You're going to get their attention."

"Milton! You fall in line behind Easton, then cut north on the I-476 loop before you get to the airport, see?" He drew colored markers on the screen map like a TV commentator explaining a play. "Your troops get off at the offramps to the western suburbs. You'll make their way into Philadelphia from that direction."

"Johnny Park is going to take his brigade off-road," Agnew said jocularly. He made some vigorous marks with a colored pen. These appeared duly on the screen map, an arrow stroke due north from Wilmington on surface highways to reach US-1, another arrow stroke along that historic highway from the southwest into Philadelphia.

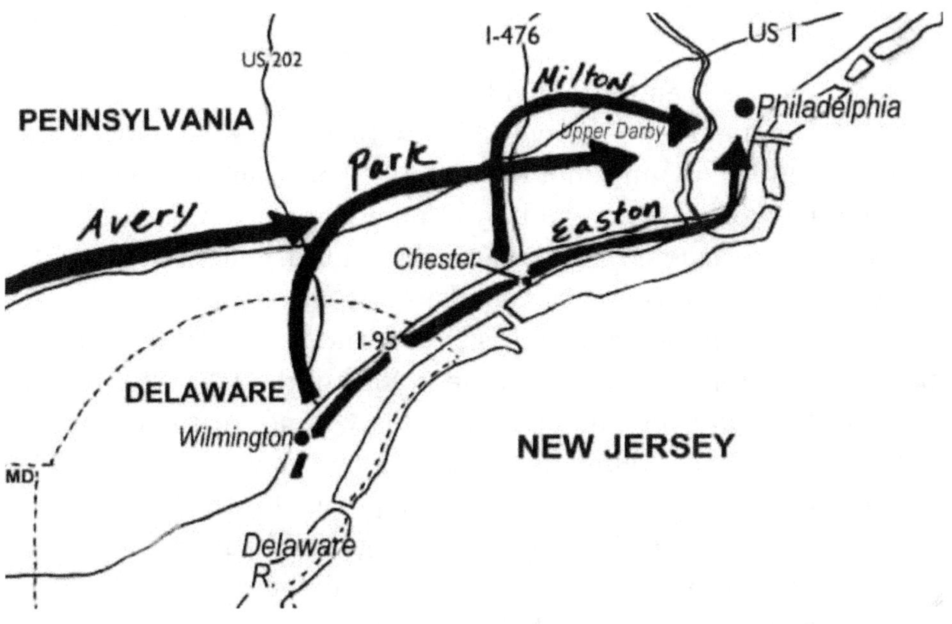

"That's it," Agnew summed up. "Feint on the east along the river, everybody else swing around to the west and find the unguarded spots in the enemy defense." He drew a big red circle around center city Philadelphia. "That's our goal. We're going to send a message. Tonight the nation is going to see our troops on TV at Independence Hall and the Liberty Bell. And the message is—" Agnew pounded his palm with a fist, "the USA will not tolerate the misguided antics of a bunch of half-assed liberal politicians."

"Don't forget to send some of our boys up the statue of William Penn on top of City Hall," Agnew called after his commanders. "That'll make a news picture, all right."

Returning to his temporary brigade headquarters, Gandhi found most of his troops had dismounted and were milling around convenience stores and fast-food restaurants. They were supplied with MREs, but civilian eating habits were irresistible on what was for most of them their first military outing.

"Get them back in the trucks," Gandhi snapped. Officers began to scurry around giving orders. A few soldiers looked embarrassed. Most of them tossed plastic wrappers onto the pavement and climbed onto their trucks carrying giant size softdrink cups. They'd be more serious, Gandhi thought, if we told them where they were going. Of course I would have to know that myself. He hoped the enemy would show up soon. Nothing like being under fire to make soldiers act more military—if they don't completely fall apart.

Gandhi's brigade split up along the half-dozen roads that led north out of Wilmington. Gandhi's command car was on a divided highway full of shopping malls, cross streets and traffic lights. Military police were supposed to control the traffic but the MPs were not always at the right spot, and civilian traffic was not scared off by the army advance. If anything, news that the first battle of the war was about to happen had brought out the populace to watch, and since there were no sounds of firing and nothing seemed at all dangerous, civilian cars and commercial vehicles cut into the troop convoy, and turned across the highway into their normal shopping places.

It was like a parade except there was no parade route and onlookers piled up more or less by accident where they happened to find something military to watch. TV news trucks were arriving, and only the general confusion kept Gandhi from getting close enough to vent his fury in person.

After an hour of slogging through this suburban Sargasso Sea, Gandhi managed to divert most of his trucks onto the smaller roads of the Brandywine Valley. They wound up and down pleasant green hills, amid large grassy lawns and stately woods that signaled gentlemen farmers and the truly rich.

Passing the stately green hillsides in his staff car, Gandhi was carried back in his head to the houses he had known growing up. The houses his adoptive parents had talked about and those they had visited; even those where they had not been invited were referred to with dignified admiration and an air of collective pride.

Estates in the Brandywine Valley were famous among the old American elite, where generations of brothers and cousins had competed in decorous ways to spend their vast fortunes: one cousin had built room after room onto a hillside mansion to house an ever-growing collection of antique furniture; another cousin built garden after garden in every style in the world, a museum of gardens from fountains to topiary to Chinese pagodas.

Gandhi's adoptive parents were much more interested in such things than his own father and mother. She was a civil rights idealist and she treated her gray New England colonial as something faintly to apologize for. His father was more of a blur to him, and anyway they were both gone before he had reached the age of ten and he had moved to a bigger, newer mansion where the beauty of houses and their gardens was a constant topic of conversation.

Up a gracefully wooded hillside, Gandhi could see from the Humvee's window the outline of massive rooflines among the trees. Suddenly he wished the CSSA army were over there, occupying these sheltered treasure homes. They would open fire on us, we would fire back, infantry would advance in battle formation, riddle the walls of the super-wealthy with automatic weapons, toss in grenades—

He saw himself running through the corridors past drawing rooms of carefully collected Federalist furniture. The battle in his head was a mixture of childish play in these houses far too big merely to live in, and a Korean orphan feeling his true identity as an outsider.

They reached US-1 and turned east. It was malls and civilian traffic again. No sign of Avery's brigade; it was hours behind, slogging its way along secondary roads ever since Baltimore. Gandhi's car passed the old Brandywine battlefield, on a hillside above the highway: George Washington's troops had fought the British here in the Revolutionary war, failing to stop another invading army coming up from the Chesapeake and into Philadelphia. In those days they had to find an open field and march within distance of seeing the whites of the enemy's eyes to have a chance of hitting anything. Gandhi wondered how close his troops would have to get, whatever the superior power of modern weapons was officially supposed to be.

Dusk was settling in, and the traffic was not improving as they reached the Philadelphia suburbs. Nighttime was not a bad time to make an attack. But only if your troops know what they are doing, and your officers are capable of keeping control, keeping contact, finding their way without a mapped-out plan. Gandhi weighed the chances of getting lost in the capillaries of suburban streets with this makeshift crew.

From his Humvee, Gandhi scanned the twilight. The pleasant middle-class suburbs had given way to grittier neighborhoods. The lead trucks of Gandhi's brigade were inside the I-476 ring, the Interstate bypass circling Philadelphia on the west. He ordered his driver to pull over in front of a pizza parlor. Gandhi began to call his troops to a halt, ordering them to bivouac in malls and parking lots, working hard to map out everyone's location so they would be able to move as a coherent force in the morning. Early before dawn would be the time to move forward. The enemy couldn't help know we're here. But he couldn't believe they were any more capable of moving at night than we are.

Milton's brigade was supposed to turn off from I-95 onto I-476, beginning the pincers movement around the west side of the city. But the CSSA had anticipated the move. A mile in from the entry to this Philadelphia ring road, all lanes had been blocked by disabled cement trucks, garbage trucks, city buses. A heavy armored force would have tanks equipped as bulldozers, plus combat engineers who could blast such obstacles out of the way. But General Agnew's hastily assembled force of National Guards was little more than a riot-control force in trucks.

Milton's brigade had driven into a cul-de-sac, with the exit ramps blocked. It was the typical construction of an Interstate highway, cement median divider, hillside cuts, a man-made gulley with sound baffles to shield the surrounding residences from traffic noise. A hundred or more heavy army trucks had started up the divided highway before they reached the first barrier, and now they would laboriously have to back out, provided that some space could be made for them in the jam on I-95. Milton and his officers were busily diverting as many troops as possible off I-95 onto surface roads, without a clear sense of where they would be going next.

At this moment, CSSA troops opened fire, from the slums alongside the Interstate at Chester.

★

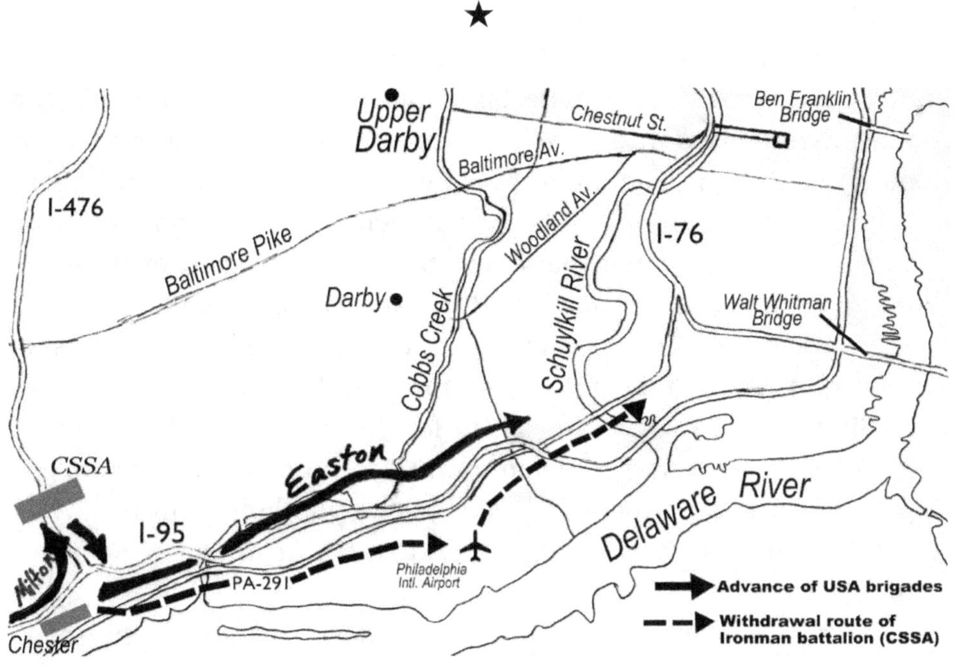

Southern outskirts of Philadelphia

"Hold your fire," Colonel Ironman Johnston said. "Hold fire. Wait for my orders." He stalked along the trash-strewn alleyways from one squad to another, repeating the command. The Interstate-95 highway was barely yards away behind a cracked concrete barrier wall and weed-choked chain-link fence. All lanes were jammed with slow-moving olive green trucks of the USA forces advancing north. For once Ironman had nothing in his mouth, no seeds to chew, no energy lozenges to suck; the chant of battle command took its place.

"Chester. Shee-it," Sutphen said. "This be where I was busted for drug dealing."

"You dumb enough to get busted first time you open you mouth," JaMichael Kilson said. He belonged to a different gang, from north Philadelphia.

"You don't know shit about Chester. We had this street organized. Everybody in black hoodies, white T's. Meet the customer right off the freeway, someone else pick up the package from the back lot. Lookouts, getaway routes, everything."

"White-T pussies," JaMichael said. "Pussies think they rule the street."

"Shut up," Newton Crawford said. He had First Sergeant stripes on his gray uniform and a black beret instead of the regulation kevlar helmet the others were wearing. "Nobody's in gangs no more. That's history. You're Ironman Battalion, that's all."

"Ironman Battalion," Sutphen enunciated. "Ain't no gang can stand up 'gainst Ironman Battalion. Shee-it, one squad of Ironman Battalion can take every gang in Philadelphia, all together."

"Ironman Battalion be every gang in Philadelphia," another soldier said. A ripple of laughter went through the line.

"Shut up," Crawford said. "Wait for the order to fire."

Ironman reappeared. "Listen up. In a minute our snipers are going to start firing—snipers only. The rest of you hold your fire. Wait until the Federals start coming out of their trucks, then your officers will tell you when to shoot them."

There was a sharp crack of M14 Munitions Disrupters, armor-penetrating rounds designed to break engine blocks. The highway trucks stopped moving. Here and there an engine hood belched steam or burst into flames. Troops in combat camouflage spilled onto the highway lanes, milling around. Some were beginning to aim weapons towards the east side of the freeway, the Chester side. Others were climbing the median to the west side, taking cover across the highway.

A shout of "Fire!" came from up the line and the Ironman Brigade let loose with their M16 semiautomatics in the direction of the convoy. Deafening noise filled the air like a gap torn out of time, although it was only a few seconds before the firing faded raggedly as the thirty-round magazines emptied and soldiers fumbled to replace them with full ones.

Firing began again, in shorter bursts. Ironman and a few officers paced the line, urging restraint. The Federals had taken shelter on the other side of their trucks, and a rattle of fire started coming in the direction of the Chester alleyways. There were surprisingly few bodies lying in the highway, considering they had taken fire from hundreds of M16s at close range. "You're firing too high!" Ironman was shouting. "Keep the muzzle down, tap off a burst." Here and there he snatched a M16 from a soldier in disgust.

Most of the human targets were gone from the trucks in front of them, and incoming fire had fallen to sporadic. "Hold fire," Crawford said. "Hold your fire!"

"Bunch of pussies out there," JaMichael said. Everyone was elated. "Ironman Battalion," Sutphen said. "Rule the Interstate."

Up the line was the sound of someone screaming, someone who no longer had a knee, someone who took a bullet from an unlucky angle, maybe someone who had dropped his kevlar armor vest because of the heat. There were sounds of crying and screaming from the other side of the freeway fence, too, gradually seeping in among the noisy babble of victorious voices. Firing started again from some distance, up the freeway, down the freeway, coming in on a slant. The sound of .50-calibre machine guns rapped at them, their bullets making a heavy impact on the shabby walls and fallen porches where the Ironman Brigade took cover. There was a whoosh and blast of rockets and fragmentation grenades. The Federal troops had not disappeared.

Then it was a steady noise punctuated by screaming, and Ironman's voice intoning, "Hold your fire. Now, tap off a burst. Now. Hold your fire."

Sutphen was thirsty but he had forgotten his canteen. Most of the men around him were out of water. Someone passed a Pepsi can.

At dusk, Crawford approached Ironman to report that half of his company were out of ammunition. "That's why you've got to keep telling them to hold their fire," Ironman instructed, "except when you have a really good target."

Federal reinforcements kept coming in. Ironman ordered a withdrawal to the Philadelphia airport. A parallel road ran along the river side of the Interstate. The Federals were sending trucks north on the southbound lanes and gradually seemed to be unclogging the jam on the northbound side. The side road would be exposed from the freeway but the Federals might not be capable of covering it with accurate fire.

Several dozen school buses, hastily painted with the rainbow emblem of the CSSA, were parked on the far streets of Chester, away from the firing line near the freeway. In these the Ironman Brigade had arrived for their first combat, and these would evacuate them to their new position. Crawford was to keep a platoon to cover their withdrawal.

"Retreating in good order is the hardest thing to do in combat," Ironman lectured. His tone implied: pass it on, tell them over again, make sure the men understand. "Retreating makes you want to hurry, then everybody's running. That's when you take casualties. No running, just orderly phased withdrawal." Crawford saluted, tall and proud in his beret. He would pass it on.

"Shee-it, everybody else get buses but us?" JaMichael said. "How far we gotta walk to this fuckin' airport?"

"We going by Cadillac," Sutphen said. "Ironman limo. Orderly phased withdrawal."

The airport was seven miles north of Chester, across shabby industrial properties and bare marshes. In the fading light, the Federals were firing from the freeway at the CSSA buses. One bus was hit, then another. Their flames lit up the road, while shadowy troops dismounted and began firing back.

Crawford's platoon, marching in the dark, overtook a burned bus. The firing had moved away to the north. "Y'all still wanna ride?" Sutphen said. "Ironman moves on iron feet. *Comprende*? Orderly phased withdrawal."

It was deep night when the platoon reached the airport. Ironman Battalion, eight hundred strong minus light casualties, occupied positions in the parking garages across from the darkened terminals.

Inside the parking structure, a noisy dispute was going on over night-vision goggles. Platoons from different companies of the battalion had clashed in the dark. One man had been shot by friendly fire. His body lay on the pavement while a pair of medics worked over him. An unruly circle crowded around.

"Night-vision goggles!" One platoon's sergeant was saying. "If we had 'em this wouldn't have happened. You assholes got all the night-vision goggles for the whole company."

"Bullshit," said a wide torsoed black man, evidently a companion of the wounded man. "The nigga who shot my man was wearing goggles. I saw him take them off."

"What the fuck good are they anyway?" a third soldier intervened. "Makes everything just green weirdness. You oughtn't be pointing guns at us in the first place, that's why you got shot."

"You from the Fourth Street, ain't you? It ain't no fuckin' goggles. It's you Fourth Street boys."

The antagonistic platoons had been recruited into the Ironman Battalion from various rehab and diversion programs. Crawford did not know them but he thrust himself without hesitation between the sides. "Put your guns away!" he shouted. "What you been hearing all day? Hold your fire! Wait for orders."

Most of the soldiers complied. Backing away, they left one man forward on each side, the sergeant from the platoon that had done the friendly firing, and the victim's buddy. Each held a M16, hands at triggers, pointing not yet at each other but a little down and to the side.

"Put down those guns," Crawford said.

No one did.

Abruptly Ironman was in the circle, looking so steady that he seemed not to have moved at all. "Gangs are history," he said. "I can't turn back the clock for you. I can't give you a car to drive around with your Fourth Street crew until you catch somebody from the Sixth Street crew who's not looking. And then the Sixth Street crew can drive around for weeks looking for somebody from Fourth Street." He motioned the non-combatant soldiers to back up to the side of the parking garage. "There's no gang fighting and no revenge in this battalion. If you want to fight among yourselves, you're on your own. No payback."

He pointed to a vacant row of parking spaces. "Sergeant Brown"— reading the man's name tape—"take your gun and stand down there. Private Ligardo"—motioning the other belligerent to the far end of the row—"stand there." The men stared at him, open-mouthed, Ironman unrelenting. They took up their positions, ten yards apart, M16s pointed at the floor.

"On the count of three, fire. At this distance, one of you should be dead. That will make one less trouble in this battalion."

There was a sound of firing from the highway.

"Are you ready?" Both Brown and Ligardo looked around. "If you're not ready, what are you waiting for?"

Ligardo shook his head. "It coulda been an accident."

"It's those fuckin' night-vision goggles," Brown said. "You can't tell friend from foe."

Ironman let them hang for a long moment.

"Get back to your units," Ironman said. "We've got some fighting to do."

The Federals had brought up mortars and found the range of the airport parking structures. Showers of cement were starting to pour down from the upper stories. Ironman ordered another withdrawal. This time they would pull back along the surface roads, across the high ungainly bridge over the Schuylkill River where it flowed past the oil refineries into the Delaware River. I-95 had already been blocked, heavy trucks overturned on the lanes of the elevated highway where it curved around the southern point of Philadelphia at the defunct navy yards. The Ironman Battalion would pull back into the southern end of the city, in a position to pick off any Federal traffic that tried to descend off the highways in that direction.

The school buses that survived the orderly withdrawal from Chester would not be used to ferry the Battalion any further. They were attracting enemy fire, so Ironman ordered them to be driven out in one direction as decoys, while the troops went another way on foot. It was three miles from the airport to south Philly.

"Shee-it. Don't we get no time to rest?" JaMichael said.

"Pussy," Sutphen said. "Why you think they call us Ironman?"

★

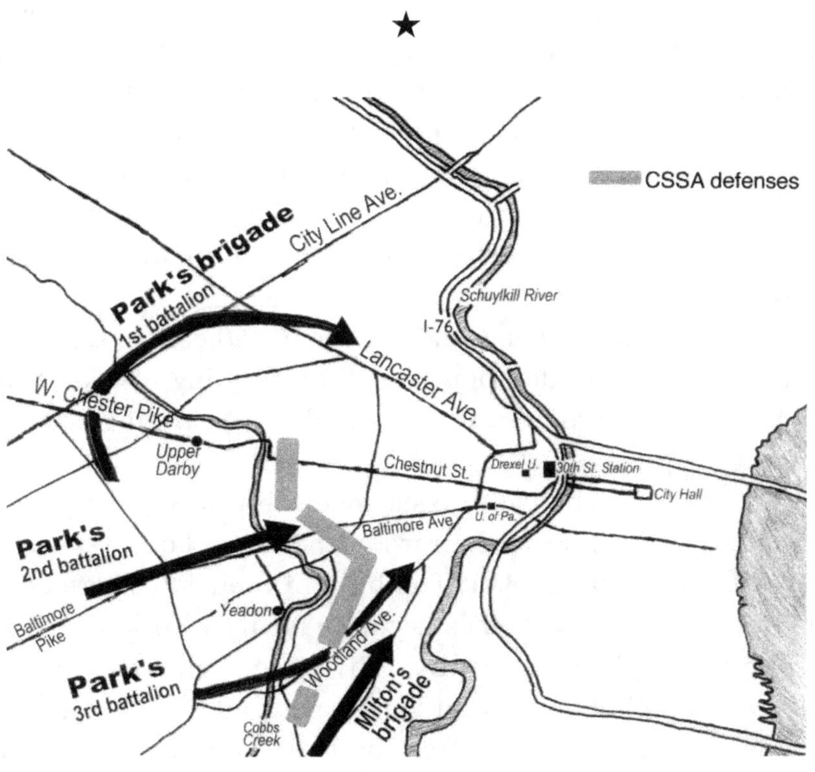

Gandhi Park dozed a little in his command car but he was up at 3 a.m. He slept very little during combat, even though it was important to get some sleep, otherwise you made bad decisions and after a while you couldn't even see things right. Nobody slept for three days during the first advance into Iraq in March 2003 but then they had to call a halt because after that even amphetamine pills can't keep you going. Gandhi didn't like pills and a half hour dozing now and then seemed to do the trick. Most of the soldiers should be awake from nervous energy, since today would be their first real combat. But they had thought that yesterday too and the strain of the stop-and-start driving and the frustration had them snoring even in uncomfortable positions on the truck beds. Gandhi let them sleep a little longer.

By 4:30 advance scouts pushing through Upper Darby and Yeadon, where the Philadelphia trolley lines ended, were exchanging shots with CSSA defenders.

"Get General Agnew on the line," he told his aide. It was hot and steamy already although the sky was barely starting to lighten. There were plenty of trees around the two-story wooden houses in this modest suburb behind the convenience stores and auto shops where the trucks of Gandhi's brigade were parked, broadleaved deciduous trees that seemed to crowd the air and make breathing oppressive. This was a half-assed operation without good intelligence, Gandhi thought.

Late last evening, when General Agnew had called, the message had been a simpleminded pep talk. "You're going to take it to the hoop tomorrow," Agnew said. "Right down Chestnut Street into Center City, Philly."

"Yes, sir. What about the resistance the CSSA put up on I-95 around the airport? I heard their troops performed quite strongly."

"It's all in the game plan. The bulk of their forces are concentrated over there. And that means you're facing a weak spot, Johnny boy." Agnew laughed ebulliently. "Give me a call when you make your breakthrough. I don't want you hogging all the glory. I'm going to land my helicopter right in front of the Liberty Bell, so I can raise your hand as you cross the finish line."

But now, in the early morning when Gandhi called headquarters again, General Agnew was still asleep, and there was no information about where Milton's troops were exactly. They were supposed to make a swooping move up I-495 into the western suburbs, but that had been blocked and they seemed to be piled up south of the airport. Avery's brigade was still somewhere down US-1, far to the south. To hell with them, Gandhi thought.

His concern was to get his own battalions in order, spread out left to right, so that they wouldn't clog the same few roads. Another tricky point was the trucks. Once the soldiers dismounted for combat the trucks had to be held far enough back so they wouldn't be under fire, but if resistance were light the trucks had to be available so the troops could make some speed in their advance, otherwise they would be marching five miles or more before they got to center city.

If this were just quelling a riot they could ride up to the flashpoint and that would be it, but riots don't have enemy commanders organizing defenses and positioning forces in reserve for counterattacks. Where to park the trucks was a boring detail but Gandhi wasn't confident that most of his staff officers were into it. God help us if we have to pull back in a hurry, Gandhi thought.

"The bottlenecks are at Cobb's Creek," he told his battalion commanders over the secure link. Each sat in a command vehicle somewhere, in the half-dark interior of a Humvee lit up by nothing more than the glow of a map on the onboard computer screen. Cobb's Creek was a narrow park that snaked up the west side of Philadelphia and marked the city limits. It was just a wooded gully, dividing the up-and-down hills of the scruffy western suburbs from the long flat slope of west Philly where a grid of streets rolled down towards the Schuylkill River and center city. "Once you get across there will be plenty of parallel streets to travel on. But Cobb's Creek Park has roads only in four or five places."

"No worries," said Col. Metzger. He had the second battalion, in the middle. "We can get across the creek on foot if we have to. That way we can loop around back to secure the roads for the trucks. If the enemy is holding the bottlenecks."

"Let's see if the enemy has figured that out," Gandhi said. "What do your forward patrols say?"

A pause on the line. "Uh—they're just moving out now," Metzger said.

"Let's get a move on," Gandhi said, irritated. "Col. Norton, status report?"

Norton, who had first battalion at the northern end of Philadelphia, said quietly: "We're under way, sir. No resistance so far. Advance units are on City Line Avenue past Cobb's Creek without having to dismount."

"Col. Soule?" He had third battalion, in the south. They were supposed to come up Woodland Avenue, along the cemetery. "Rolling, sir," Soule said. Gandhi supposed they were, perhaps only from this very moment. Give it time.

Half an hour later, there was noise of firing ahead, and battle reports began coming in. There was stiff fighting on Baltimore Pike and the other roads in the center crossing Cobb's Creek. The enemy isn't completely incompetent, Gandhi thought; they're not going to let us drive down Chestnut Street and the main boulevards into the city.

He had planned for this. That's why he had ordered First Battalion to flank still further north, initially by proceeding east on City Line Avenue, the dividing line between the slums of west Philadelphia and the affluent suburbs of the Main Line. First battalion should be about ready to turn southeast onto Lancaster Avenue, he thought impatiently, to converge along the triangle hypotenuse on the area behind Drexel University and Thirtieth Street Station. It was a grungy, crime-ridden area, Gandhi remembered, where most travelers kept their car windows shut tightly and their doors locked. He wondered what the jaded, poverty-level inhabitants would think of the sound of M16s instead of the random pistol shots that punctuated their daily lives.

The laconic Col. Soule was on the secure link. "Breakthrough on Woodland Avenue, sir." It was the southern end of the front, a bit of a surprise.

"Any resistance crossing Cobb's Creek?"

"Nothing. We're just now taking heavier fire." The trucks of Third Battalion were well on alongside the greenlawned cemetery and amid the blocks of old frame Victorian houses before the troops dismounted and went forward against CSSA fire.

"Keep going. I'll move some of Metzger's companies in behind you."

Gandhi got Second Battalion on the link. Col. Metzger was not happy at the order to send troops south to Woodland Avenue to exploit the opening. "I'm having a hell of fight here, General. I need everything I've got, and more if you can give it to me."

"That's just the point, Colonel. We're going to bypass the heavy resistance."

"But I'm making headway. I'll have them on the run if you give me a chance."

Gandhi demanded specifics: what units, how far had they gotten. Col. Metzger grunted out a disjointed list. It was all platoon-size formations, Gandhi recognized, getting through Cobb's Creek Park on foot. But without transportation they were moving much slower than third battalion in the south.

"Send Charlie Company around to the Woodland Avenue crossing," Gandhi said, cutting off discussion.

"But General—"

"That's an order."

Gandhi now had another worry.

First battalion in the north was coming down Lancaster Avenue on trucks and starting to pick up enemy fire. Big gaps had opened up between the center and the north and south salients. Gandhi wondered if the enemy was aware of this, and if they were capable of taking advantage of it.

He kept his headquarters back behind Cobb's Creek, since he needed to keep tabs on each of his advance formations, and if he passed the bottleneck there was no guarantee he could cover the whole front or avoid getting trapped in traffic. Being a forward commander was glamorous and Gandhi wished he was out there at the head of a column, but the art of generalship was moving all the pieces around and you couldn't do that if you were just one of the pieces.

The radio system was working securely and all the command vehicles had computers, but officers did not always know where they were or report in very regularly or accurately. Normally GPS coordinates would solve that. But GPS had been knocked out in the cyberwar and still hadn't been restored. The Lancaster Avenue force in the north seemed to be spreading out against resistance but once the troops left their trucks, it wasn't clear whether they were advancing, retreating, or just maneuvering through the side streets.

It's probably the same on the other side, Gandhi told himself. The enemy commander doesn't know any more about what's happening out there than I do.

Suddenly, urgently, everyone was on the line at once. Metzger, of course: "I'm in a hell of a firefight. I need backup, ASAP. I need—"

"Where's Charlie Company?" Gandhi said.

A tiny pause. "Can't tell you right now, General. I've sort of lost track of them."

Gandhi was not surprised. He switched to Col. Soule. "We're going backwards," Soule said. "I'm getting hit from the front and left."

"Where is your transport?"

"Parked back along Woodland Avenue."

"Can you get to it?"

"Not sure. Enemy might have gotten around behind us."

"See if you can fight your way back to your vehicles," Gandhi said. "I want Third Battalion to fall back and regroup towards Cobb's Creek."

It was a well-planned counterattack, or maybe the enemy was just lucky. The main roads of West Philly formed an arrowhead, with Chestnut Street as the shaft, pointed east, and Lancaster Avenue slanting down from the northwest and Woodland Avenue slanting up from the southwest. The CSSA counterattack came in the lower triangle between Chestnut Street and Woodland Avenue. In west Philly smoke billowed up from the weathered brick rowhouses with their gritty white columns and two-story porches.

It was the heart of the black ghetto where back in the 1980s a militant group of Afro-nationalists had turned a house into an urban commune and bombarded their neighbors with loudspeaker noise until the city finally intervened. The police had tried to flush them out with tear gas grenades but only succeeded in setting the block on fire, leading to a dozen deaths, a sudden switch in sympathies, and years of lawsuits and recriminations. No lawsuits this time, Gandhi thought. Just acts of war.

The fighting was getting heavier and it wasn't clear how well the troop formations were holding together; company commanders had lost touch with many of their platoons. Platoons were getting split up into squads and even smaller pieces. Not many casualties, but a shortage of medics and no clear path of evacuation. Just how hastily this operation had been prepared was becoming apparent. Some units were running out of ammunition. Gandhi had ample supplies in the reserve line behind Cobb's Creek but it wasn't clear exactly where the troops were who needed ammo and how the trucks would get it to them.

"I can't get Col. Soule on the link," Gandhi's communications operator said. There could be a lot of reasons for that, Gandhi thought. "Get me whoever you can in Third Battalion."

"We're being attacked from the south," radioed the C.O. of Bravo Company.

A lieutenant in Alpha Company said: "We're being ambushed. The CSSA has a big force out there, just laying in hiding."

"How many?" Gandhi said.

"They're popping up everywhere. Looks like a whole brigade."

"What streets? Be specific."

"How do I know? It's every street. Look out, incoming!" A burst of explosions, and the call ended.

A hidden CSSA force, laying in ambush? Casualty reports were coming in from panicky voices. Finally Gandhi heard Col. Soule's unflappable tones. "We've made contact with General Milton's brigade. Some friendly fire casualties. It's quieting down now."

Once the threatening troops had advanced into range of recognition, it dawned on Soule's forces that they were wearing the same USA battle uniforms as themselves. It was elements of Milton's brigade which had siphoned off from the Interstate and were trying to make a pincers move into Philadelphia from the southwest. Dismounted from their trucks at the sounds of firing ahead of them, Milton's troops had no direct radio communication with Gandhi's forward units. Computers in the trucks should have helped but someone on the brigade staff had gotten worried about CSSA hacking into their system and insisted on clearing everything through General Agnew's headquarters.

The friendly fire had finally stopped. But now there was another problem. Companies from Milton's brigade were driving into Gandhi's own logistics in Darby, jamming the bottleneck from the west side. Milton's forward troops were out of touch with their own brigade headquarters, and messages that came through were slow and outdated.

Gandhi called Col. Soule again. "I've changed my mind, Colonel. Withdrawing Third Battalion towards Cobb's Creek is no longer feasible. I want you to attack due north. Smash the CSSA counterattack. Use Milton's troops as your reinforcements."

"I'd be happy to do that," Soule said. "But I'm getting a lot of flack from Milton's company commanders. No one knows where General Milton is, and they're telling me they can't move without a chain of command."

"Put them on the link to me," Gandhi said.

One of Milton's company commanders came on. "Welcome to the battle, Captain," Gandhi said. "You're just in time to help us turn things around."

"Yes, sir," the captain said. "But I need authorization from General Milton."

"You're under my jurisdiction now. And I'm assigning you temporarily to Colonel Soule."

"I don't know, sir. Can I have that in writing?"

"You'll get it in writing, pinned on a body bag!" Gandhi exploded. "Your battalion is dispersed. And it's not the only one. We need to get reorganized, or we're going to lose this battle. You want to win, don't you?"

"Yes, sir. But—"

"Then get your troops together and get moving. We're making an attack. And if you've got ammunition, I want you to share it with Soule's men."

Gandhi repeated the conversation half a dozen times. The ball was rolling, assent was building up. We've got a fighting chance now, he thought.

What happened next was hard to picture. It was not a neat map in a Civil War history book, where Yankees and Rebels were arrows moving from well-marked position to position. Gandhi's Third Battalion and elements of Milton's brigade—unclear just which ones—were making their way along the residential blocks of west Philadelphia, firing up the street where smoke and noise suggested the enemy had been, taking cover behind stoops and trash bins, retreating around the block, sometimes running away, sometimes advancing, sometimes stuck to a spot on the sidewalk.

Third Battalion no longer had a chain of command. Colonel Soule had disappeared from the communications link again. Maybe killed, maybe leading from the front, maybe overwhelmed with dashing about trying to repair the lines of authority that alone would give his unit existence as a fighting force.

Gandhi sporadically talked with this captain or that lieutenant, but the small units were scattered and mixed over hundreds of city blocks. "I've lost three quarters of my men," an officer told him. "I've got one squad left out of the platoon." A captain said: "Ninety percent of my company is missing."

"How many confirmed dead?"

"I can't say, General. They're just not here."

"Well, are there a lot of bodies on the ground?"

"Uh, not right here. There was one back on the street corner. But I didn't stop to see if it was one of ours or the enemy's."

"How many at your medical collection points?"

"We've been moving fast, General. I can't say where the medical points are."

"It's probably not as bad as you think, Captain. Try to get your men together. That will make everybody feel better." The numbers were vague, impossible to tell what was double counted, rumored, or confirmed killed and wounded. Gandhi told himself these things were always exaggerated at first, and even in the heaviest fighting troops rarely took more than twenty percent casualties, which left plenty to keep on with the battle if they didn't get panicked. Given the quality of the troops on both sides, it was doubtful that many bullets were finding their targets.

Retreating troops started filtering back westward through the Cobb's Creek bottleneck on foot. These had no formation at all, Gandhi's Third Battalion, Second Battalion, Milton's forces, all disintegrated to the level of individual soldiers, at most little buddy knots of threes and fours. Gandhi did his best to reorganize them, find their officers, get them back into some kind of chain of command. His staff looked for assembly areas, in strip mall parking lots, preferably further back from the fighting. Disorganized troops were worse than useless; they could destroy the organization of troops still in functioning order.

Never reinforce failure, the adage said. Gandhi wanted them out of the way, while reserve forces could take their place on the advance without getting infected. He decided to pull the empty trucks back from Woodland Avenue, to outside the Cobb's Creek bottleneck; at least they would have a semblance of availability for coordinated action.

Milton's troops kept arriving from the rear as well. Their organization was choppier than Gandhi would have liked, but they would do. He cleared the bottleneck and ordered them forward, pinpointing the position of the CSSA defenders as best he could.

One of Milton's battalion commanders showed up, Colonel Simmons. "I'll take over now," he said. "These are troops from my command."

"How do you know they're yours?" Gandhi said. "There are elements of several different battalions from Milton's brigade here."

"Of course they're mine," Colonel Simmons said. "A colonel in General Milton's brigade can't come under a colonel in someone else's brigade."

Gandhi sighed disgustedly. "Let's get General Milton on the line."

Milton's headquarters was still out near the airport. Luckily, Milton himself took the call with only a few minutes delay.

"I'm trying to keep my forces together," Milton said. "You can see the point of that, can't you General Park?"

"If we had time that would be great," Gandhi said. "But the battle has mixed everything up, and we need to improvise. Now. While we can save the situation."

Milton paused. "I'd like to help you out," he said. "But we'd better clear it with General Agnew first." They all huddled on a conference call.

"I knew you fellows would call me when you got in trouble," Agnew said. "Now, don't panic. First I want to know about the numbers. How many have you got on your front, Johnny boy?"

Gandhi estimated: "I have about seventeen hundred troops on the Woodland front. Plus an unknown number from Milton's two battalions, two thousand tops. Minus some casualties, and stragglers who made their way back outside the bottleneck."

"That's thirty-seven hundred," Agnew said. "Not sure it's enough to risk an attack. The enemy must have at least that many in west Philly, maybe twice as much."

"Our attack is already under way," Gandhi said. "We're making progress. They're not backing us up, we're backing them up. We can't lose the momentum."

"All right," Agnew agreed. "You got it, Johnny boy. I want you to hit 'em with everything you've got, all thirty-seven hundred."

"Not thirty-seven hundred," Gandhi said, making a mistake. "There's probably five hundred stragglers I've pulled out of action."

"Pulled out of action? You gotta be kidding, Johnny, I always heard you were a big tough guy."

"Let me explain something, General," Gandhi started to say. "You can't mix fresh troops with defeated troops, it only—" Another mistake.

"Do you want to make this attack or don't you?" Agnew shouted over the line. "I want all those men going forward, do you understand? Col. Simmons! I want you to hold your troops until General Park has sent all his troops forward, including these so-called stragglers."

Gandhi said "Yes, sir!" and hung up.

The southern front was essentially stymied. Gandhi put his staff to work getting the stragglers reformed as best possible. Wherever a platoon could be put in some semblance of strength it was sent forward. Finally Col. Simmons was cajoled and shamed into sending some of his own companies across the bottleneck. At least they started in good order, Gandhi thought. However long that will last.

Further north, the center of the line was desultory, static, neither side making much effort. Still further up, in the Lancaster Avenue area, fighting was not going well, but not as confused as the south. Then, around noon, good news at last. Avery's brigade was arriving up US-1, slow, very late, but in good formation, thirty-five hundred strong. No point in reinforcing chaos, Gandhi concluded, hoping Agnew would keep them away from the southern salient. He pointed Avery's advance troops to the northern flank, following his own First Battalion down Lancaster Avenue, then called Agnew's headquarters.

"Yes, things are going fine on the southern salient," he said. "Slogging on through." It was a lie but at least it wasn't the complete opposite of the truth. "What we need now," Gandhi said, "is a left hook to finish them off."

"We're in luck," Agnew said. "I can tell you confidentially that Avery's brigade is here, and coming in just the direction we need. We'll roll up the CSSA and be at City Hall by this afternoon. Bring it on!" Agnew said. "I knew that chewing you out would light a fire under you, Johnny boy."

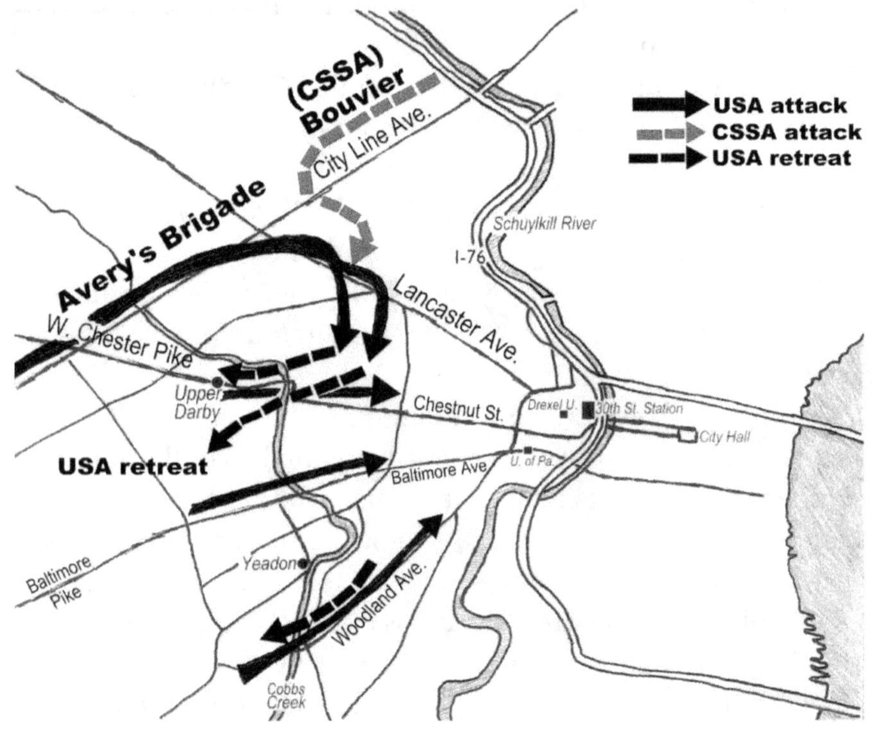

Avery's brigade did in fact roll up the northern end of the CSSA line. Cobb's Creek was no longer a bottleneck on the north, and the combination of Gandhi's First Battalion and the three battalions of Avery's were effectively sweeping all the CSSA troops from that part of the city. Avery's force paraded up City Line Avenue and down Lancaster Avenue and the streets running south, driving CSSA resistance before them. Gandhi kept direct radio contact with Avery's battalion commanders as well as his own First Battalion; they had made contact on the ground, had their streets divided up for coordinated advance. The fresh troops had dismounted south of Lancaster Avenue, with trucks following behind. All going well.

Then all was not going well. Avery's trucks, bringing up the rear of the advance, were being hit from their own rear. A CSSA force had come out of nowhere. At least brigade strength, it seemed, coming southwest on City Line Avenue, no doubt having arrived at the freeway exit from I-76.

A mirror game being played on the CSSA side, it was their own lagging reinforcements coming down from northeast Pennsylvania or New York State. If the CSSA reinforcements had arrived half an hour earlier, they would have met Avery's parade on City Line Avenue head-on.

Now Avery's forces had turned south, right turn down the grungy avenues of northwest Philadelphia. CSSA reinforcements, under General Bouvier from New York, it later transpired, had only to turn left into the same grungy avenues. The CSSA troops were going full speed, still mounted; Avery's trucks were edging forward slowly, trailing their dismounted troops. Momentum changed in a flash, in the crack of M14s disabling Union trucks, in the rattle of machine-gun fire hitting the rear of the Union columns, still in close formation as they marched towards what they thought was the retreating combat zone in front of them.

At Gandhi's headquarters it took time to sort this out. A babble of excited reports, calls for help, angry accusations. Gandhi's first thought was friendly fire, somehow, but it soon became clear that the two Union brigades in the north were not clashing. There were no more reinforcements; Avery's were the last reserves, thrown in for the knockout punch.

Ironically, Avery's brigade, the best organized force on the battlefield, still in near-perfect order, was unraveling like an old sweater. Unable to go forward, unable to go back the way it came, its troops began to scatter, through side streets, vacant lots, trolley yards and deserted gas stations and faded carwashes. Back to the west was the direction of safety; back they hurried, pursued for a while by enemies in trucks who dismounted, fired, remounted and caught up with them again. Well-disciplined rifle squads should have been able to stop the pursuers, but well-disciplined squads were few and far between; the brigade had lost its composure so quickly that its command structure was left in its wake, officers running after their troops, undignified, authority lost, struggling just to keep up.

Agnew's command post, back at Wilmington thirty miles away, caught the infection. "I'm ordering you to pull out," Agnew phoned Gandhi. "Same as I'm ordering Easton and Milton." The conversation was curt, the ebullience and loquaciousness gone.

"There needs to be a rearguard to cover the retreat," Gandhi said. "My First Battalion is in a position to do it." They had their own sector, further east than the streets where Avery had been caught from the rear; they still had their organization and would fight their way back, slowly, leaving Bouvier's CSSA forces to exult in their victory.

Extricating Gandhi's Second and Third Battalions from southwest Philly was more of a problem. CSSA forces here were just as disorganized and offered no pursuit, but Gandhi's chains of command were as vague as finding directions in a dream. Milton's command had disintegrated too, as expected. Fortunately most of the trucks were assembled on the west of Cobb's Creek, although they were overloaded with Avery's troops, who had lost virtually all their transport.

When the last Union troops on the field pulled out—Gandhi's First Battalion—they growled at Avery's stragglers and refused to talk to them. Gandhi himself posted MPs at the last remaining trucks to make sure his own troops boarded first.

At the White House Situation Room, Secretary Madigan tried not to gloat. General Harris was not so charitable. "Next time we'll do it the right way, Mr. President."

"Just an old-fashioned, behind-the-woodshed butt-whipping," Jennings said. "My daddy used to say it hurts him more than it hurts me. I dunno if it's true or not. What's our casualties?"

"Still coming in," Madigan said. "Several thousand. A lot of them may only be missing, no real bodily harm."

"But harmed in the spirit," Jennings said.

"It's not all bad," Madigan said. "War is a serious thing. I think a lot of young men learned that, and it's going to make them better soldiers."

"A lot of us learned it," Jennings said. "It ain't easy."

"Patience, preparation, organization," Madigan said. "Next time we'll be ready."

"God is sending us a message," Jennings said. "There's got to be a meaning to this. He's trampling out the grapes of wrath. That means us too, not just the enemy."

He rose from his swivel chair at the head of the mahogany table, marched to the front of the room, signaling for the information screens to be switched off. The room lights came on. He stopped between the stanchions holding the American flag and the blue flag of the Presidency.

"God isn't all enthusiasm and good intentions. He's the Jehovah of the Old Testament. God will forgive us, but first He's gonna take us to the woodshed."

Madigan looked a little smug. "God can be stern," Jennings said. "Even with you, Mr. Secretary."

Belatedly, as Union forces made their way back southward along I-95, a pair of CSSA F-16s appeared in the sky south of Philadelphia. They flew in low over the convoy, but dropped no bombs, fired off no rockets. Like dogs snarling at a retreating enemy, in this case dogs who had arrived too late for the fight. Perhaps they had orders just to see the enemy out of their territory; perhaps they were reluctant to bomb the highway, mixed again with civilian traffic. From the south, another pair of fighters appeared, USA F-15s. Both pairs zoomed to fighting altitude, covering the stretch of Delaware River between Wilmington and the mouth of Delaware Bay in a couple of minutes. Turning west, as on a dare, the CSSA planes broke Maryland airspace. Over Havre de Grace rockets were fired. One CSSA fighter was downed in Chesapeake Bay. The remaining fighters circled, headed for home.

Down below, in Philadelphia and Wilmington and Baltimore and Washington and everywhere, anti-aircraft missiles were being wheeled into place. The real war had begun.

First Battle of Bull Run, 1861

As spring 1861 turned to summer, Northern politicians and journalists clamored for the Union to march on Richmond and end the rebellion. The regular army was tiny and enlisted volunteers were untried. In late July, a force crossed the Potomac and headed south, accompanied by marching bands and Congressmen making speeches. The Union commander McDowell had jumped from Major to General in one day; now he had almost forty thousand troops to control. Against him the Confederates had twenty thousand led by Beauregard, the victor at Fort Sumter, in a defensive position behind Bull Run creek—not far from where Dulles airport is today. Beauregard placed most of his troops on his right (the east end of his line), guarding the bridge and several fords across the water. McDowell's plan was to feint an attack straight ahead, while sending large forces under cover of night in a loop to catch the Confederate line from the west. It was a good plan and it worked well at first. Surprised and outnumbered in the morning attack, the Confederates fell back struggling to form up their defenses.

Around noon things started to go awry. Federal troops had used up most of their ammunition in the attack; logistics lines lacked the glamour and élan of the marching vanguard and so were neglected. The Federal volunteers, satiated with adventure and initial victory, were growing tired and thirsty. Charges by Federal units and counterattacks by the Confederates had mixed the combat formations together; the battleground was turning into a shapeless mêlée.

There was another Confederate army, ten thousand strong, at the northern end of the Shenandoah Valley, fifty miles away by railroad. It was supposed to be held in place by a Union force of superior size, but Joe Johnston, the Confederate general, bluffed the raw Union forces under their elderly commander, a politician from Philadelphia, and siphoned off most of his troops toward the rail hub at Manassas, behind Bull Run. The last of Johnston's forces arrived in midafternoon, just as McDowell, directing from the front almost like a sergeant, launched a final attack to turn the end of the Confederate line. Unfortunately, this put their own backs right in the path of Johnston's fresh columns.

It was sheer luck; Johnston and Beauregard, ill-adjusted in combined command, had given a series of contradictory orders for counterattack at the other end of the battlefield, but the Confederates were saved from disaster because they were too hard pressed to carry them out. Johnston's late-arriving troops disembarked from the trains in marching order, unaffected by the chaos on the ground. Their attack sent the Union troops into a disorderly retreat, which grew into a panic as more and more joined in. By nightfall they were fleeing back towards Washington, leaving their artillery and stores behind, with almost two thousand dead and wounded, and over one thousand ignominiously captured in the rout. Panic infected the Union capital; Lincoln conferred about whether to evacuate. But the Confederates had also lost about two thousand in the fighting, and were too disorganized to follow up. They celebrated instead. Lincoln soon brought in more troops, and both sides settled down for a long serious war.

In the hot hours of the morning, when the Confederate line had almost broken under the Union assault, a brigade under General Thomas Jackson was sent forward to hold a hill at the left end of the line. Jackson was a professor at the Virginia Military Institute, a former West Point graduate eking out a living in civilian times. Intellectual things did not come easy to him; he had literally sweated and prayed his way through his classroom exams at the Academy. The same determination held in all things; he was a strict disciplinarian, a health fanatic, a hypochondriac given to medical nostrums and known to suck lemons in combat. He claimed religious voices talked to him from on high in crucial moments. One of those moments was on Henry House Hill that Sunday morning.

As Confederate formations melted into little segments, Jackson's men repelled the oncoming Federals with steady, disciplined musket fire. "There stands Jackson, like a stone wall!" called one of the Confederate commanders, just before he was shot in the wavering traffic. The story was picked up by the papers; the nickname stuck. Stonewall Jackson was the rock of discipline in the midst of lines of command unraveling and bonds of unity disintegrating as the hours of fighting mounted. In Jackson's first battle, he did nothing spectacular; but above all other forces, his troops did not come apart; under his orders they held their fire until the enemy was too close to miss; neither victory nor defeat broke up his ranks.

Combat, like prolonged heating in a furnace, tends to melt whatever is inside it for long. The organization that breaks down first loses; the organization that breaks down less, wins.

YEAR TWO.
TECHNO-WAR

SECOND BATTLE OF GETTYSBURG

EASTCOM, an undisclosed location in Virginia. May.

"How much longer before we get this war off the ground, Bob? The good people of the US of A are getting mighty impatient."

President Joshua Maccabee Jennings in his rumpled white suit intruded in the war room, flanked by Secretary Robert Madigan. Battle headquarters looked like a television newsroom.

Rows of desks with monitors and keyboards. Telephone handsets with long kinky accordion cables; desk microphones on slender metal stalks. Styrofoam cups, plastic water bottles, a clutter of notepads, printouts, manuals, half-eaten food: signs of a staff that had not been away from their desks for hours. Higher officers sat at the center desks, talking into handsets, all the while eyeing the computer screens of the system called HOME. Behind them stood staff officers, awaiting a word with the higher ranks, or scurrying about carrying messages and files.

Officers wore blue-green battle dress mottled with camouflage splotches. No rows of decorations over the left breast pocket like those worn on official uniforms at congressional hearings and press conferences; this was war, and everyone was in combat mode, with minimal display of rank and ceremony.

Except that battle headquarters was two hundred miles from the front, the distance from central Pennsylvania to southern Virginia. Camouflage uniforms were of no use for blending into forest leaves or netting shadows, no use at all in electronic warfare at the center of a giant communications grid. They were purely symbolic, carrying the message: we are all part of the team. As more and more of the military inhabits the administrative tail rather than the combat tooth, the uniforms of all ranks and functions have grown alike; desk jockeys far from the front take on the markings of infantry grunts.

"This is an exercise," Madigan said. "A computer game for the battle, not the battle itself."

"How many times have you boys played this thing?" Jennings snorted. "You ought to have it figured out by now."

"We're getting HOME fully programmed, Mr. President. It will be worth the wait. Remember the lead-up to the Iraq invasion in '03?"

"I remember six months of sitting around twiddling my thumbs. Hasn't anything improved since then?"

"HOME is the greatest computer in history. Getting everything connected is what takes time."

"Yes, yes," said Jennings. He clapped Madigan around the shoulders, part bear hug, part sheer physical dominance of six foot five over five foot ten. "You boys and your games."

"Mr. President, let me introduce Major Debra Zielkowski." Madigan stopped a tall blonde officer of serious demeanor.

"Good to know you, Major Zukowski." Jennings pumped her hand. "Tell me something. Off the record. What's really going here?"

"Zielkowski, sir. We're in our final simulation."

"Mighty pleased to hear it," Jennings boomed. "And what is your part in this operation, Major?"

She glanced warily at the Secretary, who nodded her the go-ahead. "I am tracking the location of enemy forces."

"So where is he?"

"They're spread out from Hagerstown, Maryland to York, Pennsylvania. With reserves around Harrisburg, Reading and Lancaster."

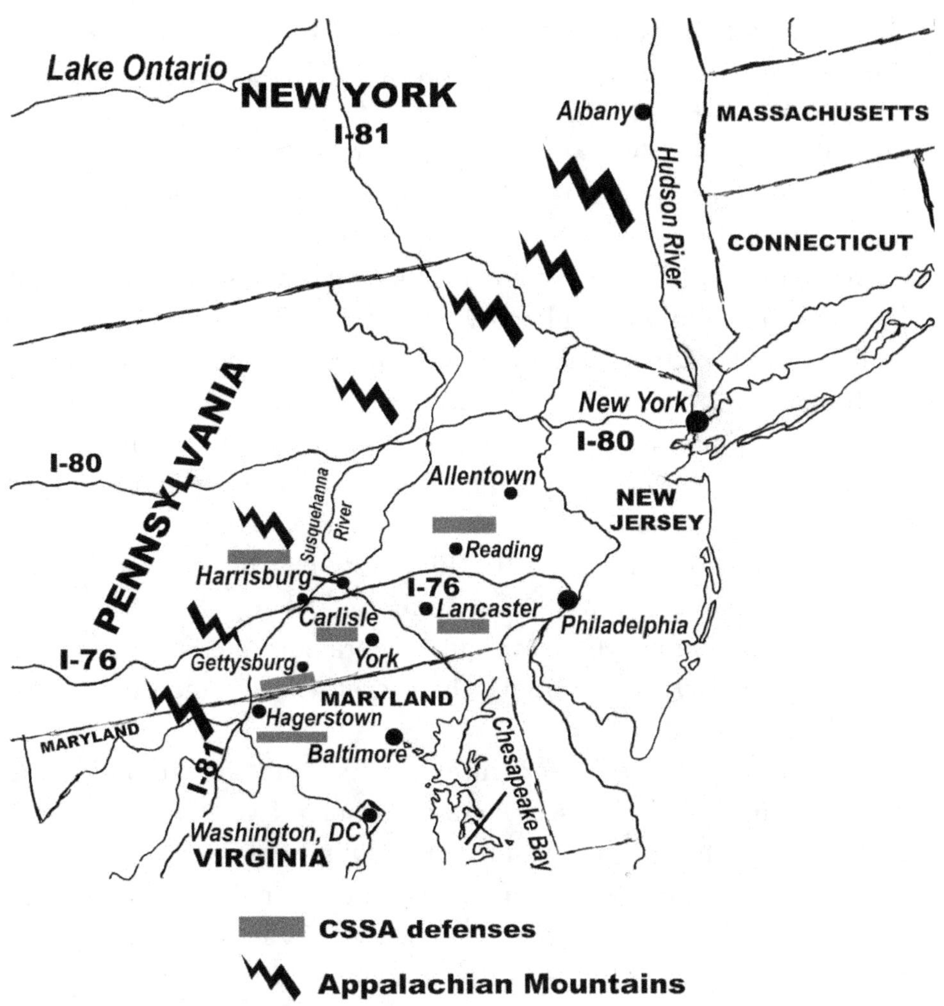

Jennings peered at the indicated map. "How many are there?"

"Altogether we estimate about eighty thousand troops in the theatre of operations. A thousand tanks, eight hundred APCs, four hundred artillery pieces, three hundred attack helicopters."

"Eighty thousand rebels, against a hundred thousand or so Union, right?" Jennings tilted his head back thoughtfully. "Almost the same numbers as the battle of Gettysburg in 1863. And Gettysburg is smack-dab in the middle. Couldn't the turning point be there again?" The President was feeling a speech coming on.

"It depends on how the battle shapes up," Madigan said. "Some of the fighting might be at Gettysburg."

"As I recall, Gettysburg was the place where all the crossroads come together, and Robert E. Lee and General Mead raced each other to get there the firstest with the mostest."

Madigan rolled his eyes slightly, passing off to Debra for a reply.

"Modern doctrine is multilevel attack," she said. "HOME is programmed to hit the enemy everywhere at once."

"Wouldn't it be better to concentrate our forces and wipe 'em out where we have 'em outnumbered?"

"Battles aren't like that anymore. Concentrating is too dangerous. Today's munitions are so lethal that you can't risk putting many forces in one place. So we spread out, just like they do. That's why the CSSA forces cover a front of seventy-five miles with a depth of one hundred miles behind it."

"That must spread 'em pretty thin. How can they cover all that real estate with only eighty thousand men?"

"Men and women, Mr. President," Debra corrected.

Jennings guffawed. "So that's the secret. One women makes up for ten fighting men."

"Technology makes up for the numbers. And the technology is run from command centers." Debra held herself very erect, six feet tall even in flat shoes, very military looking in her blue-green combat dress. "As you know, Mr. President, women don't serve in combat ground forces, although there are some of us in aerial combat. Most women are helping run the battle from back here"—she gestured around the room—"just like most of the men are."

The President nodded, humbled, impish.

"It's called defense in depth," she continued. "The enemy uses cover and concealment. Woods, hill contours, digging into pits. Buildings are best, since they obscure most of our sensors. A fluid defense, dispersed in depth. As we penetrate their lines, our forces become vulnerable to counterattack from the reserves they have dispersed fifty or a hundred miles back."

"Then how do you know when we've won? Seems to me somebody has to end up owning the battlefield."

"It doesn't work like that today. Our aim is to destroy their army, not to gain ground. That's why we strike everywhere at once. Coordinated air strikes, missiles, artillery, battle helicopters. We hit their command posts and communication centers deep in their territory, the same time we hit their forward units with our armor. And we hit their reserves so they can't come up. We disrupt their rear areas, top to bottom, starting at the top. Their combat units can't support each other if they can't communicate."

"Hold on a minute," Jennings asked. "Can't the enemy aim at our communications and command and all that and cut us off too?"

"They try to. We use the same tactics on offense as they do on defense. Disperse to reduce vulnerability. Coordinate different weapons platforms to suppress their fire while our ground forces are moving."

"I'm glad somebody finally mentioned that word," Jennings said. "Just when are we moving out?"

She hesitated, voice trailing off, having talked too much. A four-star general had come up to flank her on the left: General Curt Harris, Chairman of the Joint Chiefs of Staff, protruded his lower jaw. On her right, a three-star general, Lieutenant General Billy Jo Maddux, commander of Operation Liberty Bell, so long in preparation.

"Thank you, Major." General Maddux stepped between her and the President, dismissing. "We're almost ready, Mr. President. You understand that no useful purpose would be served in talking about precise places and times. Surprise is of the essence."

"I appreciate that, Billy Jo. I just came down to give you fellows a poke in the ribs. Making sure you're not just playing video games." Jennings gestured at the computer screens that lined the walls, laughing. Maddux smiled pleasantly, a nice man, very mild-mannered for a general. Harris moved his jaw as if transferring a wad of imaginary tobacco from one cheek to another.

"In God's good time," General Maddux said, meeting Jennings' eyes. Speaking to the President in his own language. "His time is near."

"Praise the Lord," Jennings boomed, nodding. "As I recall it took us three weeks to get from Kuwait to Baghdad in '03. That's about three hundred fifty miles. At that rate we ought to be in New York in a week or so—once you get this thing rolling." He beamed in every direction around the room, clowning. "Can I put the victory parade on my schedule? I believe I have an engagement open."

Madigan was unamused. "It's a poor analogy. The Iraqis were an outdated army fighting against the world's most advanced. They didn't get a single plane in the air. We controlled the airspace, smashed all their communications from day one. It was Soviet technology of the 60s and 70s against American technology of the 21st century. Now we're fighting troops with the same weapons as ourselves."

"Then how do you know we'll win?" Jennings was grave, no longer joking.

Madigan shook his head, dispelling doubt. "Better coordination." Remembering how the Pentagon had split, twelve months earlier, over the issue of transformation. Better off now without the traditionalists obstructing things. The period of reorganization was a blessing in disguise. "Finally, we're completely computerized. HOME will have full operational control now."

"So be it. With the Lord's blessing." Jennings bear-clasped him briefly, then turned to address the room. "Brethren and sisters. Let us pray."

Captain Tom Napoli swooped the helicopter upwards, banking to the left. Gave orders to fire on the row of tanks dug in behind the Emmetsburg Road, while he took out the buildings and missile pits at the end. Rockets exploded on the battlefield, shaking the helicopters in the air. He expertly rode the blast, veering towards Gettysburg National Park Headquarters and the embankment beside it.

Thinking: just like the practice simulations we did. Just another video game.

But there is something extra here, something very un-video-game-like. It is the pumping in his chest, pounding under his rib cage. It is the sudden pressure in his forehead, as if his head was inflating inside his helmet. It is the short panting breaths that he can't control, breathing him like a bellows pumped by an unseen hand. It is the burst of adrenalin that is racing his heartbeat. The scene is getting eerie in Tom Napoli's head; he can feel the reverberations of the blasts throwing him around in the air, but he hears nothing but a dull muffled sounds from a great distance.

The world is rushing past his eyeballs, and at the same time he is floating, detached in a bubble, pulsating to his own rhythm.

Coming into his first combat, he has wondered the universal question of all soldiers about themselves. Now that the moment has arrived, he cannot answer which he is: coward? or brave? The bubble in which he is hanging is neither, but an ambiguous third space that borders on both. On one side lies terror and paralysis; on the other is frenzy, heedless bravery, going berserk in a headlong dive to the front where death lies waiting for the incautious. Tom holds himself suspended in the middle of the bubble. He is starting to get used to it; the tension is becoming exhilaration.

Seconds earlier he could scarcely grip the controls, his fingers like wads of cotton padding. Now they felt firm again, real helicopter controls, a real trigger for the cannon under the Apache's nose. No game controls ever felt like this.

On the panel in front of the helicopter control stick, the bright blue and green screens of HOME glowed at him with reassuring constancy. The battle outside the helicopter's skin was safely ordered in here, taking the form of a circular green compass with himself as the dot in the center. Blue icons surrounded him, fluttering this way and that: his troop of helicopters, veering at targets, taking evasive action, sailing in the blast just like he was. A different set of icons in menacing red showed enemy installations, more stable on the screen since they were on the ground not moving.

An adjacent screen tallied hits and losses: one of his helicopters had been hit, spiraling to a crash alongside Park Headquarters. Eleven enemy tanks and APCs were knocked out. The Stinger battery, whose SAMs had been exploding around them a moment before, was partly disabled. Somewhere another SAM battery was opening up.

In front of Napoli and lower down in the cockpit nose sat his gunner and copilot, Lt. Billetts. A taciturn man, like Tom Napoli, all business. Billetts was calling out headings. His voice broke in on Tom's eardrums with a loud crackle, like a dead speaker suddenly coming on at high volume. The soundproof bubble of the first shock of combat had been almost like being deaf.

Now there was someone else in his world. Billetts' voice was saying nothing personal, but it was the most reassuring sound Tom Napoli had heard in his life.

"Ground battery at 11 o'clock four hundred meters."

"Got it."

Another rocket exploded nearby. The Apache shuddered, its frame giving a palpable groan as it wallowed clumsily out of control. It rode sideways, dangerously angled. Hung for a moment on the edge of death. Hung, settled, righted itself.

The noise of its engines cut into Napoli's consciousness with an ear-popping sound like turning on a switch. Another bout of temporary deafness ending, back to the world of humming sounds that meant purposeful movement in space.

HOME's blue screen was beeping and flashing a message at him:

FIRE STARBOARD ROCKET 2 AT SET COORDINATES

On some weapons platforms, HOME could fire weapons on its own, without going through a human operator. Apaches were not yet set up for full computer control of firing. HOME took in all available sensors, picked targets, tuned homing systems on the rockets to the proper destination. All that was left for the helicopter crew was to pull the trigger. This was Billetts' job. Napoli was about to shout a heads up when Billetts released the rockets. A whoosh of white flame departed from under the Apache's right strut and the rocket arced gracefully down in a deadly rainbow curve of grey smoke. Dirt spattered high in the air where it hit the ground, then cotton balls of smoke billowed up, hiding the Park Headquarters from view.

HOME's blue screen was again flashing, calmly announcing:

TARGET HIT

**PRELIMINARY DAMAGE ASSESSMENT PENDING —
ESTIMATE 4 MINUTES**

Napoli pulled his eyes from the screens, swung his head to the view from each side window. His helicopter troop had settled into more regular patterns, less jerky, the battle winding down.

Two helicopters out of his original ten had been hit; one crashed, one making its way back to base.

The row of tanks and APCs that had looked to him, flying into battle, like a giant zipper about to close—how long ago was that? in another phase of his life—were sending up ugly black clouds of smoke, with the harsh smell of diesel. Orange flames glowered through at the base of those thick midnight splotches.

Hard to see anything down there. General Meade's cannon, the Civil War monuments, the wide green lawns of Gettysburg National Monument had disappeared beneath a layer of smoke, a shallow sea of man-man fog with columns of unearthly black clouds roiling up from it. Napoli turned his head from one angle to another, taking in every view from the cockpit of bulletproof plexiglass. The ground view was ugly but the sideways panorama magnificent: seven helicopters of Captain Napoli's troop flying a big slow circle over Gettysburg, looking for new targets.

For the first time in his life the Apaches seemed to him comic. Viewed from the front they were like some kind of cartoon mouse, with fat cheeks and a bubble nose—these were the heavily armored forward gun compartments—and two bulging ears alongside the plexiglass head—the engines on either side of the cockpit. Looking like a goofy kid with a propeller-topped beanie—this was the rotors rising from the center of the helicopter, surmounted by a radar dome looking for all the world like the mushroom where Alice had met the caterpillar in Wonderland. Tom Napoli laughed in delight.

Billetts looked at him, surprised, laughing too. Lightheaded with the end of their first battle.

"Hey! That was close," Tom burst out. Uncharacteristically: normally he did not chat, did not joke around; he did his own job with a minimum of words and expected others to do the same. In the troop he was known as the Iceman.

"Hey! It sure was."

"We blasted those suckers. Hey! Hey!"

"Hey! Hey-hey!" A chorus. More laughter.

"When we started rolling sideways, I thought—fuck, our ass is cooked!"

"Amazing," said Billetts. "That's what I was thinking."

"Alright! Hey!"

"Hey-hey-hey!"

HOME's screens were again demanding attention, beeping and flashing. Napoli and Billetts both quieted down and attended to them. HOME was summarizing the battle status of Apache Troops Alpha and Charlie as well as their own Troop Bravo. Between each update came the message:

CONTINUE MONITORING SCREEN FOR FURTHER DETAILS

HOME seemed jealous of attention to anyone else. Just now Tom was enjoying flying the Apache as never before, enjoying the view from its floor-to-ceiling windows of his troop floating over the smoky battlefield. He was willing to check HOME from time to time, just not every moment. But HOME grasped at him with psychological tentacles. Keep focused on me, not on what's outside, it insisted wordlessly. Texts and icons came and went on the green and blue screens; but the screens were always glowing from the control panel, always the same electronic personality behind them. HOME was steady and reassuring, all right. At the same time, annoying.

Never before had Tom felt so centered in his own body, riding the excitement of pure confident emotional energy. For once in his life, he was happy to share a buzz of dialogue with his copilot. Watching the world outside the cockpit's transparent walls, minutes ago so dangerous and now so beautiful. But HOME did not want him in any of those spaces; nowhere but in its own hyperspace, a world made up purely of information, a world in which his own helicopter, his own body, did not exist except as a electronic flicker in an infinity of circuits.

Screw you, said Tom voicelessly, addressing HOME. You're just a fancy video game. When your icons get shot, they drop off the screen, filed under CASUALTIES. When we get shot, it's real three-dimensional steel and explosives flying through the air. Right there, *there*—he jabbed his finger into the third dimension to prove it.

Tom Napoli does not think all this in so many words. A new kind of tension is stretching him out like a rubber band. One end is an invisible ribbon attached from the center of his head through his eyeballs to HOME's screens. At the other end, centered in the middle of his chest and radiating out into his arms is his desire to fly the Apache, to watch the rest of his troop in the air around him, to see Billetts's face, to watch whatever he felt like except the control panel. HOME feels like a drug injected into his brain he is fighting to shake off.

"HOME can be a pain in the ass, can't it?" he said to Billetts.

Before he can answer, the blast of battle again surrounds them. Rockets and machine-gun fire are streaming up from beyond the row of burning armored vehicles clustered along Emmetsburg Road. The rubber band pulling him to HOME slackens.

Napoli is centered in his own body, flying his helicopter, fingering the trigger of the under-nose cannon. The cockpit's front windshield slants downwards over the Apache's pug nose so the pilot can see the cannon slung underneath sending a stream of bullets to its target. The image flashes in Tom's mind: like a man pissing bullets from a metal cock.

Small arms fire rattles on the armored shell of the Apache, making a terrible racket, doing no damage. The slightly nauseating smell of burning diesel fuel from the defeated army below fills his nostrils.

"What a stink, hey Billetts?"

Billetts does not reply. He is slumped backwards unmoving, his head dangling. His exposed throat is bright red and a dark blotch of blood is soaking the front of his flak jacket.

At the same moment Napoli becomes conscious of another smell, burning electric wiring. Somewhere in the cockpit systems are going down, ceasing to function.

HOME's blue and green computer screens are lighting up at EASTCOM battle headquarters, and this time it is no simulation. It is five o'clock on a May morning, and a map of the central Pennsylvania countryside is becoming covered with moving blips of light. Other screens zoom in on local sectors, kill boxes where the enemy will be attacked. Still other screens are posting columns of numbers, planes in the air, missiles on their way, positional headings.

First action: in the middle of the front, blue icons are moving up on Gettysburg. A row of ten Apache attack helicopters, probing the CSSA line. Red target icons light up, ground vehicles caught in the helicopters' infrared sensors and relayed back to HOME's computers. A row of tanks, dug in alongside the Emmetsburg Road, the address spelled out in standard MapFinder fashion. Immediately, the signature of missiles firing off from the Apaches appears on the screen, and a counterfire of surface-to-air missiles from a ground battery hidden until this moment. One of the helicopter icons disappears, along with most of the tanks. A second exchange of missiles; more tank icons are gone, and so is the SAM battery. The first skirmish of the battle of Second Gettysburg is over.

How many humans are dead, or who they are, does not appear on the computer screens. The programming does not yet encompass this; the priority is not high enough; perhaps it never will be; perhaps it would not be good for morale. What is linked together through the computers are the blips on the screen, the vehicles of war, firing, targeted or knocked out. The purpose of this first skirmish of the battle has been to draw the enemy weapons out of their hiding in electronic darkness and to show where they are, so that they can be destroyed.

USA probes are appearing all over the map now, filling the computer screens that line EASTCOM's war room, and all the auxiliary computers in nearby rooms feeding information into HOME.

General Maddux is at the central desk, flanked by his aides. He leans forward intently, watching the screens but at the moment doing nothing, issuing no commands, merely following the plan as it played out, this time in real time, after dozens of simulations. Later there will be adjustments to make, options to take; but war gaming has gone through most of the things that can come up, and the computer program is set to follow a prearranged path, unless it is overruled.

Each echelon of command has undergone an exhaustive set of practice simulations; every commander knows what he will do because he had done it before, seen it on the screens, seen the outcomes; has sat in meetings where the different scenarios have been explained in PowerPoint presentations on big screens, confirmed on laptops sitting on their own desks.

It is why the buildup for this battle has been so long in coming, months after month, while General Maddux and General Harris have gotten everything right, checked every contingency, checkmated every possible CSSA countermove, while Secretary Madigan peered over their shoulders, and President Jennings has blundered impatiently around the war room in his rumpled suit and big clumsy body.

The world's biggest reality show was beginning. Every level, from General Maddux at the center of EASTCOM, to the lowest tank commander and helicopter pilot, was watching the same battle unfold. There are hundreds of views that HOME can show, and not everyone watches the same view at once; but it is one single television program they are watching from different angles and different degrees of closeup, viewers and simultaneously actors of the same show.

Watching the screens, General Maddux repeated to himself phrases from the endless meetings of past months, slogans he has announced and that have gone reverberating around the staff meetings, finding their way into every PowerPoint presentation.

Maximal impact on enemy nerve centers. Sever the brain from the body.

Take out its communications, command, control, computers and intelligence. Blind its eyes so its units fumble in the dark even in broad daylight. Create the fog of war for the enemy, while rising above the fog ourselves. Render the enemy deaf and dumb, unable to hear, unable to receive reports from command, unable to send information up the channels. Unable to call out for help; no reinforcements on the way, no counterattacks because the enemy army no longer functions as an organization lending mutual support to its parts. Reduce them to little cells, ready to be picked off.

Lethal as their weapons may be, they are useless if they are firing alone in the dark. That is why the weight of the first attacks were aimed at the enemy's nerves and sensors, rather than his fighting forces. The little helicopter assault at Gettysburg was just a probe, to bring their command system alive.

Maddux surfed from one screen to another. Everything at this early phase was going well. He allowed himself the luxury of being professionally bored.

This will be faster than any campaign in Civil War One, he was thinking. They couldn't help slogging it out through attrition. We've perfected blitzkrieg. The Germans studied Stonewall Jackson's campaigns before they overran France in 1940. All the blitzkriegs since World War II have been ours. The long left hook out of the desert from Kuwait in '91. The dash to Baghdad in '03. They'll study the early Iraq campaign in the War Colleges for years to come. That campaign, and this one, Operation Liberty Bell, commanded by yours truly.

Maddux regarded himself as a military intellectual, a soldier-scholar, despite his hick-sounding name, Billy Jo, given by rural parents, and accepted without comment by fellow southerners while he was working his way up from Arkansas and Texas A&M. He was proud to know who Clausewitz was, proud of his expanded horizons that embraced not just American patriotism but the historic military art.

Snotty northern intellectuals always made his palms sweat, and self-consciousness made him angry at himself for being ashamed of his southern accent, but too proud to change it. Snotty northern liberals with their blogs and their op-ed pieces, who don't even know there is a world of great military thinkers who stretch back to the ancient Chinese general Sun Tzu, whose doctrines are taught in all the War Colleges but not in the Ivy League snob colleges. They call us bigots.

Maddux rankled in his inner thoughts. They're the ones who are prejudiced against southern accents. For them, Tommy Franks' great campaign in the Gulf War will never be in the history books, because their library is closed. We'll show them.

Get yourself focused, Billy Jo Maddux told himself. Everything looks OK. Bomber fleet in the air: B-52s carrying precision-guided bombs to knock out the headquarters of O'Leary and Rosenfeld. Cruise missiles, faster on their way to targets, are not yet launched; they should arrive simultaneously with the gravity bombs dropped from the planes. Politics by other means. The aim is not just to defeat their military, but bring down the CSSA government. Not just a battle; a campaign to win the war. It was worth taking a year to plan Operation Liberty Bell, worth whatever it takes to get everything right.

All levels: check. HOME displayed a big map of eastern North America, Illinois to Maine. Cruise missiles were now launched, their blips on the screen joining the bomber blips, heading for Chicago, New York City, Albany, even Boston. The screen dazzled with impacts piling up in the lower Hudson Valley.

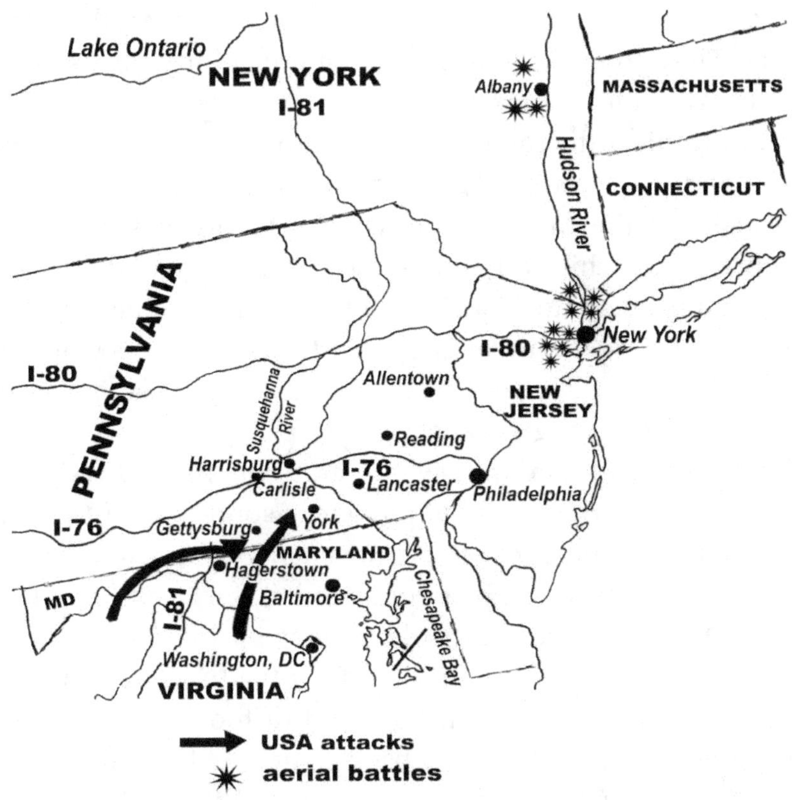

For the first time in over sixty-five years, USA forces did not have control of the air, because they had split their air assets down the middle, and the two halves had been fighting it out for almost a year, and suffering considerable attrition in the process.

Bombs and missiles by now should be hitting the government centers in Chicago, in New York, and elsewhere. It was a bit tricky. Their triple-A—anti-aircraft-artillery—is as good as ours. Patriot antiballistics systems to shoot down incoming rockets; SAMs to take out planes. The question is, is our offense better than their defense? We'll soon find out.

Maddux spoke to an aide, called for detailed assessment on New York City targets. Not much available yet. The enemy had fired some Patriot ABMs; several of our missiles had been intercepted. Others were getting through. Too early to tell.

Shock and awe, like Colin Powell said in the first Gulf War. It's the psychology of it. You don't have to knock out everything to have an effect. They could have lots of communications hardware left. It always turns out afterwards that air strikes never do as much damage as you think at the time. But you can paralyze them psychologically—keep them worried about what's going to hit them next.

He checked the theatre map again. The green screen showed thick clusters of white blips over New York City and Chicago indicating munitions impacts. He rapidly checked damage estimates. Nothing much yet. The inflated optimistic assessments would come in later in the day. He expected little on that score. General Maddux prided himself on being a realist.

The harder question was: where are their battle headquarters? EASTCOM had worked up its intelligence sources, and battle plans allocated a large component to hitting enemy command.

General Stevenson Bouvier commanded the Northeastern Army of the CSSA. There were plenty of interviews with him in the enemy press, plenty of sound bites on rebel TV. Maddux flared his nostrils in disgust. Bouvier was a rich boy, rare in today's army, although common enough in the old army back before the Korean War. Patton had been a rich boy too, but Bouvier was something else, a political general. His family was related to the wife of a previous president, back when the liberals held the presidency; he'd been expecting to be jumped to Chairman of the Joint Chiefs of Staff, if the liberals had won the last election. Expecting, no doubt, to make a reputation as the liberal reformer of military institutions, the anti-Madigan, and to ride that reputation into the Presidency, or at least Secretary of State or some other cushy job. Stevenson Bouvier was not what General Maddux thought of as a professional, dedicated to the military art.

Again class resentment rankled in the background. Billy Jo Maddux from Arkansas—like Major Debra Zielkowski, who stood behind him with a sheaf of notes, daughter of anti-communist immigrants from the Ukraine—was typical of today's army, unfashionable people who believed in their country as their highest value. Even Jefferson Gray had risen on the army like an elevator out of the ghetto. He had gone over to the other side, but Maddux half forgave him; it was an understandable motive, not to abandon your own people.

But Stevenson Bouvier was another species, if loyal to anything, loyal to fashionable ideas and fashionable people. Born with a silver soundbite in his mouth. Maddux mentally congratulated himself on his witticism. Nevertheless Billy Jo Maddux had a sour feeling in his stomach, remembering Bouvier's manner when he was only a Colonel, with a smiling way of speaking that made his superior officer feel that in some indescribable way he was being mocked.

Amazing that Jeff Gray, as commander of all the CSSA forces, would put up with Bouvier in an important command. But then, he probably had no say in the matter. The CSSA is just loosely stitched together. Their watchword is local control. A fancy way of saying the politicos call the shots, each for the benefit of their home district. They won't be calling it much longer, Maddux said to himself.

The stench of burning electric wiring filled the helicopter cockpit. Captain Tom Napoli made a hurried check. Flight controls still working, sluggishly. Most weapons operative, except the ones Billetts controlled. Fuel doesn't seem to be leaking.

HOME was glowing calmly, green screen by blue screen, on the front panel. In a few seconds it displayed a reassuring message:

APACHE BRAVO TROOP LEADER HIT

DAMAGE LIGHT

ALL SYSTEMS FUNCTIONAL EXCEPT PORT SIDE
ROCKETS

The ground fire was still coming.

For the third time this flight, tension was pulling Tom Napoli in opposite directions. Should he pull out of the battle, evacuate Billetts back to base? Don't know how badly he's hit. Medics might be able to save him. Or keep up the attack, until we're ordered back? Our mission is to draw enemy fire, smoke them out into the open so that the heavyweights can hit them. We've done that.

But where are the heavyweights? No Air Force strikes have arrived yet. Ground armor will take time to get here. The battle's still on. Outside the window, Napoli watches the rest of his helicopter troop in action, wheeling to new positions on the battlefield, firing rockets.

Is he a coward after all, turning tail when the fighting gets tough? Napoli imagines himself back at base, safely on the ground waiting when the rest of his helicopters come in. Greeting the brave ones who performed their mission all the way to the end.

Tension pulling him like a rubber band towards the forward edge of the battlefield. Tension pulling him in the other direction: his new bond with Billetts. Suddenly, the only man he ever cared about. His closest friend! The Iceman thawing in combat fire, his humanity opening up.

"Billetts!" No answer. "Bill!"

No sound from the frontseater.

Is he already dead? Thought he saw the body move—just the copter lurching? Heavy fire outside. Take evasive action. What if I get him back to base, find out he's already dead? But never can tell. Lots of stories about medical miracles in Iraq. Last minute surgeries. KIA is way down in US wars since helicopter evacuations came in. But does a copter evacuate itself?

The tension is making Napoli angry. Longing to release it, he blasts off the nose cannon in the direction of flashes in the ground fog below.

Call HOME. Let it decide. What is policy on wounded crewmen? Depends on the situation. HOME must have it programmed in. But what program? Evacuation of wounded takes precedent—objective: minimize combat deaths. Or mission takes precedent—objective: win the battle. But Billetts' body is still slumped two feet away. HOME can decide, has already decided. Just need to radio in, find out what their decision is.

Napoli opens his mouth, but no voice waves agitate the air between his lips and the radio microphone curving forward from his helmet. It's my decision, he thinks, not theirs. He's my friend. It's my mission. Decide it yourself!

He pushes down on the stick, veering towards the battle line. Catching up with his troop.

Before he can locate a target, HOME's blue screen begins flashing again:

APACHE TROOP BRAVO: RETURN TO BASE

MISSION ACCOMPLISHED

A tally of enemy targets destroyed follows.

Napoli speaks into the microphone. *"Apache Bravo leader to base. I have one casualty. Frontseater unconscious. Looks like a throat wound."*

"Roger, Apache Bravo leader. Make top speed evacuation. You have priority landing. Medivac unit will be standing by. Over."

Swinging the copter around and accelerating to a hundred thirty knots, Napoli leaves his troop to follow in his wake. The body beside him looks dead. HOME's green and blue screens glow serenely on the panel. As the landscape of southern Pennsylvania scrolls beneath him, leaving the acrid smoke of Gettysburg battlefield behind, Captain Napoli is unsure whether he has experienced a victory or a defeat.

Where is HOME? Its data exist in hyperspace—which is to say, nowhere in particular: just a huge number of electronic files with a program that can jump from any file to any other, in any order what-soever. Its worlds are as infinite as the combinations the computer has been programmed to make.

Not to say that HOME has no ties to the three-dimensional world of time and space. Its tentacles are everywhere.

In the sky, for instance, over the northeastern section of North America, where the air war is progressing. Where USA fighters and bombers are striking at government buildings in Albany, NY; evading and countering anti-aircraft artillery and surface-to-air missiles at Route 128 around Boston; dogfighting CSSA fighters over the north-ern New Jersey approaches to New York City. All these USA aircraft have their sensors, and all of them are sending data back to HOME.

But although these make up hundreds of tentacles they are not the biggest ones. HOME's links to the combat planes, if we could make them visible as streams of data flowing through the atmosphere back to USA bases on the ground, are like raindrops in a storm. The aerial battle is taking place ten thousand to twenty thousand feet up, two to four miles high; from the airspace above it comes a river of data, several rivers, mighty Mississippis in the sky.

What is up there? At first glance, a half dozen commercial air-liners, flying in seemingly blissful ignorance above the battle below. On closer look, there is nothing blissful or ignorant about them. A couple of Boeing 707s, the ordinary vehicle of coast-to-coast airline travel, droning rather slowly just under thirty thousand feet, making a mere 350 miles per hour. A little odd, since airliners generally fly in the mid-30,000s, and their timetables usually keep them over 500 miles per hour, hurrying to an on-time arrival at LAX or JFK. These Boeings are not in a hurry, not going anywhere in particular; if we could hover in the air like angels, we would see they are accompa-nied by a ring of fighter planes like the palace guard surrounding the queen. These are the aerial centers of the air battle: AWACS, Airborne Warning And Control System.

Each AWACS plane is surmounted by what looks like a giant frisbee disk elevated on struts a dozen feet above the fuselage—one reason why the plane is relatively slow. It is a rotating radar dome thirty feet in diameter, which can track any plane at any altitude up to two hundred miles away. Inside the plane, where normally two hundred passengers would sit, a dozen electronic specialists are tending equipment that can sort friendly aircraft from enemy aircraft, sending out information that guides the friendlies on their flight paths—and keeps them from colliding with each other as they zoom through combat—while targeting their weapons on the hostiles. Other equipment brightens the radar signals, straining out ground clutter that would confuse a lesser radar system.

All this mighty stream of data is not only showering raindrops of information back at the planes under its control in its area of sky, but is flowing in a torrent back to HOME, where the data will become mixed and matched in an even larger combination.

Why mixed? Because radar is only one mode of perception, one sense; and HOME has all five senses of a human being, and more. It is not just an eye, but a brain—if a brain is the locus where all the sensory circuits intersect, and connect with the motor circuits that execute action and in turn provide feedback on the updated situation—and so on endlessly in the loop that makes up conscious thinking.

Five senses, classically: sight, sound, smell, taste and touch. HOME shows that there are many more senses than this. Radar is a kind of sight, but it is something like the sight of a bat—although that is really sonar, sending out sound waves of high-pitched squeaks and listening acutely for their echoes, which the bat brain forms into an image of the world—blind in some dimensions, hyper-acute in another. Radar can see through clouds, fog, storms, day or night, any weather. But it sees in blurry images, and sees best when its target is moving.

Another set of HOME's eyes, besides AWACS, are circling the battlefield higher up, above forty thousand feet. These too are Boeing 707s, called JSTARS, but instead of a frisbee dome towering over its tail, each carries a sleek canoe-shaped cylinder slung under the front of its belly. This looks like a torpedo or a rocket, but it is another kind of radar antenna. Like a bat, it sends out signals and then reads them on the rebound, in this case reading the frequency shift of the returning signal for clues as to what it has encountered. JSTARS means Joint STARS, but it has nothing to do with astronomy. It doesn't look at the stars but tracks vehicles on the ground. It can see them, electronically, out to a hundred fifty miles away, preparatory to attacking them: STARS means Surveillance Target Attack Radar System, and it is Joint because it works jointly with other systems to put together a composite picture from many kinds of sensors.

JSTARS can track six hundred vehicles simultaneously, if they are the size of a car or bigger. But its vision, too, is rather blurred, and it cannot tell what kind of vehicles they are—only what direction they are moving and how fast—nor what kind of weapons they are carrying, nor even if they are friend or foe. Other information needs to be jointly integrated into the system to sharpen the picture. And JSTARS is usually blind to stationary objects; something like the way a bird, by playing dead, can mystify a cat, which sees rather poorly (among other reasons, being color blind) and which must wait for the prey to move in order to pounce on it.

At the moment, JSTARS has relatively little to do. The CSSA army isn't doing much moving. Icons are active around targets sites in New York and Boston—firetrucks trying to contain the damage of the USA aerial attack. The battlefields in central Pennsylvania show mostly helicopter flights—our own; and now tanks moving forward. A few enemy vehicles are escaping toward the north.

To improve on the eyes of JSTARS, we need to turn to HOME's other sensor inputs. One of these is circling the battlefield still higher up, at sixty-five thousand feet, above the level where most planes can operate. This is Global Hawk. It can stay aloft for two days at a time; and it can skim the lower fringe of outer space, because it carries no human crew. It is a UAV, an Unmanned Aerial Vehicle. It is, quite literally, a robot eye in the sky. Its eyes are much better than human eyes, much better than the radar eyes of the human-crewed vehicles circling so much closer to the earth. It takes video images and beams them back to the ground—electro-optical images like photographs enhanced to bring out the significant contours of ground objects viewed from twelve miles up. These are daytime photos, dependent on cloud cover and weather conditions. At the moment, the weather over central Pennsylvania is fair, scattered clouds—but there is heavy smoke cover, especially over Gettysburg battlefield.

Global Hawk has another set of eyes that see through the smoke: infrared (IR) sensors that make images out of contrasts in heat. The IR sensors are showing numerous bright conflagrations under the smoke: these are one source of HOME's messages of near total demolition of CSSA hardware, now adding up to fifteen hundred tanks and armored vehicles, three hundred artillery pieces of various kinds. Unlike in JSTARS radar images, vehicles do not have to be moving for their infrared signatures to appear, although the hotter they are the brighter they glow, so vehicles with their engines turned off have a better chance of evading detection.

Human bodies, too, give off an infrared signature, but too weak to be seen from thousands of feet in the air. But since IR sensors are ubiquitous in all branches of the USA military, there are plenty of sensors nearer the action: tanks moving up on Gettysburg from the south, armored personnel carriers full of infantry ready to dismount to clear the battlefield, each man carrying his own night-vision goggles which give IR images, not to mention IR sensors on their automatic rifles.

Whatever CSSA troops have survived the helicopter assault, wherever they are dug in or hiding, will soon become heat images on the screens of numerous weapons, and data integrated into the files of HOME.

Sight, sound, smell, taste, touch. The senses integrate, blend into one, because HOME can translate whatever it takes in, and output it as visual images on a screen, or as columns of numbers, or bars of a graph. For that matter, HOME could translate it all into the auditory dimension as high frequency squeaks, if it wanted to represent the battlefield into the brain of a bat.

At present, visual output will do. Infrared, of course, is not really an image; strictly speaking, it is the human sense of touch, the feeling of heat; although we think of touch as a contact sense, up close to one's body, heat travels at a distance and we do not have to put our hand in a fire to feel it. Infrared sensors make touch into a distance sense, like eyes, and going touch one better, store it in an image that stays constant on the screen as long as we want to keep it.

Sight and touch, yes; what about sound, smell, taste? Sound is being recorded by Army Intelligence operatives tapping into telephone systems, and monitoring cell phones on the enemy side of the battlefield: a fairly reliable signal of enemy preparations to move, or attack. Here too the CSSA forces are surprisingly quiet on the battlefields of southern Pennsylvania, although there is more chatter further to the rear, perhaps a sign of panicky retreat.

Smell and taste might seem trivial in war; more important for love and dining, for sniffing flowers and perfume and savoring well-prepared food. But smell and taste are chemical senses, buds in nose and mouth that react to different kinds of chemicals carried in the air or put inside the cavities of the human head. HOME is not very interested in these kinds of chemicals, but some of its sensor links inspect other sorts of chemical vestiges. Combat infantry carry machines that analyze swipes on a suspicious civilian's hands, revealing whether he has handled explosives; one step away from the suspicious wife smelling liquor on her husband's breath. HOME does not have much information, yet, on the chemical smell and taste of the CSSA forces; but it will come.

If HOME had emotions, it would be feeling very good about itself right now. But if HOME were a person, he or she (or probably a sexless neuter *it*) would be a very modest personality. HOME is not at all egotistical, since it is a team player, a team made up of sensors, weapons, supplies, vehicles, human beings, and computers. Better yet, HOME is the very team-ness of the team, HOME is the collective in the individual, the part of our selves that is bigger than ourselves, the soul in each of us that is part of the bigger Soul beyond.

HOME constitutes a religion of its own, giving assurance and security; it is omniscient where we are limited to our local views; omnipotent since nothing can overpower the forces of the whole marshaled into unified effort; supremely good since it has no petty self-interests. Though it sees our mistakes, it is merciful in correcting them since they all figure in the perspective of the larger plan.

"I can smell victory," General Maddux said. "These things look harder in the planning phase than they turn out to be. We're imposing system collapse on them. It'll be the three-weeks-to-Baghdad campaign all over again."

It is the second day of Operation LIBERTY BELL, and all is right in HOME's world. HOME is even more efficient than usual. Its estimated times for full reports keep getting shorter and shorter, and the reports are all good.

"Praise the Lord!" intoned President Jennings, visiting the war room. "God's enemies are flattened everywhere, like the wheat of the fields when the thresher comes. I have to admit, boys"—gesturing around the assembly of generals and officials, pivoting clumsily like a bear on hind legs—"there was a time when I thought this day would never come."

General Harris was silent, grinding his prognathous jaw.

"Praise the Lord," General Maddux said. "But please keep in mind, Mr. President, we've had less than thirty-six hours of combat. There's still a lot more to come."

"Didn't we take Gettysburg?"

"Yes, we did. The entire enemy front from Hagerstown to York has caved in. Their forces in western Maryland are withdrawing to the west, crossing over into the mountains of West Virginia. Their forces to the east are withdrawing back across the Susquehanna."

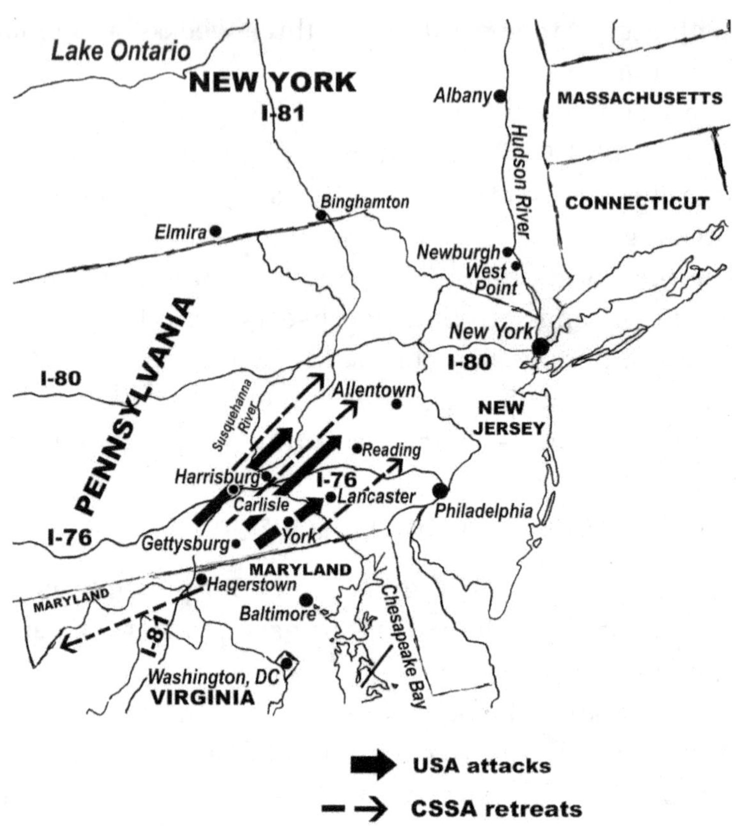

Jennings indicated the line of that river on HOME's map display. "Those are the Susquehanna bridges, I-76 at Harrisburg, aren't they? How come they haven't been knocked out?"

"The Air Force could knock them out, easily," said General Harris. "But we have a lot of targets to hit, further back. Anyhow, we'd have to rebuild the bridges, since our own ground forces are almost in position to push across right now. In fact, we've dropped in special ops to keep the rebels from blowing them up. Sometimes we move so fast that destroying enemy infrastructure would just slow us down."

"We're into their defense in depth," said General Maddux. "Their reserves are probably dispersed for another hundred miles or more, back to Allentown, P A, and Elmira, New York. The next step is to take them out."

"Can they counterattack us?" Jennings squinted at the screen. "Y'all thought about that?"

"We're hitting them all over the battlefield, wherever they stick their heads up," said Maddux. "More importantly, we've pretty much silenced their command and communications centers. The way they're responding, it looks like we've been pretty effective."

"You mean we've knocked out New York and Albany?" Jennings' face perched on the edge of a smile of righteous triumph.

"Not yet. Aerial battles are still going on up there. But their air wings are not putting up as much of a fight as we thought they would. We anticipated they would ferry more fighters to the Eastern theatre from the Midwest and West Coast. And their ground fire isn't very effective. It looks like our offensive air capacity beats their ground-to-air defense."

"No surprise there," Harris said.

"In another day," said Maddux, "we should have complete dominance in the air."

"Anything in the situation that worries you?" Jennings looked around the circle.

He was met for the most part by smiles and confident shakes of the head. Harris frowned disdainfully at this show of good cheer. "I'd be happier if we pinned down exactly where their battle headquarters is. You can deal with the politicians. I'd like to blast a few traitors in their command posts."

"I saw a TV interview with General Bouvier just this morning," Jennings said. "He claimed their battle was going well. That they've driven back our attack, and shot down hundreds of our planes."

"It's propaganda," Maddux said. "We've analyzed the video. Probably it was made days ago, and released to the media today by arrangement. It doesn't mention anything specific, except the air attack on New York, which was pretty much a given."

"We're going to post the video on HOME," said one of the computation specialists. "Our troops will get a kick out of it."

"What I have in mind," Jennings insisted, "is whether the video gives any clues where it was made. Where Bouvier's headquarters is."

Maddux turned to the back row of officers, cued Major Zielkowski. "Probably not too far from New York City," she said. "Slick production, probably by media professionals, not by military photographers. Interior rather posh, not a genuine battle headquarters." Pause to let the contrast sink in with the Spartan functionality of the present scene. "We think probably Bouvier is in the vicinity of Elmira or Binghampton. Or maybe as far back as Newburgh—George Washington's old headquarters—or West Point. They might be counting on our sentimentality not to bomb those locations."

"Are we bombing them?"

"We're hitting everything where there are indications of military communications," Maddux said.

"That's fine," said Jennings. "By the way, Major—" looking past Maddux, indicating her part in the proceedings was not yet over, "you're an expert on what the enemy is doing. Is there anything that bothers you about the information you're getting?"

"It looks very good, Mr. President." She watched him cock a quizzical eyebrow. "Just one thing."

"Yes?"

"The tally of enemy equipment destroyed and captured. We had estimated they had about three hundred battle helicopters. But so far there are less than a dozen reported downed or taken on the ground. It's way out of line with the numbers of tanks and artillery pieces—we've destroyed over seventy-five percent of our original estimates. Same with APCs—we've knocked out six hundred of the original eight hundred."

"Probably the original estimates were off," Maddux said. "See if you can fix that, Major," he said over his shoulder, turning to face Jennings. "What I'm wondering about, Mr. President, is whether it is really Bouvier over there."

"Who else would it be?"

"Jefferson Gray."

"That's ridiculous," said General Harris. "Intelligence reports show Gray is at Chicago. He's planning a big offensive in the Midwest. Probably trying to crank it up while we're concentrating here in the East. Good reason to get this over with as fast as possible, then transfer forces to the Central theatre of operations." Meaning, among other things, out of General Maddux's command.

"I wouldn't trust those intelligence reports too much, Curt," said Maddux. "You've got to think of the psychology of it. Jeff Gray never liked to be out of the action. He knows the big showdown is here, in the East. I have a feeling he's over there, somewhere."

"Jeff Gray is leaving Bouvier out to dry," said Harris. "He's got his own front to worry about."

"We'll sort it all out, in a week or so," said Jennings, amiably intervening. "In God's good time. We'll look back and pick up the pieces, and see how it was all prearranged from Above."

He turned to go. "One last thought, good people. As the battle winds down, let us be especially careful. We don't want any civilian casualties. Nothing to taint our great victory in the eyes of God—or the media."

It is the third day of battle, and Lt. Gabriel Napoli, Army of the Coalition of Secular States of America, is still alive. His location is some miles to the west of the spot next to the Gettysburg National Park Headquarters where he had commanded a SAM battery two days earlier. He is in the midst of a CSSA unit he has never seen before, in a farmhouse in the folds of the narrow valleys that crease the foothills of the Appalachians.

Gabriel has been getting plenty of sleep. First involuntarily, thanks to a concussion when missiles had rained down from a helicopter attack that first morning. He woke up, hours later, to find himself at a medical collection post, waiting to be evacuated to a field hospital. The CSSA medics were moving the wounded much more slowly than usual in the US Army, since no helicopters were operating on their side of the battlefield; but ambulances pulled up from time to time, with big red crosses painted on their roofs for visibility to aircraft, and loaded the most severely wounded.

There was some low moaning and bursts of slurred talk, but the wounded were for the most part quiet, the first act of the medics being to inject them with morphine. The shrieks and cries of the wounded, which observers of the First Civil War had found so horrifying, were largely missing, except for the first moments before the medics arrived.

Gabriel had not been loaded on an ambulance. Except for a splitting headache and overall wooziness, he seemed to be bodily intact. A soldier in the gray battle dress of the CSSA had helped him to his feet, and led him off to a waiting pickup truck. Gabriel sat in the flatbed as the soldier went back for more. Eventually the truck was full of unharmed and lightly wounded men. The pickup truck was painted in civilian colors, without military markings, and it followed the red-crossed ambulances off the battlefield, skirting the rules of war.

After a few miles, the pickup left the ambulances and turned onto a back road. It crossed fields, sped in the shade of clumps of trees, went up and down the roller-coaster of little hills that made up the central Pennsylvania countryside, crossing tiny one-lane bridges over miniature ravines and brooks. For a while they passed what seemed to Gabriel a huge number of smoking carcasses of vehicles, burnt-out tanks and artillery pieces. In the midst of the worst headache of his life, the thought grew in him: it was a devastating defeat. He tried to sink back into sleep.

Eventually, they were unloaded at a farmhouse. Gabriel recognized several soldiers from his unit, tried to nod at them. He could scarcely hold up his head. No one spoke or made eye contact. They seemed ashamed to be seen by anyone.

The soldier who had first guided Gabriel from the medical outpost was standing over him, explaining the accommodations. His voice came from far away, and Gabriel could hardly bring himself to give it any importance. The name tag on the right breast of his uniform said ALFREDSEN, and he had the insignia of a sergeant.

"Just rest easy, Lieutenant. Ain't gonna be shit happening round here today. You and your men get some sleep. There's food when you want it." He indicated packages of MREs. Sgt. Alfredsen, looking very old and moving heavily, helped him unwrap it. Mechanically, Gabriel started to eat. He hadn't realized how hungry he was.

"Where are we? What unit is this?"

"This is Second Artillery Brigade, CSSA. Looks like you're artillery too. More 'n likely you'll be folded into us. Your unit took quite a beating."

"How'd your guys do?" Gabriel was starting to feel like a lieutenant again, getting a briefing.

"Far as I know, we ain't lost nothing. We're laying low. Dug in deep. Outta harm's way."

"That's great for you," Gabriel had said. Anger woke him up a bit.

"Shit, Lieutenant. You ought to know them holy-army fellas over there have anti-battery radar. Soon as we fire, they can pick it up. Relay the location right away to their own artillery. Half the time their counterfire is on its way before our shells hit the ground. And they've got a precision fix, while we're just aiming in their general direction. Don't it stand to reason, the second guy to fire has the advantage in this game? That's why we're laying low."

"They didn't tell us that. Our mission was to fire at incoming copters. We did it. And we got blasted." Gabriel glanced around the room at the rest of the survivors, still heads down. Tried not to think of the others at the medical collection point.

"That's the army for you," Alfredsen said. "Somebody has to make the other guy start in firing."

"But why us? Why not hang somebody else out to dry?" Gabriel looked down, wishing he hadn't said it. The answer was obvious, if you were a soldier.

Sgt. Alfredsen acted as if he had not heard him. "Anyhow, you guys don't have to do nothing for a couple days. Orders are to lay low." He held out a palm full of pills. "Take a couple of these. Get some sleep. You'll be good 'n' rested in a couple days, when new orders are coming in."

"New orders? What orders?" Gabriel nevertheless took two of the pills, put them in his mouth.

So Gabriel slept, deep in the hyperspace of dreams, where nothing made sense. The distant thunder of battle was still going on the second day when he stirred himself to eat. The third day, battle sounds had receded, except for the occasional streak of US Air Force jets overhead. They paid no attention to their position, streaking to unknown targets far to the northeast.

He found Sgt. Alfredsen poking at the keyboard of a laptop, hunt-and-peck method with two forefingers. He seemed to be looking for sports scores, oblivious to the fact that most sports leagues had cancelled their seasons during the war, or perhaps wishfully overlooking the fact. Alfredsen was desultorily jumping from one blog to another where fans argued with sportscasters over the merits of players.

"I didn't know you old codgers surfed the web," Gabriel said, smiling. "Shit, you don't even know how to type."

"I'm checking for orders, you wet puppy," Alfredsen said, not looking up.

"I'll bet you are. Why don't you use the radio? It's encrypted."

"We're supposed to stay off the radio til we get a code message. And no cell phones. Them holy-army people are monitoring call volume. Even if they don't know what it means, they'll know something is up, and they can figure out more or less where we are. We're supposed to been wiped out."

"How long are we going to lay low? And what are we going to do when time is up?"

"Don't know yet. I figure it's got something to do with them decoys."

"Decoys?"

"Yep. Phony tank hulls. Phony APCs, phony artillery pieces. Commander had us bury them pieces all over the place. Shit, some of them was dug in right next to you on the Emmetsburg Road in Gettysburg."

Gabriel was stunned. "Christ, they didn't even tell us. We were defending a bunch of decoys. And getting blasted for it."

"Well, if you think about it, Lieutenant, somebody has to be alive round that part of the battlefield, or the other side's gonna catch on there ain't no soldiers there. You gotta decoy 'em into the trap."

"What trap?" Gabriel was angry again. "We're the only ones who got blasted in that battle. We're the ones who ran away."

"Battle ain't over yet. Commander said set out that first bunch of decoys where they can spot 'em easy. Second round of decoys we've still got hidden, deep." Alfredsen waved his arms toward the hillsides of this abandoned mining district. "Them decoys are coming out when we get the order."

"I get it," said Gabriel, suddenly eager. "We'll uncover the decoys, lure the US army in, and then blast them. We've got plenty of real artillery and tanks dug in back here too, right?"

"Sure nuff. Least I think so. My job ain't with the real stuff, just with them decoys." Alfredsen leaned back with a prideful grin. "Rest of this here army don't even know about us."

"Well, you sure fooled me," Gabriel said. He wasn't certain whether to be rueful or pleased at the larger organization whose scheme was just now revealing itself.

"If you can fool your own army, you can fool the other fellas. Think about it. Would you want just any soldier who got picked up by the enemy to spill the beans to 'em? Blow the whole plan. This way everybody has their own orders. Chances of them finding out the whole plan are way low."

Gabriel's depression, which had weighed on him with the loginess of too much sleep, was no longer there. Suddenly he felt clear, elated, alive again. "When's the order coming?"

"Ain't here yet. That's the army for you. Hurry up and wait."

Gabriel wandered around. He began rousting the troops he knew, checking on them, telling them to be ready for action. Acting an officer again. Trying to spread his good mood; feeling a little success as his troops began to revive.

A Colonel Brassley in the gray army uniform of the CSSA appeared, introduced himself to Gabriel. He was for the time being folded into the special artillery unit. Sgt. Alfredsen had the communications link and would explain how the orders were to be carried out. In this meantime, just wait.

After a long boring time, darkness fell. Alfredsen was at the laptop again. Beckoned.

"It's here. Look."

"*Will the Red Sox ever make it back to the World Series? Last season they were dead and buried. But remember, it is written: On the third day, he rose again from the dead. That sounds like prophecy, doesn't it, Bosox fans?*"

"That's just some baseball nut."

"Nope. That's the code. On the third day, he rose again from the dead. Check the baseball chatter, commander said. That way, it ain't gonna be no mistake, somebody quoting scripture like that."

"I'll be damned," said Gabriel. "That is clever. So you suppose everybody in our army is getting this message right now?"

"Not so sure about that. This here message is for us, to put out second phase decoys. Colonel Brassley is getting this same message, and probably some other ones too. Other units have their own codes and their own websites they're supposed to check. Anyhow, I figure we'll be hearing pretty near everybody round here up in action by tomorrow morning."

Gabriel and his unit of survivors from the Gettysburg battlefield spent the night getting decoys into position. They hoisted them out of disused mineshafts, wheeled them out of old barns and silos, uncovered them from the rubbish piles of discarded machinery and rusting autos that surround the rural settlements of America. Pickups, tractors, flatbed trucks were pressed into service. From time to time Gabriel's men boarded pickups to other parts of the landscape, uncovering hidden decoys planted almost all the way back to Gettysburg and Carlisle.

Most of the decoys were light and easy to move, far lighter than the tanks and artillery they represented; but they had plenty of metal plating to attract JSTARS, and little engines designed not so much for mobility as for heat, so that the heat signature would glow in the infrared sensors of the enemy. Some were radar units, but stripped of the expensive electronics, just designed to send out signals to attract antiradar missiles and confuse the enemy into thinking something significant had been hit.

Gabriel noticed there were decoys of just about everything, but with one omission: no decoy helicopters. He asked Sgt. Alfredsen about it, as they settled into cover, while dawn began to brighten.

"Decoy of a tank is easy," Alfredsen said. "Just build that big square frame, put a turret on it. Decoy of a helicopter—that's a screwy mess. And them rotors fifty feet long—how you gonna get that inside a mineshaft? How you gonna haul something like that on a truck? The only way you can get a helicopter in here is by flying it in—and if you do that, it's gotta be a real whirlybird, not a decoy."

"Don't you suppose the enemy will notice?" Gabriel said. "They might figure something is up."

"Nah," said Alfredsen. "That's the army for you. When things get going, they can't think of everything."

With daylight the battle picked up. There were explosions in the distance. Through field glasses, Gabriel could see tanks moving on distant hills, unsure whose they were. USAF fighters were back, no longer passing overhead but swooping on strike missions against ground targets. But now the CSSA Air Force had put in an appearance. There were dogfights in the medium altitudes, sweeping under the high cumulus clouds that threatened rain later in the day.

"It's about time," Gabriel said. "Where were our planes when we needed them back at Gettysburg?"

Union forces had advanced considerably beyond their location in central Pennsylvania, around Carlisle. The battlefront, if such could be said to exist in a multilevel attack, was fifty miles ahead, beyond the Susquehanna bridges. But because this had been an attack in depth, with air, helicopter and ground forces against CSSA defenses dispersed in depth, there were plenty of pockets of fighting all through the zone of advance.

USA helicopters were droning here and there, Apache attack helicopters, troop-carrying Blackhawks and ungainly heavy transports. Gabriel could make out the places on distant hills where MLRS—Multiple-Launch Rocket Systems—were firing, by their characteristic sequence of blasts, one after another as the rockets took off from the bank of tubes, leaving a parallel set of smoking arches in the sky.

"Here's the cat-and-mouse game," said Sgt. Alfredsen. "Them fake radars we set up are out in that direction. They'll be sending out radar signals about now. Some of them USA fighters up there"—jerking a thumb at the sky—"will be releasing HARMs. Homes in on a radar signal and takes it out. Those suckers weigh eight hundred pounds and fly 1600 miles per hour—about Mach 3. Ain't no escaping a HARM once it fixes in on you." High-speed Anti-Radiation Missile meant exactly what it was.

"So what's the point of drawing their fire?" said Gabriel. "We can't knock down their jets without giving away where our radar-guided weapons are."

"Well, HARMs're so heavy that a jet fighter can't carry more'n two of 'em at a time. We've got a bunch of fake radars out there, and we'll keep on drawing their fire til there ain't no more HARMs coming in. Then the coast is clear for us to open up. Besides, them HARMs sometimes mix up which radar they're firing at. Might get diverted if they cross another radar source on the way in. 'Specially likely since there's so much radar out here on the battlefield, and the frequency spectrum that radar operates in ain't that wide. If we can get those HARMs firing round their own positions, when the enemy is in deep like this, we're gonna be the beneficiary of their fratricide."

Sgt. Alfredsen was busy with his laptop for a while, searching the civilian blogs where CSSA communications were hiding in broad daylight, like a thief in an enormous crowd.

"Looks like that round is over for now," he said. "Cat and mouse. Now who's the cat and who's the mouse? Next step, we're gonna take out their anti-battery firing systems."

Their observation post was outside a farmhouse, under cover of a trellis of blue morning glories. Through his field glasses, Gabriel could see a USA howitzer pull into position on a nearby hillside. It looked like a tank self-propelled on its treads, but with an enormous flat turret like the layer of a wedding cake, with a huge gun barrel pointed at a forty-five-degree angle into the sky. On its roof tall antenna rods and radar panels protruded at crazy angles in the air. Nearby a truck had deposited a load of artillery shells. They sat on the ground with their cone-shaped points upward like a flock of fledgling birds with greedy steel beaks waiting to be fed.

"We're opening up with some of our own artillery," Alfredsen said. "Starting in with some remote-controlled pieces, some of our old junkier equipment, with their crews dug in at a distance. Cause they're gonna get blasted as soon as them holy-army fellas pick them up on their anti-battery radar. That's the bait. Once they start firing, we'll get a fix on them with our own anti-battery radar—hit 'em with some artillery that they don't know about cause it ain't fired yet."

Near the USA howitzer on the hillside opposite, soldiers were carrying more shells to the stockpile, stripping them from their paper wrappings. They winced as the howitzer fired with a shock wave that penetrated even the stoutest earplugs. What the howitzer was aiming at could be as much as twenty miles away beyond the horizon broken by green Pennsylvania hills. The rounds flew off into the distance.

Within seconds, there was an enormous explosion on the hillside. The howitzer disappeared into a billow of dust. Fractions of a second later began a series of bright flashes on the side where the ammunition dump had been. The earth shuddered as Lt. Napoli and Sgt. Alfredsen buried their faces as deeply as they could into the garden.

When the explosions subsided across the way, they made their way to the civilian pickup truck hidden in the leafy driveway and started along the tiniest of country roads, heading west. Gabriel drove while Sgt. Alfredsen searched the laptop. In the height of the battle, with control of the air contested between both sides, it was likely no one would spot them for anything other than a civilian vehicle fleeing its home, or care to hit them when bigger targets were at stake.

"That's the army for you," Sgt. Alfredsen said. "Them fellas over there are used to playing against amateurs. Used that anti-battery radar against them Iraqis, who didn't know what they was up against. Hell, they forgot we have the same equipment they do. And if the equipment's all the same, who wins or loses depends on something else." He tapped his forehead.

CSSA equipment was beginning to appear, dug into the fields, sometimes even coming towards them along the little country roads. Gabriel pulled aside several times to let them pass. The CSSA army was heading east, moving onto the battlefield's flank. A counteroffensive was under way.

"Decoys are all used up," Alfredsen reported. "They want us back at base, to pick up ammo for our mobile artillery."

USAF planes were becoming sparse in the sky. CSSA helicopters were now visible, flying to the attack. Wave after wave came on towards the southeast, like a flock of metal albatrosses diving for a school of fish. They must have been hidden out of range, several hundred miles to the north or west, Gabriel thought. Apaches have a range of two hundred sixty-five miles; they could get here in under two hours, flying top speed; probably refueled somewhere near the battlefield, if we had refueling dumps prepared.

Enemy fire was still coming in sporadically. A CSSA artillery piece was lumbering across the field on its caterpillar tracks, except for its gray paint looking a great deal like the green USA howitzer that had blown up when Gabriel and Alfredsen had lain in the garden half an hour earlier. As the pickup sped down the little gravel road, it suddenly veered in the shock of a nearby blast. The CSSA artillery piece disappeared in a billow of dust.

Gabriel swung the wheels of the pickup into the direction of its sideways skid, regained control, lurched back onto the road and came to a stop, breathing hard. "They're not playing like they're up against amateurs now," he said, when his breath had subsided enough to talk.

"Course," said Alfredsen, "we're both rolling the dice. Even when the odds are stacked in our favor, every once in a while they're gonna get the jump on you."

They came out on a medium-size highway. More tanks passed, APCs with their turrets open, CSSA soldiers in gray riding outside, taking risks in the hot weather, with the battle still in the distance.

Parked alongside the road was a Humvee, hidden from the air under a clump of trees. Standing by the door was a tall black man, white-haired, in gray battle dress. Five stars on his collar indicated a high-ranking general.

Soldiers on the passing vehicles turned to look and wave, swarming out of the turrets.

"Jeff Gray! It's Jeff Gray!"

Jefferson Gray, General of the Armies of the CSSA, said nothing. He gave no orders. He smiled gravely, waved. Extended his arm, pointing a finger down the road where the armor was advancing. Advancing, it seemed now to every soldier who saw him, to undoubted victory.

★

It was the fourth day of battle, and Captain Tom Napoli was tired. The landscape of northeast Pennsylvania looked summer green beneath the plexiglass of his helicopter cockpit, but Napoli barely noticed. He had been awake almost continuously for seventy-two hours, keeping himself going on pills distributed at base, and by drinking caffeinated energy drinks. Behind the buzz in his forehead, there was nothing he would like more than to lie down and sleep. But the snatches of sleep he had managed were each time soon interrupted as the battle unfolded over the past three days.

The whole Union army was tired, but it was a good tiredness. They were elated with their rapid advance into enemy territory, elated with a sense of impending victory. Like the rush to Baghdad in 2003, they felt themselves closing in on the enemy capital—for in the minds of these Southerners and Midwesterners, New York City had always been the capital of the alien cosmopolites of the North. They had broken the enemy line and had gone more than a hundred miles in three days.

Aerial strikes and advance helicopter assaults were closely followed up by a ground assault that stretched multiple columns of armored vehicles across the Susquehanna bridges and into northeastern Pennsylvania. Advance units were probing as far as the New York state line near Binghamton. Like a runner getting second wind as the finish line comes into view, they kept themselves awake, on excitement, pills, and enthusiasm.

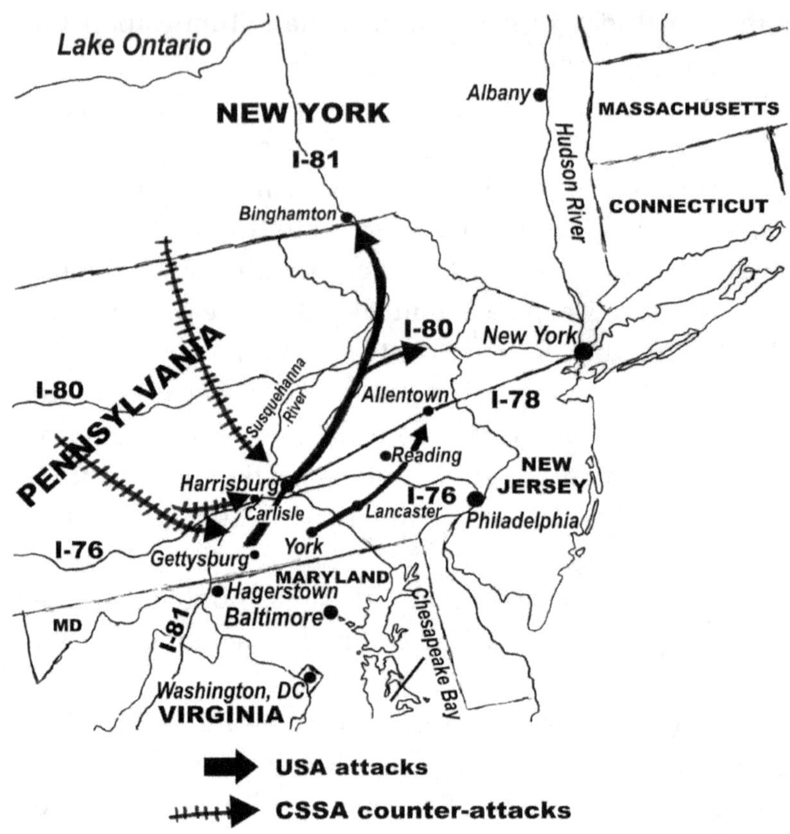

Captain Napoli's helicopter unit had relocated the second night to a forward operating base near Lancaster, Pennsylvania. The FOB was on the east side of the Susquehanna and in the midst of the Amish country. The Amish, who avoided modern technology, were still there tending their chickens and cows. They were in no panic to evacuate. When Tom Napoli brought his helicopter in for a landing he could see their horse-drawn buggies hugging the side of the road, ignoring military trucks and armored personnel carriers just as they had ignored tourist automobiles. Their horses trotted along the pavement wearing leather blinkers to block the side view. Inside the roofed box-like cabs, men in spade beards grasping leather harnesses and women in folded white caps stared straight ahead.

This morning Napoli's helicopters were part of a lead force probing CSSA defenses around Allentown, on Interstate-78 near the New

Jersey border. From there it was just another seventy-five miles to Newark and the approaches of New York City. Before they took off, their battalion commander had given them a headsup, to be ready to move FOB again that evening if all went well.

The blue and green screens of HOME glowed at him reassuringly, giving their flight plan and updating distant battle conditions. Napoli's annoyance at HOME had receded. He was too tired to hassle with it. Easier to just let HOME take over, like running on autopilot. The pills he had taken and the energy drinks he had chugged kept his eyes open, but back inside his head there was a strange pressure that made everything seem a little unreal. He could function all right, as long as he didn't have to stand up or move around; just sit here, deep in a groove, inside the cockpit with HOME's screens glowing in front of him.

In front of Napoli's knees was a new gunner/copilot, Lt. Gunderson. Gunderson was a chatty sort, but Napoli ignored him. Billetts was dead—dead on arrival back at base the first day, probably dead already when Tom Napoli had agonized over what action took precedence in the heat of combat. He didn't want to think about it, didn't want to talk to anybody. Not going that route again.

"Hey, Captain," Gunderson began, "we're crossing I-76 down there. Reminds me of the time I went to Philly with my high school class to see the Liberty Bell."

"Button it," Napoli said.

Halfway to Allentown, HOME beeped and blinked at them.

APACHE BRAVO LEADER: MISSION CANCELLED

PROCEED WEST FOR NEW MISSION

Flight coordinates followed, directing the entire helicopter wing towards the Harrisburg area.

"Attack called off," said Gunderson. "Wonder what's up?"

Napoli said nothing, wheeling the helicopter onto a new course. The green-and-tan patchwork quilt of Pennsylvania farm country below looked placid, but here and there were puffs of smoke. At higher altitudes in the sky there seemed to be more streaks of jet activity than usual.

HOME's green screen, zoomed in to nearby range, showed the orderly blue icons of Napoli's helicopter troop, with Alpha and Charlie ranged in usual formation alongside them. Jumping to a larger scale, another screen showed the sky over Harrisburg becoming active, not just with friendly blue icons but with the red icons of the enemy. Napoli had seen little of the enemy in the air for two days. HOME's reports on hostile aircraft had showed up only when he brought up screens for distant fronts, the air battles over Albany and New York City. And even those battles had quieted down yesterday.

He jumped to the Albany and NYC screens briefly, caught a picture of skies as crowded as he had ever seen before, a veritable traffic jam of blue and red icons. He caught only a glimpse, because HOME was beeping and flashing a new message. Translated out of the jargon of military code, it said:

> **APACHE TROOP BRAVO: PROCEED TO I-76, EAST AND WEST OF SUSQUEHANNA BRIDGES**
>
> **MISSION: PROVIDE SECURITY FOR CONVOYS**
>
> **ENEMY GROUND ATTACK INTERMITTENT**

HOME's ground map was now showing heavy traffic on the Interstate for over a hundred miles of central Pennsylvania. All lanes had been commandeered for traffic traveling east, except one westbound lane for vehicles returning empty for supplies. Tanks were being carried on flatbed trucks, moving faster that way, saving fuel, and avoiding tearing up the pavement by these sixty-ton monsters. It takes twenty thousand vehicles to move and supply an army corps, and many of the trucks were oil tankers, carrying diesel fuel to forward resupply dumps. An armored attack more likely grinds to a halt from lack of fuel than from enemy fire, so the oil tankers crowded the highways behind the armor, the long logistical tail of the snake behind the deadly fangs at the head of advance.

USA air superiority still seemed to be holding, despite isolated dogfights with CSSA fighters. HOME had a tally of what was happening up there, but Napoli and Gunderson were busy now with the ground screen. Hostile artillery was firing west of the Susquehanna, menacing the convoys on the bridge approaches. HOME picked out a target for them, and they hurried across the wide dark waters of the slowly winding river, skirted the tops of the wooded hills that loomed up suddenly past the river bottom and burst into the open farmland beyond.

A rocket launched off from beneath Napoli's helicopter. Two miles away came a blast on a green hillside, and a beacon of smoke billowed up.

Then another smoke beacon, and another. Napoli's troop dispersed, chasing targets on both sides of the Pennsylvania Turnpike. There were dozens of hits, leaving the landscape dotted with smoke beacons, like some great Indian powwow. Surprisingly, shelling of the convoys did not let up. From time to time traffic stopped; then transport troops cleared the wrecks from the highway and the columns started moving again.

Gunderson could not keep his mouth shut. "Where the hell are these guys coming from? There weren't supposed to be so many CSSA over here. Didn't we clean everything out two days ago?"

Tom Napoli had another worry. Coming at them from the northwest was another troop of helicopters, Apaches like their own, but painted in the gray of CSSA, with its rainbow emblem on the side. He glanced at HOME's green screen: two, three times as many hostile copters as his own wing.

"Get air fighter support, fast!" he called to Gunderson. The front-seater typed furiously at the computer keyboard. Simultaneously, breaking radio silence, Tom radioed to base.

For the first time in Tom's experience, HOME was slow in responding.

The answer came back on the radio: *"Base to Apache Bravo leader: We've got nothing overhead to cover you. Hold on. Checking other sectors."*

The CSSA copters were maneuvering into a multilayered formation, peeling off to attack each of the scattered pairs of Napoli's Apaches. Apache attack helicopters are designed for ground assault, tank-killers above all, and their rockets are positioned to be fired forward. The cannon beneath the cockpit, too, although it swung a wide arc from side to side, was not designed to fire at targets behind them. In short, neither side was really equipped for air-to-air combat against other attack helicopters; that was what a strike fighter would come in handy for.

Tom had two choices: to fly straight at the oncoming enemy copters, firing at them while they fired at him, a kind of High Noon duel in the sky. If he could break through past them, he had a chance to open up some distance until help came. But they had him outnumbered, and the chances of winning the duel were not very good. The other choice was to dive, do some extreme terrain masking, confuse the infrared heat-seeking missiles that the enemy were about to fire at him, just as he was about to fire at them.

He released a burst of silver chaff to mislead the enemy's tracking system, and banked sharply, plunging into the shadow of a wooded hillside.

Next moment came the flash and shock of an explosion.

For a second he thought they were on fire.

Then he saw his mistake. The helicopter on fire was his wingman, which had taken a missile, probably intended for themselves. When he banked sharply, Napoli had dropped under his companion helicopter, and the enemy's heat-seeking device had rammed into the nearest target.

As his wingman spiraled downwards to end in a blaze of forest fire on the hillside, Napoli swooped into a little valley, hugging the contours of the hill. A shower of leaves from the treetops spun around them in an accompanying whirlwind. Like a crazy drunken rural Saturday night spree in a pickup truck, Napoli skimmed from one little valley into another. Miraculously, the CSSA copters had lost him, temporarily.

He barked into the radio. *"Apache Bravo leader to base: Where the hell is air cover?"*

The answer seemed to take forever.

"Base to Apache Bravo Leader: Communications glitch with Air Force fighter cover. Communications temporarily out in all sectors. Take evasive action until further notice."

"Evasive action!" Tom cursed. "Gunderson! Get a message to HOME. Where the hell are our fighters?"

Strangely, HOME's screens seemed to be updating rather slowly. The same picture hung on the green screen for several seconds, before updating jerkily to new positions. And strange icons were appearing on the screen: not the familiar blue and red icons for friendlies and hostiles in nearby flightspace, but what looked like tiny ribbons of text in a blur of colors, like shreds of paper pasted in the screen.

"Something's the matter with HOME," Gunderson shouted. "Green screen is flickering. Now it's frozen."

Napoli shook his head vigorously from side to side, like a man trying to clear his breathing passages when coming up from prolonged submersion in deep water. "Fuck HOME," he said. "Keep your eyes on the airspace. And get me a heading back to base."

HOME is down. The green and blue screens in every USA military vehicle, every helicopter, every aircraft, every command post, are featureless. No information is coming through, no position reports, no orders from headquarters. The screens are dull gray.

In the war room at EASTCOM, excited voices:

"HOME is down. Repeat, HOME is down. Access emergency backup."

"Give me a minute. Can't get it. Shit, backup is down."

"Try another way into the system. Everybody!"

"What seems to be the problem?" says a higher-ranking voice, deliberately calming.

"HOME has shut down. We're searching for ways to get it back up and running. So far, nothing is working."

"How about auxiliary backup systems?"

"We're trying that. We're getting some flickers, but just garbled. Whatever caused HOME to go down has contaminated the backups too."

"Hardware problem anywhere? Any indication of power outage at crucial components?"

"Can't be. HOME is distributed over hundreds of computers, all interlinked. It's some kind of system overload."

"Get Madigan over here. This is his baby."

"Secretary Madigan is at the Pentagon, sir. Shall I call him?"

"Tell him to get his ass on a helicopter ASAP. This looks like a number one meltdown."

"Shall I call the President, too, sir?"

"Better wait on that. Let's find out what's going on here before we have him stepping into the picture."

General Billy Jo Maddux was napping in an adjoining room. Like everyone else, he had been awake most of the seventy-two hours and more since the campaign began, snatching half-hour catnaps here and there. He took his place behind the desk at the central console. Blank screens stared back at him. Useless. He stood up again. "I need battle reports, ASAP."

"Last reports, fifteen minutes ago, there was activity all over the place. Pace picking up. Can't tell what's happened since then. It's all stored in HOME."

"Can we extrapolate?"

Aides located some memory files. "Best I can do, General. Hourly position by position changes, snapshots of the campaign developing over the last three days. Last in the sequence about an hour ago."

Maddux peered at the sequence of screens. "Ground action all quiet until this morning. Then a sharp acceleration in enemy activity west of the Susquehanna, spreading east of the river. Exponential rise in calls for close air support. Then blank. If we assume the trend has continued—or even just plateaued—there's an overload on our air support in that region."

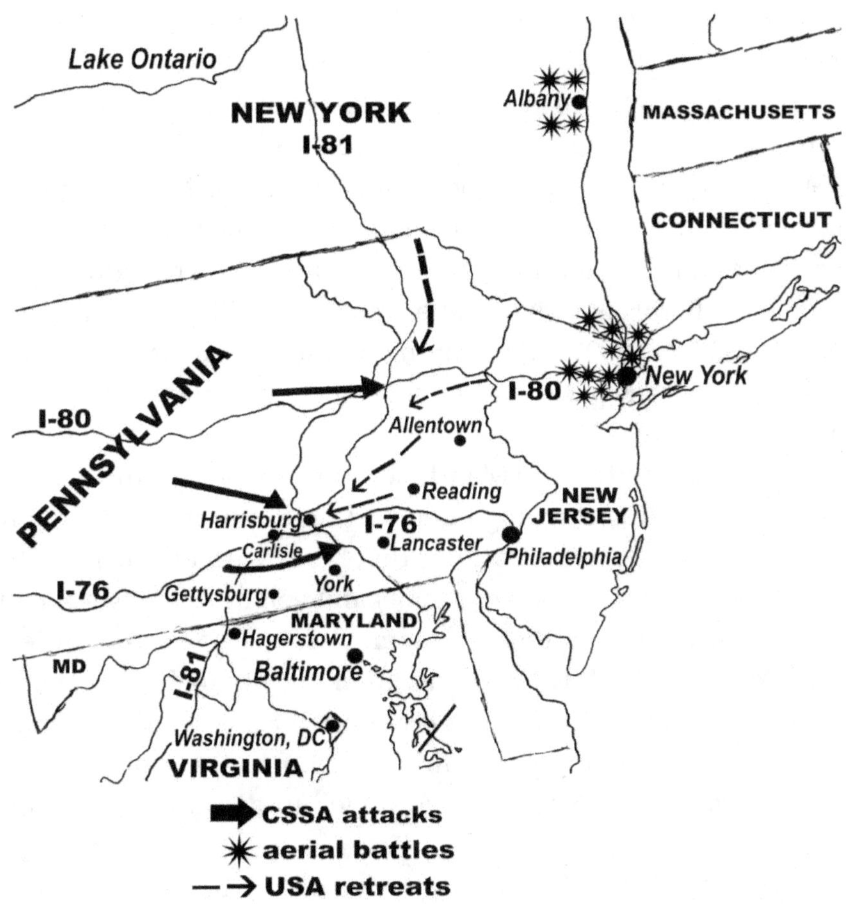

"Look at this one, General. It's the hourly sequence for the deep air strikes on presumed enemy governmental and C4ISR centers around Albany and New York City." That is, Command, Control, Communications, Computers, Intelligence, Surveillance and Reconnaissance—the package of administrative functions.

The sequence showed an initial spike, the first morning of shock and awe. Then a steady flow of air-to-air battles, dropping the third day. This morning—the fourth day—there was a sharp upturn in surface-to-air attacks, as if hitherto hidden or unused anti-aircraft weapons were now turned to the skies. HOME had automatically ordered more counterstrikes, a barrage of anti-radiation missiles. Enemy air-to-air attacks were rising sharply too. Then blank.

"There seems to be an awful lot of activity in just three kill boxes, doesn't there?" Maddux said, pointing to map grids, one around Albany and two in the lower Hudson River approaches to New York.

Aides nodded. "HOME must have ordered that."

"Well, maybe that's one good thing about HOME going down, because you can't have hundreds of aircraft cheek by jowl in a small space. There must be a traffic jam in the sky out there right now."

"Even if HOME is down, the air battle is still probably in good order. AWACS and JSTARS are flying on the perimeter, and they can control all the flight paths and target selection. They've got systems to prevent fratricide."

"Up to what limit?" said Maddux. "AWACS can handle hundreds of aircraft, including tracking enemy aircraft and missile launches. We've got five AWACS aircraft out there, but with all the density in those kill boxes, I'm not so sure they can keep everything straight."

"There might be another problem, General," a second aide put in. "AWACS and JSTARS send all their inputs to HOME, besides feeding them to the aircraft in their region. If HOME is down, I'm not sure what effect it will have on air-to-air communications."

"You mean AWACS won't revert back to direct control over its planes?"

"Hypothetically, it should. But once you modify a computer network to integrate independent systems, if you cut out the new component, the subsystems don't always go back to operating like they used to."

"Swell," said Maddux. "All right, start contacting every unit out there in the battle zone the old-fashioned way. Call them on their radio links. Start with the AWACS. And start getting a aircraft-by-aircraft report on everybody in or near the overloaded kill boxes."

"HOME has been handling all the radio traffic, sir. It will take a while to reorganize a bank of radio operators and set up a new tally for their reports."

"Get on it. The sooner we start the better."

"One more thing, General. We've been keeping radio silence over that part of the battlefield. There's no indication the enemy has broken our encryption, but they can tell where there's a concentration of radio activity."

"I don't care!" Maddux, mild-mannered Christian, almost swore. "Don't you think he knows already when he's got us in a box? Now we've got to get ourselves out."

Secretary Madigan arrived. Grim-faced he heard the briefings. He interrupted with a few technical questions, but seemed less intent than usual on embarrassing officers who gave long-winded explanations that didn't get to the point. Madigan was pondering.

"There's a flaw in the system design," he said. "The question is, how deep in the architecture of HOME is it? And can we get a quick fix, or do we have to write it off for now, and take the time to redesign it?"

"There's a flaw all right," Maddux said. "It's overloaded. There's a limit to how much one computer can do. It's not the mind of God. No matter how much memory it has. We're calling on it to guide too many weapons platforms at once."

"It's designed to handle extremely high levels of complexity, Billy Jo. We're not talking theology here. This is a nonlinear system. It can make multiple adjustments, and make them faster than any of us sitting here."

"But not an infinite number of adjustments in a very crowded situation. Don't you see it, Bob? The enemy has suckered us into those kill boxes. Maybe the simultaneous spike in ground activity on the Pennsylvania front is part of it too, just to put more pressure on the computer. They know us, Bob—they know you. Their staff used to sit in this very room. They know how much you've built this organization around HOME, and they deliberately set out to test its limits."

Madigan's usual sarcasm was in abeyance. Not one to fall back on rage, he became colder, thoughtful. "It's one possible theory," he said.

The officer in charge of computers, Brigadier General Grotweil, was quick with an alternative. "It may be just a glitch in the program. We didn't have time to test everything out before the politicians hurried us into action."

"Damn right about that," put in General Harris. "Politicians need to get out of the way and let the professionals do it right."

"More precisely," Brigadier Grotweil continued, "it could be a combination of glitches. A couple of little things, each minor in itself. When they all happen at once, there could be a unpredictable interactive effect."

"That's true," said Secretary Madigan. "It might not be anything deep in the architecture at all. Remember the Three Mile Island incident back in 1979? Nuclear power plant—just outside of Harrisburg on the Susquehanna—started to melt down. Turned out there were two causes: a pipe that got clogged and raised the pressure in the reaction chamber; and a control panel dial that happened to malfunction at the same time. The operator read the panel, which said pressure was going down, when it was really going up. So he turned the pressure up to compensate. They finally figured out what was wrong, and got that situation under control. In the end, there was no meltdown at Three Mile Island. I don't think there will be a meltdown now."

"We're checking it out," Grotweil said.

"How long will it take?" said Madigan.

"Ten point seven hours—rough estimate."

Late in the afternoon there was an announcement. HOME was up and running again.

A cheer echoed through EASTCOM, from the war room to the surrounding rooms and corridors. Anxious computer operators stood and slapped each other's shoulders.

General Maddux pushed through the happy throng to his seat at the central console. The green and blue screens were glowing again. At first glance, things had not changed that much since this morning. Still very high activity everywhere. He brought up the Albany and New York kill boxes in as close detail as possible. The screens looked fuzzy. Was it because there was so much activity in them that the image couldn't resolve all of it? Or was HOME still experiencing some kind of glitch, some kind of overload?

He called to an aide, asking her to check the positions of the AWACS and JSTARS around the forward aerial battle zone. The reply took longer than usual to come back, a minute, two minutes, five minutes.

"What's taking so long?"

"Uh, negative, General. Can't locate any AWACS or JSTARS at the positions last recorded. They may have moved to new locations. We're checking how fast and far they could have gone."

"Have we been able to raise them on the radio?"

"Negative, no radio contact. There were ten AWACS and JSTARS assigned to those battle positions this morning. No reports from them. No data coming in since HOME went down."

"Is HOME getting anything from them?"

"I don't think so. Checking. Our aircraft out there don't seem to have any guidance. They're on their own."

"Get General Harris over here," Maddux said.

General Curt Harris, dark-jowled, was chomping a cigar, against all regulations.

"Curt," said Maddux, "I think all the AWACS and JSTARS have been shot down."

Harris glowered angrily. "What are you talking about?"

"You heard me. All our flying air control systems are dead. We're activating their GPS tags." Ordinarily the global positioning tags on the AWACS and JSTARS planes were turned off. Even with their highly impenetrable codes, these Air Force eyes in the sky were so valuable that standard battle procedure was to allow no chance the enemy might locate them by tracking their GPS receivers. "Here's confirmation. One of the AWACS is down on the ground, over western New York State. At least one JSTARS has crashed in the Atlantic ocean. They're probably all out."

Harris was speechless, for once, not out of surliness, but stunned. "This can't happen," he finally growled.

"I think they've been targeting them. Possibly when HOME went down, they were able to get some kind of communications signature that told them where the AWACS and JSTARS were. Possibly also the fighter escorts that cordoned them had been thinned with all the attack support HOME was pulling into the kill boxes. Jeff Gray probably had the sectors where AWACS and JSTARS were flying deliberately cleared of CSSA fighter threats, to sucker them into a false sense of security. Suckered HOME, that is. Then when HOME went down, he sent in more than enough fighters to knock them out." He imagined the slow-flying 707s loaded with electronic gear, against CSSA's most agile jet fighters.

Harris finally spoke. "Jeff Gray, you say?"

"Yes, I'm sure it's him. Bouvier would never have figured this out. Anyway, our Air Force is now flying blind."

An aide came up. "More reports on surveillance aircraft, General. The Global Hawk flying at high altitude seems to be down too."

Brigadier Grotweil came up and confirmed the downings. "I think this explains why HOME came back on. When all the aerial surveillance systems went out, HOME's information intake dropped back below overload level. On the other hand, HOME doesn't have anywhere near as much information now, so the picture it's giving us is pretty spotty."

Maddux gave a sardonic shake of the head. "Jeff Gray is something, isn't he? You come at him with a knockout punch, and he pokes you in the eye. In both eyes."

President Jennings arrived in the war room soon after. "I hear you boys have been having a little trouble. But you've got it under control now, of course. Am I right?"

Secretary Madigan was silent, withdrawn into his own head, deep in thought. Harris had regained his voice.

"Mr. President. We can take care of this without civilian interference. Just like we would've in the first place."

Jennings gave him a long slow glance. Then he walked around the Chairman of the Joint Chiefs and peered at the screen showing the central Pennsylvania front. "Susquehanna River around Harrisburg, isn't it? See, I remember my geography, even those Yankee states. Seems to me, last time I was here, we were talking about the Susquehanna River bridges."

He pointed at the screen. "Guess my civilian eyes aren't seeing everything they ought to. But doesn't it look to you like there are no more Susquehanna bridges around Harrisburg right now?"

Maddux stepped forward quickly. In his concern for the aerial kill boxes, he had overlooked the ground situation behind the front of the offensive. The Susquehanna bridges were gone. Probably blown up by CSSA forces when USA air cover had disappeared.

Jennings took his arm, almost gently. "So now, Billy Jo, maybe you can tell me how many of our troops we have trapped on the east bank of the Susquehanna?"

"Probably fifty thousand. Two armored divisions, plus mechanized infantry. Don't know how much of our logistics component made it to that side of the bridge. We've been out of contact since morning."

"I know that. Can they fight their way out?"

"Depends on how much fuel and ammo they have. I don't know yet how many of our armored vehicles were able to refuel before the aerial attack began. Some of our fuel tankers were hit around the Susquehanna bridges, but we don't know how many."

"Can we get them out by air?"

"Troops maybe, not equipment. We'll have to check our helicopter force. We know there were major helicopter battles on both sides of the river. Also, it depends on how much air cover we have, and how much Jeff Gray has in the air against us."

"Gray has to have taken a pounding, too," Harris put in. "Two state-of-the-art Air Forces have been going toe-to-toe for four days. Our aircraft losses are substantial, but so are his."

"You might as well hear the worst, Mr. President," Maddux said. "It's not just our ground forces. It's the aerial assault on Albany and New York."

"The decapitation of their government and communications structure and so forth?"

Maddux pointed to the map. "These are what we call kill boxes, Mr. President. Our battle plan—the one that was executed by HOME—tells aircraft what box to enter, and what targets to aim at in it. Somehow, we ended up with about eight hundred combat aircraft in those kill boxes this morning."

"Sounds like a lot. You're telling me it's a traffic jam in the sky, something like flights stacked up over O'Hare in a holding pattern? Only they're firing away while they're holding."

"Something like that. Simplest way to put it is we were lured into an ambush in the sky. We've lost two thirds of our bomber force. Probably lost four hundred fighter planes. Reports are coming in now."

"And how did we lose all these planes? The other side got better pilots than us?"

"We're not sure yet how they were downed. Enemy opened up with huge amount of ground fire, surface-to-air missiles, same stuff we've got. They were keeping it in hiding until we got too many planes in the kill box. And probably there was a lot of fratricide—our antiradar missiles launched in such a dense airspace that they homed in on our own planes. It looks like the enemy kept just enough of their air force around to lure us in, but made it look like a soft target for three days. Then they flew in massive reinforcements from the West at the last minute. Like I said, we made a massed frontal attack in the sky, and got mowed down."

Jennings dropped his bulk into a chair. "We've got a lot of souls to pray for," he said. "May the good Lord receive them in Heaven, for they died in His great cause."

He raised his voice, preaching to the room. "God is testing us. He is testing our faith, and our will to fight through adversity. God is sending us a message. We've put too much faith in worldly things. We've been worshipping a false idol—this computer called HOME. It's only a dead machine, yet we treat it as if it had a soul superior to our own. The nearest thing to God in this earthly world is the human spirit: our mind, our will, our human judgment. Exalt the spirit, and God will bring us the victory."

"I appreciate your perspective, Mr. President," Secretary Madigan said. "But HOME deserves the benefit of perspective, too. Of course it's only a machine. But we put the best human intelligence into it. We've learned a hard lesson today. We've learned that HOME has a weakness, and we're going to fix it."

Jennings got to his feet. "We'll talk more about that later. Meantime we've got to take care of the mess we're in. When your hound dog pukes on the kitchen floor, the first thing you gotta do is clean it up." He looked around the circle of generals. "You fellas have any suggestions?"

"First thing is to save the Air Force," Harris said. "You can't fight a modern war without an Air Force. I'm pretty sure the other side won't have air superiority, since he started with fewer aircraft than we did, and he took pretty heavy losses too. So nobody is going to be doing much fighting, until they get their air forces back to strength. We need to go into a defensive mode for a while and rebuild."

"Bob?"

"I agree with Curt. Both sides are battered. They're not going to invade us, anyway. Jeff Gray wanted a defensive battle. He wants to tire us out from attacking the North, just like Lee kept parrying Union forces from getting to Richmond. We'll have time to get the computer system working the way it's supposed to work."

"Seems to me I've heard this argument before," Jennings said. "Are you sure your faith is in the right place, Bob? Are you in love with that machine, or is it just your ego you've put in there?"

"With all due respect, Mr. President, we've been hurried along faster than was wise. We were pressed into action, for political reasons, before we had a chance to fully test the computer system."

Jennings looked from one to the other. "Curt wants to wait for a year. Bob wants to wait until we fix the computer—say, wait for a couple of months or so. Billy Jo, how long do you want to wait?"

"The problem is out there right now on the battlefield," Maddux said. "What does a good general do when his forces are overwhelmed? He counterattacks. Grant was a master of it. He always kept forces in reserve that he could bring up at the right time."

"Do we have any reserves we can use?" said Jennings.

"Yes. We can transfer forces from Kentucky on the central front. We can move more forces up from our North Carolina and Georgia bases."

"How soon can you move?"

"Right now. If we can strike into Pennsylvania, we'll catch Jeff Gray on his flank. Our current situation is like the Battle of the Bulge in 1944. Both times, we were attacking successfully, deep into enemy territory. He launches a counterattack when we don't expect it, as if he's been luring us in, then cutting us off. How did we solve that problem in '44? Patton's counterattack on the flank of the bulge, turning the tables again."

Maddux held the president's eyes. "Like you said, Mr. President, we're being tested. The human spirit rises to the occasion. With God's help."

Jennings was beginning to beam. "Sounds good, Billy Jo. But can we move all those forces in here fast enough? Seems like they've got some territory to cover."

"I've got a reserve force right here in front of Washington, ready to go. They can be in Pennsylvania by tomorrow morning. I know what you're thinking—leaving Washington unprotected. But the same time, forces from Carolina will be on their way to take their place."

"Attacking without air superiority?" Harris said scornfully. "That's suicide."

"We can pull enough air forces from Washington to cover the attack. Probably we don't need much, since the CSSA won't have much left in the air either."

"Both sides fighting without air support? That's not modern war." Harris snorted. "Puts us back to pre-World War II days. Back to the trenches of World War I."

"Back to Civil War One," Maddux said.

"Never mind the history," Jennings said. "Can we still win this battle?"

"It's in God's hands," Maddux said. "I believe we can win it. It doesn't need a miracle, just a fair chance."

It was four-thirty in the morning when President Jennings heard the bedroom phone.

"Mr. President? Pat Buckley." The National Security Advisor. "I think you'd better come look at something."

"Bad news? Well, praise the Lord at all times, anyway."

"It's not good."

"Is it Maddux's counterattack?"

"No. That's going all right. Something else."

In the office, Jennings in pajamas and slippers was met by Buckley and Louise Carter, the Presidential Press Secretary. She held out a press release.

"It's the Reuters office in Philadelphia. From their war correspondent in Lancaster, Pennsylvania."

The headline read: AMISH VICTIMS OF USA ATTACK. The story went on to say that five Amish civilians were killed when USA soldiers opened fire on their horse-drawn buggy. Dead included a father and mother and three children.

Jennings blanched, sat down heavily. "What happened?"

"Yesterday around midday—during the computer blackout—one of our Apache helicopters was returning to base and crashed into an Amish farmhouse. Apparently the pilot was wounded or stressed out or something and he hit the house. There was some ground action in the area, and our infantry thought the copter had been shot down by CSSA forces hidden nearby. When the buggy came galloping out with the family in it, our troops opened fire. Some of the soldiers say they ordered them to stop, but they didn't. The reporter interviewed some other Amish who said the soldiers just shot them without warning."

Jennings closed his eyes, saying nothing, apparently praying.

"Are there pictures?" he said finally.

She handed them across. Photos of a dead horse with tangled leather harness, a black lacquer-sided buggy overturned in the road. Photos of a young man with a black spade beard lying with one arm around the bloody corpse of a child, a girl in a folded white cap. Photos of the mother and another child, lying in a heap with dripping red blotches on their pinafores, while a USA soldier in mottled blue-green combat battle dress and a M-16 automatic weapon hanging from his shoulder reaches down to touch the bodies. Photos of Amish buggies trotting peacefully down country roads, juxtaposed with USA armored vehicles passing them—apparently human-interest shots taken on an earlier occasion, included here for background to fill out the pages of the story.

"Has the story already gone out?"

"It's been picked up by all the wire services. It will be on the morning television news. It's already being broadcast in Europe. Everybody will have it, north and south."

"The question is," said Buckley, "whether this is the big story of the day. They've been running the story of our offensive as top news. That's been pretty much the same every day until now—USA advances in Pennsylvania. Plus bombing around New York, air war over New York, lots of pictures of skyscrapers with planes in a distance. The press doesn't know what's happened in the aerial kill boxes yet. They may never find out. They just think it's a colorful fireworks display. I don't think they even know about the Susquehanna bridges and the forces cut off on the east side of the river. So, unless we tell them—or the CSSA military announces a big victory, which we will deny—this will be the lead story."

"We could start damage control," said Carter. "Play up the guerrilla-style warfare practiced by the CSSA. Their hiding in civilian installations, using civilian vehicles. Maybe leak a story about CSSA soldiers wearing Amish clothes, using children as human shields."

"No," said Jennings. "Absolutely not. This is an aberration, not American policy. I want a full investigation. Cordon off the area. Interview all witnesses, military and civilian. Relieve those men of duty. Make sure every officer up and down the command prosecutes this to the fullest. I will tolerate no cover-ups."

"But Mr. President—"

"And investigate the helicopter pilot who started the whole thing. Test him to see if he was on drugs or something."

"With all due respect," said Buckley. "We can't interview civilians and do a forensic investigation, because it's in the middle of a fluid battle zone. A battle in which we are in disarray, and very likely in retreat. If we don't pull our troops out of Lancaster, they will soon be prisoners of the CSSA. And it's more than likely that the helicopter pilot, if he isn't badly wounded—and I've heard no reports that he was—is busy evacuating troops right now."

Jennings pondered. "All right. Get me Maddux."

General Maddux was on the line shortly.

"Mr. President? Things are going okay. We have a division well out into Maryland, crossing the Pennsylvania line."

"Billy Jo. Listen to me. We're going to have to stop the advance."

"Stop the advance—but why? So far, air cover isn't going to be any problem. They're not strafing the roads, and we've mustered enough aircraft to cover a push all the way to the Susquehanna. If you give me another division from the Washington defenses, we can cross the river lower down, and push one wing up through Lancaster to Reading. We've got the initiative again."

"Can't do that now, Billy Jo. Louise will explain it to you. Or just catch the morning news."

"But Mr. President. Our advance units are already at Gettysburg. With a rapid advance we'll drive Jeff Gray into a corner. And we can rescue thousands of our troops who are stranded out there."

"Just hold your forces right there at Gettysburg. We can rescue the others by helping them make their way back to base."

"But Mr. President—"

"You'll understand tomorrow, Billy Jo. Let's just say we were overtaken by events."

An announcement went out to the press that the USA had won the first big battle of the war. The offensive had recaptured territory from the secessionists, beginning a process that would end with the re-unification of the entire United States. It was fitting that the victory should liberate America's most sacred battlefield, the Gettysburg National Military Park.

The atrocity of the Amish family was grieved as a profound tragedy by President Jennings, Secretary Madigan, and Chairman of the Joint Chiefs Harris, and was accepted as such by the USA media. In the CSSA, the media ran the story for several days, denouncing the vicious methods of the USA forces in deliberately targeting innocent civilians. Since a scandal only keeps on growing when an entire community joins in denouncing it, the atrocity soon faded into the backlog of recriminations that one enemy has against another. There were plenty of casualties of a more ordinary sort for people on both sides to grieve about.

Inside the Pentagon, in time it became common to say that President Jennings lost his nerve over an imagined press reaction; and that if not for the Amish incident, the campaign would have been a success, and we would be knocking on the doors of New York City. In this way, the fact that the US Air Force had been removed as a real factor in the war, and that the US Army lost two armored divisions and many of its best-trained troops, was excused and covered up, and the military professionals who planned the campaign were able to save face, at least in their own eyes.

The collapse of HOME was never mentioned in the media of either side.

CSSA forces too had taken heavy casualties: at least thirty thousand troops and much of its heavy battlefield equipment were lost, along with numerous combat aircraft. The economy of central Pennsylvania was devastated, and there were heavy material losses to the infrastructure of the lower Hudson Valley. What had started out as a lightning war of maneuver by the most modern high-tech weapons turned out to be a battle for ground taken at tremendous cost; indeed, a classic example of attrition.

In this way the campaign that was called Operation Liberty Bell became known as the Second Battle of Gettysburg.

There was, however, no second Gettysburg Address. The great orator Joshua Maccabee Jennings did not feel it was appropriate.

Fredericksburg 1862

Abraham Lincoln, eager to avoid yet another winter of delay in restoring the Union, and sensing the disheartening political mood after the failed campaigns of the second year of war, in late fall of 1862 pushed for another offensive on Richmond. General McClellan was slow, insisting his troops were not yet ready, not yet reorganized and adequately supplied. McClellan was dismissed; General Burnside was put in command of the Army of the Potomac with orders to march.

The main road south from Washington to Richmond—what is now I-95—crosses the first big river in Virginia, the Rappahannock, at Fredericksburg. Down this road and its parallel railway Burnside moved an army of one hundred fifteen thousand. The Confederates had only a few thousand troops at Fredericksburg, but they destroyed the bridges and sniped at Union forces from buildings on the riverbank. While Burnside delayed for three weeks to bring up pontoons and put them across the river under fire from the sharpshooters, Robert E. Lee brought up his army of seventy-eight thousand and positioned them on a ring of low hills above the city: inferior forces but occupying a superior defensive position. Union troops finally crossed the river on the night of December 11 and occupied the now-evacuated town. On the 13th, Burnside had everything in position for a two-pronged attack.

On the Confederate right, where the river bends southeast of town, the Federals laid down heavy artillery bombardment in the morning, then in the afternoon attacked with a few divisions. These were driven back by Stonewall Jackson's counterattack. Burnside's main attack came on the Confederate left, marching through the town and up a long sloping hill. Below the crest, four thousand Confederate infantry occupied a sunken road behind a stone wall, with artillery further up commanding the approach. It was virtually trench warfare, artillery and massed rifle fire pouring down on the long horizontal lines of Federals marching up the gradual slope. Fourteen brigades in succession made the attempt—about forty thousand men; none reached the top. After six hours, in the gathering dusk, Burnside gave up. Two days later, he pulled his demoralized troops back across the Rappahannock. The Federals had lost thirteen thousand men, the Confederates five thousand.

The Union loss was a relatively small proportion—about 12% of troops engaged—and victorious armies sometimes have taken worse. But here nothing came of it, and the pointlessness of it all dragged the Union army down, even among the majority who were not hit. On the other side the Confederates were pumped up with confidence and emotional energy, ready for more victories. It was the first great lesson in the futility of frontal assault against the lethality of modern firepower. Next year, the Confederates would show they had failed to learn the lesson, when Robert E. Lee himself sent twelve thousand men to almost certain death in the desperate, magnificent, futile Pickett's charge across the battlefield at Gettysburg.

YEAR TWO, CHAPTER TWO.
BATTLE OF CARIBOU FOREST

The Governor's office, Helena, Montana. July.

"**A**mputate the salient. It's their obvious weak point," Montana Governor Don Blastings said. He clumped heavily across the room in his motorcycle boots, pointed a diamond-ringed index finger at the wall map.

Blastings put his hairy hand on Kansas and extended an up-curved middle finger across Colorado and Utah. "The Utah-Colorado salient—that's what the military calls it, ain't it? It sticks out into the soft underbelly of the West like a giant prick. I say, cut if off." He made a chopping movement along the east side of the Rockies and grinned at the assembled CSSA leaders.

"Whatever turns you on, Don," California Governor Duplessis said from the depth of his armchair. "I'd say it looks more like an open drawer. Inviting somebody to slam it shut."

The easterners, Chairperson Rosenfeld of New York and Vice Chairperson O'Leary of Chicago, caught each other's glances.

"Let's not overreach ourselves," Rosenfeld said. "We've beaten them pretty badly. Gettysburg was the downfall of a Southern army—again. And General McConnell did us all proud in west Texas, and Missouri." A suave smile and a deferential dip of the chin toward Duplessis. "Not to mention the bungled Southern attack on Philadelphia. I say it's time to negotiate."

"Negotiate what?" Minnesota Senator Tim Birkenstock said. He wore running shoes and a T-shirt with a rainbow across the chest. "We're winning. We just want to be left alone. Free from religious tyranny and sexist, racist, homophobic, pollutionist social policies."

Rosenfeld cut him off. "So let's make the peace, Tim. There's been bloodshed enough."

"All right," Birkenstock said. "Let Jennings renounce his war of aggression. Let him recognize the CSSA as a sovereign state. The UN and the EU are ready to recognize us. Canada already has. And Iceland."

"It ain't gonna work," Blastings said. "All the big battles have been on our territory. We've won, but they're still the occupying army. They're still in Gettysburg, you know."

Rosenfeld shrugged. "We're still in El Paso and Fort Bliss."

"We could make a trade," O'Leary said, bulldog-faced, perking up and sitting forward. "Give them back west Texas if they give us back that little bulge of Pennsylvania around Gettysburg. Of course, we have a lot more of Texas than they have of Pennsylvania, so they would have to throw in something else. How about financial indemnities, paid into the Treasury of the CSSA?" The Treasury was located in Chicago.

Blastings jabbed his finger at the map again. "You guys haven't been paying attention. The USA has a general named Achilles Cruz, who took Warren Air Force Base at Cheyenne around the time McConnell hit Whiteman AFB. Only Cruz didn't leave. He brought more forces up from Denver and has been creeping along the Interstate, heading west across Wyoming. Laramie, Rawlings, Rock Springs, one after another. Took him most of a year, but now he's got I-80 all the way to the Utah border."

"Can't we stop him with air attacks?" Birkenstock said.

"Like they say, you gotta put boots on the ground some time," Blastings said. "Our air forces are too evenly matched. We attack, they dogfight, everyone goes home, Cruz keeps creeping forward. I-80 ain't worth much to them—right now, it's just a road to nowhere, as long as we hold the line in Idaho and Nevada. But it used to be the big Interstate across the country, San Francisco to Chicago. That leaves only one big east-west road across the top of the CSSA, and that's I-94 across Montana. Cruz has already sliced off the bottom of Wyoming. Look out, if they keep on slicing further north, our Coalition is going to be cut in half."

Rosenfeld looked thoughtful. "We can treat southern Wyoming as another bargaining chip. It's not necessarily all bad. You can't negotiate with the other side by humiliating them. We give up something, they give up something, we compromise on something. I'm not saying we're going to get a peace treaty right away, and full recognition from the USA. But it starts the ball rolling, builds up good will."

"Good will, my ass," Blastings said. "You know where Cruz is now?" He jabbed a finger at the map again. "If you've ever been out on the road in my part of the country, you'd know I-80 comes out of Wyoming into the corner of Utah, driving out of the mountains down into Salt Lake City. But that ain't where Cruz is. He took the cutoff, Route 30 up across the border into the corner of Idaho. His advance forces are in Pocatello right now."

Rosenfeld followed him to the map. Like most easterners, the only parts of Idaho familiar to him were the fashionable resorts, up at Sun Valley and the lakes of the upper panhandle. The dry corner of the Great Basin that was the southern part of the state had no more interest for him than the barrens of Nevada.

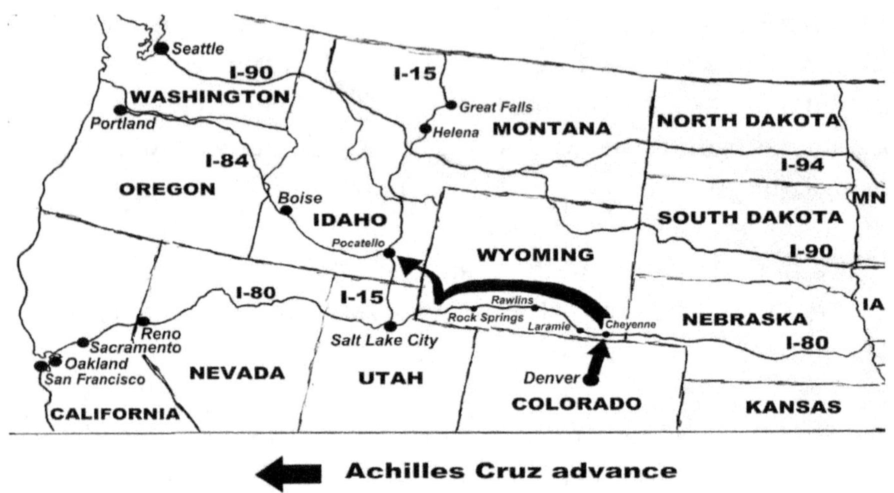

Duplessis nodded, lounging in his chair, the big cat toying with the mouse. "We're keeping an eye on him." General McConnell was back in the West, his Midwest expedition over, his forces treated by the Governor of California as his private army.

"Cruz's forces can't be that large," Rosenfeld said. "If it's serious, we can stop him. Meantime, we should go ahead and negotiate. A two-pronged approach is always best."

"Hit him hard," Blastings said. "Drive him back to Salt Lake. And start taking back I-80."

Birkenstock leaned forward eagerly. "How about taking Salt Lake City? Secular forces liberating the Mormon Tabernacle. That would show them."

Blastings raised two brawny arms and nearly pounded his own chest, reverting to professional-wrestler mode. "Like I said, it's sticking in our face. Cut it off before it gets any bigger."

"Let's think about this rationally," Rosenfeld said. "Suppose we do take Utah, and even Colorado. That makes us an occupying force.

They're not going to welcome us. They could mount a guerrilla war. It would turn into a war against terrorists, making us fight a dirty war. What would that do to our moral posture?"

Birkenstock was nodding vigorously, marching to music he understood. Duplessis was still languid, a feline expression on his enigmatic face.

O'Leary said, "But it would be a big bargaining chip on our side of the table. Think of what they'd have to pay to get Utah and Colorado back."

He glanced at the woman sitting beside him on the sofa. She was wearing a tailored business suit of serious gray, buttoned jacket stretched by her ample bosom, skirt at her crossed knees, long legs and high heels plain and severe. She had been dressed with expert advice, makeup and hair very controlled, the respectable side of elegant. Her face had a pained expression, and she wriggled in her seat, bored with keeping quiet so long. O'Leary shook his head in a brief warning and smiled encouragingly.

"At what cost to ourselves?" Rosenfeld said. "We'd have to hold onto it long enough for them to see they couldn't drive us out of there. And we'd be responsible for the welfare of the people we've captured. It's like taking prisoners in a battle. It seems great at first, but it's a big burden to load ourselves with."

"So we'll take no prisoners, right, Everett?" Blastings slapped him on the shoulder. "Tell you what, you go ahead and negotiate with Jennings, while we take care of Achilles Cruz."

"I think it's just a bluff," Rosenfeld said. "What the military calls a forward defense. Keep an eye on Cruz, while I set up negotiations. The Canadian government has offered to act as intermediary."

The meeting broke up. O'Leary introduced Rosenfeld to the woman in the business suit. "I'm completely with you on negotiations, Everett. Something good can always happen. And this is one of the best negotiators I know, Marisa Santa-Anna. She's on my staff."

Rosenfeld looked at her appraisingly. "Of course, Ms. Santa-Anna. You're welcome to join the delegation. But you might find it a little boring in Canada."

Marisa smiled demurely, her full lips pursed, catching Rosenfeld's eyes then dropping her own eyelids to half slit. "I can do more than that for you, Mr. President—" she cooed." Mr. Chairperson. Mr. Everett."

O'Leary said, "Marisa and I have been talking about opening another diplomatic front. Unofficially. Just her leading a small delegation. To Washington. Talk to people, get the lay of the land. Open up possibilities."

Rosenfeld looked at her for a moment, then shrugged. "Go ahead. I don't think I need to know about this. Yet."

"You have the forward position," General Cruz said. He walked with Brigadier General Gandhi Park along the edge of a hillside field lined with willow trees. Until three weeks ago it was a picnic ground. Now it was crammed with the portable modular huts of a USA military encampment. Armored vehicles parked under camouflage nets; anti-aircraft rockets peered at the soft blue-green horizon. The pleasant outskirts of Pocatello, Idaho, little shopping malls and modest family homes, sweltered in the July midday heat.

"That's where I want to be," Gandhi said.

"Any problems I should know about?"

"Little skirmishes almost every day. Especially in the evenings. Mostly air incursions, drones, a few enemy helicopters. Nothing we can't handle. Every once in a while kids in pickup trucks firing off a burst."

"Sounds like my days as a teenager. Old country custom, driving along the highway with a two-by-four, knocking over mailboxes."

"I wouldn't know about that," Gandhi said. "I didn't grow up in the country."

"How about enemy drones? Same as we've got, I suppose." Gandhi nodded. "Since GPS satellites were knocked out, they must be relying on drones for surveillance."

"That's their problem," Gandhi said. "All this high tech never works as well as it pretends."

"Just be ready to attack, though I can't tell you yet when or where."

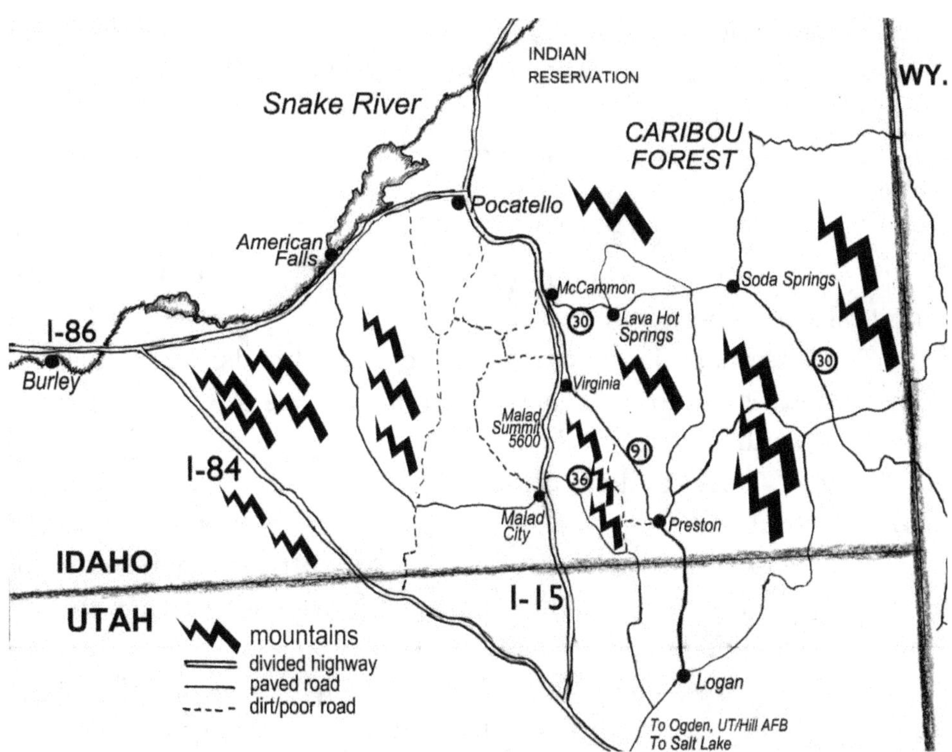

"Not even which direction, north or west?" Pocatello sat the junction of two highways, the one I-15 continuing north into Montana, the other I-86 heading west along the Snake River, across to Boise, up through Oregon to the Columbia River valley and the coastal cities of the Northwest.

"I can't move until the Utah governor sends me more troops, and the Pentagon sends some decent air cover. But when we get it rolling, we have strategic options. Go north to cut off the western CSSA from their land route to the East. Go northwest and take out the economic heartland around Portland and Seattle. We could even start in that direction, then swoop down on Reno, on into Sacramento and San Francisco. We're sitting on a strategic juncture. Just being here gives the other side plenty to worry about."

"It's an old historic route, isn't it?" Gandhi said. There was a faint ripple of a breeze, blowing the grass like waves of a golden sea lapping the distant hills. "The Oregon trail. The pioneers came the same way we did, Route 30 through the mountains. When they reached this spot, they must have known they would make it. Just follow the big river snaking to the northwest, until you reached the Columbia, then follow it to the sea."

"You know a lot about America."

"Growing up in a foreign land does that. You pay attention to things. You can't take as much for granted."

"I grew up in these mountains," Cruz said. "In Colorado. We don't take it for granted."

"The Interstate highways follow the old railroads," Gandhi said. "Pocatello was a railroad junction before it was a town. The past is buried beneath the present."

"I know. The first intercontinental railroad was joined by a golden spike, just outside of Salt Lake City." And now, both were thinking, now it's the enemy frontier, dividing two countries. A hawk circled gracefully over the valley. The two generals watched the horizon in silence for a moment.

"We fought over it before," Cruz said. "It's worth fighting over again. The most beautiful land on earth. It's our country, mine and yours."

Gandhi said nothing. He was thinking of a trip he had taken to Korea when he was a college student. He had gone with a group of Korean adoptees, orphans brought up in America by American parents. They were on a mission to rediscover their identities. They had received a big welcoming ceremony in Seoul, heard a lot of boiler-plate speeches, went out in the evening in large groups and got sickeningly drunk together. Then they came back to America. I'm glad I came back, Gandhi thought. He looked at his prosthetic arm. Even with this.

Cruz was in his helicopter flying over the grassy valleys and the forested hills of the Caribou National Forest. The concrete ribbon of Interstate-15 unreeled below, curving east and then south towards McCallom, where the old pioneer trail curved out of the mountains, coming from Wyoming. He flew upward past the town of Lava Hot Springs and then to Soda Springs, up in the mountain gap where Cruz kept his helicopter cavalry and where he had his headquarters. Thinking of a phone call he had received last week from President Jennings.

"I'm mighty pleased to talk with the only one of my generals who's done anything worth diddly-squat," Jennings had said. "I don't need to tell you we've been taking a beating in the East. Worse'n that, there's talk of peace negotiations. That means permanently breaking up our great country, handing the half of it over to those atheists for ever and ever— well, anyway til God sees fit to punish them. That's why we need a victory in the West. You see, Achilles?"

Achilles saw, wondering to himself whether the Pentagon brass would get wind of Jennings talking to him outside of channels.

"I appreciate your I-80 campaign," Jennings said, "all the way across that great state of Wyoming, winning it back for the US of A. Now I want to tell you, Achilles, in case you're wondering why you didn't get as much publicity for that great victory as you are rightfully entitled. You sort of snuck up on those atheists, without them really knowing what you were doing, and I knew that's the way it had to be. But now, I need a big, finger-licking victory. Deliver me that and I'll guarantee you all the publicity you want. You'll be a national hero."

Thanks, Achilles said, he would rather have more air support.

"I know, I know. We're run down in that department, stretched mighty thin, just protecting what we've got. But you've been doing OK without much air, haven't you? Has the other side been bombing you much?"

Intermittent. The CSSA Air Force was stretched thin too, and Cruz had enough interdiction and surface-to-air to keep them from holding up his advance. But clearing three hundred miles of remote highway was one thing; concentrating troops for a big battle was another. Modern battle was air-intensive, he explained, pretty much all flying artillery.

"Let me know when that big battle is about to happen," Jennings said, "and I'll bust every butt in the Pentagon to get you what you need. Just between you and me, how soon will it be?"

Cruz was not ready to move until he had more troops. Those were supposed to be coming from Idaho, but the Governor and the National Guard commander were not helpful. Could the President send another thirty thousand of the regular army for the Idaho campaign?

Here the President was not so sure. "If God Almighty would let me walk on water," he laughed, "I doubt that he would let me move those big Texas armored divisions away from the southwestern front. Not to mention the Governor of that great state of Utah, Mosiah Moroni Young, who wants every last man from the regular army in Oklahoma and Colorado stationed at St. George protecting southwest Utah and the road from Las Vegas. He's scared to death of Californians rolling up I-15 into Salt Lake. Just between you and me, Achilles, you're going to have to take what you can squeeze out of Mosiah Moroni and do the job on your own. Shoot, the enemy can't be every place at once."

It was the worst part of being a general, Cruz thought, talking to the politicians. Especially politicians in uniform. Every day for the past three weeks he had the same conversation with General Orrin Hawp, commander of the Utah National Guard. Forces were always about ready to start. But instead of heading up I-15 to reinforce Cruz, Hawp said, wouldn't it be better to send them out the diagonal spur of the Interstate further west, I-84? Then they could rendezvous at Burley, or Twin Falls.

Cruz tried cajoling, tried agreeing with Hawp's plans, anything to get him moving. Next day it would be the same conversation, in another form. How about Cruz moving on ahead, with Hawp's forces coming behind to reinforce him? There couldn't be any CSSA resistance in the southern part of Idaho, otherwise we'd have heard of it by now. Why not push ahead to Mountain Home AFB outside of Boise, knocking out their only air base in this part of the country? With that in Union hands, the defensive perimeter would be reached, Utah would be secure. Then the campaign would be over, wouldn't it? Cruz came to confine himself to asking just what units Hawp had in what state of preparation, and exactly when they were moving out.

It was like chewing through a thick piece of steak that turned out to be all fat and gristle.

Cruz's helicopter settled onto the air field at Soda Springs. An eagle's nest at almost six thousand feet. Clear waters of the reservoir mirroring snow-streaked peaks rising to eight thousand feet above flower meadows of vivid blue-purple. Cruz's own sharp-eyed birds of prey, the helicopter cavalry, were nesting around the lush green field, scouting duties largely done before the heat of the day.

It was awkward to have his bases spread out along a single highway, like beads on a string, fifty miles from south to north along I-15 on the other side of the mountain wall. But with the striking power of modern munitions, big troop concentrations were too vulnerable. In any case it was unclear which way the battle campaign would go. Cruz had positioned his headquarters where he could reach them all equally fast if he needed to.

He put in a call to Governor Mosiah Moroni Young. Might as well get this over with.

"I'm glad you called, General Cruz," the Governor said. "General Hawp told me how much you're helping him defend the great State of Utah."

"I hope we're not misunderstanding each other, Governor," Cruz said. "When the President calls up the National Guard, they become part of U.S. Armed Forces. The chain of command runs through the military theatre commander. That commander is me."

"Of course you are, General. But you have to appreciate my position. Utah sits out here all alone, the only state of the Union on the western side of the Rockies. We're dead in the middle of enemy territory, except we have the deserts to protect us. Did you ever hear of the State of Deseret?"

"Isn't that what Utah was called before it became a U.S. territory, back in the 1840s?"

"We're the Church of the Latter Day Saints," Mosiah Moroni Young went on. "What you call Mormons. We came out here to escape persecution. Our great prophet, Joseph Smith, was killed by a lynch mob in Illinois in 1844. I have to tell you, there are Mormons who aren't happy with President Joshua Maccabee Jennings and his Christian USA. You call yourself Christians, but you don't appreciate that we are the true church of Jesus Christ in America. Did you know that Jesus appeared here after His resurrection, two thousand years ago? And that the lost tribes of Israel settled this land, six hundred years before that?

"Look, I'm just a soldier doing my job," Cruz said.

"This relates to your job, General. What war do you think you're fighting? Did you ever hear of the war between the Nephites and the Lamanites? You'd call them the white men and the Indians. It's all there in the Book of Mormon. The Lamanites were one of the tribes of Israel, whose skin turned dark as punishment for rebelling against the Lord."

"I'd say we're fighting the Coalition of Secular States that's trying to break up the Union."

"Confederations and idolaters. What does it say in the Book of Mormon? Nations that uphold secret combinations and covenants shall be destroyed by the Lord. It's all there—read the Book of Ether, Chapter 8 Verse 23. This has all been predicted."

"All right, so it's been predicted," Cruz said. "You want to win the war, don't you? And that means the army has to be unified under one commander, otherwise it's disorganized and ineffective."

"I had a vision," Mosiah Moroni Young said. "The angel came and stood by my bedside while I was praying. His feet did not touch the ground. He told me, the time has come to reestablish the State of Deseret. The true state as it was, not just these boundaries set by the United States for the state of Utah. Did you know, General, that where you are right now, in the Bear Lake Valley of the state of Idaho, was originally settled by people of the Latter Day Saints? And all the surrounding country, out to Pocatello. This is LDS country. It will be reunited into the State of Deseret. And down into Arizona, where Mormon families live in the ways of the ancient patriarchs. And the corner of Nevada, too, that is LDS country from ancient times, though now it is the site of that modern day Sodom and Gomorrah called Las Vegas."

Swell, Cruz said to himself, now I'm supposed to fight for somebody's religious empire. "With all due respect, Governor, I don't need to know the overall strategy," he said aloud. "I need to win the battle right here in what is called Idaho. And I can't win it if I'm pulling one way and General Hawp is pulling another. I need his forces to back me up."

"You should subordinate yourself to General Hawp's command."

Cruz had trouble keeping himself from swearing into the receiver. Speak to him in his own language, he told himself. "You still recognize the Old Testament of the Bible, don't you?"

"It is valid as an earlier revelation. Just as the book of Mormon, revealed to the prophet Joseph Smith by the angel Moroni, is another Testament of Jesus Christ."

"Then you know that the downfall of the people of Israel was when the kingdom was divided," Cruz lectured at him. "The northern kingdom of Israel went its own way and were conquered by the Assyrians. Then the southern kingdom of Judah was swallowed up by Babylon. The weaker state cannot cut itself off from the stronger, if it wants to survive. Maybe you could ask the angel Moroni about that, when next you see him."

The governor paused. "Yes—he visits me almost every night," he said slowly.

"When you see the angel, tell him that General Cruz is sent by the Army of the United States, and that behind him are two million troops. How many troops does Utah have, Governor?"

"I'll tell you what the angel says."

"Tell him General Cruz is his instrument, and that he needs twenty thousand troops from the Utah National Guard, moving towards Malad City, starting tomorrow."

Politicians! Cruz said to himself, after they had hung up. If this didn't work, he would call Jennings again tomorrow. Maybe Joshua Maccabee would get the line of command straight, would know how to talk to Mosiah Moroni. Or maybe they would cancel each other out. Achilles Cruz needed a drink.

Three a.m. Forward Operating Base, Utah National Guard, outside Malad City, Idaho.

"*Warning, warning,*" said the voice inside Specialist Jared Smith's earbud. "*Unidentified helicopter traffic, twelve o'clock, thirteen miles. Closing fast. Enemy armored vehicles, eleven o'clock to one o'clock, multiple columns, eleven miles.*"

The handheld screen flashed the same message. Jared touched the screen. A map came up: a filigree of roads amid dark spots for hills: bright yellow dots of traffic speeding down the roads; other dots in red, representing air traffic, approaching more rapidly. He touched again, brought up a visual image, zoomed for a closeup: armored personnel carriers, heavy tanks rolling across the fields. Zooming still closer: the mouth of a cannon became visible, emitting flame as a shell departed in his direction.

"Warning, warning, enemy tanks opening fire," the computer voice said. *"Closing to three miles. Take evasive action. Recommend counterattack with all available weapons."*

"Counterattack!" Jared said aloud. "Fire anti-tank guns. Launch Apache helicopters!"

"Smith!" Sergeant Page's voice broke in. "Get off that video game and pay attention to the UAV feed."

Reality filtered into Jared's consciousness. Heavy sweat ran down the back of his neck, under his battle dress. The Ground Command Station felt hot and clammy, even though the air conditioning was pumping, dripping condensation from the vents overhead. He and Sgt. Page were seated side by side with barely inches between, inside a square windowless box on the back of an army truck. Electronic equipment crammed the drab beige space.

Three monitor screens filled the wall in front of them, along with dozens of instrument dials and control switches. One monitor showed a map display that traced the flight path of their pair of Hunter Unmanned Aerial Vehicles. A second monitor gave video feed from the UAV's onboard TV camera, a real-time view that would have been full lifelike color if this were daytime. Another monitor was switched to infrared night surveillance, picking up heat sources on the ground, which could be computer enhanced and compared with templates of possible sources, then turned into identification messages. Just now the monitors were showing nothing interesting, as far as Spc. Jared Smith could see.

Sgt. Hiram Page was the remote-control pilot of their pair of over-sized toy model planes. But just now the UAVs were on automatic pilot, as usual when nothing was happening, programmed to patrol systematically over the terrain between I-15 and the diagonal spur of

I-84 cutting through the mountain ranges of the Sawtooth National Forest fifty miles to the northwest. There were many threads of little roads and unpaved tracks between the Ground Command Station and the outer fringes of the UAV's patrol territory, crossing the grasslands and the mountain valleys that became steadily more barren further west, where southern Idaho turned into the fringes of the Utah desert.

"Shit, there's a lot of roads to cover, considering there's nothing there," Jared complained. "And why are there so many people driving around, at this time of night?"

Sgt. Page put down his book. "Watch your language. Truckers like to drive at night. Especially when it's a hundred degrees in the daytime. And I'd say not much cooler in here right now."

"Don't they know better than to drive in a war zone?" Jared said. His hands moved habitually back to the video game, then stopped under Page's disapproving stare.

The three weeks they had been encamped at Malad City had not been what Jared expected. Instead of rushing into combat, blasting away, escaping death, maybe getting wounded, coming home to show off his bandages and tell his friends about it—instead of the wonderful story he was getting ready to tell, it was nothing so far but sitting in this hot little room being bored.

Even the Idaho locals seemed to know nothing was going to happen—they went right on driving around in their pickup trucks, going to work, shopping, going to parties, whatever they did for fun out here in the farm country. While he and his unit were on combat alert, no leaves allowed, full combat dress all the time. It was getting old. Everybody knew nothing was going to happen.

Eventually new orders would come down, the Utah National Guard brigades and the rest of the Idaho expeditionary force would move somewhere else. Maybe we'll find the enemy then, Jared thought, reaching for his video game. Or maybe we'll be sitting around somewhere else being bored.

"Hey, look at that!" Jared said. The infrared display showed a green blob on a road twenty miles away, the thick penumbra glow of a ghostly balloon. "Something really big. A tank, or a tank on a HET, by the speed it's moving." A heavy equipment transporter moved tanks on a giant truck bed with a lot less fuel.

"That's probably just construction equipment. Somebody getting ready to work on the highways soon as it gets light," Sgt. Page said.

"Don't you think we ought to call Captain Squires?"

Sgt. Page swiveled in his chair towards the closed door at the back of the command station, then shook his head. "Squires about bit my head off last time I went to him in the middle of the night with one of your false alarms."

"We could blast that tank-hauler right now," Jared said. "Our Hunter has a laser-guided munition on each wing. I'd sure like to see what that looks like hitting its target."

"Grow up," Page said. "This is no video game. Those munitions aren't cheap, and this is the only Hunter team on the whole front. This is valuable property. You talk Captain Squires into wasting one of those on a useless target and they'll take it out of your hide—and mine too."

"Look," said Jared. "There's another one. That's an awful lot of traffic on that road. Could be a whole enemy battalion."

Sgt. Page peered at the screen. "In the first place, a battalion is much bigger than that. And that reminds me, that was the second time you got me in trouble with the higher-ups. Two weeks ago, when our reinforcements from Fort Carson arrived at night, you thought it was an enemy attack because they were driving around on the west side of I-15 looking for places to park. That alert went all the way to General Cruz, and the Captain was definitely not happy about what came back down."

Page looked at the screen again, shook his head definitely. "See, they're coming from the south. Probably the reinforcements from the Utah National Guard that everybody's been waiting for."

He opened the door, reached back to pick up his book, and started outside. "That AC unit sounds like it's about to break down. I'm going to get the tech to work on it. Keep your eyes on those monitors, Smith, and stay away from that video game."

There was definitely traffic out there, Jared could see. Some of it was coming up the little roads from Utah, and some of it was looping almost due east now, on Highway 37, heading toward Malad City.

He'd like to see what the IR feed looked like for the roads closer in, all those little back roads in the farm country and in the mountain valleys on the west side of I-15; some of them coming out of the Indian reservation outside of Pocatello.

But the Hunters were on autopilot, and they were sweeping the area further west, cruising quietly at 110 knots, methodically sending in strip after strip of video of a aerial view several miles wide. If Sgt. Page were here, he could take over manual control and bring the UAVs nearer their own positions, to see what could be coming up on them in the dark.

Jared was tempted to climb over to Page's seat and take the remote pilot controls; he had seen him operate them often enough, how different could it be from a video flight simulator? But if Page caught him, there really would be hell to pay.

Jared picked up his video game. It was almost brand new, called "Civil War Two." It was the most realistic war game Jared had ever seen, and he had been playing war games ever since he was four years old. Not just monsters or unrealistic icons, it had the sight and sound of real war, from the monitors and map displays on down to the video feed as you actually experienced it. At least, how Jared expected to experience it, since he had never yet been in combat. The voice in his earbud started up again, *"Warning, warning—"*

"Smith, what did I tell you?" Sgt. Page was back. The AC units were working no better, and a blast of hot air had entered the command station while the door was open. "Give me that video game."

Jared resisted having the book-sized game tugged from his hands. "Listen, Sergeant, it's no worse than that Mormon shit you're always reading."

"Watch your language!" Page put the Book of Mormon down hurriedly on his seat and ripped the video game away from Jared.

The command station monitors were bright and full of green glowing shapes, moving rapidly. The Hunters had gone on methodically covering their swath of territory, scanning nearer and nearer to the USA Army front along I-15, and the volume of traffic heading their direction was now plain to see.

"That's disobeying a direct order, Smith," the Sgt. said. "I'm putting you on report, as soon as this shift is over."

"Why don't you put me on report right now?" Jared tried to stand up in the cramped space. There were scarcely room to swing a punch. Jared landed a glancing blow and Page pushed him back into his chair.

The command monitors were now flashing bright red messages:

> WARNING, ENEMY TROOP VEHICLES IDENTIFIED,
> TEN O'CLOCK TO TWO O'CLOCK, CLOSING TO THREE
> MILES. WARNING —

"Listen, Sergeant, you're the one that lives in the land of fantasies. Do you really believe that shit about the gold tablets and the angel Moroni appearing in the middle of the night?"

"It's a revelation of God's power," Page said. "He only reveals himself to the godly. If you would just straighten out and grow up, Smith, you could hear Him too."

In their jostling, a switch had been hit. The Ground Control station computer had switched to audible mode. The computer voice rang out:

"*Warning, warning, alert, alert! Enemy fire incoming!*"

An explosion shattered the wall of the Ground Control Station. The monitors went out and then everything in Jared Smith's consciousness was dark.

Most of the troops were asleep in their windowless pods, the portable quarters of the well-equipped modern army, with air conditioning on and doors shut. Soldiers who weren't asleep were listening to music on headphones or playing video games, sealed off from the hot night. Chattering of helicopters came near. Soldiers shrugged, swore, turned over to burrow their heads deeper into bedding. The military was always moving something day or night, among bases strung out over fifty miles with mountains in between, commanders flying in and out, shifting reinforcements and logistics. The helicopters persisted overhead.

Then—

Pods were rocked by blast waves, shuddering on their raised plank foundations.

Rockets were streaking down from the night sky. Helicopters parked on the improvised landing field were hit first, along with officers' command vehicles, communications vehicles, and anti-aircraft artillery. CSSA forces had their sensors too, their drones and helicopters with onboard video and telemetric feed; they knew the standard operating procedures of the US Army, knew what to look for and where to find it. Munitions stores were hit, cooking off secondary explosions and sending rockets and artillery shells at unpredictable angles and directions.

Multiple fragmentation bomblets were ripping the pods' walls. Soldiers were running in the dark now lit up like a fireworks show. They dragged bloodied companions, called each other's names.

Captain Dave Witmer was outside his pod when it began, returning from the row of latrines at the edge of the meadow. Through his night-vision goggles the scene unfolded like an old low quality film in green and black. The trampled grass streets of the pod city were a jumble of half-clothed soldiers, running this way and that, unsure which way to go.

Witmer started back to his pod, automatically seeking his sidearms and his secure handheld radio. Maybe just seeking his sanity in the mêlée, he realized, seeking a fixed starting point.

His pod didn't seem to be there anymore—the huts had crumpled this way and that, tipping against each other, making jagged roadblocks across the once military-neat rows. He needed a chain of command, needed his First Sergeant, needed his lieutenants to report, needed the platoons of Company C to fall in.

He thought he recognized a man from his company, grabbed at his green-tinted form in the rushing crowd. The man did not stop— he had no night-vision goggles, did not recognize his commanding officer, or could not hear the captain's voice in the blast or the rush of his own adrenalin.

Witmer made another failed attempt to accost a man. A third attempt was more successful—Staff Sergeant Robbins, in T-shirt and shorts, but in boots and carrying an M4. Together they patrolled an intersection at the edge of the pod city, pulling men they recognized out of the crowd, getting them in some sort of order. Not everyone stopped, but for those who did, the drill formation seemed to calm them.

"Collect the wounded!" Witmer yelled. A man fell at his feet. Blood was soaking his shirt. He sat up nevertheless when Witmer touched him. "Better not move," Witmer said. "You could lose all your blood, if it's bad."

"I'm all right," he said, getting to his feet. "I don't feel a thing."

Not everyone was so lucky. A man was lying outside a crushed pod in a contorted position. Something looked indescribably weird in the green of Witmer's NODs. Witmer tore off the night observation devices. The next fireworks flash showed the man's belly was open with the entrails hanging out.

Witmer found a medic hurriedly bandaging, tournequetting, injecting morphine. Witmer dragged him to where the man with the torn entrails lay. The medic shook his head. "Nothing I can do about that one, Captain."

We need stretchers, Witmer thought. But where? Witmer sent a man in the direction where the battalion medical station had been.

The rockets out of the sky had stopped; the CSSA attack helicopters had finished their opening phase and moved on. CSSA transport helicopters had landed, half-circling the camp on west and south, discharging enemy infantry. Enemy ground vehicles were arriving too from the spiderweb of little country roads, more and more infantry beyond the edge of the meadow, laying down increasing fire.

Small units of the First Utah brigade had pulled together into firing lines and now there was a firefight. But not for long. The defenders took casualties; their fire slackened. As enemy fire increased, zeroing in on resistance points, the ill-formed platoons and squads pulled back, first scurrying, then running.

Where were the heavy weapons? The Utah brigade had tanks, armored personnel carriers, mobile artillery. As yet, it had hardly been able to mount a heavy machine gun. The crowd of bodies milling in the camp streets was no longer at cross purposes, no longer individuals searching for buddies, it now had a direction—the motor pool.

Armor could save us, Witmer thought. The enemy couldn't possibly have any armor out here, it was a sneak attack, made with helicopters and light transport vehicles filtering through the surveillance zone. Since the rockets stopped, there had been nothing but small arms fire, enemy machine guns and light mortars at the most.

The unorganized mass of soldiers had much the same idea—armor was shelter. And the motor pool was where they assembled whenever they left their base. Modern infantry never traveled anywhere on foot; they were always delivered in vehicles, then dismounted if need be to fight.

The sky was lightening. NODs were no longer needed, not even useful in the transitional light. The motor pool resembled a sports arena at the end of a game mobbed by championship-starved spectators, except instead of tearing up the grounds for souvenirs they were mobbing the rows of parked armored vehicles. Most of the tanks were still up on the beds of heavy equipment haulers, but every wheeled Stryker and tracked APC was the center of a little crowd, clawing and pulling at each other. Idiotic! Witmer said to himself. They need to assemble their crews, get their firepower into action before the enemy gets here, instead of fighting among themselves.

Then he realized: the enemy was here. The mob of bodies tussling like rugby scrums wore two different uniforms, the grey-uniformed CSSA and the green T-shirts and green-and-brown battle dress of the USA. One group would climb on top of the vehicle or open its rear combat door; the other side would grab their legs and try to pull them off. The CSSA troops had guns while most of the USA troops did not, but it made no difference since they were too close to fire. The CSSA were using their guns not to shoot but as bludgeons to smash their opponents' arms and heads. It wasn't just that it would have been massive friendly fire either way. The range at which soldiers were used to firing had been crossed, diminished to nothing, and now it was easier to grab and kick and punch, a game of king of the mountain whose aim was not glory but fighting for their lives.

At the end of the row of parked vehicles a tank had started up and began to move. Its turret swung toward the ant-pile swarming the APCs. Whose? The big gun leveled menacingly, but it was the turret machine gunner who fired, raking the row of APCs and sending the ants falling and scurrying in the dim light. Witmer had a sinking feeling it had been captured by the CSSA. Now they had armor, probably would get more. Could we bring any of our own armor into action?

The intermingled armies separated. The CSSA withdrew temporarily to one side of the field and began laying down a regular fire. USA troops began to form up behind the armor. One APC came into action, then another. We have a chance, Witmer thought. He picked out the nearest parked vehicle in the motor pool and motioned his little squad towards it.

Before they could break into the open, the roar of CSSA Apaches was again overhead, flying so low the blast of sound and wind pummeled them into the ground. Tank-killer rockets arched down in rainbows ending in booming flashes. When Witmer looked up, the APC he had chosen was lurched on its side with its treads torn off.

The CSSA helicopters were gone, chattering up the valley, seeking other targets in the dispersed USA camps. Creating maximal havoc, Witmer said to himself. Their helos are spread too thin to hit everything.

A truck came in their direction, its canvas-covered bed holding only a few soldiers. Witmer flagged it to a grudging halt and got his squad on board. Crowded in the front cab were four soldiers, most of them without their shirts. The sun was coming over the mountain peaks and the first rays made them look bloody, like caricature red Indians in war paint—or maybe their own wounds, though Witmer couldn't see exactly who was hit. Muscular young bodies all piled close to each other. Their talk was a stream of obscenities, and Witmer was enough of a good Mormon to be put off by it.

Then he realized: they're babbling, the same words over and over. He was feeling lightheaded himself. It seemed insane to let himself be driven by these kids. Not much else he could do right now. He found a place to lay down in the truck bed and let the flow carry him where it would.

Vehicles were streaming out of the motor pool and onto the road. The crowd had a new goal: the Interstate highway. It was the obvious place, the road they had come in on during the drive from Utah, and the backbone that linked the USA positions together. There were two on-ramps, just north and south of Malad City. The Utah Brigades were all camped in a scatter of sites in the farmland west of Malad

City; there was no room on the east side of the highway, where the hills jutted up almost from the side of the road. Vehicles pouring out of each of the camp sites converged in a traffic jam; the two brigades' seven thousand troops were served by almost two thousand vehicles, not just combat armor but trucks and service vehicles. As many of them as possible had now started up and were heading onto just two roads—most of these large ungainly vehicles crowding the onramp on the south edge of town, the mindset being to head south on I-15 to safety in numbers.

Soldiers had crammed inside APCs, beyond their usual capacity of nine. Larger numbers jammed onto trucks. Still more were clinging to the outsides. Traffic slowed the vehicles to a walking pace. Soldiers on foot were streaming out of the camps, catching up and climbing aboard, helping each other on. Both sides of the little two-lane streets were full, traffic all heading in the same direction.

Stop and start, with inevitable collisions. A man's feet were run over by a wheel. Limbs were caught and dragged in caterpillar tracks. Bodies jumping on and off were crushed between vehicles. Some drivers stopped to let their passengers climb down and pull the accident victims away; but vehicles further back in the queue pressed forward, in a howl of shouts and curses.

A little trickle was getting through, onto the highway. Then all forward movement stopped. Word was shouted up the line: I-15 South is blocked, the enemy is there. CSSA helicopters, whether inadvertently or by design, had let a handful of APCs and trucks onto the highway, then had hit them with rockets. The disabled vehicles blocked all the lanes. Ordinarily the army would bring up an armored bulldozer to clear them out of the way, but anything that might have been available was caught in the crush approaching the on-ramp.

In desperation, vehicles began to descend the on-ramps in the other direction—the lanes of I-15 were still open northwards. Malad City FOB was the southernmost in the chain of bases, Virginia was the next FOB, they would join forces, finding safety in numbers.

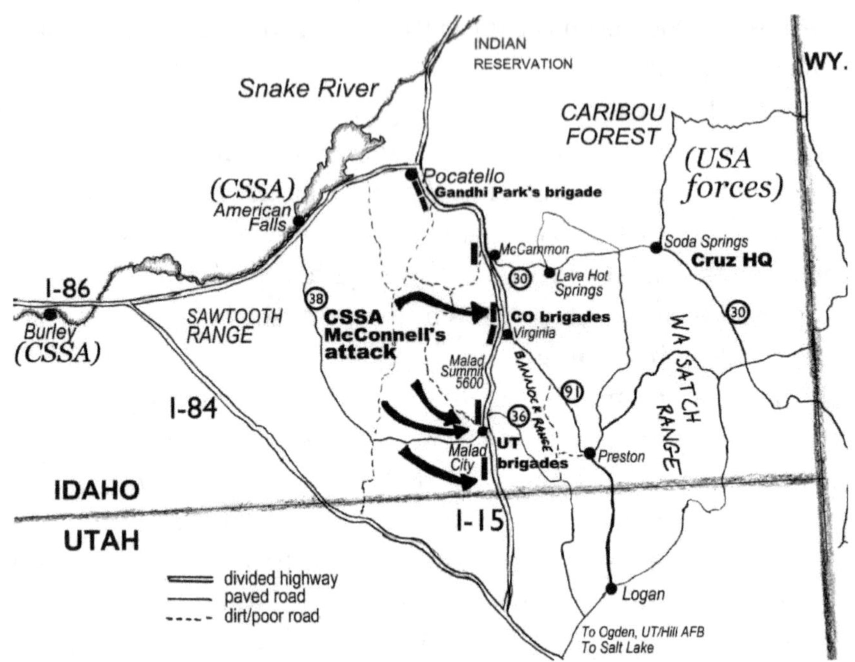

CSSA attackers, although a smaller force than the two Utah brigades, were pressing them hard from behind. The traffic jam had slowed the pace of the Utah brigades so much that the CSSA troops hardly needed to remount their own light transport; they advanced on foot, raking the mob of retreating Federals with M-16 fire, exploding rocket-propelled grenades among the vehicles. The traffic jam on the on-ramp was loosening now, water finding its drainage now that the Federal vehicles had turned north, using both northbound and southbound lanes of the divided Interstate.

The exit columns were picking up speed, APCs accelerating to 60 miles per hour on the open road, trucks and cars among them. Here and there soldiers clinging to the outside of vehicles slipped and fell off, too exhausted or wounded to hold on. Their comrades sometimes shouted to stop for them, but the momentum of the column was set and no one stopped.

It was twenty miles from Malad City to Virginia. Halfway there, Interstate-15 funneled into a narrow valley, and climbed to Malad Summit between a pair of nine-thousand-foot mountain peaks. Ordinarily northbound traffic would descend from the summit into the farmlands of Marsh Valley, with its filigree of little roads south of Virginia. What the columns fleeing from Malad City did not know, was that the FOB at Virginia had been overrun too, and that retreating traffic was now escaping south on I-15, filling both north and southbound lanes, heading for the Malad Summit bottleneck.

Up in the eagle's nest at Soda Springs, Achilles Cruz took in the reports with grim detachment. The lethargy was gone that sometimes took hold of him when dealing with the routine hassles of military life, and that made him want a drink when he talked to politicians. He felt fully engaged, certainly not cheerful but very clear-headed and focused. There was a lot to focus on.

The forces at Malad City were disintegrating. Not too surprising; they were raw troops, without battle experience in this young war— but then most other troops in a suddenly expanded military were battle-raw too, without falling apart. The Utah brigades at the south end of his line, closest to the Utah border, could not help but be infected by the dilatory attitude of General Hawp and the political wavering over what role Utah forces would play in this campaign. No one had told them anything directly, but they knew.

The brigades at Virginia were also being attacked, the same sudden helicopter rockets out of the pre-dawn sky, the same abrupt intrusion of CSSA infantry in their camps. The defenders were regular army forces, two brigades from Fort Carson, Colorado. Their command structure was holding up better; perhaps they had a little more warning time. It was impossible to tell how many attackers there were; everyone was exaggerating the numbers, probably because they were overwhelmed.

The attackers seemed to know what they were doing; communications and surveillance were the first things they hit, creating high-tech blindness and turning it into old-fashioned wild-eyed panic. Reports were conflicting about whether the enemy had armor or not. Cruz guessed not, although his own armor at the Virginia camps was paralyzed and useless; some of it overrun and possibly captured and turned against them.

One thing was clear: for the present, the enemy had control of the air. The helicopters belonging to the Malad City and Virginia brigades were destroyed on the ground or inoperable. CSSA attack helicopters had little opposition, although some might have been hit by ground fire. The only thing limiting them was that most had exhausted their rockets and were returning to their forward base to rearm. Where? It was a point of vulnerability that could be attacked.

Cruz was in contact with Hill AFB in Ogden, Utah, and F/A-18s were on the way. But they were not the only force in the daylight sky. Their CSSA counterpart from the Mountain Home airbase near Boise was only two hundred seventy-five miles away; and Cruz's staff computers were full of reports of air-to-air duels. These were by now old antagonists, matched up repeatedly in the air war of the past ten months that had taken such a toll from both sides.

Today was already shaping up as the familiar story, equally matched and extremely expensive high-tech machines fighting to a stalemate and eliminating themselves through mutual attrition, thereby turning the battle over to lesser weapons and more traditional maneuvers.

Cruz called for additional support from the fighter bases in eastern Colorado. They would send what they could, though shorthanded, with other commitments. The usual excuses. The Texas and Gulf Coast bases were equally unhelpful, and the Midwestern front had its demands and priorities. The only good thing was the CSSA seemed to be playing it the same way. They had air backup in coastal Oregon and Washington, and over in California and Nevada; but thus far they were only matching the USAF tit for tat, leaving it to the ground forces.

It was McConnell's style of attack, Cruz said to himself. Get in on the ground, grab the glory for himself. The old Confederate cavalry raid in the night. That meant the CSSA forces were probably undermanned, relying on surprise and psychological shock. He could ride them out.

Col. Dietrich, commander of Cruz's air cavalry regiment, entered the Soda Springs headquarters. "General, we're ready to go. All fueled up and armed. Awaiting orders."

"Keep it reined in for now," Cruz said. The blond officer standing in front of him looked especially solid this morning, silhouetted against the crisp blue morning sky. The purple meadows felt unusually still.

"But we're getting slaughtered down there. They have no air support. We're all we have left."

"That's the point, Karl. I can't tell if McConnell has thrown in everything he has in the air, or whether they're waiting for you to go in, and strip us bare."

"But how are we going to find out?"

"I'm authorizing a limited recon for now," Cruz said. "No more than three helos. Get me a good read on the road between Malad City and Virginia, and whatever is coming from the west. Don't fight it out. Hightail it back here if there's any trouble."

"And the rest are just going to sit here on the ground and wait for the enemy to show up?"

"I'm not sure McConnell has enough forces to hit this far back, or if he does, he'll have to skimp someplace else. Keep all triple-A at full readiness." Cruz cuffed Dietrich on the triceps. "Don't worry, Karl, you'll have all the fighting you can handle when the time comes."

Cruz put in a call to General Park over the secure link. "Gandhi, what's the situation in your sector?"

"Dead quiet," Gandhi said. "I haven't heard any action between here and McCammon."

"What does your recon show for enemy forces north or west of you? I don't mean reports from the drones—I mean confirmed by your own patrols."

"Same as before. Enemy forces at American Falls about twenty-five miles outside Pocatello, and a bigger concentration eighty miles west. They're not moving in this direction."

"And north? Any sign of forces from Montana?"

"There is considerable enemy force at Idaho Falls, fifty miles north. Rumors among the civilians here are that some of them are Montana National Guard."

"What estimated numbers?"

"Elements of a couple of brigades at Idaho Falls. A battalion at American Falls. There might be more, dug in and concealed."

"They might be waiting for you to move out to reinforce the battle in the south. Then the rebels could join forces at Pocatello, and be in position for another offensive."

"Do you want my opinion, General?"

"That's what I'm asking for, Gandhi. I'm just thinking out loud."

"I don't think the forces up here are McConnell's. They've been sitting here for months, and that's what they're used to doing. McConnell has brought in his own strike force, and it's not big enough to hit all our camps at once."

"So I take it you are ready to move."

"We're mounted right now. My helos can be on their way to the relief of Virginia in ten minutes. Armored columns will be right behind them."

Cruz was silent for a long moment, as if sending a message of calm to his subordinate. The sun was high and the clearing in the high mountains was starting to get hot. "All right. Move them out, except for a skeleton defense to hold Pocatello. But I want you to move only as far as McCammon, until further notice."

"Yes, sir. Are you expecting the next attack will be at McCammon?"

"Frankly, I'm not. I have the feeling they want us to feel overwhelmed and cut off at the north end of our position. They're leaving open a line of retreat going east from McCammon: Highway 30, over the mountains to Soda Springs, and all the way back to the Wyoming border." Cruz explained slowly, projecting his calm—but getting the feeling Gandhi Park didn't need it.

"That's what I'm getting from their pattern of helicopter and fighter/bomber attacks," Cruz went on. They've cut off I-15 south of Malad City, and Highway 36 east, so there's no escape except north. And they're attacking traffic on Highway 91 on the southeast side of Virginia, so nothing can get out that way. It looks to me that they want to trap the four Utah and Colorado brigades between Malad Summit and Virginia, while they try to panic our three brigades at the north end of the line. That's why they've left Route 30 open—they want the Wyoming campaign force to go back the way it came."

"So I am to reinforce a stand at McCammon?"

"I didn't say make a stand. I want you to prepare for an attack."

"I'm ready to roll into Virginia right now. It's only another ten miles. I could get there in time to prevent the encirclement of the Colorado brigades."

"No," said Cruz. "I want you to wait. I know that sticks in your craw, General. But remember the rule: don't reinforce failure."

At noon the USA forces at Virginia were still resisting. Cruz had marshaled reserves from the Preston area, down Route 91 near the Utah border, sheltered behind the Bannock Range. The situation at Malad City was beyond repair. Stragglers were coming into the Preston area on foot, over the mountain passes and canyons. For now they were just a nuisance, demoralized individuals creating pathetic scenes on the road, as Cruz's reserve troops went forward on Route 36, heading for the juncture at Malad City. But they were just putting up a forward defense, preventing the CSSA from driving further into the Union rear supply areas.

Cruz sent bigger mechanized forces up Highway 91, heading towards Virginia from the southeast; but these too were told to proceed cautiously, their numbers too small to fight the bulk of McConnell's army; at best they were to harass it on the outskirts of Virginia, screening the counterattack to come.

The counterattack would need fresh forces, full-scale combat brigades. These had been ready in Utah for weeks, while the generals and politicians had argued as to their route and strategic objective. Cruz had alerted General Hawp already in the early morning, and received a promise of reinforcements. Yet Hawp's tone of voice was not reassuring. He was still holding back, waiting for something. It had to be Governor Mosiah Moroni Young, still dreaming of his independent State of Deseret.

It was time to settle this once and for all. Mosiah Moroni had to be made to understand that Utah could not survive a crushing loss just across the Idaho border, leaving the CSSA with the momentum to roll down I-15 into Salt Lake City. The situation could be retrieved, but Utah forces had to join Cruz's forces in a pincers attack that would drive the CSSA out of southern Idaho. Momentum could swing either way, but the time was now.

Reports were coming in from Virginia. The CSSA had scored a big victory at Malad Summit, and were driving north and east. They had reached the triangle of highways south of Virginia. They had cut off Highway 91. There was no longer any escape to the south or east.

Things had gotten bad enough so that even Mosiah Moroni Young should get the message, Cruz thought. No point in waiting any longer. He put in a conference call: He wanted General Hawp and Governor Young on the line, simultaneously. As an afterthought, he had his executive officer call the White House and ask the President to join them. Arguing as one man's voice against two politicians and religious fanatics was not a contest Achilles Cruz was confident he could win. Joshua Maccabee Jennings had promised to help him when he needed it. He was calling in his cards.

Thick black cloud-pillars rose in the air like angry smoke signals on both sides of the Interstate outside of Virginia, Idaho. Our fuel dumps burning, Captain Witmer thought. Miraculously, he and Sgt. Robbins still held together a squad-sized group, all that was left in organized form of Company C. They had abandoned their truck in the traffic jam at Malad Summit. The young soldiers in the cab had stopped cursing, but they refused to get out of the cab. They were still piled together, looking less bloody and more dirty, when Witmer glanced back at them as his squad picked its way among the rocks. It turned out to be a good move. Half an hour later, they had gone less than a mile on the rough terrain. A sudden racket behind them made them look: CSSA attack helicopters were back again, having replenished their munitions, and now were rocketing the stalled traffic relentlessly. It reminded Witmer of photos from the early railroad days in the West, when buffalo herds were slaughtered by passengers firing from trains.

The helicopter attack let up for a few minutes when several USA F/A-18s flew in to harass the harassers. But only briefly. CSSA fighters were soon on their tails, and the aerial battle swooped off to higher elevation, leaving the CSSA Apaches to resume their deadly work. The enemy helicopters should have been targets for the Utah brigades' triple-A, but no one had thought to bring it along in their hurry or if so had abandoned it in the crush.

From the distance of the rocky hillside Witmer's squad had a good view. Spectators of our own battle, he thought. Well, better than being over there where everything is completely useless.

A trio of USA helicopters approached from the mountains to the northeast, moving at top speed. Witmer felt a little flicker of relief, then realized it was not enough. From the rear of the traffic jam on the highway, where CSSA ground forces followed the retreat at a deliberate pace, ground-fired SAMs streaked up at the Union air patrol. The trio of helicopters quickly retreated. The CSSA is picking up our abandoned weapons and using them against us. The enemy fires our equipment, Witmer thought; we don't.

Witmer's little troop made their way at a distance from the road, hugging the hillsides, then scrambling across the farmlands that widened out at the bottom of the pass. Somewhere ahead there had to be intact USA formations, a solid wall of organization that they could merge with. For four hours they had been marching in the hot sun, throwing themselves into ditches when enemy helicopters passed overhead. Among ten men, they had four M4 carbines. Witmer kept looking to scavenge a sidearm, but he had seen nothing.

From time to time Witmer spotted CSSA units fanning out across the fields, heading northeast in pickups and captured USA Army trucks. Firing at them from a distance would be a useless gesture.

Reading his mind, Sgt. Robbins said, "How about setting up an ambush, Captain? That way we'd pick up a vehicle, and some weapons."

"If we don't blow the car all to hell," one of the soldiers laughed grimly. His name tape read: JACK. It was his last name, not a first name. "And if we can stop a truck with an M4."

"We need to get some weapons first," Witmer said, "then get a vehicle."

The heat was in the 90s, making shimmering waves in the air distorting the geometrical rows of crops like a bad case of astigmatism. Half the men looked severely sunburned, their faces turning ugly purple-red. No one carried any water, and no one had had any food since the previous evening.

"Might as well attack anyway. " Jack said. "Take some of them down with us."

"Button that, Private," Witmer said. "We're not on a suicide mission." He motioned the group forward. "There's a stream up ahead. We can get some water."

In late afternoon, they reached a bigger road, about a mile outside of Virginia. In the distance off to the left, I-15 seemed to have opened up again. All the traffic was going north, in an orderly fashion. All military traffic. It was quieter too, no more firing nearby. CSSA helicopters passed along regularly but the fighting seemed to be over. High in the sky, they no longer looked like black scorpions but more like buzzing flies.

Witmer listened for sounds of firing in the distance, anything coming from the north side of Virginia. Any USA forces still putting up resistance, a goal line they could aim for.

The road ahead ran east-west, connecting I-15 on their left to Highway 91 angling in on the right. It had intermittent traffic, mostly heading east, where there should be signs of battle—if the CSSA had not already encircled the town. But that direction too was quiet.

As Witmer's squad climbed up the little embankment out of the field, a USA Army two-and-a-half-ton truck bore down on them, heading west. For a moment the same thought flickered in their heat-dazed minds: friendly forces, rescue! The truck slowed to a halt. A CSSA soldier leaned out the window. The door opened and the gray-uniformed soldier stepped out, waving an M4 casually as if he were directing traffic. "OK boys, end of the line. Get in the back with the rest of them."

Witmer blinked ferociously, clearing the sweat from his eyes. From behind him came a shot. Sgt. Robbins had hit the soldier in the middle of the chest. As he crumpled to the road, Witmer ran forward and grabbed the M4. The touch of the gun in his hands was the sheerest pleasure he could remember. His muscles came alive as he hefted its weight and felt the trigger.

Shouts came from the back of the canvas-top truck and a pair of CSSA soldiers dropped over the tailgate. Witmer, Robbins, and the rest of the squad who had weapons opened fire on them simultaneously. The two guards were down on the pavement. Two of Witmer's squad were still firing, emptying their ammunition clips, the bodies bouncing from the impacts.

The silence that followed exploded in Witmer's ears like a giant vacuum pressure jar popping. A dozen USA prisoners who had been crouching for cover on the floor of the truck were sitting up and leaning out cautiously.

"Americans!" Witmer yelled. "We're USA." A few of the liberated prisoners began to climb out.

The CSSA truck driver was still in the cab. He could have driven off but he seemed paralyzed. A pistol sat on the dashboard in front of him but he made no move toward it. Witmer was pulling him out of the cab when another truck pulled to a halt. Then another, coming from the opposite direction. A whole convoy of captured trucks filled the road, loaded with USA prisoners.

Witmer stood with the pistol in one hand and an M4 in the other. His squad was looking at him. Then their gazes dropped to the ground. They made no move as CSSA soldiers swarmed around them, taking the guns from their hands.

Witmer suddenly felt limp as a dish rag. He could barely put one foot in front of the other as he and his squad, shuffling like zombies, were motioned into the back of a truck and driven away.

Prisoners were gathered in a big field on the far side of Virginia, alongside what had been one of the USA camps. The town was completely under CSSA control. Hundreds, maybe thousands of USA soldiers were standing listlessly in a sorry semblance of a parade-ground formation. Wounded men were collected in thick rows, lying on the ground waiting for attention. Medical care was short in supply and slow in coming. A few CSSA soldiers walked among the fallen and defeated, passing around bottles of water.

Guards patrolled back and forth. Witmer thought they were laughing and joking but the sound came to him far away from the other side of a thick glass barrier that was his head.

Sounds of cheering filtered through. The guards came to attention, looking very proud and military. CSSA soldiers crowded into the field, waving their arms at a figure standing very erect in the back of a jeep. It was General McConnell.

McConnell was pumping his fist in the air, a broad grin on his face. The crowd responded with a rhythmic chant: "Mick! Mick!"

McConnell let the troops go on for a few minutes, enjoying themselves, playing half cheerleader, half celebrity idol. He was bareheaded and had let his hair grow long into a blonde mane that shone in the late-afternoon sun. The low-angled light blazed from his blue-glazed reflective sunglasses. Instead of regulation camouflage battle dress he wore a military dress shirt, without the row of service ribbons but crossed with the leather straps of a shoulder holster showing an ivory handled revolver.

He hushed the cheering with a cutting gesture. "Soldiers of the California Seventh!" A roar. "Soldiers of the Second Idaho!" Another roar. "And from my heart—Marines of the First Marine Expeditionary Force!" An agitated segment of the CSSA crowd waved fists back at their general. "This is your victory." More cheers. Write it down, he said, the name of the Battle of Caribou Forest. Future historians would add it to a proud list. He went on, telling them there was more work to do. Telling them the strategic significance of clearing the Northwest from this enemy invasion.

McConnell turned and gestured toward the USA prisoners. "This is what remains of the enemy army. Treat them well—they were doing their job. Though not half as well as you've being doing yours." The CSSA crowd laughed. The prisoners looked even more wilted. "I know we've been a little short on food, but we can probably find plenty of it around here." The crowd, some of them chewing candy bars, laughed again. "So save some of it for our guests. And medics! That's where we're really short. Fortunately our casualties are light. So I want all medical officers to detail what medics they can spare to look after the defeated enemy."

Two USA officers were brought forward, captive under escort. Brigadier General Young of the First Utah, Brigadier General Sandoval of the Colorado forces. They saluted McConnell stiffly, reluctantly accepted his outstretched handshake. There were no swords to hand over, and today most ranking officers did not even carry sidearms, unless it was part of the theatre of leadership—some commanders thought that heroes were good for the troops. Surrender was less ceremonial now, but the forms were still useful on both sides, a way of easing the situation.

"You will join me for dinner, of course," McConnell said.

It took place in a commandeered restaurant, a steak house alongside the highway. Officers of both armies sat in a long row made up of formica-topped tables pushed together, covered with paper tablecloths bearing the restaurant's advertisements in bright red designs. General Young, a good Mormon, declined the ceremonial liquor, but he raised his water glass dutifully as McConnell and his staff offered toasts to future friendship, to America, to the great state of Idaho, and to the coming of peace. Other more partisan toasts brought cheers and standing ovations from the CSSA officers, while their Union captives sat silently.

Conversation became fragmented and convivial. General Sandoval grunted occasionally, taking his liquor and drinking a good deal of wine with his food. McConnell's dinner party included the three women officers who were among the USA prisoners. The two younger and better-looking of them were seated to his left and right. McConnell alternated his attention between them, cheering them up, inquiring about their battle experience, their military careers, their romantic lives, offering compliments, making smooth witticisms. Captain Melody Klimp, a transport officer in one of the Colorado brigades, kept up a frown as best she could. Her own commander, General Sandoval, was sitting directly across, looking on disapprovingly.

On the other side, Lieutenant Tamara Wilson was telling McConnell about the hassles of inventorying every piece of battle equipment in her brigade with only forty-eight hours notice before they moved out. She was a plump young woman in her early twenties, with thick black hair and graceful oval face of mixed-race parentage, her skin a deep perfect tan. "Sounds like you need a break," McConnell was saying. "A little R and R."

"I didn't come to Idaho for vacation, you know, General," Tamara said.

"I know you didn't. But now you'll have some time on your hands." Their thighs rubbed under the table.

"I'll bet you're a very busy man, General." She didn't move her thigh away.

"A good officer has to find time for everything," he said.

General Sandoval broke his silence. "What arrangements have been made for my troops' sleeping quarters tonight, General?"

"About the same as my troops," McConnell said. "Most of them are sleeping on the ground. These camps have been pretty torn up by the fighting."

"And the officers?"

"We'll find something for you." McConnell called a staff officer. "It looks like General Sandoval is ready to retire. Find something appropriate for him."

Sandoval stood up. "We're not done yet. Achilles Cruz is still out there. You'll see tomorrow."

"If so, we'll have a really good party tomorrow night," McConnell said. He was holding Tamara's hand under the table.

Casualties were not as light on the CSSA side as McConnell had said. Witmer saw CSSA wounded, too, and a crowded field hospital marked with red crosses on the tops of tents and vehicles. Burial details were collecting bodies, while leaving others for later: their own dead first, the enemy dead when they got around to it. It had taken six hours to take this place, there must have been considerable resistance. McConnell had been boastful, or making a positive impression for his troops. That's half the art of being a general, Witmer thought.

The prisoners' guards, too, were not uniformly happy in their victory. As evening wore on, a tone of bitterness was heard in their voices. There were quarrels over distributing food. The USA captives were doubtless hungrier, having been driven from their camps before breakfast; but the CSSA must have had a hard few days of it in their sneak attack, and some had been lying concealed in the hills for over a day waiting for everything to get into position. Many of the prisoners of war were reduced to shameless begging, holding out their hands and grasping pathetically at the CSSA soldiers passing among them handing out MREs. The guards reacted to the begging by becoming progressively more jaded.

One guard, isolated in a sea of outstretched hands, jerked the sack of MREs back abruptly. "If we take any more prisoners tomorrow, we won't be able to feed ourselves." His companion flung the contents of his sack into the crowd, setting off a scramble. "Bunch of animals," he said.

Medics for the Union wounded were sparse in the crowd. Occasionally a nurse circulated among the hundreds lying on the meadow, with an armed guard at her side. Most of the wounded were still waiting for aid.

"They're going to kill us," a prisoner said. He was from one of the Colorado brigades, with grimy face and blood soaking his sleeve.

"They won't kill us," Witmer said. "There are laws of war. We're all civilized."

"Civilized." Pvt. Jack squatted on his heels, looking like an Indian. "The US Army massacred plenty, in these same mountains. Drove the Nez Perce to starvation, up in Yellowstone. Same thing with the Sioux. Massacred men, women, and children at Wounded Knee. Left the wounded out in the snow to freeze."

"Indians did it too," a bearded soldier said. "The Fetterman massacre. All eighty killed. Custer's regiment. Two hundred dead, not a man left alive. You know how that is, all killed, no wounded? When the Modocs ambushed settlers, the bodies were mutilated. They tortured the wounded to death."

"Those days are past," Witmer said. "No one's going to torture anybody."

"Then why don't they send a medic?" the Colorado soldier said. "They're leaving us out to die."

Pvt. Jack drew a long knife from under his shirt, displayed it deliberately. "They didn't search me. I'm going to take some of them with me."

"Put that away," Witmer said. "The guards are jumpy enough as it is."

"I'm a Modoc," Jack said. "They never beat us. We fought seven battles. Beat the white man every time. Then the eighth battle, we were down to forty warriors. The army had five hundred. We could go on killing them, ten to one, and they'd still outlast us. We gave up and went to the reservation. Except for seven warriors they hung, after we surrendered."

"The Modocs were murderers," the bearded soldier said. "They killed white men right in the middle of a negotiation under a flag of truce."

"So did the white man. When the army negotiated with the Apaches—"

"Go to sleep," Witmer said. "Give the rest of us a break."

The men were still arguing as Witmer fell asleep. The moaning of the wounded trailed off into a sound he was making in his own head. He dreamed of air raid sirens, shaped like round metallic disks, like electrodes attached to patients' chests in a cardiac test. Women were circulating among the sleeping soldiers wearing metal disks like breast plates. Big-breasted women looked like Valkyries. Norse mythology, Witmer murmured to himself, women on the battlefield, picking up the dead.

He awakened to the sound of distant explosions. The dark night sky had faded to gray dawn. Bombs were falling south and east of town. Sounds of aircraft, rockets, artillery. Nearby, the heavy rumble of armored vehicles as their engines started up.

"Prisoners, everybody on your feet!" A thin file of guards stood across from them in the meadow, automatic weapons levelled at them. How few they looked, facing thousands of prisoners. Guards menaced prisoners who were slow to rise, poking guns at them, looking for signs of resistance. Some of those still lying on the ground were wounded men, others too despondent or groggy to move. The guards began shouting at each other. If one of them fires accidentally, they'll all fire, Witmer thought.

CSSA vehicles were moving on the roads, picking up speed. The whole army was in a hurry. The explosions were closer. The prisoners began milling around, agitated by the approaching firing. Little conspiratorial mutterings about rushing the guards. Private Jack, the Modoc warrior, gestured to Witmer with his knife.

"Prisoners, down! Everybody on the ground!" the guards now yelled. They seemed even fewer than before.

"Now's the time," Private Jack whispered hoarsely. Witmer motioned his squad to alert. Sgt. Robbins and a few of the others were ready to fight. The guards were pointing their guns directly at them.

A jeep drove rapidly into the meadow and screeched to a halt. It was General McConnell.

"Put your guns down," he said to the guards. "We're letting the prisoners go."

The sergeant in charge of the guard protested. "They've got weapons, sir. They're getting ready to rush us."

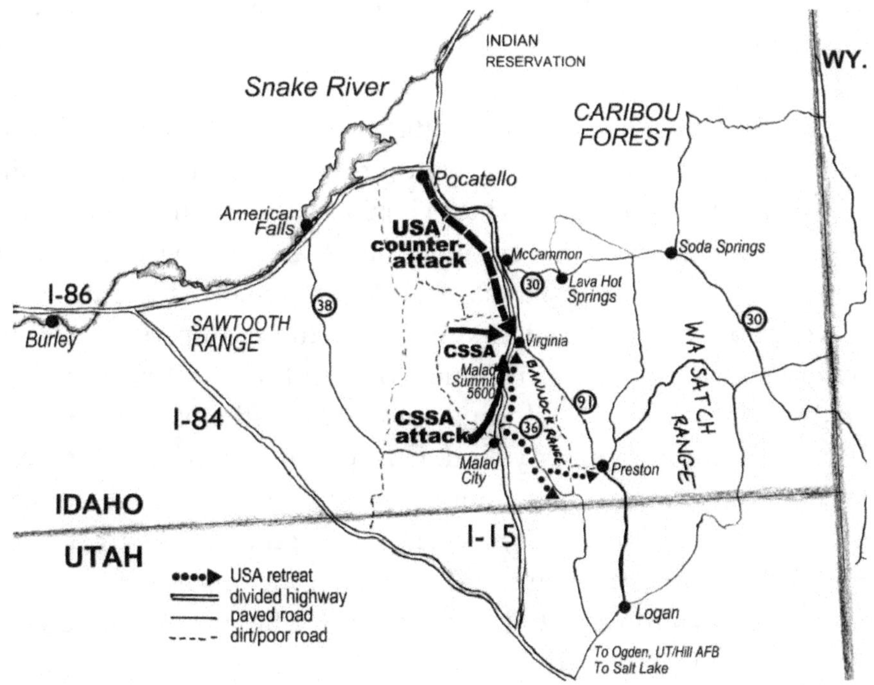

Firing was coming from a new direction, this time from the north. Cruz has counterattacked, Witmer thought. And the firing from the south and east must be reinforcements from Utah.

"We can't hold onto them, Sergeant," McConnell said. "We have to move out, and we can't take them with us."

"Can't we push them along in front of us, so the enemy can't hit us?"

"We don't use human shields," McConnell said. "Not in the Marines. And not in my army command. Is that understood, Sergeant?"

A staff officer gave orders for the prisoners to be dispersed and the guards withdrawn. McConnell's jeep had rushed away. The prisoners were mostly up on their feet now, with as many of the wounded capable of moving on their own or with help. Ripples of life flowed through the crowd like a patient waking from anesthesia. Excited knots were planning bold attacks or desperate escapes. But there was no overall direction, no chain of command, scarcely any officers and those scattered among the debris of many broken units. Some of the men wanted to stay where they were, some wanted to help the wounded, some wanted to move towards friendly lines, others to get away from the firing. For the present, the currents cancelled each other out.

The CSSA was mounting an attack. All the roads around what had been the prisoners' camp were crowded with vehicles going north towards the sound of firing. Then a wave of helicopters roared in from the north—the USA counterattack—and rockets began crashing down onto the nearby streets. CSSA armor was dispersing across the farmland, spreading out, taking cover. Tanks and APCs rumbled their massive frames onto the meadow. Anti-aircraft rockets were streaking upwards and exploding among the helicopters.

"They're ours!" Witmer yelled. How could he tell the helicopters we were Americans, prisoners or recently so, amidst these armored vehicles captured by the CSSA, whose insignia were still those of the USA Army? He had no radio, no communications of any kind, no American flag to wave to let them know who was down here.

Firing intensified on both sides. The prison camp, on the northwest side of Virginia, was directly in the line of approach of Cruz's counterattack from McCallom. Both sides were throwing more and more firepower into the area.

The freed prisoners were running, without knowing which way to go. Witmer resisted the impulse to run with the others. He had his squad, his squad could save him—not to save him from this impossible attack of friendly and hostile fire, but to save his coherence of mind, an officer taking refuge in taking care of his men. He motioned his squad to drop to the ground, stay put rather than run without a direction. It was hard to see where anyone was.

A blast struck nearby and Witmer was thrown by the concussion-wave. Dirt was flying high in the air, descended covering half his body. The whole world was going dark. Then light returned and the crash of battle seemed further away.

Witmer could feel nothing below his knee. He lay still and tried not to look at where his foot should be.

A wounded soldier crawled over to him. It was Pvt. Jack. "Captain. I didn't finish telling you about Wounded Knee."

"Not now," Witmer gasped.

"I have to tell you. How it started. The Sioux were surrounded by thousands of US troops. Big Foot was wise, he agreed to surrender. Their women and children were starving. The Sioux were prisoners, like us. They were giving up their guns." Jack was breathing hard. He didn't seem to be able to stand up. But he wanted to say something important to Witmer. "Then one of the Sioux warriors fired a shot. The Seventh Cavalry went crazy—remember, they were Custer's old regiment that was beaten by the Sioux at Little Big Horn. The cavalry killed everyone they could. They couldn't stop firing. They even shot each other in the crossfire." He pointed to the Union helicopters overhead. "It's happening again."

"It isn't," Witmer said. "It's a mistake."

"I'm here for a reason," the Modoc said. He had his long knife out. "I'm going to get one of them before I go."

"Let it end," Witmer said. "Revenge goes on forever."

"So be it," Pvt. Jack said. "It's the way of the warrior." He started to crawl laboriously towards the nearest CSSA tank. He could barely move.

"Meet your Maker in peace," Witmer murmured. But the Modoc warrior was no longer listening. His body, at least, was dead.

General Cruz's helicopter flew in low in the late-afternoon light. There was massive destruction all along the roads from McCammon to Virginia. The distant view was glorious as usual, the mountains brooding in their blue shadows to the west, lit up in bright warm colors to the east, one mountain range behind the other. But closer it was a wreckage of vehicles, crashed helicopters, smoldering buildings; strewn bodies could be seen from the air. General Park's victorious armor were posted at intervals, presiding mutely over the scene. Medical details were picking up the bodies, sorting out the wounded, leaving the dead for disposal. Judging from their uniform patches, the most of the dead were from the Utah and Colorado brigades, the prisoners taken in yesterday's battle.

Gandhi Park was waiting in a command car.

"Why didn't you let me go in yesterday?" Gandhi said, "When I could have saved some of them?"

"If I'd let you attack yesterday, the CSSA wouldn't have been caught off guard today," Cruz said. "And who's to say you wouldn't be one of the prisoners?"

"Maybe I should be." Gandhi looked the bodies scattered off into the distance. "I gunned them down. It was my order to fire the rockets."

"I gave the order, General," Cruz said. "You just passed it on."

"Just following orders. Well, that's what we do."

"War is hell," Cruz said. "You know who said that—William Tecumseh Sherman. Do you know why he said it?"

"Because war really is hell. And the hell of it is giving orders that you later wish you hadn't."

"If your enemy is no pushover, you have no choice when you get him on the ropes. If you don't take that moment when it comes, it'll turn around and bite you."

Gandhi nodded. Ferocious as he was in personal confrontation, there was a level of responsibility in command that he was just as happy to pass on to someone else. Someone as steady of purpose as Achilles Cruz. He looked out to the west where the CSSA forces had retreated. "What about the pursuit?"

"Are you up for it?"

"I've got some armor left. Helicopters pretty badly depleted. And what happened to our air cover this afternoon? It was all right this morning."

"We mustered everything we had. Some of it flew in from Texas and Louisiana. I wouldn't count on it for now."

"The CSSA are covering their retreat with an armor force near the Indian Reservation. My forward columns have been probing them. There's no soft spot, but we could smash what's left if we had a pincers movement coming up I-84 and cutting in behind them."

"My thought exactly," Cruz said. "General Hawp's Utah reinforcements were supposed to be doing just that."

"Were supposed to be?"

"They stopped. Took the wrong roads, recaptured Malad City, then stopped. Didn't get behind them." Cruz shook his head with disgust. A call was coming in.

"That should be Hawp now."

But it was Governor Mosiah Moroni Young. "General Cruz, I congratulate you on your great victory. The State of Utah thanks you."

"It's not over yet, Governor. We still have an opportunity to finish them off."

"Utah has shouldered the brunt of this, General. I sent you all my helicopters. We have suffered grievous losses."

"The enemy is in retreat. If General Hawp would just send everything he has under my instructions, we can catch the rebel army from two sides and destroy it. There's still time—"

"Let's not overreach ourselves, General. We have driven the enemy from our borders. They won't come back this way again. We have retaken the ancestral lands of the State of Deseret. It is enough."

"With all due respect, Governor. The rebellion is still on. The Union has not yet been restored."

"I had a vision, General Cruz. The angel mentioned your name. You have served God's plan. And now you should expect to be promoted to a bigger theatre. I believe President Jennings wants you for the New York front."

Getting kicked upstairs, Cruz said to himself.

The governor went on. "I have ordered General Hawp to bring back the bodies of Utah's fallen sons. We will honor them for their glorious deaths at the hands of the enemy. I will be sorry if you can't attend the ceremony."

★

Big Bill O'Leary took the call in bed. He got up, wrapped the sheet around him, and pulled it off the bed. Marisa Santa-Anna did not bother to cover herself, but lay there admiring her outstretched legs and stroking her volcano-shaped breasts.

"Bad news," O'Leary said. "At any rate, a change of plans. The pressure is off Jennings to negotiate with us."

Marisa frowned. She was running her fingers below her rib cage and squeezed at a suggestion of loose flesh. "Oh. How's that, baby?"

"McConnell's attack in Idaho failed. It's a big Union victory. Heavy casualties on both sides."

"McConnell. Big egotist. Big know-it-all." She giggled. "Big everything, though, if you know what I mean."

"Our army had to retreat. The only good thing is, the Union army isn't trying to follow up. We didn't knock off Utah, but they didn't split the CSSA, either."

Marisa yawned. "Come back to bed, big boy."

"And oh yeah, McConnell is missing."

Marisa sat up abruptly. "I hope he's dead!" She threw herself facedown on the pillow.

O'Leary sat on the bed, pondering. Marisa opened an eye, observed him sideways. O'Leary was writing on a note pad. She rolled over on one elbow, arching to show off her breasts. "McConnell was better than you in bed."

"I'll show you." O'Leary fell on her heavily. He was a bit paunchy and out of shape, but had the vigorousness of an important man used to making people do what he wanted. After a few minutes of pounding, he raised his bullet-shaped head, now a brighter-than-usual shade of florid. "You've got to go to DC," he panted. "Tell them I could make a deal. I could bring Illinois and the whole Midwest back into the Union. Find out what they'll promise me."

"Who, Jennings?"

"No. Not Jennings. He's not your type."

Marisa reached up and hit O'Leary's chest abruptly with both fists, pushing him away. "All men are my type."

"Maybe. But some men dedicate their cock to God."

"Who, then?"

"There's political opposition over there. There always is. I hear the Secretary of Defense, Madigan, doesn't get along with Jennings too well."

"Madigan? I've heard his name on the air bases. The generals hate him."

"He might not be your type either. A nerdy tech-head. Gets his rocks off on computer gadgets."

"Don't worry, big boy." Marisa was in his face, making little smacking sounds with her lips. "I'll find someone who'll make a deal with you."

Both were thinking: and with her.

Shiloh. April 1862

It was a successful surprise attack. Confederates routed half the Union army and sent it running to the rear in panic. Yet the entire army did not come apart. Enough Federal formations held together until nightfall, losing ground but not their organization. Massive reinforcements arriving in the dark shifted the balance and turned the momentum. Next day the Confederates were pushed back by superior numbers and driven from the battlefield. It was a battle of morale, of dominating emotional energy one day and losing it the next.

General Ulysses S. Grant had been ordered to advance up the Tennessee River, a gateway into the deep South. At Pittsburg Landing near the Mississippi border, Grant's forces made camp on the west side of the river, over fifty thousand strong, and waited to be joined by yet another Federal army, approaching across the river from the northeast, moving slowly under General Don Carlos Buell. Twenty-five miles to the south, at Corinth, Mississippi, the Confederates concentrated their own army. It was big enough to counter one of the Union forces, but not two of them. The Confederate commander, Albert Sidney Johnston, tall, handsome and magnetic, was a war hero of the former Texas Republic. His plan was to hit Grant before Buell arrived, to drive Grant's army into the swamps west of the river where it could be cut to pieces.

Before dawn on April 6, a Sunday morning, Federal pickets were shocked by the entire Confederate army. Almost forty-five thousand troops had somehow marched, unperceived, within a mile of the Federal camps. By 6:30 a.m., they had overrun the camps on the right side of the road, eastward towards the river. On the left, General William Tecumseh Sherman had a half-hour notice and was able to get his troops out of their tents and into line. Sherman's headquarters was at Shiloh Church, a rough-hewn log building at a farmland crossroads, destined to become the Confederate headquarters, and to give its name to the battle.

It was two different battles in one. On the right, one of Grant's divisions disintegrated completely. Some Federals ran three miles, ending up cowering under the bluff at Pittsburg Landing, clamoring to be taken on boats to safety. Reserve troops moving forward encountered a rush of broken regiments, shouting "You'll catch hell." "We are whipped." "The rebels are coming!" Hundreds on hundreds rushed by, singly and in squads of a dozen, wounded on foot or carried on stretchers, but others unhurt, without their guns and knapsacks, having jettisoned all equipment. Officers with drawn swords tried to make the fleeing troops halt; cavalrymen galloped after them and threatened to shoot them if they did not stop. But no one stopped.

The soldier's-eye view is chaotic. Roads are full of heavy six-mule wagons carrying wounded, unnerving the unwounded with their cries of pain; the woods are full of blue coats and gray coats, artillery batteries hurry here and there with horses at the gallop; there is a din of musketry on the front, while shells shriek and burst over their heads; the air is thick with the smell of burned powder, smearing their faces. A man stands at the roadside, throwing up his hands and yelling: "For God's sake don't go out there; you'll all be killed. Come back! Come back!"

But elsewhere on the field, it was a day of punches and counter-punches, the armies like two boxers, neither backing down. Grant's huge forces were encamped across an arc five miles wide; the spread isolated the panic on the right and allowed other formations to fight their own battles. Grant sent his rear divisions forward to buttress the center, where they collided with the onrushing Confederates at a dense oak thicket that soon got the nickname the Hornet's Nest, after the sound of buzzing bullets from unseen rifles. Casualties piled up as Confederates sent in wave after wave of attack from late morning until midafternoon, all repulsed. Sidney Johnston shifted forces, throwing punches on both flanks.

On the left, where Sherman put up strong resistance, Johnston reinforced, then attacked again. Three times Sherman made a stand, even managed to counterattack in the early afternoon, but each time was forced to withdraw by heavy casualties and relentless pressure. There were a series of natural barriers, creeks swollen by rain, sunken roads allowing good cover for defensive rifles, steep ravines; Sherman held up the Confederates at each one but each time beat a strategic retreat. By late afternoon, Sherman and the left-side divisions were backed up to the last road parallel to the river.

The right side, already weakened, was crucial and here Johnston personally commanded from the front. His aim was to drive the Federals away from the river, out of reach of Buell's reinforcements. The flank attack stalled temporarily around noon at a peach orchard where the Confederates had to face murderous fire crossing open fields. Then in the early afternoon, success: the corner of the line was turned. The Federals formed another battle line a mile back, at a pond soon called Bloody Pond—in the end, same story, and the Confederates had driven on through all the way to the bluff over Pittsburg Landing. Grant massed what artillery remained on the top of the bluff and the Confederate attack slackened, with the light fading at 6:30 p.m. The Union center, too, gave way; the Hornet's Nest was surrounded from all sides, and what remained of several Federal divisions were forced to surrender, their generals captured.

Grant's army was almost finished; one more determined charge might have taken the landing and sealed off the river. But Confederates had taken heavy losses too. Among them was Albert Sidney Johnston, killed by a stray bullet—quite possibly friendly fire from his troops behind him. He was replaced by Beauregard, the victor of Fort Sumter, commanding from the rear at Shiloh Church. Beauregard, like most of his army, believed victory was assured; his troops were tired from a long march the previous day and a long day's battle that had advanced the front four miles; his men were hungry and ammunition needed replenishing. He called his troops back into the captured Union camps for the night. They would finish off the Yankees in the morning.

By evening the tide was turning, although not everybody knew it. All afternoon the crowd of panicked troops skulking at the landing had increased to several thousands. An officer rode back and forth on the top of the bluff, waving an American flag, pleading: "Men for God's sake, for your country's sake, for your own sake, come up here, form a line, and make one more stand." No one responded except for one man saying, "That man talks well, don't he?"

General Grant himself arrived with his bodyguard of twenty-five cavalrymen, pleading with the stragglers to make one more effort to redeem themselves. Finally he ended with a threat: if they did not return to their commands, he would send his cavalry to drive them out. Fifteen minutes later cavalry swept the beach, but most of the skulkers climbed up the bank to hang by the roots of trees, and when the cavalry had gone were back at their old places.

Even as reinforcements started to come across in steamboats, Buell's army finally arriving in the dark, the mob had to be kept away by bayonets as they waded out to the boats. Guards cleared a path through the gaping crowd for the new troops to hurry up the winding roadways towards the battle line above the bluff, in a torrent of voices: "It's no use." "Gone up." "Cut all to pieces." "The last man left in my company." The disembarking troops insulted and shoved them. Here and there in the crowd the mood began to waver, and a few voices called out welcome: "Good for you." "Go in, boys." "Give it to 'em, Buckeyes."

Materially, in fact, everything had changed. In the dark, Buell arrived with the first half of his Army of the Ohio, and gunboats massed on the river to shell the former Union camps now held by the sleeping Confederates. By 9 a.m., Grant launched an attack, no fancy maneuvers, just straight ahead all along the line. With twenty-five thousand fresh troops and full ammunition supplies, he now had a two-to-one advantage. It was a grinding battle of attrition, not so much a boxing match like the previous day but just unrelenting forward pressure. The Federal center stalled at the Hornet's Nest, same place as yesterday only facing the other side, with the woods already cut by shells and the underbrush burned and full of dead and wounded of both armies. Beauregard, still counterpunching, launched counterattacks on right and left, temporarily blunting the Federal advance. But he and his army now fought tediously, the enthusiasm and elation of yesterday having evaporated. By 2 p.m., the last counterattack petered out.

Beauregard massed artillery just south of Shiloh Church, covering the retreat of what was left of the Confederate army, back on the Corinth Road on which they had come. Theoretically a pursuit would have crushed the defeated army, but Federal troops were too exhausted to do more than bivouac on their reclaimed campgrounds, now looted and trashed and littered with bodies. Firing ended spontaneously around 5 p.m., no one having given the order.

A total of twenty-four thousand were lost on both sides: the US thirteen thousand, the Confederates over ten thousand, the biggest bloodletting of the war so far.

What caused the panic and disintegration? Could it have been the horrors of combat, the blasted and mutilated bodies surrounding them, the terrifying sounds of enemy guns, the cries of the wounded that made battlefield a very scene of Hell? But casualties were heavy everywhere, and the most steadfast soldiers had more than those who ran most quickly. No, it was something else, something in the collective mood within each troop, that disintegrated in a moment, or held together, a mood communicated back and forth with the enemy too.

Listen to the sound of the oncoming Confederates, rushing forward shouting as they surrounded the Hornet's Nest, filling the woods with their rebel yell before they are seen: "Down would drop first one fellow and then another, either killed or wounded, when we were ordered to charge bayonets. I shouted. It was fun then. Everybody looked happy. We were crowding them. Their lines waver and break. They retreat in wild confusion. We were jubilant; we were triumphant. Officers could not curb the men to keep in line. Discharge after discharge was poured into the retreating line. The Federal dead and wounded covered the ground."

On the Federal side, an officer: "There is a shock as the men crowd on each other, a waver, then all discipline is lost, the Union forces break... and a mad race for the landing and shelter of the gunboats is made, while the Confederates with cheers and yells follow fast and follow faster." An ordinary soldier: "The enemy flank us and are moving to our rear; some one calls out, 'Everybody for himself!' The line breaks, I go with the others, back and down the hill across a small ravine, with the howling, rushing mass of the enemy pressing in close pursuit. The striking of balls on the tents gave a short, cutting sound that terrified me. The striking of the shot on the ground threw up little clouds of dust. The hair on the back of my head was standing straight up, and I felt sure that a cannonball was close behind me, giving me chase as I started for the river. In my mind it was a race between me and that cannonball. I never ran so fast before."

It is not just fear of death, because death had been with them all along. It is collective fear sending contagion from one man to the next—as William James said, feeling afraid because you are running away more than running because you are afraid. The mass of fugitives have one idea, reach the landing and get across the river to safety. They support each other in their idea, even try to recruit others to join them, to discourage fresh soldiers from going into the fight; they refuse to change their mood even as reinforcements arrive and others can see the tide of battle is turning. Only at the end of battle on the second day do the last Union skulkers give up their hiding places on the landing.

The moods of attacker and attacked are reciprocal. The Confederates whoop to terrify their enemy. When they succeed, they are elated, when the enemy runs away they run forward. What is a nightmare race for one side is a joyride for the other.

An incident: in the pell-mell retreat from the Hornet's Nest that first afternoon, the Federals are outrun by an artillery team galloping past, horses and men hauling a single cannon at reckless speed. Something peculiar about its uniform and colors—it becomes clearer when the team halts, the gun is unlimbered and fires grapeshot point-blank into the retreating flood. It is Confederate artillery in their midst. But no one attacks it, although it is in easy range of swords and bayonets; and even though gun-tenders have vulnerable moments when they must reload, and normally troops would make a mad scramble for the deadly cannons in those short breathing spaces. No, the fleeing Federals are incapable of fighting even to save their lives; they are dominated and the Confederates who chase them feed off their despair. What terrifies one side emboldens the other.

Did the generals make the difference in winning or losing the battle? Grant did little to win the battle except that he refused to lose it, holding out until help came and then launching the simplest of counterattacks. Beauregard may have lost it with one mistake—not finishing off the victory by sending his right wing ahead to take the landing, putting it off until tomorrow while his troops got a much-needed rest. The Confederate generals closest to the landing late in the afternoon wanted to push ahead, feeling victory in their grasp. The Union soldiers opposite them on top of the bluff believed they were doomed. In the setting sun they can see the glint of rifle barrels and bayonets of the Confederate formations, seemingly endless marching of one line after another; a Union soldier loads his gun and lies flat with head down, awaiting what seems sure defeat, wondering when someone will raise the first white flag.

But Beauregard is miles to the rear, surrounded by a crowd of aides, receiving congratulations. The troops nearest him believe they have already won; the general catches their mood. Federal prisoners taken at the Hornet's Nest are stacking their arms, lowering their colors, officers handing over their swords in all the traditional ceremony of surrender. Confederate soldiers wandered away from their units as the excitement spread, eager to see the captives with their own eyes. Officers called it the proudest day of their lives; boys jumped up and down, thinking the war is over. Soldiers became busy exchanging their inferior muskets for the Yankees' new rifles, settling down to loot the Union camps. Beauregard, full of empathy for his men, shares their mood. It is the collective mood; the general does not rise above it.

The mood dissipates over night. Without the flush of excitement, the Confederate troops are merely tired in the morning, hung over from their emotional binge. They held the emotional energy on that first day; their surprise attack in the first dawn gave them the initiative, and they still held it at nightfall. It was not just Buell's army arriving that gave the Federals the renewed advantage of numbers; the crucial moment was gone, the mood on both sides had dissipated.

There was still a hard day's fighting to come. The Confederates, although much more heavily outnumbered now than the Union divisions had been anywhere on the first day, broke into no general panic; they fought back tenaciously, and their final retreat was made in good order. There were no Yankee troops yelling and charging on their rear; today the Federals too are merely methodical, pressing their weight of numbers. When the second sunset comes, the Federals settle into their recaptured camps, more in exhaustion than elation, surrounded by the dismal carnage.

And the surprise attack that started the whole thing? Surely generals as competent as Grant and Sherman would have constructed defenses for the camp, would have scouted the roads to the front to prevent the entire enemy army from marching near without giving an alarm. In fact both Grant and Sherman had pooh-poohed reports of enemy threats the previous day, asserting that what their scouts had sighted were no more than skirmishers. It was a failure of intelligence, and for the usual reasons: there was an overabundance of information, contradictory and with no easy means to tell false reports from true; the Union army had been encamped for several weeks, building up forces for an attack; skirmishes and raids happened every day, thus far without consequence; its mindset was to advance, not to receive an attack, and so no defensive fortifications were built. In short, Grant and Sherman were careless and overconfident.

Or was it was the way armies operated in the 1860s, when information was gathered by horseback and rains turned roads into mud, clogging everything to a near-halt? Under modern conditions, with today's technology of long-distance surveillance and communication, a surprise attack by large forces should be impossible.

YEAR TWO, CHAPTER THREE.
BATTLE OF ST. LOUIS

West side of St. Louis. August.

"What you got there, Private?" Sgt. Sutphen said.

The white soldier had a plastic bag, with several dozen glass tubes inside, the size of laboratory test tubes. He made a move to throw the bag into the shrubbery and thought better of it. Sutphen was backed by four M4-carrying guards with the black triangle Ironman patch on their shoulders. At a silent head-shake from Sutphen they encircled the shot-up car where the private was crouching. The name tape on his gray CSSA battle dress read "TRAVIS." He was grimy and stained with sweat. It did not look like he had been wounded.

He held out the bag to Sutphen. "Here you go, Sergeant. I confiscated this off a drug dealer back there."

Sutphen ignored his outstretched arm. With deliberation he walked around the car, surveying the spread-out line of soldiers holding positions along the burned-out street. It had been a residential neighborhood in west St. Louis. Sidewalks lined by maple trees rows, now sadly blackened to midwinter in August. Lawns twenty yards wide where old-fashioned children's swings hung from branches of ancient trees. Red and tan brick houses with fanlites over front doors, black shutters setting off white-crossed window frames. Double-decker porches screen-walled for hot summer evenings, not just for decoration but for use.

CSSA armored vehicles were parked in driveways well back from the street, taking cover under pretentiously pillared car porticos that survived the heavy shelling. Battle noise was gone for the time being. In a wide branching tree down the block a huge flock of birds started up a mighty chirping whenever a soldier walked by.

Sutphen wheeled abruptly on Pvt. Travis. "You scored this where? This be a nice white neighborhood. Ain't no drug dealers round here."

Travis looked weary in the summer heat, whether from too many days of battle without sleep, or the aftermath of the drug. "We came through north St. Louis, in the ghetto, before they sent us to the battlefront. Last week, whenever that was."

Sutphen tore the plastic bag from his hand. "Bullshit. Somebody fronted you this, soldier." Two of the guards pinioned Travis. "You gonna tell me who?"

A wary clump of nearby troops had gathered as onlookers. Guns dangled from their hands, but they watched carefully, keeping their distance from the smart-looking Ironman guards with the black triangle patches.

An officer arrived, Captain Tomkins, the company commander, two vertical bars on his kevlar helmet. Sgt. Sutphen did not salute.

"I'll take care of this, Sergeant. There'll be no drug dealing in my outfit. Platoon commander! This man is under arrest."

"We ain't no MPs, Captain," Sutphen said. "Your unit's new to the Ironman command, ain't it. We be IDC—Ironman Discipline Commissioners." He tapped the black triangle above his left bicep. "We take orders from Ironman himself. And Ironman orders are, anyone who fucks up our battle-ready instrument gets punished. Immediately."

"I agree completely, Sergeant. I won't tolerate any soldier in my unit who isn't ready to fight. This drug addict will be court-martialed."

"No time for court-martial. IDC takes care of business immediately. That means here and now."

Captain Tomkins started to protest, but hesitated before the purposeful menace of the little phalanx of black triangles. His unit, the Eleventh Illinois Brigade, was newly formed, and this week in St. Louis had been their first combat. He had heard of the exploits of Ironman Johnston in a string of battles: the brigade that always held its position, that moved with incredible promptness, that never lost as much as a skirmish.

Had heard, too, that the original Ironman Brigade had been broken up, scattered into a special battle discipline force throughout Johnston's expanded command, now that he was a Major General and had command of the Battle Group of the entire St. Louis area. Stonewall Jackson, they say, had marched his troops with incredible speed on the wilderness roads of Virginia because he was willing to march them to death. The instrument of his will was a special rearguard hurrying along stragglers with fixed bayonets.

Sutphen was swinging the plastic bag of crack pipes in his hand, displaying it to the troops of the Eleventh Illinois. He dashed the contents of the bag to the ground at Pvt. Travis's feet and fired a burst into it. Amid the leaping shards of glass a chemical odor rose up, rough and pungent, from the white powder catching fire.

Travis shuddered backwards in the armlock of the guards. His pants were slashed above the boot tops and a trickle of blood was starting to flow down.

"Next time I see anyone holding any dope," Sutphen announced, "I'll kill you personally."

The guards dropped Travis and he lay in a heap on the hot pavement, panting heavily.

"Be ready to move out," Sutphen said. "All of you. Ironman's troops move immediately, no getting ready time, no delay. We always get the jump on the enemy. That's why we always win. If you ain't ready to move out when the order comes, you stay behind dead."

A couple of Travis' companions started pulling him to his feet. Captain Tomkins approached Sutphen. "Sergeant, are you saying you have orders from General Johnston, that the Eleventh Illinois should be ready to move?"

"Ironman troops always ready to move," Sutphen said. "When and where, you will hear." The captain let out a little snort of breath and frowned warily. "Let me tell you confidentially, Captain," Sutphen went on, "Ironman be expecting the Feds to make a move. And we is going to make a countermove. Drive right up the Feds' asshole. Be ready."

The knot of Ironman Discipline Commissioners were back in their mobile post, an armored Humvee with the black triangle painted on its side. The heat was stifling but at least it was shade. Vehicle air conditioners were turned off to minimize pickup by enemy infrared sensors from whatever surveillance aircraft were still managing to fly.

"Back in the day," JaMichael Kilson said, "that stash be easy money." He had Staff Sergeant stripes with one rocker on his sleeve but Sutphen had the triple stripes and rockers of First Sergeant.

"There be a day when you was a bunch of street hoodlums," Sutphen said. "JaMichael be doing burglaries in his own street where there ain't no money, cause he don't like the pressure out there in the white burbs where the money lives."

"Where the cops waitin' on every street for a car driven by a black man. And Neighborhood Watch phoning in, and sitting with a shotgun in the dark waitin' for you to come through the window."

"Bullshit," Toney said. He had Staff Sergeant stripes too. "My crew done hundreds of burglaries and we ain't never seen no one waiting in the dark. It's all in you head."

"You be the crew that shat on the floor every burglary," Sutphen said. "Cause you bowels be jumpy about being inside someone's house, and you scared to use the toilet 'cause you don't like being trapped in a little room."

"How you know so much about it?" JaMichael said. "You a pussy street dealer, profiling like you tough, while every stickup dude know you be easy money. I hear Crawford hisself robbed you three times and you ain't got nuff sense so it happen again."

"Shut up," Sutphen said. "We Ironman now. There ain't nothing good about the old days."

JaMichael lounged back on the seat and closed his eyes. "Ain't nothing good about being here in St. Louis. Too hot to sleep. And nothing to keep this Ironman awake. Least the Air Force, they get amphetamine pills issued for combat duty."

"Ironman leave all that shit alone," Sutphen said sharply. "If you sleepy, it because you put impurities in you body. Junk food, processed sugar. Animal fat. You eat right, take the right supplements, you never get tired."

"I seen JaMichael eating that hot dog on the street," Toney said. "Not just hot dog, corn dog, fried in transfats. Sit in you stomach. Weigh down you bowels. Make you slow. Some day even the Feds get the jump on you. "

"I still fast enough to get the jump on you," JaMichael said. "I seen you with that box of jelly donuts."

"Shut up," Sutphen said. "This be Ironman talking. Like he said, when you or I speak in his voice, Ironman be talking to you. Whenever you lose your edge—"

"—do fasting," the others said in unison. "Cleansing. Get the impurities out of your body."

Sutphen went on, the others echoing. "The more you can do without, the stronger you are." Even JaMichael was alert, shaking off the lethargy. Five lean muscular black bodies inclined towards each other in a ring, right fists clenched, while they repeated: "Without Ironman method, you are a bunch of street hustlers. With Ironman, we are an unbeatable fighting force." They banged fists. "Ironman!"

"Crawford wants to see you," one of the guards said a few minutes later.

Col. Newton Crawford was in his command post. He had risen through the ranks at a meteoric pace, carried upward by Ironman's victories. Now for the first time he had his own independent command, no longer as Ironman's deputy, but C.O. of the First Brigade, St. Louis Battle Group. But it was not in this capacity that he addressed Sgt. Sutphen and a dozen other ranking NCOs of the IDC. There was a stand beside his desk with a flag bearing the black triangle, for Crawford was also Commander of the Ironman Discipline Commission under Ironman Johnston himself.

"Any discipline problems?" Crawford said. "Rasheed?" The ring of NCOs reported in sequence, curtly, mostly no problem, all clear. There was occasional mention of a line unit where the logistics of refueling and rearming vehicles was slow, or where the officers were not sufficiently deferential. The IDC had its own special protocol among themselves. All referred to each other by nickname, without military titles, no sir, no salutes except the banging of clenched fists.

"Sutphen, any discipline problems?" He had said nothing yet.

"Nothing we can't take care of."

"I want to hear about your problems," Crawford said. "And I want to hear how you take care of them."

"Ironman says, take care of business immediately. That's what I do."

"How many bodies have you left lying out there? And how many wounded, that end up in our field hospitals?"

"Battle quieted down day before yesterday," Sutphen said. "No more Fed attacks. They sick of the pounding we gave 'em. No enemy firing, no IDC firing."

"That's the way I want to keep it," Crawford said. "There's too many new troops in the St. Louis Battle Group. They're not used to IDC methods. Stories are getting back to the news media in Chicago. More important, stories are getting back to Jefferson Gray's headquarters. You're going to get Ironman in trouble unless you're careful."

"Ironman can't get in no trouble," Sutphen said. "Ironman be unbeatable. The news loves Ironman."

"The news loves Jefferson Gray," Crawford said. "St. Louis Battle Group is just one part of Jefferson Gray's Midwestern Front. It's Jeff Gray that's picked off the Feds, every time they've come across the Ohio River. It's Jeff Gray that lays the traps for them, that knows the enemy commander's mind better than he knows himself. It's Jeff Gray who makes the strategy. Ironman's just the one who carries it out. If you think the press won't take Ironman down, think again."

Sutphen turned to the circle of NCOs. "You hear what Crawford saying? He's got the Ironman triangle on his sleeve but he's not talking with the voice of Ironman."

"Hold out your hands and look at the color of your skin," Crawford said. "Ironman is white. He recruited you all out of that white man's rehab center, didn't he? Jefferson Gray is black. He's the greatest general this country has seen, and he's the greatest black general ever lived."

Sutphen shook his head. "Jeff Gray is good. He got that magic charm, he never lose. But nobody else knows that magic charm, and he can't teach it to you. But Ironman teaches you victory. He taught you, Crawford, and he taught me and he taught every one here in this room. And we're going to go on teaching it. Even if you kill Ironman, you can't kill the Ironman in us."

"You got killing on your brain," Crawford said. "You heard what the problem is, and I told you to take care of it. I'm telling you as Commander of the IDC. And I'm going to tell you one more thing. I am also Colonel Crawford, C.O. of the First Brigade, and if anything happens to General Johnston, I am designated as next in command to take over the St. Louis Battle Group, with the temporary rank of general, under General Jefferson Gray."

"Can't nothing happen to Ironman," voices murmured from the circle.

"Especially when you have a general who leads that close to the front," Crawford said, "there is always a successor named in advance. Ironman sent forward my name and Jefferson Gray approved it."

"Sitting pretty, ain't you Crawford?" Sutphen said. "So now you're Jeff Gray's man. We'll see, the battle still be coming."

President Jennings was watching the Midwest weather report. A storm was gathering in the Gulf, picking up moisture over the hot tropical waters, heading up the Mississippi Valley. A front of low pressure was sweeping across the continent from the northwest as the jet stream dipped south from Canada. The two fronts would intersect within twenty-four hours. St. Louis was in for a pounding.

"Seems like a bad time to launch an offensive," Jennings said. "Our brave boys are liable to be bogged down in the Mississippi mud."

"We've been waiting for this, Mr. President," Major Debra Zielkowsky explained. "That's General Maddux's plan. We'll make our flanking move just before the storm comes. We'll be in position and the CSSA won't be able to respond."

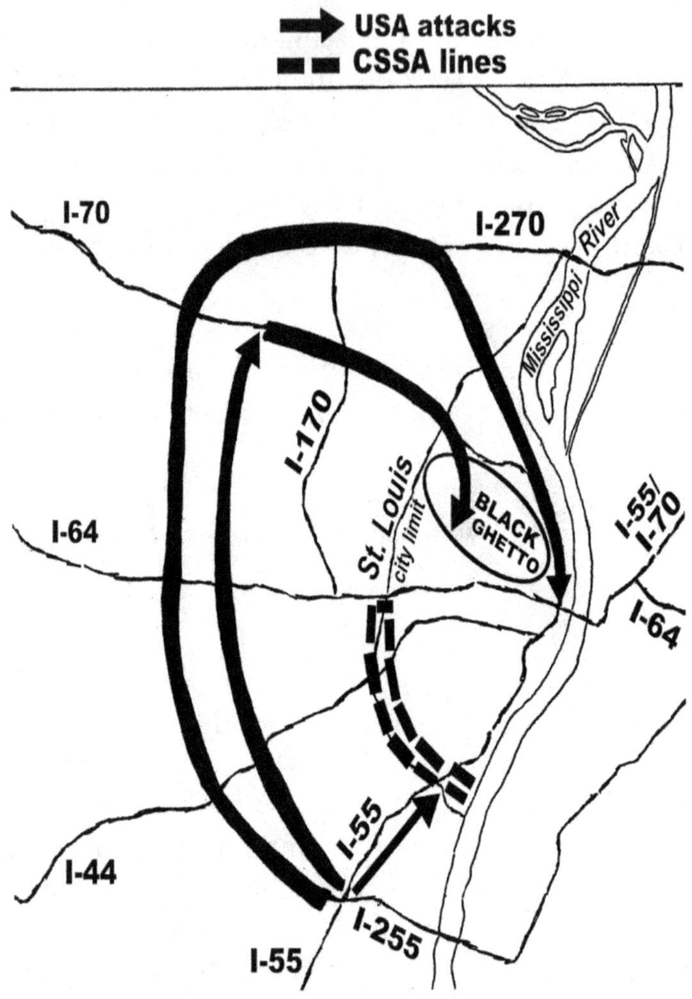

The wall screens and desk monitors of the White House situation room displayed more than a weather map. There were big strategic maps of the Midwestern Front, showing the location of all the opposing forces. Maps of the highway grid around St. Louis, like a wiring diagram in the middle of the country where all the circuits came together. Street maps of St. Louis and its suburbs. Maps plotting where enemy armor had last been spotted, where artillery trajectories had been traced, where CSSA command posts were believe to be located. Planning maps with animated arrows showing projected USA moves and potential CSSA countermoves.

"That's this doohickey right here, right Major?" Jennings pointed to one of the planning scenarios. "Now what I want to know is, how can General Maddux pull out all that armor from the south side of St. Louis, take it all the way around on the I-270 bypass, and swing in behind the enemy in north St. Louis? I mean, the enemy's got a control room over there in Illinois same as we have here. If we can see where he is, sure as shooting he can see us coming on the highway."

"That's where the weather factors in," Debra said. "It's a matter of relative speed. We move first, they move second. They can't respond until they know where we are going. And we move in good weather. They have to move when the weather gets bad. They can't possibly move as fast as we can. We have it all timed."

"But if I were General Maddux, I wouldn't swing all the way out to I-270. I'd take this highway here—" jabbing a finger at the screen, while his other hand motioned the operator to zoom in closer, "get in on I-170 and save myself a fifteen-mile loop."

National Security Advisor Pat Buckley interrupted. "Hold on now please, Mr. President. You promised the Pentagon when they set up this remote feed that you weren't going to interfere with the professionals."

Jennings clapped his hands and sat back. "Sure enough. I just get too dad-blamed excited. It is a mighty temptation, when you got everything out here on this TV show, and you can make everything happen just by pushing a button. At least that's how it's supposed to work, isn't that right, Major?"

"Secretary Madigan wanted me to tell you confidentially that the new computer system is not completely operative, Mr. President," Debra said. "It's eighty percent up and running. But there are still some bugs to be worked out."

"I expect there are," Jennings said. "That's why I'm wondering if it's a good idea to try out this new system in the middle of a thunderstorm."

"With all due respect," Buckley said, "the Pentagon asked for more time to test the system. It was you that insisted, Mr. President, that we move ahead with the attack on St. Louis."

"I know, I know. When it's only two hundred eighty miles from our border to the capital of the godless Coalition, we ought to be able to punch through and open up the roads to Chicago."

He called for the big map of the Midwestern Front on the wall screen. The armies of North and South were concentrated where the southern tip of Illinois made the point of an arrowhead clumsily chipped between the winding banks of the Mississippi and the Ohio rivers. The top of the rough triangle was more nearly a straight line, the east-west highway of Interstate-64 running from St. Louis across Illinois and southern Indiana to Louisville. General Jefferson Gray kept his CSSA army along the I-64 line, letting the Federals cross the Ohio in a half dozen places. But southern Illinois and the little slice of Indiana south of I-64 were Jeff Gray's maneuvering ground, where he blocked one Federal advance after another, usually with humiliating losses.

"Since we're making no headway against Jeff Gray down below I-64," Jennings said, "it makes more sense to gird up our loins and make a mighty effort at the city that controls the river. We get across the river at St. Louis and we're in the center of the highway grid, pointing toward Chicago, Indianapolis, Detroit, anyplace in the whole CSSA heartland. We've got more armor, more infantry, more anything than they do in St. Louis. We ought to be able to punch through. New computer system or not."

"We're all on the same page," Buckley said. "Secretary Madigan is as committed to breaking through at St. Louis as you are. Especially since the enemy invaded USA territory. I think it's Jeff Gray's idea, or his trigger man, Ironman Johnston's. They want to fight on our territory and run down our resources while we throw them out."

"That sits heavy on my heart," Jennings said. "The homes of the innocent are a terrible price to pay. But no one can hold an American city hostage. We will free St. Louis even if we have to destroy it."

He turned to the screens showing incoming feed from surveillance aircraft over St. Louis. These were pilotless drones with their TV camera images enhanced by computer to bring out the shape of objects on the ground, and others showing heat sources from infrared sensors. Operators at computer consoles typed in commands and the screens brought up aerial views made during the battles of the last week, marked white spots where fires were burning. Now the fires were out but on the latest screens the ground was becoming harder to see, everything fuzzier, more blurred.

"It's the high humidity in the area," Debra said. "Sensors never work as well when there is heavy moisture." Cloud cover was visibly socking in the city, blotching the video feed with swatches of dirty gray. "It could get worse if there is an electric storm."

One of the feeds, from the western perimeter of the metro area, showed big columns of heavy vehicles crowding the highways, both the Interstates and the surface streets, heading north. "Our armored attack," Buckley said.

"Right on time, anyhow," Jennings said. "I gotta hand it to your system, Major. Just like you said. But answer me this. If I'm looking at it, the enemy has got to be looking at it too. I know we went through this before, but it still bothers me like a flea on a hound dog. Jeff Gray ain't dumb. He knows we're coming. What makes you so sure he can't do nothing about it?"

"It's like playing chess," Debra said. "Your moves don't have to be hidden for them to work. Once you take the initiative, the opponent has to answer whatever you do. And we have the initiative. It's right there on the screens: we are moving and they aren't."

Dull blotches covered more and more of the video feed. It was harder to tell what was moving on the ground. The operator switched to infrared, but the light blobs wavered imprecisely. Then the feed cut off entirely. The operator tried another feed, with momentary success. But the quality was dropping everywhere. One feed after another was inaccessible or hard to read. "It could be something wrong with the line," Debra said. "And the battle is starting up. That means more enemy interference. Also they may be targeting our drones."

"Battle reports are fine," Buckley said. "Our left hook has been launched. According to ground commanders, our advance forces are already penetrating St. Louis from the north. Resistance is light. And we are launching our right feint along the river from the south, to hold Johnston's forces in place. We'll cut him off from the river and destroy him."

"And the rains came and the waters rose," Jennings said. "And the hosts of the idolaters were confounded utterly."

★

A CSSA tank was hung up on the cement highway divider. On one side its treads were spinning off the ground. The caterpillar tread on the other side, still in contact with the pavement, had managed to rotate the seventy-ton vehicle more and more fixedly onto the barrier. The engine was roaring and grinding but all the engaged tread was doing was digging a sinkhole into the pavement, crumbling the edges of a widening crater that was rapidly filling with water. Rain was coming down steadily and splattering in the oil-slicked pool like a dirty fountain in a abandoned park.

Behind the M1A1 Abrams tank the highway was crammed with armored vehicles. The swing of the Federals' left hook had gone through and now the CSSA was following them with their own swing, starting west and then north and now it was coming into the home stretch going east. The CSSA advance into northern St. Louis had taken over both eastbound and westbound lanes of the highway, but the hung-up tank was turned sideways and its twenty-six-foot length and twelve-foot width blocked a lane and a half on each side of the barrier. There was room on the outer lanes and the shoulders but tanks and armored personnel carriers acted much like civilian traffic slowing at the scene of an accident to gawk, or out of contagious feeling of an upset in the collective flow in this metal herd.

Armor traveling in road formation are supposed to maintain strict separation distances and in any case drive slower than civilians. A fender-bender among tanks and APCs is ever harder to sort out than among cars, since armored vehicles accelerate slowly and take considerable time to warm up if an engine is cut off.

A few tanks were filtering around the edge of the accident but the bulk of them were slowed as badly as a downtown L.A. freeway in afternoon rush hour.

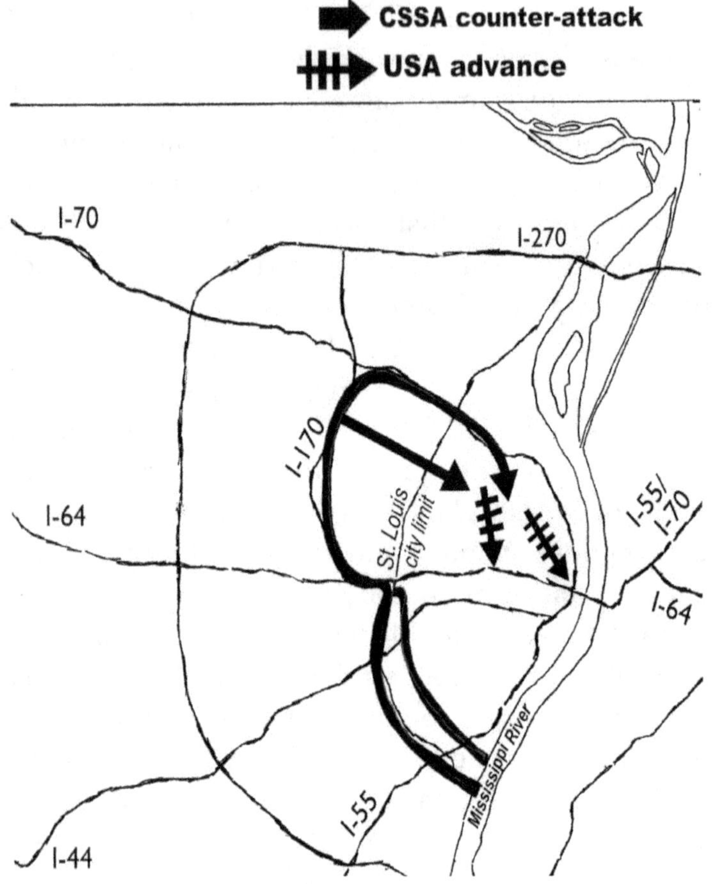

A knot of soldiers had dismounted their vehicles and were clustering around the disabled tank, shouting in the rain. A neighboring
tank was attempting to bulldoze the hung-up vehicle off the median
barrier, but accomplished little more than digging the crater deeper
into the pavement. The rescue vehicle backed up, forcing a tedious
chain reaction of other vehicles backing enough to give it room, and
was getting ready for a flying start at bulldozing again.

Col. Bracken, the ranking officer on the scene, was swearing.
"Damn lucky this rain is keeping enemy helos from flying. We'd be
pushovers for a rocket attack. Hurry it up—this weather won't last
forever!"

A Humvee pulled up along the shoulder, coming from the east,
from the direction of the front, ahead of the traffic jam. General

Ironman Johnston got out. He scowled at Col. Bracken's salute. "It's a temporary problem, General. We're working on it and we should have it—"

Ironman wheeled and gestured at the nearest tank commander. "Aim your main gun at the concrete barrier and blast it through."

"Sir! A M1A1 is impervious to even a point-blank impact. We can't destroy the vehicle, and I don't see how that's going to clear the highway—"

"I didn't say aim at the tank. Aim at the barrier and take it down."

"Now, sir? Hadn't the column better take cover?"

"I'll give you two minutes to get your gun in position. Starting now."

Ironman vaulted the barrier to the westbound lanes. Armored vehicles were slowly filtering past the chokepoint, and the highway ahead was almost empty, just silhouettes of distant vehicles making dark masses in the gray splattering rain. Ironman gestured vigorously for the armored vehicles at the head of the queue to move faster. When nothing happened, he jumped athletically onto the side deck of the lead tank and flung himself headlong against the front hatch where the tank driver's face was staring out. The man startled at this apparition of a face in the rain, its every muscle hard-set and quivering with intensity. The driver momentarily looked paralyzed.

Ironman resisted an impulse to punch him in the face. Instead he gestured to him to raise the headphones from his ears, the bulging earpieces also serving as noise blockers. "Get a hold of yourself, soldier," he shouted over the engine noise. "I'm your C.O., General Johnston, remember? Accelerate to top speed and get up the highway, now!"

The tank driver had not yet recovered his composure, a sudden face inches from one's own being more disconcerting in combat than the expectable impact of enemy fire on armor. Keep the psychology in mind, Ironman told himself. Just enough shock to get them going, not so much they can't obey orders.

As the tank started to accelerate, Ironman clambered back along the deck and jumped in front of the next tank. His movements were too harsh and deliberate to be graceful but he bullied his own body to set an example for his disciples. This time he jumped directly onto the front deck and stood up to confront the tank commander at the turret hatch. He was speaking too rapidly and had to repeat his orders. He was startling people too much, Ironman told himself; he would have to play on their psychology more deliberately.

These armored troops were fresh to his command. He hadn't trained them himself, and they didn't feel like the extension of his body that he felt with his own creation, the Ironman Battalion. Giving himself positive feedback, Ironman congratulated himself for having had the patience to repeat his orders and wait for signs they had been understood. In this way he cleared away the tanks that had occupied the westbound lanes opposite where the disabled vehicle sat on the median. He stood in the pavement imperiously in front of the next tank in line, ordering it to stop.

On the other side of the median, the rescue tank was ready to fire at the median. The force of a depleted uranium shell would shatter the cement into a shower of shards. Ironman gave the gesture to fire and crouched behind the nearest tank. He made his mind deliberately clear, a moment of zazen meditation, communing inside himself.

The boom of the gun was deafening but Ironman did not hear it inside his cocoon of concentrated consciousness. The gun fired again. The concrete barrier was gone, leaving a fifty-foot gap in front of the tank. Ironman stood up, refreshed, and jumped back to the other side of the freeway.

The disabled tank had settled down, its offending tread hanging on the pavement. But the tread was off its drive wheels and the vehicle was unable to move on its own power. Ironman ordered another tank to bulldoze it into the gap in the median barrier, and then to push it all the way across the westbound lanes.

"Yes sir! All the way across? There's not much shoulder over there where we can leave it. Should I try to straighten it out so it doesn't block more than one lane?"

"All the way to the guard rail," Ironman said. "Push it over the embankment. Then everybody get the hell moving again."

The tank commander started to send word to the crew of the disabled tank to dismount their vehicle but Ironman angrily waved him to proceed with the bulldozing. "They'll figure it out," Ironman said. "If they don't, they don't belong in my army."

Rain was intensifying, strings of translucent beads curtaining off the street into an endless series of outdoor rooms with walls of water. While the bulldozing proceeded, Ironman ordered the watching soldiers back into their vehicles, ready to move out at top speed as soon as the road was clear. A knot of soldiers wearing black triangle patches had gathered, members of the Ironman Disciplinary Commission drawn like disciples to their guru. They hunched close together, impervious to the rain.

"This is our time to rule," Ironman intoned loudly. He licked the rain from his upper lip. Some of the others imitated the gesture. "Lightning storm coming. The enemy's made his move, now he's taking cover. No helicopters up there, no gunships, no drones. Big electrical disturbances will knock out their IR. Lasers are blocked. Even high-altitude radar is distorted."

"Enemy be blind," Sutphen said. "Deaf, dumb and blind."

"Both sides lose their air support, their target acquisition, their reliable electronic communications," Ironman said. "That means, advantage, us. IDC's job is to make sure everybody in these columns gets the message. Keep them moving. If they stop, they're no good to us. They might as well be dead."

"Deaf, dumb and dead," Sutphen said.

"When we get south of Natural Bridge Avenue, I will call a brief halt while we locate the exact position of enemy armor. Don't let the troops think we're stopping because the lightning storm is too heavy. It's our moment of maximal advantage. I'm sending scouts ahead by civilian vehicles and on foot to locate enemy positions. As soon as we have them, we'll move, hell or high water. And give them both."

The group extended their right arms straight out, fists meeting at the spoke-center of the circle. "Ironman!" they chanted.

"Deaf, dumb and dead," Sutphen repeated as the group hurried to their posts. "Move it out."

★

Ironman's left hook had reached the black ghetto of northern St. Louis, but the rain was letting up. Daytime darkness had visibly lightened. Rain was dripping lazily onto the junked cars that lined the streets and vacant lots amid abandoned and boarded-up houses. A soggy litter of junk food wrappers and deteriorating trash piles was slowly composting itself for the next millennium. Indoors was obviously no more comfortable than outdoors, for the street corners were starting to be repopulated with knots of black men, young and middle-aged, lounging in the drizzle. They glared contemptuously at the parade of armored vehicles dispersing itself along the streets.

"This be Crips territory," Sutphen said. He was riding in a Humvee marked with the black triangle. Every available wall space was sprayed with gang graffiti. "Check it out: Rolling 60s Crips. Compton Gangsters. 107 Hoover Crips."

"Don't shit ya pants," JaMichael said. "These be Crips wannabes. Travel all the way to L.A. to find out what happenin'. Can't even think up they own names."

"Hear they outshoot L.A. Crips five times over, any day of the week," Sutphen said. "St. Louis be the homicide capital of the nation, aside from Detroit 'n' Baltimore."

"That ain't our problem," JaMichael said. "We losing the rain. No more cover from Federal target acquisition. All shit gonna bust loose when the Feds find out where we at."

"Don't shit *y'all's* pants," Sutphen said. "Feds can't move fast as Ironman. They sensors come back on, but it be taking hours 'fore they helos and gunships flying again. Ironman know what he about."

A young black man wearing a dark blue head bandana and draped in gold chains down his open chest detached himself from the street corner. He sauntered up to a Stryker armored personnel carrier which had pulled to a halt. The pause had been reached, when scouts were probing enemy positions. The Stryker's hatch was open and the street dealer was gesturing energetically in negotiation. The Stryker squad were all white, but this didn't faze the young black man, who seemed used to having white youths cruise the ghetto in search of drugs.

Sutphen motioned the Humvee to pull alongside and got out. "Hey, whassup bro?"

The street dealer stiffened at the sight of an unfamiliar black man, even one in the gray combat dress of the CSSA. "Where ya from?"

"From Ironman," Sutphen said. "I don't bang with no amateurs."

"Amateurs? What you talkin' bout, man? This be Rolling 60s Crips."

"Crips, amateurs," Sutphen said, insouciantly swinging his M4. "This be war. Real war. We be breakin' you St. Louis record-book homicide rate in five minutes." The dealer started to retreat. Confronting a rival gang head-on was not the way street violence was carried out; most of it was ambushes and surrounding isolated intruders away from their home turf. The IDC squad had followed Sutphen out of the vehicle and were backing him in a half-circle.

"Hold on, bro," said Sutphen. "Ironman got no beef with Rolling 60s. What I want is some info."

The dealer stopped, gold neck chains swinging as he turned. He was quite young, no more than sixteen years old, tall and slender, with the faint beginnings of a moustache. Large diamonds studded his earlobes and gold covered his fingers and wrists, visual bragging of success. "Info? What it worth?"

"What's you name?" Sutphen demanded.

"Chill."

"Chill, my man, listen. What it worth be you life. You info good, I gonna let you live. You info bad, I'll be back, send my IDC boys after you."

"What you wanna know?"

"USA armor come through here. How long ago, how many?"

Chill shrugged. "Before the rain. Streets fulla them."

"How many?"

"Same's you. Maybe more."

"How many pipes you sell?"

"A couple. A century worth."

"That all? Got anything left?"

"I got plenty left, man. How much you want?"

Sutphen poked his M4 at the boy's neck where the gold chains crossed. At a gesture the IDC crew had pinioned his arms.

"Ironman don't buy that shit no more. Get that, nigga? We kicked that habit. We pure. We get high on victory. If I see you selling dope to my troops, you dead. Get it?"

Chill raised his hands to show empty palms. "Chill, man, chill, I'm cool. I on vacation til you dudes outta here."

At a nod from Sutphen the IDC crew dropped the pinion and stepped away. "All right," Sutphen said. "Where be the USA armor now? Which way they go?"

"Where they go? Down Jefferson Avenue, down Florrissant Street. They everywhere."

"Don't see none of them here now."

"That be before the rain. Since it come down, they gone."

"Tell ya what," Sutphen said. "You info be half-good, that's all. I need up-to-date, on-the-clock info. I'm giving you a big chance, Chill, my man. I need you to head down Florrissant Street, down wherever, find where USA armor be now. Come back and tell me."

"Florrissant Street?" Chill turned hurriedly but the IDC crew blocked his way. "That be Crenshaw Gangster Bloods turf. I won't live two blocks."

"Shee-it," Sutphen said. "This be war, man. You ain't gonna get killed by those slobs. Besides, I gonna send you with an escort. Ironman escort."

He turned to JaMichael. "Take this man Chill down to Bloods territory and see where USA armor at. Borrow one of them civilian cars parked round here."

"Listen, Chill, my man," Sutphen continued. "We ain't no gang, and we ain't no cops. We be Ironman. There no law higher'n us, 'cept Ironman himself. You come back with the right info for this Ironman victory, I gonna see you get a chance to join Ironman yoself."

The youth hustled off with JaMichael into the drizzle.

Sutphen shouted after him. "And stop dealing that dope! You deal any more and I'll kill you myself."

★

General Ironman Johnston sat in his command car fidgeting inwardly, although his external appearance was stern and taut. The storm was his cover, the wilderness that would hide his movement, but it had crossed him up, it was much too mild and now it was petering out before the attack could begin. The double left-hook maneuver thus far had gone as planned; General Maddux had swung his Federal forces all the way around western St. Louis, pulling out from the south and coming back in on the north; CSSA armor, with excellent timing, had shadowed them on a shorter route, swinging westward and then north and finally falling in on their tail, far enough back to be unnoticed. Maddux had planned either to encircle the rebels or to alarm them into abandoning their front and withdraw northeast towards downtown where the two armies would meet head-on, only now the Federals would be holding defensive positions and force the CSSA to attack in the teeth of superior firepower.

And now Ironman had jumped around behind them. But the rain had slowed to a drizzle and it might even be clearing up.

Ironman took a handful of flax seeds and chewed them impatiently, spitting the hulls through the Humvee's open window. The hulls lay on the wet pavement amid the flotsam of inner-city neighborhood life, soft-drink and beer cans and discarded crack pipes. There were twenty-five thousand Federal troops somewhere in the blocks ahead, hundreds of armored vehicles. As of now they should be taking up positions facing south and west; if he could move fast enough, he would hit them from the north. He had fifteen thousand troops and three hundred fifty tanks and Strykers; it would be enough. But the rain!

The thought flickered across Ironman's mind of calling Jefferson Gray. Gray was always calm, contagiously calm, and that in itself was reassuring. Since when do I have to rely on other people? Ironman thought. I'm getting psychologically over-programmed. Anyway, the less communication the better. True, the city was full of civilian electronic signals—TVs, radios, cell phones, computers, wireless—so his army was hiding in an electromagnetic forest, the advantage of urban warfare in the cybertech age. Military signals were encrypted and supposed to be secure but still the enemy might find where they were. Say nothing.

Ironman shoved another handful of flax seeds into his mouth.

Major Sorrell, his staff officer, had a report. "Scouts are starting to come back. Enemy armor at Cass Avenue and down Tucker Boulevard. Some over behind the basketball Dome. About fifteen-twenty blocks from here."

"Are they still moving?"

"Can't tell about all of them. Some have halted and taken defensive positions, facing south and west."

"What force strength?"

"Reports are fragmentary. We've located about twenty armored vehicles."

"That's not enough info for us to start the attack. Do they know we're here?"

"I don't think so. No sign of it yet."

Abruptly the Humvee was rocked by staccato impacts, the firing of a heavy machine gun. Balls were slamming on the roof and denting the hood. The windshield, designed to be bulletproof against heavy fire, was covered with white cracks that made visibility impossible. There was a sudden chill, a dropping of the temperature. The sky went dark, almost the blackness of night, a heavy twilight in the early afternoon. Ironman rapidly rolled up the side window. A shatter of broken glass lay on the Humvee floor. Ironman picked it up with his fingers—it was ice.

A hailstorm was coming down, pelting the streets with miniature white cannonballs. The windshield was not cracked, it was the pattern of the shattering ice.

"Get on the horn and get everybody moving!" Ironman said. "Open radio contact with all scouts. I want enemy armor positions relayed to fire control and get our vehicles moving forward. We can't fire from a distance on these urban sight lines, so we're going to drive right up their backs."

"Yes, sir. But we haven't acquired many targets yet."

"We'll acquire them as we go along. Get our armor out there right behind our scouts. Laser tags aren't going to work in this weather. Relay info by word of mouth if you have to."

Flashes lit up the sky ahead. Not the outbreak of battle, but lightning, and an eardrum-crackling sound like fabric being torn by a giant, plummeting down the sound registers from the high-pitched to the low guttural, and then booming reverberating thunder. Three seconds between the flash and the thunder—the lightning was only a half a mile ahead. The intervals were growing, five seconds, six seconds. Ironman made a little inflection of prayer to his private vision of heaven, which just now was unloading right on top of the Federal positions.

The radio crackled and buzzed, breaking up the voices of higher officers and tank commanders and scouts. Radio silence was thrown to the winds. Computer consoles flickered unsteadily. It wasn't going to be very precise, Ironman thought. But he had drilled everybody into what they were to do. And his IDC were out there among them, making sure his forces kept on attacking, now that the order was given.

Infrared, laser designation, precise target coordinates—that was just so much flotsam of the storm. And that cuts both ways; soon the enemy would know where we are but they wouldn't be able to do anything about it. We may not hit everything we're aiming at, but what army ever did? While the storm lasted, he was pretty sure, we would be firing and they wouldn't be firing at all. You don't have to destroy everybody to break an enemy.

The hail had stopped and now water was pouring straight down. Water descending on Ironman's army like standing under a pump, like standing under a broken water main. The street was ankle deep, a river floating with beer cans and crack pipes, and now furrowed by the slosh of armored tread and the churning of oversized tires. Ironman's army, an irresistible extension of himself, had begun to move.

CSSA armor was advancing on every street across northeast St. Louis from Vandeventer Avenue to the Mississippi River. It was slow moving in the flooded streets but there wasn't far to go, even at ten miles per hour. Scouts on foot were drenched by the downpour but now they were in contact with the enemy, emboldened by the cover of water and dim daylight, like kids running out in a summer storm to enjoy getting wet. The Federal troops were spread out in depth, dispersed as a modern army should be in the face of lethal firepower, so that after the first enemy tanks and APCs were reached there were more in the blocks ahead for over a mile.

The downpour had driven the Federal infantry to cover. Instead of fanning out in a perimeter protecting the armor, they had clustered for shelter, many of them in their APCs under the driving rain. This gave CSSA armor lucrative targets as the tanks approached the blocks where they had clear lines of fire. APCs could be penetrated by the big gun of an Abrams tank. Tanks themselves could withstand even a direct hit of almost anything. But their treads and drive wheels were vulnerable, and tanks could be penetrated from behind where armor was thinner. Pickings were especially easy in the open spaces around the monuments and public buildings of central St. Louis, at the Dome and the Convention Center and at Busch Stadium and at the Gateway Arch itself.

At least for the moment the Federal armor were caught looking south, away from the direction the attack was coming. Individual tanks were surely aware something bad was happening, but the structure as a whole was paralyzed, unable to react.

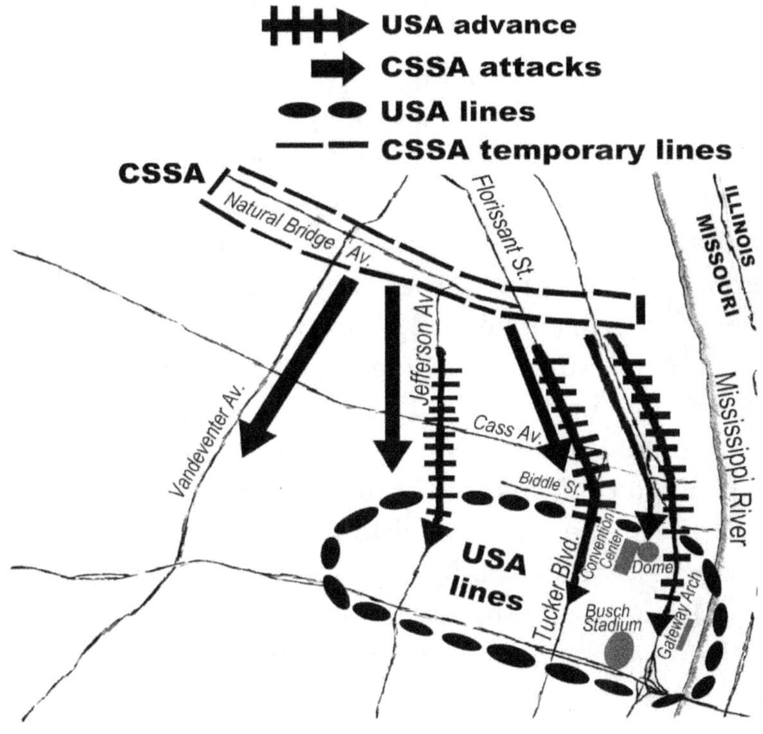

Thunder was still booming and the firing of battle at first could scarcely be distinguished from it, except there was no pause after the preceding flash of lighting. Inside USA armor, soldiers thought they were being hit by the storm. Vehicles in a lightning strike are generally safe for their occupants, the electric current merely passing over the hull to the ground. But you did not always remember this when your own vehicle, seemingly impregnable with its modern armor of compound metal-and-ceramic layers, is suddenly gaping open and rocked by the force of a million fists.

Survivors fled their damaged armor and were shot by the small arms fire of dismounted CSSA infantry accompanying the advancing tanks.

It was hard for Ironman to tell how many USA armored vehicles had been hit. Computer links were flickering on and off, and radio messages had to be shouted and repeated. But forward spotters were communicating with their tank gunners by light flashes and hand signals, and the USA forces were clearly taking heavy losses. Well, not clearly since nothing was clear in this murk, but certainly. Ironman felt it. His troops felt it.

His own losses so far were minimal. The enemy was pointed the wrong way and slow in reacting and returning fire. The worst problem was traffic. Military vehicles moving in a combat zone are always dangerous, and in any battle a fifth of the casualties could come from traffic accidents. Here they were almost all the casualties, the army driving in flooded streets with near-zero visibility and terrible communications. Heavy tanks were not likely to be floated even on a flood current but they clumsily crashed into walls and crunched the front door stoops of St. Louis row houses. The tanks mangled parked cars, and this in turn made them a danger to other tanks and the lighter APCs, and to any dismounted soldiers who happened to be wading nearby.

So far, Ironman gathered, there were only a couple of incidents of friendly fire and only one APC was seriously damaged when they fired upon by each other.

Ironman's biggest worry was traffic jams stalling the attack. He kept up a constant stream of demands to hear how traffic was proceeding, and ordered his Humvee to head towards the worst bottlenecks.

At Biddle Street, the flow of water was especially strong. A Stryker APC weighs eighteen tons but this one's wheels had slid and crashed into the side of a tank, partially knocking over a utilities pole. Both crews got out and were standing in a cluster when lightning struck. Nine men were down.

Four of them were dead, floating in the street like drowned bodies except that their clothes were shredded and singed. A couple of medics were administering CPR to the dead bodies, since lightning kills mainly by cardiac arrest and paralyzing the respiratory system and there was a chance of resuscitation getting their bodily systems going again. The survivors of the lightning strike were wandering around in various postures of confusion; some had their eardrums burst and were holding their heads, some blinded by retinal bleeding, some were kneeling and vomiting into the rain-lashed water.

A man with his shirt stripped off had a small black mark on chest and back where the electric current had burned in and out of his body for a few milliseconds. A million volts of current had coursed through the power pole and the armored vehicles, and whoever was touching these surfaces had burn marks on the part of their body that made contact. Some had burn marks around their necks where their metal chains and body jewelry had touched their flesh heated to fifty thousand degrees Fahrenheit.

More vehicles had stopped and a growing cluster of soldiers were shouting and arguing when Ironman drove up.

"Fuckin' lightning," one soldier was saying over and over. "Can't fight fuckin' lightning." IDC guards had moved in and were confronting the freaked-out soldiers.

A soldier was sitting on a house stoop with his arms clasping his knees. He was not one of those hit by lightning but he was shaking and crying uncontrollably. A pair of IDC guards with the black triangle patches shoved their way through the knot of soldiers and pulled the man to his feet. The IDC guards were burly black men. The crying soldier was a slender white boy not yet grown into his lanky frame.

"Straighten up, soldier! Get some self-respect." They slapped his face repeatedly but the boy was beyond terror and the crying did not stop.

The crowd of surrounding soldiers had hung back, hesitating while the IDC moved in. Now they surged forward and pulled the IDC guards off the white boy. The knot of men spun clumsily, like the mêlée on a baseball field after the batter has been hit by a pitch, angrier but impeded from doing much damage as they thrashed and fell into the inches-deep water.

The rain had slackened slightly to a mere heavy pour.

"At-ten-SHUN!" Ironman's voice could be heard but the mêlée did not stop. Taking an M4 from his own guard, Ironman fired a burst over their heads. The mêlée lost enthusiasm and broke apart.

The wet soldiers struggled to their feet. The hysterical soldier was still crying, but he looked with dull focus at Ironman's face.

"You're alive, soldier. Think about it." Ironman gestured to the dead bodies. "They're not. Who's worse off here?"

The IDC were looking at Ironman raptly. Their guru was speaking, revealing the magic. The other soldiers, too, still heaving deep breaths, were calming.

"What difference does it make how you get it? Lightning flashes like a thousand suns. Bomb blasts like a thousand gunshots. Your body can only die once. It's your mind that multiples it."

Lightning flashed again, and the boom came a few seconds later, near enough to shake them. Ironman pointed to the sky. "I'm not out to kill you. I'm going to make you victorious. Whether you live or die."

The boy had stopped crying, although he barely seemed to know where he was. He seemed hypnotized on Ironman's face. The rest of the troops too looked at him with mouths open.

"Victory," Ironman said. "Victory over yourself. Get moving!"

Thunder and lightning had stopped, and the rain diminished to a heavy drizzle. The sounds of battle winding down were faded, desultory and far away. Sutphen saw an isolated APC in the vacant parking lot of a McDonald's hamburger shop, and pulled over his Humvee to check. The McDonald's was closed and there were no lights, but a group of soldiers were inside.

They were huddled in a circle on the floor. The air was thick with that unmistakable chemical smell. The soldiers were holding glass tubes fitted with mouthpieces, some lighting each other's pipe with cigarette lighters, others lighting their own.

Sutphen turned on the lights. Across from him, in the midst of the group, was JaMichael Kilson. He had a set of gold chains around his neck, hanging outside the front of his battle dress. There were a half dozen other soldiers, both black and white. All of them were in the euphoric, temporarily stunned condition of a crack high.

JaMichael gestured with his pipe at Sutphen. "Have a hit, bro." He motioned towards a plastic sack of glass tubes in the center of the circle.

Sutphen waved him off. "Where you get them gold chains?"

"Where you think? I picked them up off the street."

"Off the body of that punk kid, Chill."

"He done chilled hisself to death," JaMichael said. "Dropped dead of fear soon as he reached Bloods territory."

"That be murder," Sutphen said. "Armed robbery. And now drug dealing."

JaMichael pulled himself to his feet, a little unsteadily. "So what," he said. "They'll never know who killed him, just another battle casualty. There won't be no investigation."

"You and I know who killed him," Sutphen said.

"Blow it off," JaMichael said. "Take a hit." He pulled a crack pipe from the sack and extended it to Sutphen.

Sutphen's hands were holding the M4 and they were quivering. He hadn't touched drugs in two years. A sudden movement of his M4 struck the pipe to the ground.

"Victory over yourself," Sutphen said.

He trained the M4 on JaMichael's face. "You just a street hustler, JaMichael."

The group of soldiers were on their feet. Some backed away. Others moved towards Sutphen, waving hands from side to side, talking him down. "He's your bro, Sutphen." "He Ironman too." "Chill, chill!"

Sutphen ignored them. "Just a street hustler. You going backwards. You broke the Ironman code."

JaMichael reached for his gun, but the crack cocaine made him slow. Sutphen squeezed off a burst that destroyed JaMichael's face. Sutphen turned in a semicircle, firing mechanically, like a robot. The other soldiers were down, easy targets without their helmets, their weapons put aside. In slow motion, Sutphen loaded another clip and fired some more into their crumpled bodies until the clip was exhausted. Then he walked out the door. He was crying.

Sutphen's driver was outside the McDonald's. "What happened?"

"Let's just say, enemy fire."

"Where's the enemy?"

"Dead, dead and dead," Sutphen said. "Let's get moving."

Another Humvee pulled up, the black triangle on its side. Col. Newton Crawford got out.

"Keeping order again, are you, Sergeant?" Crawford said to Sutphen. "Get back inside." A squad of guards from his accompanying car started to follow Crawford into the McDonald's but he motioned them to stay outside.

The bodies of the APC crew were sprawled on the floor in front of the food counter in the contorted positions that come from repeated firing at close range. Crawford walked over to the body with the black triangle patch and turned JaMichael Kilson on his back.

Crawford turned back to Sutphen. "I told you, you're going too far."

Sutphen said nothing. The tears had stopped. He felt nothing.

"Immediate punishment for disobeying orders," Crawford said. "That's the Ironman rule." He kicked the bag of crack pipes away with his foot. "You know it, Sutphen."

Sutphen still said nothing.

Crawford raised an M4 at Sutphen.

"They was a bunch of dope dealers inside Ironman's army," Sutphen said. "And JaMichael, right inside the IDC."

"So you killed them," Crawford said. "It doesn't look good. Ironman force has gotten too big for this kind of thing. Ironman force is going to be famous after this victory, the battle of St. Louis. This doesn't look good for Ironman. Doesn't look good for me. Doesn't look good for anybody."

Sutphen nodded bitterly. "I hear you, Crawford. One more dead body and everything be cleaned up. Just one more on the pile of casualties."

Another Humvee pulled up outside. The pair inside the McDonald's froze in a tableau. General Ironman Johnston himself came through the door.

Ironman scanned their faces. "What is it, Sutphen? I can see it in your face. It's written in your body posture. What do you want to tell me?"

But Sutphen for once was not talking.

"He's gone too far," Crawford said. He gestured to the bodies on the floor. "The IDC is getting a bad reputation. It needs to be cleaned up. I'm punishing him now."

"One killing leads to another," Ironman said. "The chain has to stop somewhere. I say stop it here."

"Ironman rule says, punish every breach of discipline immediately. He disobeyed my order. I'm punishing him now."

"It's time to rethink that rule. We can't run an army like that. You're not still in rehab."

"With Ironman method, we are an unbeatable fighting force," Crawford said. "Without absolute obedience to orders, there is no victory."

"We have the victory," Ironman said. "Now is the time to learn some psychology."

Crawford turned his M4 away from Sutphen and trained it on Ironman. "You've lost the Ironman principle," Crawford said. "You're not Ironman any more. I am."

Sutphen had found a weapon and pointed it at Crawford. The barrel wavered. "Do I shoot him, Ironman?" Sutphen asked Ironman Johnston.

"No," Ironman said. "Put the gun down, Crawford. There's only room for one man's will power here. The strongest army acts as one body and one will. That's why we win. I'm still the C.O."

"Not any more," Crawford said. "You lost your nerve, *General* Johnston. I haven't lost mine."

Ignoring Sutphen, Crawford fired a burst into Ironman Johnston's chest. Sutphen's gun followed Crawford as he strolled across the floor with deliberate ease to check whether his former commander was dead. He was.

Sutphen's gun was still shaking when Crawford turned to face him. "All right, Sergeant. You got anything to say to me?"

Sutphen lowered his gun. His hand shot up in a salute. "Ironman, sir!"

Crawford's guards and Ironman Johnston's guards were pressing at the door as Crawford and Sutphen emerged. "General Johnston has been killed by friendly fire," Crawford said. "There was a shootout here and everyone involved is dead. Except Sergeant Sutphen, who saved my life—Captain Sutphen now, because I am giving him a battlefield promotion."

Ironman Johnston's guards and Crawford's guards glanced at each other's faces, waiting for someone to show a sign of questioning. Crawford stared at each one in turn. Their faces went blank.

"A dark shadow has passed over our movement," Crawford said. "But we have survived. The Ironman spirit cannot be killed. I know I can count on everyone's loyalty."

Crawford slowly made the circuit of the group, gripping each man's hand and looking into each one's eyes.

He gave orders to pick up General Johnston's body to send North for a state funeral. "I am the Commanding Officer now," he reminded them. "You will address me as General Crawford—General Ironman Crawford."

General Jefferson Gray was visiting the front as the victorious Battle of St. Louis drew to a close. He drove through the burned-out streets in an armored command vehicle, leaning out the window, waving to the troops. They surged forward around the blasted cars and the crumpled door stoops and piles of brick rubble, shouting like fans catching sight of their favorite rock star. Jefferson Gray was white-haired and smooth-shaven and his uniform was immaculately clean, while the soldiers were young and short-haired and their faces and clothes were grubby and streaked with smoke and oil and gave off the smells of the hot city and days of battle. But he was one of them, more than one of them, their idealized self rising above themselves. They jumped and waved and pushed forward to get a glimpse and gave gang signs and Jefferson Gray saluted them with quiet dignity. The shouting went down the street preceding the car and following it for several excited minutes as the car turned a corner and went off into the distance.

In the car with him was Newton Crawford, the one-star insignia of Brigadier General on his helmet and collar. Crawford sat back and did not show himself to the troops. He was Ironman and his own soldiers were a force apart. This was Jefferson Gray's day and his own day would come.

Vice Chairperson O'Leary had come down from Chicago for the victory. He leaned out his window and let himself be photographed next to Jefferson Gray and made enthusiastic and humorous gestures when his practiced instincts told him a television camera was pointed in his direction.

A quiet spot came in the route as the car sped up to reach another segment of the battle line. Jefferson Gray closed his window and turned to General Crawford sitting in the back seat. "Ironman Johnston is dead. What a price for victory. It's like losing my right arm."

"The IDC is still operative," Crawford said. "It's the muscle and bone of Ironman. You still have that arm, sir."

"How'd it happen, again, General Crawford?" Jefferson Gray said.

"It was a friendly fire incident during a lightning storm," Crawford said. "General Johnston was leading from the front, as always. He intervened to break up a dispute, and was killed doing it."

"I understand you were on the spot, General?"

"I arrived soon after. I like to lead from the front myself."

"You need to break yourself of that habit," Jefferson Gray said. "You can't react to the big picture if you're caught up in little firefights. You need to change your style as you rise higher."

O'Leary twisted around in his seat to join the conversation. "Y'know, Jeff, we ought to think twice about what gets released to the news media. They know Ironman Johnston is dead. But it wouldn't sound good for him to be killed by friendly fire. The public doesn't understand friendly fire. They don't know how often it happens in battle—they think it's some kind of scandal."

"Friendly fire is one of the dangers you risk in the battle zone," Jefferson Gray said. "It is one more thing a soldier has to be courageous about. And lucky about, too."

"The public doesn't know that. It wants its heroes to be like TV action figures." O'Leary leaned forward. "What I'm saying, Jeff, is my people need to be in complete control of the news releases."

Jefferson Gray had turned to the window, facing away from the conversation. "In this matter. You're arranging the funeral ceremonies in Chicago. You handle all the news releases to do with Ironman Johnston. I have a war to fight."

"General Crawford could help me out with the news reports," O'Leary said. "Right, Newton? As I understand it, all the witnesses who know anything about this friendly fire shootout are in your headquarters staff."

Crawford nodded. "You have my complete cooperation, Mr. Vice Chairperson, sir."

"Bill, call me Bill. Big Bill if you like."

"Bill."

"That's enough on that," Jefferson Gray said. "General Crawford, you are confirmed as C.O. of the St. Louis Battle Group. But I want the Ironman Disciplinary Commission disbanded. Fold them back into a new Ironman Brigade, if you want. It's good for morale to have names like that."

He rolled down the window and began to wave again to the cheering crowds.

Chancellorsville, May 1863

It was the most sophisticated battle of the war. Both sides carried out clever maneuvering both planned and improvised, with good execution and intelligent understanding of what wins battles. The Federals had learned the lesson of Fredericksburg: a brute force frontal assault on a strong defensive position merely wastes troops in one-sided attrition. Union General Hooker planned to turn the tables on the Confederates, and make them carry out a frontal attack on his prepared position. To this end, he started with a wide swinging march to the west of the stalemate at Fredericksburg, crossing several rivers fifteen miles upstream and looping back to catch the Confederate fortifications from the rear. As Lee moved out to challenge the threat at Chancellorsville, about eight miles west, Hooker prepared to meet the assault in the heavy woods called the Wilderness. The Federals combined all the advantages: taking the initiative by maneuver, a battlefield position of concentrated fire against a frontal assault, plus resources to win by attrition if necessary, since the Federals outnumbered the enemy by about two to one, one hundred fifteen thousand to sixty thousand.

Deception aids maneuver, and Hooker covered his move by attacking with two army corps at Fredericksburg, while sending three corps in the great circling move to the west, with two more corps ready to reinforce them by a more direct route to Chancellorsville. Lee responded by improvising in the same manner, leaving a mere two divisions to hold the strong defensive position on the heights at Fredericksburg, and leading the rest of his army to Chancellorsville. The superior Federal forces had successfully converged, and Lee had seemingly fallen into the trap.

But Lee now went on to encircle the full sweep of the Union maneuver, dividing his forces again, sending Stonewall Jackson with two thirds of his remaining troops—about twenty-seven thousand—in a roundabout swing around the west end of the Union line, to come in behind Chancellorsville, in their rear. Union and Confederate end-runs mirrored each other, but in different rhythms: the Federals had already completed their arc and were back in compact position when Stonewall's columns appeared out of a logging road hidden in the forest. Hooker had maneuvered to make the Confederates attack him in a superior defensive position, but their answering maneuver fell on the rear of the Union army as it engaged forward against where it thought Lee would be. Stonewall had marched his troops all day at top speed to carry out this looping maneuver.

In fact, early reports had reached Union officers that Stonewall was leaving Lee's camp to begin his march, but they assumed the Confederates were retreating from the battlefield, not curving around behind it.

One Federal corps completely disintegrated under Jackson's late-afternoon attack; a corps was only one fifth of the army on the field but it set a devastating tone for the rest as it fled in disorganization into their midst. Hooker was knocked out by a falling beam from artillery fire when Confederates penetrated close to his headquarters, leaving him with a splitting headache and profound shock at this sudden reversal of his plans, which had unfolded so perfectly up to now. The Union chain of command was punch-drunk: Hooker turned over command to another general but continued for several days to give intermittent and contradictory orders.

The Confederates received a worse blow to their command. Stonewall Jackson was mortally wounded, shot by his own pickets as he reconnoitered the enemy in the dusk. He was the master of rapid movement through harsh discipline, the second being one of the conditions for the first; he had hectored and executed plenty of his own troops and now they had killed him.

The next day the Confederates pressed their advantage of momentum by attacking from two sides. J.E.B. Stuart, another aggressive commander, took over from Stonewall and pressed the assault from the west while Lee closed the pincers on the Union army from the east. It was the most costly part of the battle for the Confederates, still greatly outnumbered but carrying frontal assaults by sheer élan. The Wilderness was heavy woods with thick underbrush which caught fire in the fighting, and many wounded were burned alive. Nevertheless the Confederates had the intoxicating air of victory while the Federals fell back in defeat. As General Lee appeared at the front, an enormous cheer spread along the Confederate lines, from smoke-blackened soldiers and wounded men struggling to raise themselves for a wave and a glimpse of the general who had become a symbol of themselves, believers in their own invincibility.

YEAR TWO, CHAPTER FOUR.

BATTLE OF FOUR CORNERS

The Pentagon. November.

Marisa Santa-Ana was escorted into the Secretary of Defense's office by a pair of security guards and left alone with Madigan. She wore oversized horn-rimmed glasses and her hair was pulled back severely and piled on top of her head in a bun. Her suit was brown tweed and the skirt was loose and shapeless and hung well below her knees. The jacket bulged sideways below the armpits, too tight for a woman of her build. A gold silk scarf looped around her shoulders. The temporary security badge worn by visitors to the Pentagon hung suspended far forward over the precipice of her breasts.

Madigan said, "Brigadier Grotweil says you have something important to tell me, and you can't deliver it to anyone else. Well, what is it?"

Marisa got up from her seat at the side and walked up and down in front of his desk. She was wearing modest medium-heeled shoes, but her ankle bones made delicate hollows on either side of the Achilles tendon and set off the curves of her lower calves. She pivoted slowly for his eyes.

Demurely she turned to Madigan and smiled. "I make the interview first. Then I tell you my personal message."

"Go ahead." Madigan didn't have to tell people he was busy. Grotweil had said this woman from the Mexican TV network was very insistent. More to the point, she had been to Chicago and interviewed the heads of the CSSA and seemed to know their generals. It sounded like she was carrying some kind of offer, a feeler from the other side.

"It's so hot, don't you think?" Marisa untied the scarf and dropped it carelessly on the carpet. She looked at Madigan as if she expected him to get up from behind his desk and pick it up. Madigan merely stared from his rimless glasses.

"I can give you ten minutes. The clock is ticking."

"I represent the people of Mexico," Marisa said in rhythmically accented rapid-fire. "I represent all Hispanics. South of the border we are hundreds of millions. We are friends of Americans—if you wish to be friends with us. Already forty millions of us live in *El Norte*."

"*Yo lo sé*," Madigan said. "*Somos muy buenos amigos*."

Marisa took off her jacket and trailed it behind her with one hand as she spun a slow circle. She was wearing a pale yellow blouse, transparent enough to reveal a white strapless brassiere with double-D cups. She revolved herself slowly to display every angle.

Madigan couldn't help smiling.

"What we want to know, Mr. Secretary Madigan, is what this war is doing to us. All this fighting. Are you trying to kill us? We live on both sides of the border, you know."

Madigan came around the desk and stooped to pick up the scarf. He tossed it onto a chair.

Marisa was abruptly in his face. Her nipples touched his shirt front with the pen protector in the pocket and the gold clip on his necktie. "Yes, the Hispanic people. *La Raza*. We lived in New Mexico before you did. Before you took it away from us, because you are so powerful. Mr. Secretary *gringo*."

She spun away like a hummingbird changing course and plopped herself on the sofa on the other side of the room. "What is this terrible war doing to us? We want to live in peace. We come to America to make a good life for our families. We work hard, we contribute. We accept low wages. We take the jobs no one else wants. We travel to work. El Paso, Dallas, Denver. Now the roads are cut. How are we to get through? Artillery on the Interstate from Santa Fe to Pueblo,

Colorado. Those horrible vampire drones that come out of the sky and destroy your vehicle. Helicopters buzzing everywhere like dogs growling over your head. How can we live like this?"

Madigan sat down beside her on the sofa. "Look, Miss Santa-Ana. You need to understand. Some of the Interstates cross the front, from US territory into enemy territory. You can't just drive up there like it's peacetime."

"What about the other roads?" Marisa was animated, churning her hands like she was winding an invisible spool in the air in front of her breasts. "The road from Las Vegas—blocked. The crossing at Lake Powell dam—blocked. The roads to Cortez, Durango—blocked. What are we supposed to do—die in our cars? Walk across the desert in the heat while the helicopters shoot us?"

"It's an active front," Madigan said. She was back on her feet, strutting wildly on the carpet. Madigan grabbed her hand and pulled her back to her seat. "You can think about this strategically, can't you?"

He gestured to the wall map, using pedantry to calm both her and himself. " The highway from Albuquerque to Denver is held by forces on both sides of the border. Same thing in the west, another battle front on the road from Utah to Las Vegas. If we broke through there, we'd be in Southern California. So of course the CSSA blocks it."

"Pressure building up," Marisa said. "Where's it going to blow?" She had let her hand fall on Madigan's lap. Now she reached into his crotch and began to stroke.

Madigan twisted away, tried to concentrate on the map. "The CSSA has bases all across eastern New Mexico and west Texas. We have to protect Colorado and Utah, so we have a lot of forward bases there too. I'm sorry to inconvenience your people, but I'm sure you understand—"

Marisa was nuzzling. "I hear they're fighting around the Four Corners. What is it, *mi Secretario gringo*—a CSSA invasion of Utah? Or is the USA—" she pronounced it *Ooo-sah*—"blowing off pressure, pricking General McConnell is the butt?"

She had dug a finger into the seat of Madigan's pants.

Madigan wrenched himself from his slumped position on the sofa to his feet. He readjusted the clip on his necktie. "Interview is over. Get the hell out of here."

Marisa had made a mistake. But she never let a man get the initiative in a fight. She turned her head violently away and began to button her jacket. "You're losing the war, aren't you. You think you're so powerful, Mr. Big-*Estados-Unidos*-Secretary. I heard you lost half your armor and all your air force at Gettysburg. You got beat at Philadelphia. They whipped your ass at St. Louis."

"Your time is up."

Marisa pulled angrily at her jacket, popping a couple of buttons. She tore it off and threw it at Madigan's face. "You ripped my clothes."

"I'm sure your employer will buy you some new ones." He was about to call security to show her out.

Marisa abruptly sat down again. "I have a message."

Madigan hesitated, his finger over the intercom button. "Let's hear it."

"From O'Leary. The Vice Chairperson-something." She lifted her skirt and began to adjust the top of her stocking.

"So he's your boss?"

"The Hispanic people are my boss." She tossed her head haughtily. "O'Leary is a friend. I have many friends in important places."

"I'll bet you do." Madigan leaned back against the front of his desk, across from the sofa, watching her. She had taken off her shoe, angrily rapped the heel on the edge of the desk. It broke off in her hand, leaving the shoe completely flat.

"Well?"

"His message is a friendly one. He thinks this war is foolish and wishes it would end."

"It will end soon enough," Madigan said. "Sooner than you think."

"O'Leary can offer you favorable terms. To speed things up." She took off the other shoe and broke off its heel to match the first one. Her skirt was still high above her knees.

"What terms?"

"That's all I can say right now. The only question is whether you are willing to discuss."

"I'd have to take it up with the President."

"Sure. But don't wait too long. The terms might change."

"Depending on what?"

"How long can you go on without winning a battle? You haven't won one yet."

"There's Caribou Forest. General Cruz beat McConnell in Idaho."

"What good did it do you? You still can't break out on the Utah front. Jefferson Gray has you stalemated in the Midwest. And I hear you are destroying New Jersey but the Eastern front is just costing you men and equipment. Your air forces are almost gone." Marisa reached a hand under her raised skirt into her own crotch. She raised a finger to her mouth and began to lick it.

Madigan told himself this interview had to stop. But he merely said, "If you think we're so weak, why does O'Leary want to bargain? They have their problems too."

Marisa wetted her finger on her tongue. "Your problems are bigger. I hear you had this computer system called HOME. The world's greatest supercomputer. It controlled everything. Then it went bust." Her erect finger curled. "A big strong man like you, and he can't keep his *system* up."

"How did you hear about that? That system was top secret."

"Not secret enough. Everybody knows about it. Now you think you have a new system that's even better."

"You got that out of Grotweil." Madigan felt like strangling her. He advanced toward her.

Marisa took her wet finger out of her mouth and put it on his lips. "It went down, right in the middle of battle. Gone dead train. You boys need Viagra."

Madigan had his hands on her neck. Marisa did not flinch. "Go ahead," she said. "Some men get their rocks off by having sex with a plastic bag over their head."

Madigan expelled his breath sharply and sat down on the sofa. He was breathing heavily.

"Sure, Grotweil told me some things. Everybody tells me some things. Nobody can keep from telling me what I want to know."

"So what do you know about the new computer system?"

Marisa opened her handbag and looked at her face in a mirror. "Net war, something like that. It's the opposite of the old system. HOME linked everybody to one big computer that tells everybody what to do. Now this network war is supposed to link everybody to everybody else, so they all share all the information and make their own decisions."

"Network-centered warfare," Madigan said. "The idea isn't that much of a secret. But now we have all the pieces to make it work."

"Hardware and software," Marisa murmured, reaching into his crotch again. "They fit together."

Madigan pushed her away, gently this time. "Not everybody's sex is on autopilot," he said. "I need calm to think."

Marisa pushed down her skirt and stood up. "Thinking about trying out your new network at Four Corners?" she said. At the door she mouthed a kiss. *"Mi Secretario."*

Madigan sat at his desk, thinking of whether to have Marisa Santa-Ana arrested. It was too uncertain. Marisa might do anything, say anything about what happened in their meeting, charm some people into believing her. Let her go.

He called his assistant. "I want Major Zielkowski to carry out a security investigation on the woman who just left. Give Zielkowski everything she needs, but keep it top secret. Have her report directly to me." No point in putting a man on the job. If there was anyone immune to Marisa's spells, it would be Debra.

Southeast Utah.

The fantastic chiseled buttes of Monument Valley were passing beneath the helicopter but Captain Tom Napoli was not interested in aesthetics. It was architecture like the valley of the Nile only doubled in size. Enormous Egyptian tombs, crumpled step-pyramids, Pharoahs' thrones, nature's own Sphinxes of eroded rock. Ordinarily under battle conditions Tom Napoli's Apaches would be flying lower, below three hundred feet, staying under enemy radar and using the rock piles in the valley as hiding places, like kids playing tag dashing from one safe spot to another. But now they were in all-out hurry, riding to the rescue of the USA's forward operating base at Tuba City, Arizona. Battle orders said Tuba City was under attack from CSSA forces and was running out of fuel and ammunition. These days they were always in a hurry, Napoli thought. Somebody was always running out of something. It was getting old.

Tuba City was a hundred miles southwest of here, in the high desert south of the Utah-Arizona border, on the road to the Grand Canyon. Tuba City was a roadside poverty squat in the Indian reservation, but the US Army had to put its FOBs somewhere if it was going to advance into enemy territory. It needed forward supply dumps so it could leapfrog another couple hundred miles, each leap within helicopter battle radius, its out-and-back refueling comfort zone, until it reached the populated areas of central Arizona or threatened the routes to California. It was a war of helicopters, mainly—there was no front line, just a string of FOBs in the Utah rockpiles and the Arizona and New Mexico deserts, a string of armored helicopter pads. In between the FOBs were eighty or a hundred miles of empty space. Enemy helicopters could fly through the spaces, and it was enemy helicopters that had been attacking Tuba City, probably from their own CSSA base at Flagstaff, Arizona.

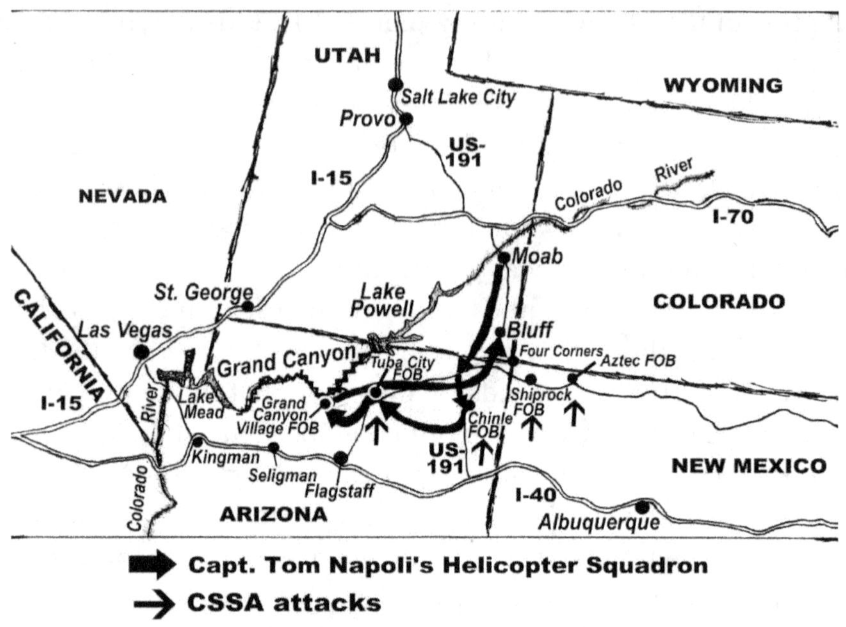

In this war of empty spaces without a front line everything had to be supplied from a distance. Especially ammunition, which high-tech armies used up in prodigious amounts, flinging around two thousand pound bombs and thousand pound missiles like giants in a food fight. And worse than ammo supplies, the appetite for fuel. It was the biggest, heaviest load, and the fastest used up, since everything you did in the combat zone used fuel, whether fighting was going on or not. And if you ran out of fuel you were caught, stuck in the nonlinear battlefield, not exactly stuck in hyperspace because when you were out of fuel you could no longer jump from place to place and the enemy had you sited and you were dead.

And that was why Tom Napoli and his four Apaches were speeding towards Tuba City, Arizona, flying down from battle headquarters at Moab, Utah not quite as fast as they could go but as fast as their accompanied convoy of Chinook transport helicopters could keep up, 140 miles per hour. One more reason to fly twelve hundred feet above the ground, over the tops of the Monument Valley rockpiles, since Chinooks were heavy and would be even slower if they had to maneuver around these massive pylons purple-red in the rising sun. There was more danger from enemy aircraft but it would be worse if one of the Chinooks, weighted with tons of helicopter fuel, were to hit one of the rockwalls or get caught in a gust and crash to the ground. Napoli's four Apaches herded along the dozen Chinooks like cowboys, like riding shotgun for a convoy of stagecoaches in the sky.

Napoli's communications operator had a message. "FOB Chinle, Arizona calling, Captain. Urgent call for help. Col. Atkins says they will be overrun within an hour if they don't get refueled. Their Apaches are holding off CSSA armor attacking through the desert from the south. But they're running out of fuel and the base fuel dump is empty. They want you to divert to Chinle."

Napoli thought of the new standing orders. Be flexible, respond to your environment. Horizontal links in the network. Chinle was sixty miles due south of where their helicopter convoy was right now; they could reach it in fifteen minutes in the Apaches at attack speed, in thirty minutes even with the lumbering Chinooks. It was almost a right-angle turn from their original flight path.

"What's the report from Tuba City?" Napoli said.

"Same as before. They want fuel. Urgent."

"How urgent? Are they under immediate attack?"

"Last attack report was 1800 hours. Eleven hours ago. Should I call and ask them?"

"No, forget it, I know what they'll say. Any UAVs out there?"

The communications operator punched some keys. "Raw feed from—" he read off some coordinates "—that's fifteen miles southeast of Tuba City—nothing. Here's another UAV at—" more coordinates.

"Just give me the bottom line. How many hostiles around Tuba City?"

"Can't see anything in the immediate area. Some engagements with enemy helicopters forty miles out."

"And Chinle?"

"Lots of raw UAV feed coming into our zone." He called out a series of coordinates. "Shit, you can get too much of a good thing here. Network-centered warfare, my ass. Somebody has to filter this stuff."

"Just answer the question. How many hostiles at Chinle?"

"Here's something. UAV feed at ten miles, on Highway 191. Enemy armor. Chinle thinks it's battalion size."

"Enemy helicopter escort?"

"Just a minute. Here's a report from ground control on the Chinle situation. Twenty minutes ago. Enemy armor escorted by four Apache attack helicopters. They think it was four. Or two. May be a couple downed. Or turned back for fuel."

"Looks like a breathing space, " Napoli said. "How hot is the landing at Chinle?"

A pause while the operator sought the answer. On the ground below Napoli's convoy the purple-red rock mountains of Monument Valley had given way to dull tan of the Arizona desert. Every minute now was taking them further from Chinle.

"Chinle is down to two choppers covering their airspace; otherwise it's just their Triple-A. No enemy fire. We can get in."

"Looks like Chinle needs us more than Tuba City does," Napoli said. He flicked on his microphone to alert his squadron.

"Just a minute, Captain, here's something." The communications operator was jumping from screen to screen. Messages from every FOB across the battle zone, from Grand Canyon Village in the west to Shiprock and Aztec, New Mexico in the east. "Damn, everybody wants something. Hostiles all over the place. Isn't anybody carrying fuel except us?"

"One thing at a time," Napoli said. "It's Chinle unless somebody says something else is more urgent. Call control at Moab."

Every second at 140 miles per hour towards one destination was making the other destination further away. Before the call to Moab went through Napoli was on the radio net to his squadron: "Cowboy Six, Cowboy. Change course to new coordinates." Using COMSEC—Communications Security code—he told them they were diverting to FOB Chinle. Maybe the flight control at Moab would overrule him; maybe they would go to Tuba City after all. Maybe somebody else would be near enough to relieve Chinle.

The operator had Moab on the air. Orders were to proceed to Tuba City. Did they know about the call from Chinle? Yes, they knew, it was all taken care of. Ask them again, Napoli said. Tell them what we heard. No, they hadn't heard that. Tell them to check higher up. Tell them to get General Park himself, all hell is busting loose everywhere down here.

"Moab says they're checking it," the operator said. "Meantime, orders are to keep your course for Tuba City."

The operator was flipping rapidly from one channel to another. Messages were coming in on top of each other. The west end of the battle zone was quieter now, out towards the Grand Canyon, but everybody east of Chinle seemed to have their own emergency. FOB Shiprock, New Mexico was under attack, impossible to tell how severe. There was plenty of UAV feed but no one in the battle zone had time to interpret it. Assessing enemy strength was supposed to be done at ground control stations at each FOB, and somebody back at General Park's headquarters at Moab was supposed to get the big picture. Then again, Moab probably has ten times as much feed as we do, Napoli thought. I'm not holding my breath til they answer.

Network-centered war is the new doctrine, the Pentagon had announced a month ago. Maximal local initiative is the path to victory. The days of centralization are over. Every local commander to have full access to all relevant information. Unit commanders to communicate laterally as need be and help each other with maximal flexibility. Be faster and nimbler than the enemy, the SECDEF's order had said.

What held it all together was supposed to be the theatre Commander's Intent issued at the beginning of the campaign and updated in daily Battle Orders. Well, the Commander's Intent was stated two weeks ago in a message from General Hawp, Commander of the Utah Theatre of Operations. Hawp had said that the operational center of gravity was dislodging the enemy from Las Vegas, thereby protecting Utah's southwest corner, and opening the road for an invasion of southern California. Our FOBs on the Arizona and New Mexico side of the border, Napoli told himself, were just a way of harassing the enemy, a forward defense until the push could come against Las Vegas. The big battle would develop at the west end of the line.

Still no update from Moab. In twenty minutes they would be at Chinle. General Park's orders of the day, issued before Napoli's convoy had taken off that morning, had said nothing about supporting a drive towards Las Vegas. Gandhi Park was subordinate to General Hawp, but operating autonomously in control of the FOBs protecting the southern Utah border, with authority on into the corner of Colorado and into New Mexico. Park published his own Commander's Intent: all units to support the FOBs across the border and extend them as opportunity and local enemy weakness provided. It was well known that Gandhi Park did not think highly of the political appointee General Hawp.

Captain Napoli was back on the air. "Cowboy Six, Cowboy. Confirming new heading." He gave the flight coordinates for FOB Chinle. "Prepare for a hot landing."

Moab sounded like a place out of the Old Testament, one of the ancient enemies of Israel where ritual abominations were offered to cruel gods. Moab, Utah was dramatic enough, a town in the bottom of a steep rock-walled valley where the roads forked. Up above the town the highways hooked into the mountainside, where natural arches pierced through orange-scarlet stone outcroppings, giving an air of the supernatural amid the gnarled mesquite and needle-spiked cholla.

General Gandhi Park's headquarters had taken over most of the town. Fuel and ammunition dumps were hidden in excavated hillsides, and Patriot missile batteries pointed at the skies against enemy aircraft threat. Rows of helicopters cramped the municipal airport. One of them belonged to General Hawp. He was Commander of the Utah Theatre of Operations, and at the moment he was reminding his subordinate General Park in no uncertain terms about the fact.

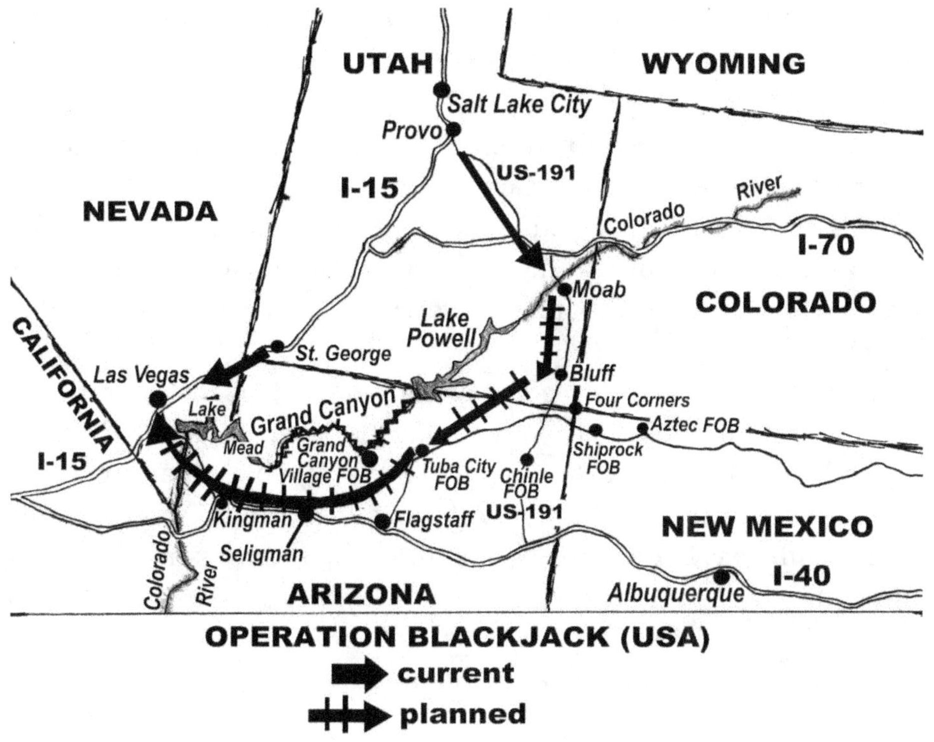

"Consider this a formal briefing on Operation Blackjack," General Hawp said. "My intent is to destroy the enemy forces at Las Vegas. That is the opponent's center of gravity. My scheme of maneuver is to keep up direct pressure on the front at I-15 west of St. George—this is the holding force that will keep the enemy's divisions in place. Meanwhile I will attack by a hooking movement, south and then west through Arizona, coming in behind the enemy lines south and east of Las Vegas. My main effort will be mounted from Kingman, Arizona northwards to Henderson and Hoover Dam, Nevada. To that end, your current task is to build up a chain of FOBs for supporting logistics, extending from southeastern Utah to Seligman and Kingman. The enemy is confronting our forces on a static front west of St. George. His southern flank is protected by Lake Mead and the Grand Canyon, which have no land crossings for a hundred fifty miles. He is expecting nothing from that direction except light helicopter patrols. My plan of operations, General Park, is to position four brigades in your southeastern Utah sphere of operation. These brigades will rapidly move through the logistics corridor set up by the FOBs reaching through Tuba City to Seligman and Kingman for the final assault on Las Vegas—"

An aide had entered the room with a concerned look on his face and was gesturing to catch General Park's attention. Gandhi Park and his staff sat in stiff postures around the briefing table. General Hawp was at the front reading from PowerPoint slides projected on a screen. Hawp gave the aide a scowl and continued reading the PowerPoint:

"—First Brigade will reach Moab by day 11 of the operation. I need not remind you that today is day 10. First Brigade will move forward to FOB Tuba City on day 14. Second Brigade will reach Moab from day 15 to day 17. It will move forward to Tuba City—"

The aide was bending over Gandhi Park's shoulder and whispering in his ear.

"Would you mind, Captain!" Hawp barked.

"Sorry, sir!" The aide snapped to attention. "Battle reports coming in."

"Battle reports. Where?"

"FOB Chinle, Arizona. FOB Shiprock, New Mexico. FOB—"

"Chinle? Shiprock? That is not our main effort. They are far from our main effort—off at the east end of your zone of operations, General Park."

Gandhi was on his feet, stepping in front of the aide. "With respect, sir. I'd better look into this."

"General Park. Sit down, sir. My briefing is not over."

"Sir, with all due respect—"

"Sit down, General!"

Gandhi stared at him a long stiff moment and sat down. He had been relieved of command before. He couldn't risk it again. At least not yet.

The briefing droned on. Component commands. Supporting efforts. Battlespace management. Timings. Operational reserve. Force protection—

Gandhi stirred again. The aide was at the door, waving frantically. Gandhi looked away for a moment, then shook his head vigorously and dashed for the door.

General Hawp frowned and went on reading the PowerPoint.

When Gandhi returned, Hawp was down to the dregs of his PowerPoint. He switched off the projector with a expression of extreme forbearance.

"Now, General. Was it something that just couldn't wait?"

"We had to sort out our helicopter logistics convoy escorts. They had an emergency call to divert to support FOB Chinle."

"And was it such an emergency after all?" Hawp said.

"They got there in time. Chinle was down to one Apache. The rest were grounded for lack of fuel. Enemy ground column got within six miles. Captain Napoli was able to cover the landing of his Chinooks and is resupplying fuel to the FOB."

"So, it's nothing."

"Not quite nothing. One Chinook was lost to enemy fire. Enemy Apaches covering the attack were hiding beneath the rim of Canyon de Chelles, east of Chinle."

Gandhi could visualize it as he spoke: a cluster of enemy helicopters hovering beneath radar level, inside the canyon walls where the Indian cliff dwellings were. One helo just barely raising up over the surface so that the Longbow radar on top of its rotor could find a target which it relayed to the other Apaches, like cowboys and Indians fighting amid the rocks and waiting for each other to stick up their head and make a silhouette to fire at.

"Napoli's squadron chased the enemy out of there. One possible enemy chopper lost, none confirmed."

"One of our Chinooks downed," Hawp said. "Carrying fuel."

"Two thousand gallons," Gandhi said. It was carried in huge rubber bladders, like a whale stuffed inside a helicopter. Gandhi had once ridden in a Pave Low copter on a Special Forces mission, where they carried their own fuel and the soldiers had to ride on top of the fuel bladder, like bouncing on a combustible waterbed. Now the fuel would be transforming into a thick black pillar of smoke in the desert air.

"Not good," Hawp said. "It's that much more fuel we need to make up for logistics support of Operation Blackjack. And one less Chinook to carry it."

"There's more," Gandhi said. "FOB Shiprock, seventy-five miles further east in New Mexico, has now come under heavy attack, and is calling for urgent refueling. They want Captain Napoli to divert there next, since he's closest."

"What's the matter with everybody?" Hawp said irritably. "Don't you have your FOBs on a regular refueling schedule, Park?"

"We did," Gandhi said. "For ten days we've been starving them while the effort has gone into logistics buildup at Tuba City and Grand Canyon Village. Operation Blackjack takes precedence—your order, sir."

"Chinle and Shiprock are your problems, not mine," Hawp said. "They're a distinctly minor element in this campaign."

"The enemy does have forces in New Mexico," Col. Ramirez put in. He was Gandhi's Executive Officer. "He's got FOBs north of Albuquerque. Our FOBs are a cordon for defense. They're protecting Operation Blackjack's back."

"Let's get back to the point," Hawp said. "Who told Captain Napoli he could divert to Chinle?"

Gandhi's staff officers looked at each other. Gandhi finally broke the silence. "Nobody. He made the decision himself, on urgent request from Chinle."

"Nobody," Hawp repeated. "I'd say that's dereliction of command."

"May I refer to the new standing orders from the Secretary of Defense, Sir?" Col. Ramirez said. "Network-centered warfare. All unit commanders in combat situations are to communicate with adjacent units and support them upon request."

"Swell!" Hawp said. "Now everybody's in charge. Nobody's in charge. Now get this. Operation Blackjack takes precedence. All local initiatives are to support the main effort. Is that clear?"

Command was asserting itself, at least in that room. How far out into the battle space Hawp's command would carry was another story, Gandhi thought to himself. With the others of his staff, he stood stiffly and repeated: "Yes, sir!"

"So where is Captain Napoli now?"

Col. Ramirez answered, jumping in before his boss, protecting Gandhi. "While we have been discussing, sir, Captain Napoli is no doubt making up his own mind. Since he supported FOB Chinle, and we haven't told him otherwise, I assume that he is on his way to support FOB Shiprock."

"That's his funeral," Hawp said. "All I care about is that the logistics are ready tomorrow when First Brigade arrives in Moab on its way to Tuba City. Get every available helicopter going on delivering fuel to Tuba City and the other western Arizona FOBs." He started to leave, heading for his helicopter.

Gandhi Park and Col. Ramirez caught each other's eye. Hawp was ordering them to strip Moab of helicopter patrols, and the whole southeast sector of the front too. Both men started to open their mouths, but neither said anything.

General Hawp stopped with his hand on the door. "Wait a minute. Where did Napoli divert from when he went to relieve Chinle? What was his original destination?"

"Tuba City," Gandhi said. "They had some enemy incursions on their perimeter yesterday. They wanted extra fuel reserves to be on the safe side."

General Hawp exploded. "You mean Napoli diverted my fuel for Tuba City so he could go to some little scrape-up at Chinle? And now he's doing it again, heading the wrong way into New Mexico?"

There was a moment of silence. "Get Captain Napoli on the line," General Hawp said. "I'm on this network too."

In the air over the northwest corner of New Mexico.

Lieutenant Gabriel Napoli, Army of the CSSA, felt excited as a teenager at a concert. General Mark McConnell, himself! Gabriel didn't believe in heroes, didn't believe in war, really. It was just what you did when you had to defend something important. Gabriel knew all that, knew that heroes were pumped up by media, knew that it was a lot of little guys, ordinary soldiers like himself who did their jobs and were the real heroes. But General McConnell! and he had seen him, passed him no more than six feet away when they embarked at Albuquerque. And McConnell was in one of the hundreds of helicopters ahead, somewhere in this flotilla in the sky, this band of pirate ships marauding behind enemy lines, flying over the most exotic landscape on earth.

The rear cargo door of the transport helicopter was open and Gabriel looked down on a landscape of pink and ochre steep-sided mesas, table-lands carved like giant Indian dwellings, like tomtom dance platforms, sand paintings. A long ridge wall formed itself in the sand barrens. As the helicopter fleet nearer, the wall turned an abrupt angle leaving a battlement at the corner rising like a cathedral spire, like a tall ship under sail—Ship Rock, New Mexico, Gabriel realized with a jolt.

Depressions in the New Mexico desert stopped short at a patch of neat rectangles of cultivated farmland greened up with irrigation, then reappeared on the other side of the farms, claw marks of some Godzilla monster circling the perimeter.

Gabriel could hardly believe this was real. Suddenly transferred to the Southwestern front, after a lifetime in small-town Pennsylvania, where whatever beauty there was in the familiar countryside had dulled to a routine of highway traffic, gas stations and shopping malls. And now he was floating over New Mexico where everything was magic, where human construction looked like shy apologetic visitors in the presence of a great and powerful goddess.

The scene framed in the cargo bay shifted: dry creek beds, the upper reaches of extinct river-canyons petered out like imprints of lizard tails, their writhing petrified in a death agony of sand. Gabriel gulped in his breath. He felt like a baby first sticking his head into the world.

Behind him in the dark womb of the transport helicopter was his SAM battery, the Patriot surface-to-air missiles he was supposed to set up at their destination. General McConnell's expedition was penetrating enemy territory, and somewhere in Utah, he gathered, they would conquer a base. They would put down fuel and ammo supplies and these would have to be defended from enemy air attacks; that was Gabriel's job. The base would be a buildup point for the real attack, a jumping-off place for leapfrogging further ahead. The final landing-place, although no one had explicitly said so, was apparently Salt Lake City or the USA military bases around it. The staging area was a place called Moab.

The Sergeant from his Patriot battery had approached the cargo door and was shouting in Gabriel's ear over the helicopter noise. "Four Corners is underneath us. The only place in the country where four states comes together."

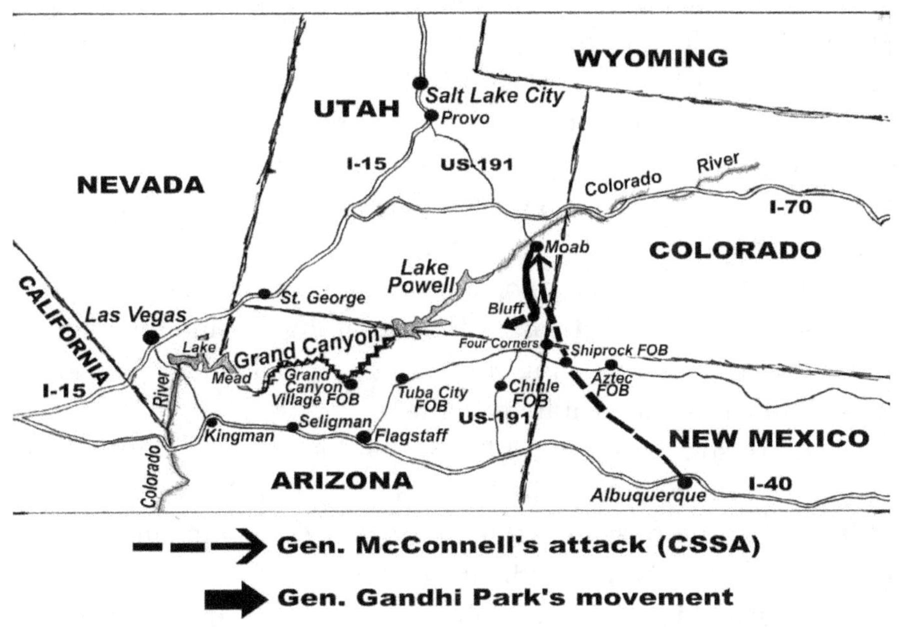

"It's not one country any more," Gabriel shouted back.

"It will be, it will be. This land can't be divided."

Gabriel nodded. More than ever, looking down at the painted landscape, this museum on desert canvas, it seemed impossible this beautiful country could be torn apart. It was like ripping a painting, made not by human beings but by the hand of God himself. Wait a minute, Gabriel thought, we're supposed to be the secular states of America. Whatever. The place imposed itself on the merely human idea.

"Now we're in enemy territory," the Sergeant continued. The fact seemed to make him nervous and wanting to talk.

"If we're over enemy territory, where's their air defenses?" Gabriel said. "Awful quiet, isn't it?"

The Sergeant looked uneasy. "Enemy doesn't know we're coming. He's not looking for us in this direction. At least not yet." He went back into the cargo hold and sat down.

It was quiet, Gabriel thought, the pounding of the helicopter propellers notwithstanding, just a background noise he was used to. He expected flying into combat would be more nerve-wracking. But not in this magic land. The landscape was so beautiful you wanted more than just look at it. But you can't eat it, you can't make love to it: he wanted to get close to it, roll down hills, play capture the flag like summer camp. It was a fantasy but what the hell, as long you're imagining let's imagine being a giant, a giant child who can roll down mountainsides. Better yet, zoom up in the air, swoop to all heights, wing through all perspectives.

Imagine what it's like to be an eagle gliding so high the ground looks like a flat canvas of abstract art, then dive inside the painting.

Art museums are nothing compared to this, he thought. Not just look at paintings, you can fly into them.

Abruptly something had him by the foot and was pulling him back into the helicopter. The burly Sergeant with a wrenching effort had thrown him against the interior wall. "Lieutenant, what the fuck! You were halfway out the cargo door!"

There was thunder now, and shock waves in the air. But there was no rain and the picture window of the cargo door was still bright and sunny.

"Firing ahead," the Sergeant said. "We're approaching the enemy position."

The watered green zone between the western slopes of the Rocky Mountains and the red Utah canyons was behind them and the prehistoric shapes of eastern Utah were beneath. There was a screech of jets overhead, and momentary flashes as rockets exploded.

"Our fighter support," the Sergeant explained, "and enemy fighters coming out to meet us." He seemed calmer now that the fighting had begun, the tense period of waiting finally over. "We didn't open up with preliminary air strikes. That would have warned them we were coming. Those are our Marine fighters from San Diego. Got here just on time. Everything looking good."

Looking good was relative, Gabriel thought. Ground fire was coming up, and helicopters were crashing into the picturesque landscape. Helicopters were throwing out chaff to distract missile guidance systems, filling the air with silvery glitter like flocks of metallic insects high in the air. Flares to confuse heat-seating sensors. Antiradar devices were jamming both sides, high tech balancing high tech. Most of the helicopters rumbled on, leaving a fraction of their numbers behind.

"You have to expect to take some casualties," the Sergeant said, voicing the thought for both of them. "If most of us get through, it's a victory. The enemy gets it worse."

The firing became more remote from their helicopter. CSSA attack helicopters were fanning out to their targets. Gabriel's own CH-57 transport helicopter was bringing up the rear of a fleet, and they had no armaments that would be of any use until they landed. Through the cargo door Gabriel could see highways winding in the rock mountains, jammed with trucks. Deep green-painted fuel tankers, heavy canvas-topped troop carriers. It was the Union army. They were stalled on the highway going into Moab. Something was blocking their way—of course! Ourselves.

The Pentagon.

Major Debra Zielkowski was supposed to get the dirt on Marisa Santa-Ana. There was dirt all right. She was a professional prostitute—a cheap whore, really, there was no other word for what she was. To be accurate, not so cheap in price. She was a hustler, taking men for all she could get. Taking them for more than their money. She had started out at the Air Force bases in the Southwest, years ago, and worked her way up to commanding officers. She had compromised the entire Southwest defenses, enough to end several careers if Secretary Madigan wanted to act on Debra's report. Moral turpitude, probably breach of security. There wasn't any doubt she was selling information to the enemy. Now she was selling herself to CSSA commanders—General Mark McConnell for one. Probably selling information along with herself. Who knows, maybe she was selling to both sides, a double agent. It was something else to check up on. What was clear was that Marisa had worked herself up almost to the top of the CSSA—she was Vice Chairperson O'Leary's mistress, the Mayor of Chicago's kept woman. The Mexican newswoman pose was just a front. Now she's here—here! in the Pentagon—doing her whoring and spying and playing the double agent.

And she was thirty-nine years old. Older than Debra by almost ten years. Debra couldn't help comparing her own erect, flat-chested figure to the pictures of Marisa in the security file. Bulging old bitch. Men were such pigs.

Debra was in the wood-paneled corridor to the Secretary of Defense's office when she was approached by two security guards. "Major Zielkowski? General Harris wants to see you immediately."

The Chairman of the Joint Chiefs of Staff as usual had an un-lit cigar in his mouth, chomping with more than his usual feroc-ity. "Major, I understand you are preparing a security report for the Secretary, on a woman named Marisa Santa-Ana. I need a copy of that report."

Debra hesitated. "Sir, the Secretary commissioned the report. I don't know that I am authorized to release it to anyone else yet."

The muscles in Curt Harris's jaw hardened, making him look even more like a squat bulldog. "I'll take responsibility for that, Major." He held out his hand peremptorily.

After a long moment, Debra put the report on his desk. Harris picked up the folder and leafed through it quickly.

"Is that all, sir?" Standing at attention made her feel very mili-tary, very clean, compared to that woman. She was proud to be part of a team. All the same, she needed to get out of this office.

"Not yet. There's some pretty heavy-hitting stuff in here, Major. Some important names could be compromised with this."

"Yes, sir."

"We might go to the press with the story about Miss Santa-Ana consorting with General McConnell. That would give the enemy a black eye. The scandal might even force him out. They'd lose one of their best generals. It wouldn't officially come from us, of course. Leak it to the press. You could handle that, couldn't you, Major?"

"I don't see how," Debra said. "I'm in computer security, not public relations. Anyway, this should be for Secretary Madigan to decide."

Harris gave her a hard stare. "I'll let it go for the time being. Madigan may not be around much longer."

"Sir?"

Harris tapped the folder. "This report confirms what I already know. Marisa Santa-Ana is a spy. She has already turned some of our people."

"Yes, the report said that was probable, at the Southwestern AFBs. You have additional information?"

"You bet I do. And from the best source. Santa-Ana herself."

"You've seen her?"

"She came to see me," Harris said. "Stood right where you're standing—until she went into her act. She told me she had been sexually harassed by Madigan, and wanted to make a complaint."

"Did you believe it?" Debra said. "She's a— a professional prostitute. How can you sexually harass someone like that?"

"I played along with her," Harris said. He tapped his hairy brow with a blunt finger. "Wiled the rest out of her."

"The rest of it, sir?"

Harris got up and circled triumphantly to the front of his desk. "She got through to Madigan. He revealed national defense secrets to her. His position is compromised. He's through."

Debra sat down heavily in a chair. "And you have evidence of this, General?"

"I have what Marisa told me. What I need is for the rest of your report to confirm it and fill in the details. We can nail her, easily. More importantly, we can nail Madigan. He's become a menace to national security."

"If I may ask, sir. What did Marisa say she got from Secretary Madigan?"

"She knew about the breakdown in the HOME system at Gettysburg, when it was put into action before it had been adequately tested. She knew about the shift in battlefield operational procedures, to this idiotic network-centered system."

"She could have heard about HOME from lots of places," Debra said. "It was widely implemented, and the plan goes back to the days before the rebellion started. And the idea of network-centered warfare has been around for a long time. We only upgraded it substantially when we put it in action last month."

"Upgraded," Harris said disgustedly. "I'd call it radically downgrading our command-and-control. Now anybody can call anybody for help. Screws up the entire system of mission planning. It throws away our whole system of computer coordination. It takes the Air Force out of the center of the picture where it belongs. Abandoning HOME and switching over to network-centered warfare is just about an act of treason."

Debra stood up. "Let me get this straight, General. Marisa Santa-Ana has classified information about the transition from HOME to network-centered battle operations, and she got this from Secretary Madigan. Do you have evidence for this?"

Harris slammed a fist into his meaty palm. "Pretty damn good inference, from what she said. At any rate, Major, we're halfway there and I need you to finish the job."

"You want me to get information that Madigan is giving classified information to Marisa?"

"It's your duty, Major. The Defense Department is teetering on the brink of destruction. Madigan used to have sound ideas about how to transform this place—he was a progressive force at one time. He understood the importance of air power in high-tech warfare better than anyone. But now he's caved in—gone over to the enemy. If we let this go on much further, we risk destruction on the battlefield. And right here in the Pentagon."

"What do you want me to do?"

"Carry on normally for a while. Go see Madigan. Talk to him about Marisa Santa-Ana. Record what he says. You've got a device on your cell phone that will do that. Report back to me as soon as you have anything."

"Yes, sir." Debra gave an involuntary shake of her head and turned to the door.

Harris stopped her. "Don't let your sympathy for Madigan sway your judgment, Major. There's a lot at stake here. There'll be a new Secretary of Defense, pretty damn soon."

At Secretary Madigan's office, the receptionist pointed Debra to the inner room. "Go on in. He'll be back shortly."

But the big desk with the flag stands on either side of it and the round seal of the Secretary of Defense behind it was not empty. Lounging in the great swivel chair was a voluptuous female form, spike-heeled legs crossed with the skirt pushed far above her knees. Marisa Santa-Ana was half-adjusting her stockings, half caressing herself.

"You!" Debra said. "How did you get in here?"

Marisa barely glanced up, merely waved her security badge on its lanyard. It gave her access to the most restricted areas of the Pentagon, the same as Debra's.

"Where'd you get that?"

"General Harris gave it to me." Marisa looked at her contemptuously. "Tell me something, *solterona*. Aren't you getting old to be a virgin?"

Debra found it hard to form words. Her tongue was dry and stuck to the walls of her mouth. "That's none of your business," she finally blurted. "I'm not a public woman, like you." She knew enough Spanish to recognize she had just been called an ugly old maid.

"Don't feel so bad about it," Marisa said. She shrugged luxuriously like she was pulling her shoulders up around her head like a blanket. Her eyes opened and she gave the lazy smile of someone wakening from a delicious sleep.

She came around the desk to Debra. "We can fix you up. First of all, do something about your hair." It was pulled back in a tight ponytail. "Let it down, grow it out. You're flat as a boy, but some men like that. Your legs are your best part, do something with them. And learn how to walk—" Marisa demonstrated, swiveling her hips with every step. "Not like this." She comically imitated Debra's stiff military march.

"Keep away from me," Debra said. "I know what you are. You're—"

"I know," Marisa said. "I'm a spy and a whore and I've seduced your boss and I've stolen national security secrets. I'm a menace to the whole system. Isn't that what you want to say?"

"I— you—"

Marisa turned her back and yawned ostentatiously. She lazily stretched, her back moving in a ripple that went up her spine to her shoulders. Suddenly she reminded Debra of a cat waving its tail.

"And now you want to find out just exactly what Mr. Secretary of Defense big man Madigan told me. What national secrets he gave me just for a lick of my hot little *coño.*" She was purring and rubbing against Debra and seemed very small and soft. Debra was horrified to find herself with an impulse to stroke her.

"How are you going to find that out," Marisa said, "by being so straight and pretending you're a man? Except you're missing one thing a man has—the thing that gets you hot over a real woman, a woman like me."

The cat had clawed her. "You can't touch me," Debra said. "I can have you arrested. We have enough to charge you."

Marisa was inspecting her fingernails. "What about your boss— isn't he the one you're supposed to get the goods on? Oh, he didn't do anything. He didn't tell me anything I didn't already know. It doesn't matter. He's on his way down. I can always tell when a man is getting bigger or smaller in the world."

Debra felt stricken. She was a team player. But who was the team? It was true. Madigan was going down. But then who else was there? Harris? She shuddered. She was losing a part of herself.

Marisa was nuzzling and purring. "Don't feel bad, *bebita.* Men are like that. They're all strong and puffed up on the outside and then they bust and go limp. They're weak on the inside. We women have to stick together."

"I'm not like you," Debra said. "You're a double dealer. You have sex with anyone."

"So what? I got no education, no money. I don't even speak good English. All I have is my ass, and I know how to use it."

"You're a traitor. The worst kind. You spy against both sides."

"So what if I make it with both sides?" Marisa said. "I'm a free woman. I don't do what men tell me. They prey on women. And they shit on Latinas. To them I'm just a dumb Mexican whore." Marisa was in Debra's face, angrily waving her hands. "Why do you take orders from them?"

Debra stepped back from her onslaught. "I don't trust you."

"See? Women can't get anywhere because we don't trust each other. You have to believe me, *pequeña,* if you want to play these men."

"You're just saying that so I won't turn you in."

"You won't turn me in."

Secretary Madigan was in the room. How long he had been there Debra was not sure.

"Sir! I have the report you requested," Debra said.

"Put it on the desk," Madigan said. "Something more important has come up."

"She's a spy working for the other side."

Marisa had insouciantly curled herself on the gold-colored couch in the alcove in a posture of utter relaxation.

"Obviously," Madigan said. "But she has some information for me."

"Sir, do you think it's wise to employ a double agent? They're notoriously unreliable. And this woman—"

"—is carrying a peace offer from Vice Chairperson O'Leary. He's willing to split the CSSA. Pull the Midwest out of the Confederation."

"But that's betraying his own team. Why would he do that?"

Marisa answered sleepily from the couch. "He's willing to deal. He wants to be Secretary of the Treasury. With a free hand for reconstructing the Midwest, you know, *mucho dinero* for the war recovery."

"Just the Treasury?" Debra said. "Not Secretary of Defense too? Are you going to listen to this, sir?"

"This is political reality," Madigan said. "It's purely a matter of cost/benefit analysis. How much would O'Leary cost, compared to how much the war is costing."

"What about the religion issue? Is O'Leary going to hold out for total separation of church and state?"

"He hasn't brought it up," Madigan said. "I don't think he gives a damn about church and state."

"Do you think President Jennings will accept this offer?" Debra said. She had forgotten Marisa lying on the couch.

"Frankly, right now, no," Madigan said. "I think he wants to crush them on the battlefield, teach the rebels a lesson. Put the fear of God into them. But if we can win a big victory, the time may be right to tell Jennings. We just have to wait."

"About the investigation. Should I call it off, sir?"

"Put it on the back burner. If anybody asks, tell them Marisa is clean."

"Including General Harris?"

"Yes, including Curt Harris. Why?"

"Sir, I need to speak to you alone," Debra said. "I was just in General Harris's office."

There was a hurried knock at the door and Madigan's personal assistant burst in. "Sorry for the interruption, sir. Urgent message from the Southwestern front. Moab, Utah has fallen to the CSSA. General Park's headquarters has been overrun."

It had been a series of conflicting orders for Captain Tom Napoli's helicopter squadron. Yesterday General Hawp himself had gotten on the horn, when they had diverted to FOB Chinle. Hawp had just about chewed him a new asshole over that move, told him his helos had better be at FOB Tuba City within the hour. There was no point in saying anything to that except "Yes, sir!" No point in arguing about the new network-centered operational orders. They were always changing procedures from one damn thing to another. You did what you had to, except when the Commanding Officer was on the line and then you did what he told you, or at least you said what he wanted to hear. They could get to Tuba City fast enough once they were airborne—it was only nintey miles—but getting four Apaches and eleven great lumbering Chinooks ready and off the ground wasn't something you could do with a snap of your fingers.

They had been in the middle of taking care of Chinle's refueling needs when Hawp's peremptory order had cut that off. At least they had left the Chinle forces with enough fuel to go on, if they didn't get hit too heavily by another enemy attack. A couple of the Chinooks were empty of cargo and could have gone back to Moab for reloading, but Tom decided it was too risky to send them back alone without escort, and brought them along with him to Tuba City even though they would be superfluous. Every helicopter takeoff used more fuel than just cruising but at that point they still had plenty, so they left in a hurry without topping themselves up—Tom hoped it would not come back to haunt them.

By the time they took off from Chinle the enemy attack had eased up. Apparently it had been lightweight, just a harassing attack, General Hawp had said dismissively. Tom wondered briefly why there had been enemy armor approaching Chinle if it was just skirmishing, but he let it go, he had too many other things to worry about. The enemy was skirmishing at pretty much all the Federal FOBs across the top of New Mexico and Arizona, but according to Hawp that didn't mean anything. We still had the initiative, and when our attack unloaded on Las Vegas, in a big sweeping circuit coming around the Grand Canyon from the south, the enemy would be scrambling to shelter while we poured in on them. Get the enemy one step behind, and never let him catch up—that's when we pick them off and destroy them.

Enemy attacks had not resumed at FOB Tuba City, either, when Tom's helicopter fleet arrived. They started to unload the rest of their fuel and ammunition supplies, routinely enough, into a swarm of ground vehicles that would carry it to protected shelters. In the afternoon, air traffic at Tuba City was becoming heavy. Hawp's orders had sent virtually every helicopter available at Moab hurrying to Tuba City. Now they were all crowding the landing field, so they were landing further and further out in the scruffy desert. Their rotors were kicking up sandstorms, making it difficult for anyone to see what was going on. The ground trucks coming to unload the helicopters had to get off the hardened roads and some of them became stuck in gullies and patches of deep sand, where they had to call for other vehicles to pull them out.

Finally the local air controller had told Tom Napoli to stop unloading and take what supplies he had left to FOB Grand Canyon

Village. FOB Tuba City had all it could handle and there was more coming in, and Napoli's squadron was occupying space at the center of the airport that could be put to more urgent use.

Tom still had four Apaches operational, still unrefueled, but with only fifty miles to Grand Canyon Village it would be alright. One of his Chinooks had malfunctioned, due to the sand storms whipped up at Tuba City, so only ten had readied for take off.

Shortly after they were down to eight. A Chinook code-named Longhorn-16 was next to last to take off. As it lifted slowly into the air, still weighted with seven tons of fuel, its pilot lost sight of the ground controller standing below in the blowing sand. Perhaps the pilot thought he was being told to make an emergency diversion to the side, perhaps he had merely gotten disoriented in the chaos of overly dense air and ground traffic, and the voices snapping with exasperation over the radio links where too many people were talking at once.

Whatever it was, Longhorn-16 had not yet retracted its landing wheels and one of them caught the rotor of Longhorn-13, which was still on the runway waiting to start. Longhorn-16 shuddered, lost its lifting force and settled back for a landing—directly on top of Longhorn-13. Its pilot and copilot were crushed in the cockpit, but the cargo area was empty, Longhorn-13 being one of those which had already unloaded its fuel. This did not help Longhorn-16, which burst into flames, and soon there was a huge pillar of black cloud rising above the Tuba City airfield.

Leaving this ill omen to guide the still-incoming logistics caravans from Moab, Tom Napoli ordered his remaining helicopters to head for FOB Grand Canyon Village. In wartime, you couldn't stop and collect the damage. The difference between winners and losers, Tom told himself, was whether you looked forward or back. Still, Tuba City was beginning to give him the creeps.

By the time they reached Grand Canyon Village, Tom was back to cold normality. Flying in was like reverting to peacetime. The Grand Canyon always came up on you suddenly. Flying low across the high table-land, the view was just a long expanse of dull green sagebrush. The canyon itself is not a monument that announces itself in the distance, but a gash in the earth that you can't see until you are right on top of it. Then the ground drops out beneath your feet, and you are looking down inside the skin of the earth.

Late-afternoon sun rays struck the sides of canyon, leaving a darkshadowed curtain on the lower walls a mile below. Tom couldn't resist circling out over the canyon rim—ostensibly to check base security, he told himself—but really, he felt like seeing it, feeling the relief of it after the human chaos of Tuba City. I'm not becoming like Gabriel, he found himself thinking, am I? The little wimp. Tom methodically assured himself there were no missile-armed enemy copters lurking beneath the canyon rim, and settled in for a landing in the wide parking lots of the Village.

FOB Grand Canyon Village had ample space for the helicopter traffic, and the vacated buildings of park headquarters and the tourist facilities comfortably housed the auxiliary mounting post for General Hawp's Las Vegas offensive. While their load of fuel and ammunition was unloaded, Captain Napoli told his crews to get a meal while he waited for orders. He didn't want to be around them while they talked over their comrades lost in the day's mishaps. According to the radio link, Moab was still overloaded with military traffic both coming and going. They were to stay at FOB Grand Canyon Village overnight.

Morning brought another windstorm of messages and orders. Return to Moab to pick up more fuel cargo. Half an hour later: Cancel that, Moab under attack. Emergency messages were coming in from the FOBs to the east: Chinle, Shiprock, under attack again. And now FOB Aztec, New Mexico, even further east. Urgent calls for reinforcements. Tom Napoli, wary of General Hawp's wrath, stuck to his main orders. But what were they? Get under way to Moab, get airborne before FOB Grand Canyon Village was attacked too—what else could he do? Tom had his helicopters fueled up at night, in fact fueled up from his own cargo bladders delivered to the FOB. It struck him as ironic that you hauled all this fuel for someone else to use, and then had to use it yourself so you could fly back. That set a limit to how far you could supply an offensive, the outer reach being where you used up all your supplies just in order to carry them. At any rate the Chinooks, empty now, could fly faster.

Morning sunrays were lighting up the far side of the Grand Canyon walls in luminous pinks as Captain Napoli's fleet headed northeast. A new series of messages were exploding over the radio.

General Gandhi Park had moved his headquarters. It was no longer at Moab, but at Bluff, Utah. Tom called up a map on one of the helicopter computer consoles. Bluff was down in the southeast corner of Utah, virtually at Four Corners, fifty miles past Monument Valley. Was he supposed to land there and pick up more fuel cargo? Yes. No. Wait—

FOB Shiprock, New Mexico was under heavy pressure and out of fuel. Shiprock was being evacuated. Captain Napoli's Cowboy squadron would do the job; the empty Chinooks would carry out troops and essential equipment.

Evacuate them where? Back to Moab. But Moab was under heavy attack, wasn't it? Tom thought. Command messages from FOB Bluff were unclear whether Moab was operational or not. Since all the helicopters and land bases were on the horizontal network, not just vertical from command headquarters downward but sharing information laterally at the front, an informal message system had sprung up—better to call it rumors.

Headquarters at Bluff was unable or unwilling to tell him whether the big base at Moab was still holding out or was in enemy hands. But the network-centered rumor system had something to say about it. Moab was getting hit by a CSSA assault that had flown in from New Mexico. It was another one of McConnell's raids.

No, McConnell wasn't with it, it was just a feint. The raid on Moab had been driven off, with dozens of CSSA helicopters downed, and CH-47s carrying Patriot missile crews too. That jogged Tom Napoli's memory: Gabriel was in a USA Patriot crew. Trying to shoot down his big brother, and missing as usual.

So Moab was safe. Tom wondered how long it would take for orders to tell him where he was supposed to go, after he had evacuated FOB Shiprock—was it going to be Moab after all, or the new base at Bluff? Or if things were dying down, maybe Shiprock wouldn't be evacuated after all. The army was always like that. Hurry up and wait. This was getting old.

The battle zone network was excited again. McConnell's attack on Moab was massive, the strength of two cavalry regiments, a hundred attack helicopters. Twenty CSSA helicopters were down. No, thirty. No, it was thirty USA helicopters that were down. Ground-to-air defenses at Moab had collapsed.

Voices on the helicopter-to-helicopter network were sounding increasingly panicked. Everyone seemed to be talking at the same time. Everyone was calling for help, calling for information, calling for orders.

The computer console was beeping and flashing. Circumventing all the radio chaos was a message from General Gandhi Park's headquarters. Translated out of COMSEC code it said:

```
Moab has fallen to CSSA forces. Battle
headquarters at Bluff, Utah is your new center
of operations.
```

Then specific orders to Cowboy Squadron:

```
Confirming previous orders, evacuate FOB
Shiprock with all available transport. Fly
evacuees to FOB Bluff and return to FOB
Shiprock until evacuation is complete. Brig.
Gen. Park, commanding.
```

They were almost over the exotic landscape of Monument Valley when the message came. Once again Tom Napoli's Cowboy squadron wheeled in the sky, changing course southeast to Shiprock, New Mexico.

Abruptly the air was full of missiles. In the clear desert air, with the sun bright and the sky bleached pale, the flashes were muted, more felt than seen, munitions streaking through the high geometry of empty space like daytime lightning. Booming explosions crashed over the noisy chattering of the helicopter rotors and sent shock waves that rocked Tom's nine-ton helicopter.

"Incoming! Incoming!" someone shouted on the squadron net, rather superfluously. In the splutter of voices, one message told what they needed to know: "Red F/A-18s at—" giving directional coordinates.

"Cowboy six," Tom said coldly, trying to impose some calm on his squadron with his voice. "Red fighters—" He repeated the coordinates. "How many?"

"Two— I think."

"Take evasive action. Scatter. Head for the rocks. Cowboy six, out."

CSSA F/A-18s were Marine Corps fighters. They could be coming from San Diego, but then again McConnell no doubt had brought his own Marine aviation support with him out to the desert. Tom's own Apaches carried Stinger air-to-air missiles but these would not be much use against fighters that could fly at double the speed of sound and turn on a dime. The F/A-18s were firing missiles that locked onto a target by using an onboard computer that would track wherever its target turned. Tom's Apaches carried radar anti-jamming devices, but these in turn sent out signals that were targeted by enemy detectors. It was a game of electronic chess in the sky, move and countermove and counter-countermove already thought out by the engineering masterminds, but now they had to play it at top speed with no time to think.

It was a matter of chances and numbers; each F/A-18 carried a maximum of four air-to-air missiles; if there were only two enemy fighters and they had already seen some action, at worst half of Tom's squadron should be able to make it to cover.

Tom released chaff and flares into the air to decoy the missiles and told his operator to raise ground control at Bluff, get what fighter interceptor support was possible. He was expecting nothing. If the battle at Moab was as bad as they said, it would have drawn most of the air support from USAF bases, and anyway they would have to come from Provo and Logan, Utah, and from Colorado Springs, each three hundred fifty miles away. No, they were on their own. He fired a Stinger in the direction of the F/A-18s, not so much expecting to hit one but just to make them wary in their attack.

One of the Chinooks was hit. A big fat goose waddling in the sky. A sitting duck for the predatory F/A-18s. Its tail rotor was dangling and the body was on fire, but it had so much air resistance that it would not plummet to earth, not so much diving but wallowing towards the ground.

The Apaches scattered, heading for the rocks of Monument Valley. The Chinooks, much less agile, did what they could. Today they were better able to fly low than when they were loaded, but they were still clumsy.

One Chinook teetered around a rock pinnacle, far too narrow to provide much cover. Then the helicopter found the safety of a huge rock-reef of purple-red sandstone—too close, its rotor scraped the rocks, the Chinook fell off balance, and crashed onto the desert floor. There was no explosion, since it was not carrying fuel this time, it just settled down to form another inert Sphinx, adding its gray-tan bulk to nature's gaudier formations in the valley.

Tom landed his Apache in a gap in the rock hills—the old Monument Valley Visitor Center. It would be hard for the F/A-18s to hit him here. He radioed his squadron. One by one they reported in. All the Apaches were safe, again. The Chinooks had survived the attack of superior flying power as well as could be expected: two were crashed, two were missing, maybe out of radio range. Tom thought about taking off to find them, since an unescorted Chinook out here alone was like a sheep away from the flock. Still, there was no point in looking until he had some idea of where to look. For now, the remnants of Cowboy squadron and its charges were scattered across the picturesque spaces of Monument Valley, halted like exhausted tourists at the end of a long day.

A little convoy of vehicles was making its way down the highway towards him. It was a long straight ribbon of asphalt, across the desert from the north where the surrounding rim of cliffs was broken through by the road to Mexican Hat, and beyond it, Bluff, Utah. Who would approach in the middle of a battle? Tom prepared to fire his 30 mm chain gun. Should he take off, risk the chance the F/A-18s were still around? The convoy was three miles away, then two.

The vehicle profiles resolved into recognizable shapes. It was a Patriot missile station, hauled by tractor cabs. It was Gandhi Park's way of responding—having no air cover flying overhead, he had sent anti-aircraft, the top of the line, capable of blowing any attacker out of the sky at a range of fifty miles. Behind the Patriot battery came a oil tanker. Gandhi was supplying his forces the old-fashioned way, by ground transport. Slower than resupplying by helicopter, but cheaper and more efficient in its own fuel use. Moving logistics by ground was risky, in these days of the nonlinear battlefield when aircraft jumped long distances and could rain down on any intervening spot. But when everything was air against air, sometimes the blank spot remaining was the old-fashioned way, on the ground.

It dawned on Tom that this was how Gandhi Park had moved his headquarters from Moab to Bluff—over the highway, getting out of Moab ahead of General Hawp's brigades moving in for the Las Vegas offensive. Did Gandhi feel McConnell's attack coming, getting out of the way just in time to avoid it, while Hawp took the brunt? Or was he just getting out of town, repositioning himself in a way that gave him some breathing room from the pressures of his superior officer? Either way, Gandhi had dodged a bullet.

One of Tom's missing Chinooks clattered in from the south. Tom radioed it where to land. Other helicopters were arriving, the remnants of FOBs at Chinle, Shiprock, elsewhere. An occasional truck or Humvee would pull in from the abandoned outposts of Arizona and New Mexico. Monument Valley was becoming a refuge and a rallying point. Gandhi's trucks and oil tankers were trickling in from the direction of Bluff, refueling and rearming the survivors. Confidence was returning, taking the place of panic. Gandhi Park's army was reforming itself, waiting for the renewed CSSA attack, defying whatever would come.

The White House.

"Network-centered warfare was a damn stupid experiment," General Harris said. The Chairman of the Joint Chiefs of Staff slammed a hairy first on President Jennings' desk. "If the Secretary hadn't caved in on the glitches with the HOME system, we wouldn't have gone to the other extreme, and this defeat wouldn't have happened."

"I went along with it," Jennings said. "I thought it was a good idea for our boys to help each other out on the battlefield, sharing information and all that. And you fellas told me it was going to work." He sat with his hand over his forehead, looking crumpled, for once smaller than his six foot five inches. "But this great nation can't stand a long string of defeats. The public is getting discouraged. There's talk of peace out there—peace at any price. Even breaking up the Union. Even letting ungodliness take over."

"It's not quite as bad as that," Pat Buckley, the National Security Advisor said. "The media is playing up General Gandhi Park for his heroic stand at Monument Valley. They didn't know about our Las Vegas offensive, so they don't know that it was broken up. All they know is that the CSSA got Moab, and we lost some forward bases on the Arizona and New Mexico side on the border. Shoot, Monument Valley is a lot better for photo ops than Moab—most people never heard of it."

"I'll get you a victory," Harris said. "Put HOME back in action, and let the Air Force run it. We'll bomb them into submission."

"Let's face facts," Secretary Madigan said. "We tried centralization. HOME was the world's greatest supercomputer. It had inputs from everything and it was going to make optimal decisions for the entire military operation. It didn't work. The system got overloaded and went down in the middle of battle."

"That was five months ago," Harris said. "Our computers are better now than they were then. We just need to beef it up some more, so it can handle more information."

"I used to think that," Madigan said. "Operational science means learning from your mistakes. We learned that complexity beyond a certain level can't be handled centrally. That's why we shifted to a network of computers, all laterally connected. We linked our fighting platforms together so they could support each other and respond creatively to local conditions."

"So what happens?" Harris said. "You get a bunch of idiotic decisions by helicopter commanders in the air, and another idiot like General Hawp who loses the big picture and starts ordering men around like a drill sergeant. That's no command structure, it's just high-tech chaos."

"The solution," Madigan said, "is obviously somewhere in the middle. We need middle-level computers for each part of an operation that can put all the battle information together with the logistics and make the right allocations. We've run two experiments—one too centralized, one too decentralized. We're closing in on the optimal computer-human interface."

"What you're saying, Bob," Jennings said, "is you need another chance. Fuss around with the computers some more, and get it right next time. But we don't have time for another next time."

"That's not all," Harris said. "I don't like to say this, Mr. President, but it is my duty to inform you that the Secretary of Defense has been compromised by an enemy spy."

"If you're talking about Miss Santa-Ana," Madigan said, "I've seen through her all along. I put Major Zielkowski's security detail on her right away."

"That's not all Major Zielkowski's report says," Harris shot back. "She can testify to serious sexual improprieties between yourself and this known spy."

"Hold on a minute," Madigan said. "You've been tampering with Major Zielkowski's report. And I know that Marisa Santa-Ana has gotten through to you. You're the one who's been turned, Curt."

"Boys, boys," Jennings said. His dour face had lightened and he was sitting back in his chair, looking amused. "Seems to me this Miss Marisa must be quite a package, to get you scuffling over her."

"That's not the worst of it," Harris said. "I don't give a fart about who screwed who. Marisa Santa-Ana is a CSSA agent who brought a peace offer from Chicago. And the one she discussed it with was Mr. Secretary Madigan."

Jennings' face went tight. "Is that true? Did you entertain a peace offer?"

"I listened to it," Madigan said. "It's my job to look at everything that affects the conduct of the war."

"Isn't that a bit out of your department? I'm the one who handles the politics."

"War is an extension of politics by other means," Madigan said. "They can't be compartmentalized like that."

"Maybe not," the President said. "But I'll be the one who decides what compartments things fit into. I notice you didn't report this peace offer to me."

"Or to anyone else, Mr. President. There wasn't time—the battle at Moab was at its height."

"This is a pretty serious breach of trust," Jennings said. He pushed a pad of paper across the desk. "I understand you fire off a lot of memos to everyone in the Pentagon. This will be your last one. I want your resignation."

Without a word Madigan made a brief scribble.

"Before you go, Bob," Harris said, "we need an understanding about what you'll say to the press. You're not going to talk about the peace offer, are you?"

"I don't see why I should lie about it, if anyone raises the question."

"Your lack of loyalty disturbs me," Jennings said. "Really, Bob—don't you love America enough to preserve it?"

"That's what I've been trying to do," Madigan said, "until I was undermined. Now I'm going to do whatever I think is right."

"Think about this," Harris said. "There are serious charges against you—sexual impropriety and connections with an enemy spy. If you start talking about a peace offer, we will be forced to make that public."

"You can't prove that. I can beat you in court."

"We don't have to go to court," the National Security Advisor said. "We can publicize Marisa Santa-Ana's background. Major Zielkowski's report could be leaked, along with some other off-the-record information. The press would smell blood in the water."

"Think of how your wife and family would take it," Harris said.

"Let's not be unpleasant," Jennings said. He draped a big arm around the compact figure of the former Secretary of Defense as he steered him to the door. "Let's just tell the press you resigned to spend more time with your family. That's the usual formula, isn't it?"

After the door closed, Harris said, "General Hawp really screwed up in Utah. Let's get rid of him too."

"Can't do it, Curt. Utah politics—I still owe the Governor." Jennings' shrugged, then guffawed. "But I can kick him upstairs. Figure out a new position for him—Commander-in-Chief of the Rocky Mountains, or something like that, where he won't get in anybody's way."

"And you'll be needing a new Secretary of Defense."

Jennings laughed again. "Not you, Curt. I've had enough trouble in the Pentagon. I need someone bland, who can keep the peace while we fight the war."

Harris frowned. "At least let me run the war my way. Unleash the Air Force. Quit crapping around with ground operations. Let the ground forces be spotters, finding the targets and putting laser tags on them. I'll set the computers for maximal Air Force impact. We'll hit everything the rebels have got—military, economic, political. I can take them all out. That'll be the victory you're looking for."

"It's not that easy," Jennings said. "We're not the only air power in this war, remember? The other side has the same stuff we have. Our Air Force is already off the leash, but it hasn't run that far from home. And that's because the rebels are sitting over there with their own fighters and their own Patriot missiles. We've just been knocking each other out of the air. We neutralize each other."

"Sure, our forces have been run down," Harris said. "But so have theirs. What I need is a big buildup. Rebuild the stealth bomber fleet. Give me a thousand more fighters and I'll break their air force, and then we'll bomb what's left until they quit. I'll give them peace if I have to make a desert out of them."

"You got any spare money, Curt? I know how much those planes cost, at a hundred million dollars a pop. And I know how many years they take. I can't wait for the Air Force building program. I need victories now. And they have to be with what we've got. And that means on the ground."

"It sounds like you don't need my services any more," Harris said.

Jennings pushed the note pad across his desk again. "Write it out, Curt."

Harris looked shocked. He did not expect his bluff to be called.

"You saw how it's done. Your letter of resignation."

Jennings took the signed note with his long arm. He sat back and smiled.

Harris rose and started to leave.

"Hold on, Curt. You've not going anywhere."

"What do you mean?"

"I'm not accepting your resignation. You'd be a loose cannon out there. I want you here where you can't do much damage."

Jennings comfortably stretched his imposing bulk. "But I'm holding onto this letter, just in case."

Utah-Colorado border. Weeks later

Lieutenant Gabriel Napoli, CSSA, is back in the air again. General McConnell's attack had not reached Salt Lake City, but happened upon a much more lucrative target, smashing up four of Hawp's Utah brigades coming into Moab. No one ever figured out exactly why all those troops were on the road in such a remote part of the rock valleys but it was a vulnerable position for them and they had been smashed. The story was going around that Hawp's army was heading towards Four Corners on its way southeast—it would be an offensive against Santa Fe and Albuquerque, eventually aiming to cut off the CSSA forces in west Texas. McConnell must have figured that out and beat them to the punch, Gabriel thought.

Moab was full of captured fuel and munitions for the Federal tanks and APCs and helicopters and gunships that were supposed to roll over the CSSA. It should have been a bastion of strength but it turned out to be the wrong location in time and space. It was the linear part of the nonlinear battlefield, and being unable to move as fast as the enemy (us!) it was caught and destroyed. McConnell doing another JEB Stuart imitation only this time we destroyed an entire army.

Gabriel's CH-57 transport helicopter is flying eastward from Moab, reinforcements for the new front in Colorado. In fact, both brothers are in the air, unknown to each other, and flying in the same direction.

Captain Tom Napoli, US Army, is pondering military trends. Two years in, and what have we got? A bunch of rebel victories. I-95, Gettysburg, St. Louis, Four Corners. Only one we won was Caribou Forest, but that didn't lead anywhere—rebels are still safe in their West Coast fortress, while we're getting pushed out of Utah.

Tom is evacuating the USA outpost from Monument Valley, as they consolidate their Colorado front. He eyes the changing landscape with suspicion. The computer screens before him in the cockpit make him feel no better.

Can't trust the technology these days. First they tell us HOME is going to eliminate the fog of war. You bet. It's great when it's great, except when it goes down with cyber attacks or overload or human error or some damn thing. And that shift to network-centered war wasn't so great either—not when you've got generals like Hawp butting into the net.

Refuse to lose, he reminds himself. We're not done with this thing yet. Two years and we're just where we started, more or less— except we know a lot more now about what doesn't work. I'm still alive, no thanks to the tech-heads at the Pentagon. Let the grunts fight it out. Bumbling through.

The nose of his AH-64 is scarred, the window bubbles pitted. But it is still flying.

Attrition, they call it. The so-called high-tech advantage is gone. Now it's just a matter of who wants it more.

A flicker of consciousness reminds him of his brother. That little punk Gabriel is winning. He always does the easy thing. He always had the luck.

Not this time. Who wants it more? I do!— *We* do!

Again Gabriel is looking down from the edge of the open rear cargo door, meditating on geology.

I'm getting older, he tells himself. Seeing into the insides of things.

A vast landscape torn by angry violent eruptions like old battlefields, shell pockets, canyon gullies like trenches, hill-cliff palisades. Leftovers from ancient combat of the earth battling against itself, punched up from below by giant fists trying to get out. Million-year artillery barrages of winds, prehistoric rain torrents, Neptune and Pluto fighting it out, the storm-gods throwing their hammers.

Pinnacles of pink rocks pass below the cargo bay. High places, where weights have been raised, potential energy of physics ready to come accelerating downwards and smash anything below. Primitive projectiles, non-human bow strings stretched taut. I'm looking at a stop-action photo of geological forces held in tension in the earth: earthquake faultlines, continental drifts and collisions, earth surface buckling, rippling, rifting. And then erosion follows: the violent battlefield, and peacetime after the shell-fire, scattering the bodies.

Edges of earth-shapes are frozen energy, not really frozen but moving at a scale far bigger than human lives. If you could gaze steadily with the eye of a giant, the landscape wouldn't be static at all, but teeming with energy, the insidious combat of geology. It would be a rapid war on the time-scale of beings whose moments are eons, whose campaigns go on for hundreds of million years. Nature's Verdun, Utah's battle of the Somme, the earth so blasted nothing grows here again.

With the eyes of a giant? Gabriel thinks. With the eyes of God, if there were such a thing.

Suddenly he thinks of Tom. Wondering if he ever looks at the scenery. Not bloody likely.

But the landscape reflects his presence unseen, like a curved and opaque mirror.

This violent earth is like Tom, Gabriel tells himself. The earth battle will swallow him up.

He's going to end up crashing in these beautiful canyons. And they won't even notice—they won't stop being beautiful. Beauty always wins over violence.

And me? I'm immune. Because I don't mind what happens. I'm the artist, looking down at these deadly depths.

Somehow I feel I'll be the one who survives.

Another chasm of soft-colored rock was opening up below. Why is this so beautiful? Gabriel wondered. America takes you back to the primordial, the pre-human. God, I love this place.

Chickamauga. September 1863

Chickamauga is the nightmare story of a communications disaster. One side makes a miscommunication at exactly the wrong moment; the other sides strikes unknowingly just where it will have maximal effect. The result: victory by accident.

But mistakes have a pattern. It is not preordained where a battle will take place, nor that everybody will be there. A battle is not a party with an invitation list and everyone comes on time. The fateful breakdown in communicating orders among the Federal divisions which led to the defeat at Chickamauga was the culmination of a series of makeshift adjustments as both sides hurried to join the action.

It all started at Chattanooga, an important railroad junction at the southeast corner of Tennessee. Federal troops under General Rosecrans managed to maneuver the Confederates out of the city, who retreated across the border into Georgia. Since no one knew exactly where the Confederates were, Rosecrans sent out several widely scattered probes to find and attack them. In fact, the Confederates were not far away, where General Braxton Bragg was gathering sixty thousand troops to retake the city.

The two sides made contact in a shallow valley divided by meandering Chickamauga Creek. Bragg's forces gathered on the east side of the creek; on the west side, some weak Federal forces briefly held them up from crossing the bridges. Bragg had a strong advantage of numbers, and he was determined to attack the Union forces while they were still divided. But in this battle, nothing went according to plan. Not all of Bragg's troops had arrived, and the night was spent in arrangements and logistics as divisions marched in and tried to find their places in the battle line. Many of the Union forces were miles south, and they began scrambling up to the Chickamauga with anxiety over being cut off by Confederates blocking the road to their base at Chattanooga.

When full-scale fighting broke out on Saturday morning, it was not Bragg who first attacked, but the relatively weaker Federals. Rosecrans, realizing he had only thirty-two thousand against a Confederate army twice his size, had decided to fight on the defensive. But top command on either side turned out to be almost entirely ineffective. Local commanders reacted to opportunities and threats on their own initiative, and soon neither Rosecrans nor Bragg controlled or understood what was happening.

Early in the morning, General Thomas, commanding the Union corps at the northern end of the battlefield, noticed a single brigade of Confederates on his side of Chickamauga creek, and decided to pick off this isolated force by sending in several divisions. Nearby Confederates troops came to the rescue. Union forces in the vicinity, in turn, rushed to the sound of firing. The battle, starting with a fairly small engagement at the north end of the line, gradually spread southward as more and more troops became engaged. It turned into a series of unplanned flank attacks, since the reinforcements generally pulled out of their existing lines and headed north towards the sound of battle, coming in on the southern flank of the enemy.

It was like a zipper closing from the north to the south. The Confederates with their larger numbers pressed forward, crossing the Chickamauga at numerous points and by afternoon were holding positions on the west side of the creek. As darkness fell the battle was essentially a stalemate.

The most important result for the Union troops was that their formal organization had gotten badly misaligned. There were supposed to be three Union corps, each comprising several divisions; but the corps commanders (Thomas in the north, Crittenden in the center, McCook in the south) had borrowed divisions from each other to throw into the emerging battle, and lost divisions from their sector because they had moved spontaneously and had slanted either in front or behind their neighbours. The result was that the chain of command was a hodgepodge; Thomas acquired informal command of all the divisions in the northern end of the line even though half of them belonged to other corps.

This set the stage for the debacle over the mistaken order on the second day of battle. Again the overall plans of both Rosecrans and Bragg were not working well. Bragg ordered a Confederate attack for early Sunday morning starting at the northern end of the line, to turn Thomas's exposed flank. But this did not get off on time, and eventually in exasperation Bragg simply ordered his commanders to attack everywhere at once. In effect this meant turning over control to local initiative, probably a realistic thing to do under the circumstances.

On the Union side, the problem was more a matter of trouble-shooting, responding to whatever attacks the Confederates made. Their attack on Thomas, in the north, failed to turn the corner, but it did excite Thomas into calling repeatedly for reinforcements, both from his neighbors just to the south, and to Rosecrans' headquarters.

Rosecrans was still trying to keep control, riding up and down behind his line and looking for gaps in the defenses. In the morning he noticed a lightly defended crossroads and ordered Negley's division to cover it. Unfortunately Negley was slow to move, perhaps because he would leave yet another gap in the line, and so when Rosecrans came back later Negley's division was still in the same place, and the relieving division—under the ill-fated General Wood—was just arriving. General Wood was chewed out for being dilatory in responding to an order; it wasn't his fault that the gap had not been filled properly but he was the highest officer on the spot when Rosecrans happened to be making his inspection, and he got the full blast of Rosecrans' anger while their staffs looked on. Wood would now obey orders no matter what.

Unfortunately for Rosecrans and the entire Federal army, the scenario repeated itself a few hours later. Thomas was taking a powerful assault in the northern sector and calling desperately for reinforcements. Further down the line, division commander Brannan got an urgent visit from one of Thomas's staff officers and pulled his troops out to rush to the rescue; realizing this would leave a hole in the line just south of Reynolds, Brannan sent a message to Rosecrans explaining what he was doing. It was becoming a game of musical chairs. Rosecrans decided to plug the gap and sent a hurried message to his recent punching bag, General Wood, ordering him to close up on Reynolds.

In the broken chain of command and the constant improvising, Rosecrans had forgotten who was where. Wood was not next to Reynolds but another whole division further south. But orders were orders; Wood consulted with his own corps commander, McCook, who happened to be present; but McCook was out of the loop now and the best they could do was agree that Rosecrans must know what he was doing and speed was of the essence. Dutifully, Wood pulled his division out of line and sent it around behind the adjacent division, heading north.

It was at this moment, by fateful coincidence, that General Longstreet's Confederate corps unleashed a massive attack on this very front. The surprised Confederates found that where they had expected strong resistance was an empty gap half a mile wide. Troops do not move as fast on a battlefield as on a parade ground, but all speeds are relative to what your enemy can do; often resistance will slow down an attack enough so that reinforcements can be brought up. But here there was no slowing at all; four Confederate divisions rushed through the gap and spread out in both directions. They reached the main north-south road behind the line which was the Federals' artery of communications, as well as their escape route north to Chattanooga.

It was a textbook pattern of a breakthough, rarely so fully realized. The Union army was split into halves. The southern segment, which included Rosecrans' headquarters, fled in panic westward into the hills, seeking another road home to Chattanooga, abandoning the battlefield. The northern half turned into a churning mass of fugitives, abandoning artillery, ammunition and supplies in their rush to flee north.

The result could have been worse for the Federals. Thomas, at the far end of the line, had built wooden barricades which thus far had repelled Confederate attacks. Now he was pushed back in the infectious confusion, but managed to keep some units in formation onto a hill in the northwest corner of the battlefield. Here collected more and more of the retreating soldiers. Not everyone was panicked and some were still willing to fight if there was a nucleus of organization. This Thomas's core of unbroken troops provided. The battle at Snodgrass Hill turned into a determined struggle. The Confederates had moved so rapidly that they had lost some of their own coherence as well, and they attacked without artillery and took large casualties in the frontal assault.

Late in the afternoon Thomas's forces withdrew in good order, having covered the remainder of the Union army as it got safely on the road to Chattanooga. The Confederates were spent, and did not pursue. The Federals lost half their army; the Confederates one quarter of theirs.

Victory in battle is a matter of organizational breakdown, but this is relative. Both sides break down to some degree in the rush and confusion of unexpected adjustments. This is Clausewitzian friction. Both Bragg and Rosecrans suffered from communications problems and lack of coordination from above; but this did not prove fatal to either side because both sides suffered equally. Until a local turning point was reached: one side broke down organizationally at just the place where the other side made a well-organized attack. It was a huge multiplier; most of Rosecrans' army was suddenly broken beyond repair. Only the survival of a segment of organization, a life preserver floating away from the wreck, saved the lives of some of these men who no longer made up a fighting force.

The End. Part One.

PREVIEW OF PART 2

"I'll tell you right now, Colonel," Gandhi Park said. "You are with me under protest. I don't like being spied on."

"My job isn't to check up on you, General Park," Debra said. "President Jennings has full confidence in you. He just wants someone he trusts to tell him what's going on. He doesn't believe the official channels."

The staff car proceeded under a gloomy pre-dawn sky, promising rainstorms. They drove through the oil refinery district, approaching the channel behind the back end of Staten Island. Officially it was a borough of New York City but geographically it was on the New Jersey side of the Hudson, an outer mudflat of Newark Bay. Union troops occupied Staten Island, and fired an occasional rocket at the CSSA battery at the narrows where Brooklyn framed Lower New York Bay from the other side. Verrazano Bridge still arched gracefully across the narrows, but no one was going to cross it in either direction without being blasted into the water. Staten Island was playing the role of a blind behind which the invasion force could gather for a crossing.

"I don't like anyone breathing down my neck."

"If that's the way you feel, why did you join the army? We're a team, you know."

"The best team in the world," said Gandhi. " As long as the civilians stay out of it."

"And the women, too? Is that what you mean, General?"

"Since we're outside official channels, I'll tell you the truth. Women don't belong in combat. They're too distracting."

"Not if men keep their minds on their work."

"Women make more work for us. We have to take care of them, on top of everything else."

"No one has to take care of me," Debra said.

Rain splattered and then drizzled as Gandhi's boat crossed into open water. The moist gray weather felt lucky, Gandhi thought, reducing enemy laser spotting and providing at least the psychology of cover, even if it did little good against radar and infra-red sensors. There were USA radar jamming planes aloft, but they would be targeted by Coalition planes and SAMs, and who knows how many would survive.

Union helicopters clattered toward the Brooklyn shore, passing north of Verrazano Bridge to draw fire away from the invasion fleet to the south.

"Have you ever been in combat?" he asked Debra.

"No. I've run plenty of simulations, though."

"Give me a break," Gandhi snorted. "I mean when someone is trying to kill you."

"We're all targets, aren't we? Precision munitions can hit us whether we're at the front or not."

"It's different when you're out looking for someone to kill," Gandhi said. "Are you ready for that?"

Debra nodded but looked away. What she liked about the military was the team, not the killing.

This part of Brooklyn, the south coast at the inner corner of Long Island, appeared denuded of troops. The landings further east on Long Island three days ago had attracted the available forces to put out the fire.

"There's a shortage of transport, sir," said one of the officers.

"You bet there is. Dismount all the riflemen until the ammo is loaded. And get it going forward."

"Are we to wait for further transport for the infantry, sir?"

"There isn't going to be any further transport," Gandhi snarled. "Get their asses in motion, right now. Requisition any civilian vehicles you can find. But don't stop and wait for fuel, because there probably isn't going to be any, unless these gas stations still have some. It's ten miles to the Brooklyn Bridge. You can hike there in four hours, if enemy resistance doesn't get any worse than it is right now."

He sent officers scurrying off to their units. A few hung back, asking questions.

"But sir. If we encounter heavy resistance, how are we at handle it without our armor and artillery?"

"Bypass whatever pockets there are. We need to get north before enemy reinforcements start coming down on us.

"Shall we wait for CAS?"

"Call it in, but don't wait for it. Our air support is stretched pretty thin."

"When can my men expect water and fresh food and medical evacuation?"

Gandhi shouted in the man's face. "Do I make myself clear, Captain? For the time being, we may be cut off on this side of the harbor. If we get to the Queens Borough line before the enemy gets their reserves in action, we're going to win. If not, we're going to die in Brooklyn. Now get moving."

GLOSSARY

AAA   anti-aircraft artillery (also called Triple-A)

Abrams M1A1   tank

A-10 Warthog   low-flying plane with heavy armor against ground fire

AH-64   Apache attack helicopter

APC   armored personnel carrier

AT   anti-tank missile

AWACS   Airborne Warning and Control System

C4ISR   Command, Control, Communications, Computers, Intelligence, Surveillance and Reconnaissance

CAS   close air support

COMSEC   Communications Security (code for radio transmission)

Crypto   cryptography security clearance

DOD   Department of Defense

EPW   enemy prisoner of war

ESI   Extremely Sensitive Information (security clearance)

F/A   fighter/attack (air-to-air fighter/ground attack bomber)

FOB   forward operating base

HARM   high-speed anti-radiation missiles (homing in automatically on radiation emission sources)

HEAT   high-explosive anti-tank (armor-piercing missiles)

HET   Heavy Equipment Transporter

HOME   Hyper Organization Military Efficiency (fictional computer system)

IED   improvised explosive device

IR   infrared

JSTARS   Joint Surveillance Target Attack Radar System

KIA   killed in action

M1A1   tank

M4   carbine

M16   automatic weapon

M240   heavy machine gun

MCAS   Marine Corps Air Station

MLRS   Multiple-Launch Rocket Systems

MRE   Meals Ready to Eat

NOD   night observation device

SAM   surface-to-air missile

SAW   squad automatic weapon (machine gun)

SECDEF   Secretary of Defense

SCI clearance   Sensitive Compartmented Information (security clearance level)

Stryker   armored personnel carrier

Triple-A   anti-aircraft-artillery

TS   Top Secret (security clearance)

UAV   Unmanned Aerial Vehicle